MIDNIGHT MAGE

THE NIGHT REALM: MAGIC MARKED BOOK ONE

CHANDELLE LAVAUN

MEGAN MONTERO

MAGIC MARKED:

Midnight Mage

Marvel Mage - coming summer 2020

Master Mage - coming fall 2020

Dear Salem,

Thank you for helping us remember the plot to the trilogy we somehow completely forgot.

ONE

ELLIE

"ALL RIGHT, Nickel, your turn! Spin the bottle!"

Nickel adjusted her *Wonder Woman* diadem and flipped her perfectly curled black hair over her shoulder. The gold diadem matched flawlessly with the shimmering makeup that gave her ebony skin an ethereal glow. "Game time."

With a wicked grin, she leaned forward and spun the empty beer bottle. Her hazel-green eyes sparkled with mischief as the bottle twirled at a nice steady pace, like she'd played this game a thousand times and knew *just* the right way to spin it. It made about a dozen laps around then slowed down. The guys in our circle leaned forward and I felt their eager, thirsty eyes on the tip of the bottle, hoping it would land on them. It passed Nickel then crawled by me, and my heart sped up to match the beat of the music filling the room. I loved my best friend but I did not want to kiss her in front of a bunch of horny boys I went to school with. Especially at one of Tyler's infamous

Halloween parties. Tyler grabbed Alex's shirt and their eyes widened.

Oh God. Gross. Please no, keep going.

Then it rolled right by and stopped on the person beside me. I sighed with relief and leaned back on my heels.

"OH!" Tyler and Alex shouted and threw their hands up.

Wait. Lao sat beside me…and the bottle stopped on him. I turned and found him sitting there in his *Green Lantern* costume with brown eyes so wide they were practically the same size as his glasses' lenses. His cheeks turned bright pink. I bit my lip to stop myself from grinning like the Cheshire Cat. To say Lao was in love with Nickel would be the understatement of a millennia.

"Breathe," I whispered as low as I could.

Nickel crawled on all fours toward him, looking every bit the lioness on the hunt, and I was suddenly concerned if Lao still had a heartbeat. She stopped right in front of him and sat back on her heels, mirroring his position. His face paled and I saw his pulse ticking in the vein on his neck. Nickel giggled and wagged her eyebrows at him, then cupped his face in her hands and pressed her lips to his.

The rest of the circle howled and smacked their hands on the mahogany hardwood floors, drawing attention to our little circle in the corner of the room.

Nickel kissed him good and hard – but then again, she had to. Tyler said there was a ten second rule, which seemed seven seconds too long. At least.

When she finally pulled back from him, she grinned. "Check that off the bucket list." Then she jumped to her feet and skipped back to her spot.

"Best day ever," Lao croaked just loud enough for me to hear. His shoulders sagged and a dopey love drunk look fell over his face. His thick black-rimmed glasses were lopsided and smudged, but I knew he didn't care or notice.

I chuckled and leaned toward him. "You alive?"

"I am now—"

"ELLIE!" Tyler shouted from across the circle.

I gasped and turned – and found the entire circle watching me with expecting eyes. *Wha— OH SHIT. It's my turn.* My stomach tightened and turned. My mouth watered like I was going to be sick. *Why did I agree to this?*

Nickel leaned closer to me. "You wanted to live a little, remember?"

I groaned and eyed the bottle like it was a venomous snake about to strike. This wasn't the norm for me. I'd never, ever, played spin the bottle before. But I was seventeen now and I was tired of being so shy. I was tired of being a wallflower. Nickel was super popular, and that wasn't what I wanted. I just wanted to have some fun.

But this is not fun.

"Come on, Catwoman, we don't bite," Charlie, a preppy soccer jock, said with a cocky grin from over to my right. "Unless you ask me to."

He didn't even know my name and I was maybe about to kiss him? *Yeah, no thanks.*

I didn't care that he was dressed as *Iron Man*, he was no

3

Tony Stark. But it was too late. I'd already agreed. I'd sat down. I'd joined the circle...and now they were watching me. Suddenly dancing with Andy and Bernadita didn't seem like such a bad idea. I should have just gone with them. So what if the dance floor was packed with people I didn't want grinding on me. At least they wouldn't be on my mouth. I shook my head. *No, you signed up for this, Ellie. Suck it up, buttercup. Mama didn't raise no bitch.*

I forced a nervous laugh then leaned over on all fours to reach the bottle. The glass was cold to the touch – or maybe my hands were sweaty. I took a deep breath then spun the bottle as hard as I could. It spun like a bat out of hell, so fast I couldn't even count how many times it went around.

Instead, I sat back and scanned my potential lip-mates. Luckily, this was Tyler's Halloween party and even though he'd only learned my name tonight, I at least knew who everyone else was. They were all kids from my school, but I only *knew* two of them personally. Nickel and Lao were two of my best friends...everyone else didn't know I existed until tonight. There was only one person in this circle I was okay with having to kiss, but I secretly suspected that was a product of his *Loki* costume because Tom Hiddleston did things to me – even when it wasn't really him.

I surveyed the rest of my potential victims and my stomach tightened. Next to Lao was a girl named Katie, dressed as a barbie doll. Beside her was Mickey, a tall unassumingly handsome boy wearing his own football jersey as a costume. Then there was Tyler, *aka* Zeus for the night, and his best friend Alex who wore kickass glowing devil horns. Melinda next to him, whom Charlie had already spun on and kissed, was rocking the hell out of a *Princess Peach* costume.

Nickel threw her head back and laughed. She clapped her hands. "Damn, Ellie, you don't have to spin it so hard."

My cheeks warmed. I grimaced. "Sorry."

I eyed the bottle and held my breath, but it was still spinning. Nausea rolled up my throat. I wrapped my arms around my waist and tried to hold myself together. *Oh god. Just stop already and put me out of my misery.*

The bottle wobbled in a circle two times then stopped *right between Alex and Tyler.* I looked up just as three guys walked through the front door and stopped right in the line of my spin.

"*OHHHHH,*" Everyone groaned.

All three of them looked to be about my age, wearing the most amazing Victorian English costumes, yet I did not recognize them. Two of them had dark hair, light eyes, and pale complexion...but my gaze froze on the third one. The one in the middle. The one standing directly in line with my bottle. My chest tightened. He was breath-takingly gorgeous, with light green eyes and sandy blond hair that was longer on the top and hung over his fore-head a bit. He was tall, too. At least six-foot-four. His eyes were sharp and sparkling with light...and looking right at me.

I gasped.

Tyler cupped his hands around his mouth and shouted, "Step through door number three, contestant."

The boy frowned then glanced to his two friends.

"Wait, does she kiss *him*?" Lao hissed.

Nickel jumped to her feet. "Well, that's how the game works. Where the bottle stops your lips pop!"

WHAT?

My eyes widened but I couldn't look away from him. *I can't kiss him. He's a total stranger.*

Nickel slid her hands under my armpits and scooped me up to my feet — then *pushed*.

I stumbled forward and kicked the beer bottle, sending it flying right into Charlie's lap. The guy, the outrageously pretty stranger, watched me with narrowed green eyes as I stumbled over toward him. My heart pounded so loud it actually drowned out the sound of the party around me. I felt like I was walking the plank, but I was *not* Captain Jack Sparrow. I didn't have tricks up my sleeve to get out of this.

"*Ellie, Ellie, Ellie,*" the circle chanted behind me, slapping their palms on the floor. "*Ellie, Ellie, Ellie.*"

I heard Nickel's voice in my mind before the party saying, *badass is a mindset. Adopt it and its yours.* She was right. I could do anything I wanted. So why was I freaking out that I had the perfect excuse to kiss a complete stranger without it being weird?

But then I got close to him and saw the light dusting of freckles across his high cheekbones and his perfectly tan complexion. He had thick eyebrows that were a few shades darker than the dirty blond hair hanging over his forehead that I was dying to run my fingers through. His light green eyes scanned my face and I saw his confusion clear as day. I looked at his mouth and my heart stopped. I felt its hollow echo through my bones. *You can do this. You can do this. No big deal. He's gorgeous, how awful for me.* I pushed my shoulders back and held my chin high. *Just do it. Nike style.*

I met his eyes and whined under my breath, "Mistakes were made."

He scowled and opened his mouth, but I didn't give him the chance to speak. I reached up and took his jaw in both my hands and dragged his mouth down to mine. Heat exploded inside of me and I pulled him down closer. We stumbled a few steps and then his hands landed on my waist, steadying us. He smelled like the crisp fallen leaves in a forest on an autumn day. I inhaled him in. In the distance, I heard the circle counting to ten but I was lost to him. I slid my tongue in his mouth and groaned. He tasted like cool mint and I wanted more. His lips were smooth and silky, and they felt like Heaven against mine.

"...EIGHT...NINE...TEN!"

I pushed back from him, gasping for air like a fish out of water. My vision was blurry and had those little black squiggles all over. My body felt light and weak like I had a sudden flu and needed to lay down. My heart thundered in my veins, every pound against my ribs felt like I'd been punched. I looked up at him and shook my head. *What the hell was that?*

He blinked, licked his lips, and shook his head, all

7

without taking his eyes off of mine. "What the bloody hell..." he breathed.

"Okay, I like this place a lot," his friend with the chocolate brown hair and sapphire eyes said with a sideways grin. "Let's stay."

I smiled at them like this was absolutely no big deal *at all*, even adding a wink for effect, then spun around and forced myself to calmly walk into the crowd. *Oh my god, oh my god. I can't believe I just did that.*

"Ellie!" Nickel yelled after me with a laugh. "Ellie, wait! Where are you going?"

"To throw things off counters like a normal cat!"

TWO

ELLIE

I STOPPED in front of the snack table and frowned. *Do I want something sweet or salty? Or do I want something...sweet? Like cool mint?* I glanced over my shoulder and spotted *him* on the other side of the kitchen, leaning against the wall next to his two friends and some scantily dressed girls. But he was watching me. He hadn't taken his eyes off of me since I kissed him. Even in the chaos of the party my eyes somehow kept finding his.

I sighed and turned back to the table, trying to think about snacks and not how delicious he was. *Food. Focus on food, Ellie.* There were more options than I knew what to do with. My first instinct screamed brownies but at *this* party I was afraid of what was in those brownies, so it wasn't worth the risk.

"Heads up!"

I flinched and turned toward the sound just as a pizza delivery guy sat four pizza boxes on the table to my left.

The second he took his hands off of them the wolves descended. It was a free for all, a panicked mad-dash for fresh pizza. Later if someone asked, I'd pretend I wasn't involved. I scrambled through the crowded kitchen with my eyes locked on the prize. My stomach growled. I reached for a slice, but my hand collided with a much larger, tanner hand. Electricity shot up my arm. I hissed and yanked it back, shaking it out.

"Sorr—" I looked up and froze, my mouth going numb and dry "—y."

It was *him.*

The boy I kissed two hours ago.

My breath left me in a rush. Heat rushed to my face. My gaze went right to his lips and my mouth watered. That kiss replayed in my mind and I wanted desperately to drag that pretty mouth down to mine again. His lips curved into a crooked sideways grin that sent my pulse fluttering into la-la land. I looked up and found his soft lime green eyes watching me.

"Sorry, sorry, I just saw pizza and I don't know I guess I got excited and I just went for it—" I slammed my mouth shut. *Stop making it worse.* My face was on fire. "Sorry."

He arched one eyebrow and his eyes twinkled. He opened his mouth —

"Oi, Stellan!" The brown-haired guy who came with him grabbed him by the arm and dragged him away from me. "Come and have a look."

Stellan.

What a name.

I stood there like an idiot watching him get dragged away from me. His eyes stayed locked on mine until he was yanked around a corner. I sighed. "Damn it."

"Okay, the moment we've all been waiting for..." Tyler shouted to the crowd while standing on a chair and holding two pieces of paper. "We've got our two finalists for the annual costume contest! Everyone gather around!"

My stomach tightened and butterflies danced around.

"Ellie! Come on!" Nickel emerged from within the crowd. She grabbed my arm and tugged. "Let's get up there."

I groaned and grabbed a few cookies as she dragged me away. "Must we?" Two hours of catcalls and vulgar feline related pick-up lines and I was ready to go home and burn my *Catwoman* costume. Maybe dig into a pint of mint ice cream and relive the time I kissed a hot guy but didn't talk to him afterward. *Damn it.*

"Yes. This is it. I can feel it," Nickel said as we found a spot at the front of the crowd. She bit her lip and shimmied, then looked down at me and winked one green eye. "This is *our* year."

I frowned and glanced down at myself. This was the first Halloween that my costume was subtle. I even wore my own clothes. Well, I wore *Nickel's* top because I didn't own anything as revealing as *this*. The leathery black material hugged my chest like a vice grip, which was good since she hadn't let me wear a bra with it. Between the skin showing through the rows of rips in my black jeans and the strappy crop top, I felt naked.

"I don't know, Nickel, there's not much to my costume this year…"

Nickel, whose real name was Nicole, giggled and leaned down close to me. "Exactly my point."

I rolled my eyes. "Oh, so I have to be sexy in order to win a costume contest?"

"At a party full of hormonal teenage boys?" Bernadita jumped in front of us to get out of the way of a herd of hockey players rushing toward Tyler. She scrunched up her nose and narrowed her hazel eyes at their backs. "I'd say yes."

Nickel sighed and shook her head. "No. First of all, *I* dress sexy every year and I've never won. Secondly, because our group costume is *sick* this year."

I scoffed. Easy for her to say. Her beautiful dark brown skin made the gold armor of her *Wonder Woman* costume really *pop.* She was magnificent, as always.

"Don't make that face, Ellie." Bernadita swatted my hand and shook her head at me, making her burgundy curls bounce around her petite shoulders. She gestured down at her costume made of green leaves. "Yes, obviously Nickel looks like a goddess…but this year, we really stepped it up. I mean, *hello,* Poison Ivy wished she had hips like *mine.*"

"*I* wish I had hips like yours," Nickel said with a chuckle.

"*Nicole.*"

We all turned at the sound of her real name…and found Andy standing there with her hands on her hips. She shook her head. "We've talked about not inflating her ego any more, she's too feisty and dangerous as it is. And as you can see, prison jumpsuit orange really isn't my color."

I threw my hand over my mouth and laughed. This year our group decided to dress as *Justice League*, and even though I preferred *Marvel*, I had to admit it was worth it just to see straight-laced, super conservative Andy cosplaying *Harley Quinn*. I loved even more that she chose to go with Harley from the *Suicide Squad* movie from when she was in prison. The money spent on her *Puddin* choker was money well spent.

"That's impossible to do, Andy." Nickel tossed her hair over her shoulder. "Now, where are the boys? Everyone is about up here and since we're going to win, the boys need to be here."

The boys. Crap. I'd lost sight of them about half an hour ago when I went for more snacks. They weren't the most confident, outgoing sort of boys. They preferred comic book stores and science labs. Although, I wasn't much better. We were all nerds. The only reason we got invited to these parties was because of Nickel. She was ridiculously popular and dragged us along everywhere she went.

Which was sometimes awesome, sometimes torturous.

Nickel was five-foot-nine regularly, but in her heels tonight she was taller than most of the boys. She pointed to the far wall. "I saw Lao trying to blend in with the drapes over there."

"*Green Lantern*, green drapes. I get it." I chuckled and shoved another cookie in my mouth.

When I glanced in his direction all I saw was *him*. Stellan. He stood smiling with his two friends. When our eyes met, his lip pulled up in a sexy smirk that twisted my insides and made it hard to swallow my cookie. I chewed faster, hoping my cheeks weren't puffed out like a chipmunk. I turned back to my friends. I quickly brushed off my top lip, praying he hadn't taken notice of the crumbs clinging there.

Bernadita wagged her eyebrows at her. "Keeping tabs on your future husband, Mrs. Liu?"

"He's probably still trying to recover from that kiss." I giggled. *Just like me.*

She shrugged. "He's a dork and adorable. He's got a chance to make that happen. But if you tell him I said that…"

I swallowed the last little bit of my cookie, then put my fingers in my mouth and whistled. Lao turned and spotted us. We waved for him to come over and his cheeks flushed. He tapped the others then led them through the crowd and over to us. Normally, in school, no one moved out of their way. But as *Batman, Aquaman, The Flash,* and *Green Lantern?* Smooth sailing.

Sherman grimaced at the people crammed in all around us. "Can we leave after this? I'm hungry."

"There's food here—"

"*Andy.*" Sherman closed his eyes and shook his head once. "Food that has been sitting out for more than two hours has a higher contamination rate and given the amount of hands in said food I will have to pass and *insist* on getting freshly prepared sustenance."

"OKAY, YOU READY?" Tyler screamed, the veins in his neck bulging.

The party went nuts. People held their drinks up in the air and fist pumped with the other hand. The music shut off mid-song. Tyler stood on chair that probably cost more than my parents' rent. Even in the dim lighting, his pale skin was nearly the same color as the toga draped around his body. A golden leaf crown tangled with the messy brown hair on top of his head. He was killing it dressed as the Greek God Zeus. He even wore the strappy sandals to complete the outfit.

He waved his hands for the crowd to quiet down. "All right, the moment of the year...my darling Hera and I have counted all your votes throughout the party to narrow it down to the top two costumes."

I popped up on my tiptoes and whispered to Nickel, "do you think she knows that Zeus cheated on Hera every day with anything that moved and that Tyler is no better?"

"I'm not sure the caption on Pinterest told her all of that." Nickel winked.

"The top two are..." Tyler drummed on his stomach for a few seconds, then held up the pieces of paper. "And I can't believe I'm about to say this in real life...the Avengers and the Justice League!"

Oh my God.

That's US.

My jaw dropped.

"See! I told you!" Nickel grabbed my elbow and dragged me toward Tyler, leading the rest of our group closer to the front.

"Avengers assemble!" Tyler shouted and waved his hand. "Up here by me, dudes!"

The party was cheering like this was Superbowl Sunday.

I stopped beside Tyler then turned to face the crowd. My heart leapt up into my throat. They were all staring at us. Every single person. I hated being the center of attention. Although, I had to admit, Nickel's sexy makeover on me tonight was giving me a boost of confidence I wasn't used to. At least now when they stared at me, I knew I looked good. Apparently, you can wear cat ears as long as you've got the skimpy clothing to go with them. Otherwise you're a weirdo. Not that I knew from experience. *Nope.*

"All right, all right, all right. Settle down." Tyler looked down at me and bit his bottom lip. Then he *purred* and my stomach turned. "Okay, so you all know, since this is my party, at my house, I get to pick the winner. You've narrowed it down to the top two for me and I have to say you've done a brilliant job this year. I mean...*meow, Catwoman.*"

I curled my hands up in front of me and hissed.

Which was apparently the exact *wrong* thing to do because his eyes flashed with excitement. "Hera, my love, the coveted trophy, please?"

Hera, also known as Monique, sashayed up to him in her see-through toga and handed over a crystal skull the size of my head. She blew a kiss at her boyfriend like she hadn't just seen him flirting with me or sitting in a circle playing spin the bottle in front of half the school.

He smacked her ass as she walked away, then he held the crystal skull trophy out in front of him. "Now, I have to admit, this was a tough call. Both teams here gave quite a run for gold. I mean...*Fat Thor, amiright?*"

The guy whose name I didn't know - some jock - jumped out in front of his group and danced with his fake-fat stomach. I wanted to roll my eyes, but he even had a bowl of guacamole and chips. I couldn't hate the attention to detail. I may have even taken a picture with him earlier to share on my cosplaying Instagram page. *Not that I have one of those.*

Tyler calmed the cheering crowd again. "Yeah, you guys look fantastic. But without a *Black Widow* or *Scarlet Witch*, I'm not sure how you could beat out the sexy ladies of the *Justice League!*"

Every single guy in the party raised their drinks, splashing beer onto the people around them as they screamed like the mindless teenage boys that they were.

"Congratulations to..." Tyler held the crystal skull trophy up over his head. "The *Justice League!*"

My jaw dropped. Everyone cheered and hollered. Even the guys we beat. My heart fluttered with excitement. This was every nerd's dream - going full cosplay and winning a costume contest at the most popular guy in school's party. I couldn't wait to tell all of my friends at the comic book store.

Bernadita squealed in my ear and jumped up and down.

Hewie leapt out in front of us and snatched the trophy from Tyler's hand. He held it up and yelled, "YES! Thank you!"

The snotty girls at the front snarled at him, but everyone else's gaze was on us. *The girls.* I felt each and every guy undressing me with their eyes. A cold chill slithered down my spine and I shivered. *Okay, I'm done with the attention now.* I was glancing toward Nickel when my gaze landed on a pair of pale green eyes. *Stellan.* He raised his cup toward me and gave me a nod. My cheeks heated and I wanted to go talk to him, to hear the smooth timber of his voice once more.

Sherman pushed his way past Bernadita to stand beside me. He tapped my best friend's shoulder between repeatedly whispering her name, "Nickel. Nickel. Nickel. Nickel—"

"*Yes,* Sherman, what?" Nickel snapped.

He blinked. "Can we go now?"

"Sherman, we just won the contest," Lao grumbled. "We can't leave *now.*"

"Actually, we can. And we should." Nickel reached out and wrapped her arm around my shoulders. "These babes are getting too much attention from lusty, slutty boys and I don't feel like ruining my good mood by having to castrate a bitch. Come on, we outties. Ladies, link up."

I grabbed her hand then reached behind me and took Andy's - who squeezed Bernadita's hand like her life depended on it. Once we were linked up, Nickel charged through the crowd like the true alpha she was. I glanced over my shoulder and found the guys dancing their way behind us. Well, except for Sherman, who looked more like an alien than *The Flash* as he scurried to catch up. Ravi was using *Aquaman's* trident as a dance prop. Lao was getting creative with his bat wings. Hewie was fist bumping everyone we passed with the crystal skull. Behind him, Stellan —

Stellan? I wasn't going to get to talk to him. But I had to. After that kiss I just needed to know where to find him. To at least get his last name so I could find him on Facebook. I glanced over my shoulder, but he was too far away. There were no less than fifty people between us, I'd never get all the way over to him before my friends walked out the door. *Damn it.*

"Wait, Nicole! Where you going?" Tyler shouted, reminding me of why we were leaving.

We were just about to the front door, but she stopped and smiled over her shoulder at him. She batted her eyelashes. "Just going outside for some fresh air."

"Okay but wait!" Tyler wiggled his way through the crowd until he got to us. "Before I forget, we have to get our picture together."

Every year the person, or group, who won the costume contest got their picture taken with Tyler and Monique...and then it was blasted all over social media, seen literally by the entire student body. And if that wasn't enough, it was always blown up and hung in the cafeteria. *Why?* I hadn't figured that out yet.

CHANDELLE LAVAUN & MEGAN MONTERO

Tyler whistled. "Yo, Alex, do the honors, man?"

Alex grinned and handed his beer to the busty, mostly topless girl beside him, then he held his hand out and took Tyler's phone. He held the camera up. "Strike a pose!"

Now *this* was a moment my friends and I were prepared for.

No cosplay was complete without being able to pose like the character in question.

I struck my best *Catwoman* pose and held it.

"Okay, I took like ten." Alex held the phone out to Tyler. He looked at me and nodded. "This is gonna be your hottest party pic yet, Ty."

I glanced over my shoulder to where I last saw Stellan – but he was gone. My heart sank. Now that we were about to walk out the door, I realized I didn't want to leave yet. I hadn't gotten to talk to Stellan, though he hadn't exactly tried to speak to me either. He'd had his chances. He probably just wasn't interested. He probably was worried I was some stage five clinger after that kiss.

Tyler grinned. "Hey, Nicole, give me your number and I'll text you the picture."

"Your girlfriend has it." Nickel arched one eyebrow then spun toward the door. She glanced over her shoulder. "Ask *her*. Come on guys, let's go grab tacos."

I grabbed my leather jacket off the coat rack by the front door and slid it on - then paused. I needed to use the bathroom. The pressure in my bladder was waving its arms at me for attention. But the bathroom was in the back of the apartment, past like a hundred teenagers. My friends were all standing at the door. I sighed and skipped over to join them. Our favorite taco place was a block away by Columbus Circle. I could wait until we got there.

We slipped out of the apartment just as the elevator doors across from it were opening. We jumped inside and crammed in. I hit the button for the first floor, then the one to close the doors.

As they closed, Stellan and his two friends stepped into the hallway and pale green eyes found mine. My heart fluttered. He held his hand up and leapt toward the door. I cursed and dove for the button to open the doors but they closed in my face. I groaned and sulked back against the wall. *Why didn't I get his number? Or at least his last name so I can find him online? Maybe Tyler or Alex has it.*

Ravi turned his back to the doors and grinned. "Guys, this is really going to help our street cred. So... you're welcome."

"*You're* welcome?" Bernadita arched one eyebrow and put her hands on her hips. "You think *you* did that? Please, as Shakira once said, these hips don't lie."

"I know I'm no Jason Momoa..." he gestured to his stomach where he had one ab instead of the eighteen Momoa had. "But I've been begging you to let us do Justice League since the movie came out. Aquaman is *finally* cool. All of this naturally tanned skin is finally paying off. Thank you, India!"

The doors opened behind him. Nickel smiled and stepped forward. "Let's go, Ravi."

In all the excitement and meeting the hottest guy ever, I

forgot I needed to pee. He could talk all he wanted as long as we were moving. The others were still arguing about who won us the contest when we stepped out onto the sidewalk on 61st Street. It was only October in New York but that wind ripping up the street was bitter. Ice-cold air slammed into my face, prickling like glass shards against my bare skin. I shivered and zipped my jacket closed.

We stopped at the corner of 61st Street and Central Park West as cars and cabs sped by in a noisy blur. I looked over to my right where a good-looking guy with skin even darker than Nickel's stood in a pristine white suit. He had massive white angel wings hanging off his back, and I knew he had to have spent a ton of money on them because they looked legit. He stood there double fisting tacos - actually, he had at least two in each hand. I grinned. I liked his style.

And then I saw the guys he was talking to and I recognized that chiseled, scruffy jawline instantly. *Stellan? What? How?* I frowned and glanced back at the building, then spotted a red exit sign. *He must have taken the stairs.* I turned back to him and found his gaze locked on me.

My pulse fluttered. He was stupidly gorgeous, his sandy blond hair and bright green eyes both glistened in the neon lights from the buildings around us.

My breathing grew tight. I licked my lips and took a step toward him.

"*ELLIE!*"

I jumped and turned toward the sound of my name - and found my friends on the other side of the street. I cursed and sprinted over to them. Nickel, Sherman, and Lao were up ahead...*inside* Central Park.

"Wait, where are we going?" I froze on the sidewalk beside Bernadita and Ravi. "I thought we were getting tacos?"

Ravi rolled his brown eyes. "Did you not hear Sherman in the elevator? He doesn't want tacos."

"So we're cutting through the Park—"

"*Through?*" I groaned and wiggled around. The pressure in my bladder was about to explode. "I have to pee. I didn't know we were going through. I can't hold it that long."

"Well, where you gonna go?"

"Not in Central Park at night." I spun around and spotted a hotel right across from us. "Look, The Emerald Hotel. I'll just run in there and go real quick, then meet you back here."

Bernadita pointed behind her with her thumbs. "Just let me tell Nickel—"

"I'll be back by then!" I scurried back to the street then paused. "Just wait for me inside where Nickel is now!"

THREE

ELLIE

"ELLIE!"

I heard her call out for me, but I didn't wait. I high-tailed it across the street and through the front doors of the hotel. There was some kind of party going on in the lobby, so I stopped the closest person and asked where the bathroom was. The girl, a sexy Cleopatra, pointed to the far-left corner. I thanked her and pushed my way through the crowd, begging my bladder to just hang on another minute. How could I have let it get this bad? Oh, I knew, sexy green eyed minty flavored distractions happened. And now I was suffering for it.

But when I rounded the corner into the hallway, my heart sank. There had to be twenty women standing in line. *No, no, no. This can't be the bathroom line.* I jumped around them and hurried down the hall to where the line stopped...and then it turned *inside* the bathroom. I groaned and did a little dance that every girl knew - the one that meant if I didn't find a toilet, I was going to need a wardrobe change.

The other women were all giving me the stink eye like they would beat me up if I even thought about skipping the line. I cursed and spun around in a panic. *Think, Ellie. Most bathrooms are in the same place on each floor. Just find the stairs.* I ran to the end of the hallway to a door without a sign - *YES. Stairs!*

I pushed the door open then flew down the stairs to the lower floor. I had to go too bad to climb *up* stairs. The door at the bottom was jammed, so I threw all of my body weight into it and it flew open. Gravity took over and I slammed into the wall on the other side of the hallway. "Ouch. Ow. Shit."

In the back of my mind I knew this was ridiculous, but this was what New York did to a person with their lack of public restrooms. *Should've just gone in a bush inside the park.*

About five feet down, I saw a door that looked promising. *Please be a bathroom, please be a bathroom.*

I pushed the door open. "YES!"

It *was* a bathroom. I jumped into the first stall and locked it behind me. I'd never been so happy to find a toilet.

After washing my hands, I looked up at myself in the mirror and didn't recognize the sultry face staring back at me. Dark coal lined my violet eyes. My skin was pale against the black crop top and tight jeans. My hair was a wild midnight mess around my face. But the thing I noticed the most was how plump my lips felt after that kiss. I reached up and touched them. Even now his minty flavor lingered on my lips. But I'd lost any chance I had of knowing who he was when I'd walked away. I shook myself and stepped back from the sink. Disappointment sank into the pit of my stomach. *Maybe Tyler or Alex know him? I could ask them. I know them enough now after winning the contest.*

I slipped back out the door and froze. *Crap. Which way did I come from?* I shrugged and ran toward a bright light streaming in from another hallway. When I made it to the next hallway and turned left, I slid to a stop. *Okay, I definitely did not come this way before.* For a moment, I considered turning around and going back to find the path I'd taken before, except that made no sense. I just had to get up a level.

I stood in the middle of a bank of four mirrored elevators. My heart sank. There wasn't a single button on the elevators, but there was an opening into another hallway that was lit bright like a full moon. After a second of waving my arms around like a lunatic swatting mosquitos, I gave up and ran through the open doorway, shivering as cold air rushed over me. I fumbled for my cell phone that was tucked away in my jacket pocket then pulled it out and found a text from Nickel.

Ellieeeeee. You broke the code - and don't you dare say it's more like guidelines! You're not a pirate. We're waiting for you in the park, you've got 10 minutes before I come running in there after you.

My cheeks burned from smiling as I shot a text back to

her. I glanced up and frowned. The hallway was mostly dark, with only flickering lights in the distance. The bulb must've just gone out. I shrugged and looked to my right and spotted a set of stairs. It wasn't the same staircase, but it would work. I'd lived in New York my whole life, I just needed to get to the street and I'd be set.

When I got to the top of the stairs, I was in a grand marble room with floor-to-ceiling glass windows. *Weird. I must've come out on the other side of the building.* But it didn't matter. Just outside the glass walls the glittering lights of Manhattan were shining like the buildings of Asgard. It was near midnight on the Upper West Side, so the lack of people on the sidewalk was fairly normal. I sprinted toward the door at the far end and pushed my way outside.

There were no cars coming by, but I instantly spotted the tree line of Central Park to my right so I dashed across the street and hurried into the park. *Damn, how did I get so turned around? I was not this far from the park before. This is what kissing random strangers does to my brain. Focus, Ellie. Just get to Nickel and this is all over.* I dodged a massive tree then sprinted down the path. It was darker than it had been a few minutes ago. A streetlight must've gone out. But the moon above was shining bright and gave off enough light to see the path between the trees. It wasn't the entrance to the park I was used to taking but it would get me there.

The sounds of the city had disappeared as I ran between shadows to the spot where my friends were waiting. The path curved around a tree then opened up into an empty — *wait, EMPTY?* I slid to a stop right in the middle of the path. My friends were nowhere in sight. My pulse quickened, my heart hammering in my chest. My breathing grew tight. I glanced around but it was just me out there. The moon shining down on me put me in a golden spotlight for anything or anyone watching from the darkness. A cold shiver slid down my spine.

"Nickel?" I whisper-shouted. If she were near, she'd hear me, but I didn't want to alert anyone else to my presence.

I bit my lip and waited for a response, only to hear a symphony of crickets. I stood in the spot where I'd last seen her, yet there wasn't a person in sight. *Wasn't she supposed to be right here? This is where I saw her standing with the boys. It hasn't been ten minutes yet, either, so she should be right here.*

My hands started to shake and goosebumps that had nothing to do with the temperature broke across my skin. "Nickel, where are you?"

Nothing.

Just the eerie howl of the wind ripping through the park.

I groaned and fiddled with the zipper on my jacket. I was a New Yorker, I grew up here, and I knew that no one lingered in Central Park at night by themselves. Especially not at midnight. *Especially* not a teenage girl without a single weapon. That was asking for trouble.

But my friends had just been right *here.* I'd seen them all standing here. It didn't make any sense. We didn't abandon our own. We had rules for our group. Sure, I'd broken one by going to the bathroom by myself but there was no way Nickel would leave the park without me. Even if she came in to find me, she would've left the rest of them outside to wait for me.

My stomach turned and tightened.

It didn't make any sense.

My friends would never have left me anywhere.

Two of them would've come looking for me in the hotel, the others would've planted themselves like cement poles in the last place I'd seen them. We'd learned this the hard way in middle school. I knew I'd messed up by going alone but I'd panicked. Needing a bathroom in desperation did funny things to the brain.

But still. They'd be here.

What is happening?

"Nickel? Andy?" I licked my lips and took a few steps backward to get out of the moon's spotlight. My stomach turned and bile rose in my throat. "Sherman? Bernadita? Ravi?"

Still…*nothing.*

This couldn't be happening. No, they had to be playing a joke on me. Pranking me as punishment for running off alone at midnight. *Right. That's it. They're messing with me.*

"Guys, okay…you can come out now." I forced a chuckle despite the trembling in my body. "Very funny, guys. Come on…come out."

I counted to sixty and still nothing.

Literally a whole minute of standing in the dark by myself.

Oh no, no, no. Damn it, Ellie. Why didn't you just wait for Bernadita?

I dug into my pocket then pulled out my cellphone. My heart sank. No new messages or missed calls. From anyone. Which didn't make sense because Nickel alone wouldn't have stopped calling. My best friend was over-protective. With shaking fingers, I opened up our text thread and frowned. My text saying I was on my way back out failed to send. I frowned and hit *retry*...only to have it immediately fail again.

Okay, don't panic yet. Sometimes texts suck. Call her.

I closed the texting app and opened up the phone. Her name was third on my favorites, just under my parents, so I hit it. I hadn't even gotten the phone to my ear when there was a sharp clicking noise. When I looked down, I saw *CALL FAILED.*

The world spun around me so hard I actually stumbled back another step or two.

A large, warm hand gripped my left elbow and my heart stopped.

All of those self-defense classes my parents made me take kicked in instantly. I balled my fist like I'd been taught and swung my arm as I spun around. I couldn't see the man's face, I just saw enough to know I did not know him. He was too tall, too broad shouldered, dressed too nice.

My fist slammed right into his nose. Sharp pain shot through my hand and up my arm.

Bright neon purple light exploded between us and he stumbled back a few feet.

Everything was moving in slow motion yet in hyper speed all at the same time.

The guy shouted as blood poured onto his face. He stumbled back into a patch of moonlight, and I saw a fancy Victorian English costume and a head of shaggy, dirty blond hair. My heart stopped. *STELLAN?*

OH GOD.

SHIT.

I gasped and leapt away from him with my heart caught in my throat. I pumped my arms and dug my heels into the ground as I sprinted away, but it was like one of those awful moments in a dream where no matter how fast you ran you didn't move at all. Trees passed by me, so I knew I was putting distance between us, yet I still felt like I was alone in the park with some strange guy.

Except he wasn't a stranger, *I'd kissed him.* It was the pretty one with green eyes from the party who I kissed during spin the bottle. He'd kept a close eye on me at the party after that. Everywhere I looked there he'd been. And then he'd followed me out of the party. I thought the dude in the angel costume eating tacos had stopped him. And then it hit me. *Oh, God, did he follow me here? Was that purple light some kind of drug he was going to use on me?* My stomach turned and bile rose in my throat. My pulse was pounding so loud it was the only noise I could hear.

Oh God, oh God, oh God. What have I done? Why didn't I

just wait for them? Shit, shit, shit, shit, shit! I groaned to myself as I hauled ass for the edge of the park.

"Wait! Wait!" He yelled from behind me.

But I didn't stop. I didn't care how pretty he was or how good his lips tasted – he couldn't stalk me. *Shit, shit, shit! I'm such an idiot! This is why you don't kiss strangers, Ellie!*

I looked up and cried with relief. The lights from Columbus Circle were up ahead, I just had to get there. I'd find a cop. I'd seen a dozen of them out on the corners before I ran into that hotel. *Oh God, please be out there. They have to be out there. This can't be happening.*

My legs burned and screamed but I kept going, kept pushing. Just a bit farther. Columbus Circle was *right there,* just beyond the — I choked on a gasp and slid to a stop.

THAT'S NOT COLUMBUS CIRCLE.

Something wasn't right. I spun in a circle and stumbled farther away from the park. I didn't recognize any of what I saw. It wasn't any other part of New York City, either. *What the hell?*

Where are all the buildings? I spun around again, frantically looking for a *single* skyscraper but not finding even *one.* Right where I stood should have been a massive stone and gold sculpture. There should have been steps and a bunch of food vendors selling hot dogs and soft pretzels. Steam should've been rising up through the metal grates in the ground as the subway rushed by...but the ground under my feet was...was...*dirt.* Everything was so still and eerily silent. *Where are all the people?*

WHERE AM I?

That glass-walled shopping mall that was the center-piece of Columbus Circle was gone.

Trump tower was gone.

I didn't even see the hotel where I'd gone in for the bathroom. I saw a glass wall but that couldn't have been where I came from, it was only one floor. Where was the rest of the building? I glanced around in a panic when my eyes landed on something I should have seen instantly.

It was a damn castle.

Literally.

What in the ever-loving hell is happening?

Up ahead of me in the distance, a massive castle made of stone towered over me like an ancient skyscraper. It looked like something out of a Disney movie.

What's happening? Where am I? Where are my friends? Where is ANYONE? What the hell is going on? Oh God, did someone drug me at the party? WAIT, did Stellan drug me? He had to have. That was the only explanation for this hallucination, because this *had* to be a hallucination or I'd lost my damn mind.

The lights I'd seen were coming from these strange vintage lamps with a glittery glow. There were more of them lining the walls of the castle. But that was *it*. There were no streetlights, no lights in buildings. No lights on cars passing by - *where are all the cars?* I glanced left and right down the roads except there were no paved roads. Or at least they didn't look paved. It was hard to tell without lights. Everything was dark and black. The shadows were creeping in with every breath.

My whole body was trembling from head to toe.

My breath left my body in a shimmering purple cloud.

I gasped.

Why is my breath purple?

What is this place? Where am I?

God, he DID drug me.

I put my hands on my head and spun in circles, tugging on my hair and praying I'd wake from this horrible dream any second. I turned back toward the park and my stomach flipped. Stellan was headed right toward me...*running.*

DAMMIT.

Where am I?! What is even happening?

I panicked and glanced around. I had to get away - *but where?* The only thing I recognized was that glass wall. I needed to retrace my steps and find my way back from wherever the hell I was. I groaned and sprinted into the darkness. I just had to get there. I balled my fists so hard my nails cut little bloody crescents into my palms.

This better be a dream.

It has to be.

It's a dream and I'm about to wake up any second now...

FOUR

STELLAN

Mistakes were made.

My heart thundered through my veins, sending shock-waves down my legs.

Mistakes were made.

I pulled my sleeve up and stared down at the black markings on my left forearm. I knew the pattern so well by now I could draw it with my eyes closed. I'd seen it my whole life. In fact, I couldn't remember *not* having it. My parents refused to talk about it, but my sister used to tell me it showed up when I was a year old.

But what none of them knew was that *I knew* what it looked like when I went into First Realm. They didn't know I snuck over there every week and that while I was there my marking *changed.* Over there, it wasn't an image of triangles and circles and swirls...it was words. Words written in plain, simple English. Words that said *mistakes were made.*

Butterflies danced in my stomach and my pulse skipped.

Mistakes were made.

MISTAKES WERE MADE.

"Oh my God," I heard myself whisper. I stumbled back and the world spun around me as it all clicked. "Mistakes were made...she said...mistakes were made."

It's HER.

Her. After all this time, all the waiting, and there she was. *Mistakes were made.* When she'd first said those words, right before kissing me like her life depended on it, I hadn't thought anything of it because it was a common phrase in First Realm. Every time I went there I heard it. Weston and Shylock made a point to tease me about it every time. *I did hear that, right? I can't be going crazy right now.* I tried to will my markings to change back to the English words so I could prove it to myself, but they wouldn't. I wasn't in First Realm anymore.

Wait, what was she doing in First Realm? The last I'd seen her she was standing on the corner near The Emerald and then I saw her running out of the portal wing here in Second Realm — *WAIT. WHAT AM I SAYING? HOW DID SHE GET THROUGH?*

I looked up and my breath left me in a rush.

Purple magic swirled in the air all around me. I'd been so preoccupied by her that none of it clicked. *Purple.* Not silver. My magic was silver, a bright, shiny silver...but *this*...was purple. This was the color of — "OH MY GOD."

I felt my blood drain from my face and my stomach

turned. All those old stories my sister used to tell me flashed through my mind in rapid fire. I heard the words whispered next to candlelight as we hid in her closet. I saw the writings in that old diary she'd found hidden in the palace and the pictures someone had elegantly drawn out.

I looked back down at my markings. It was *her.* But then my gaze moved to the purple magic and my heart sank because it was also *HER.* I frowned and pain shot through my face as fresh blood dripped out of my nose. She'd punched me.

"Oi, Stellan!" Weston shouted from way off to my right, closer to the portal wing. He had his hands cupped around his mouth and pale blue magic swirled around his fingers, amplifying his voice. "What you doing, mate?"

"It's her," I heard myself whisper back.

Shylock stepped out from behind him and scowled. "Bloody hell, are you *bleeding?*"

Shite. What AM I doing? Speak to her. I looked up and opened my mouth to speak and gasped. She was gone. Of course she was gone. I'd snuck up on her in the dark at midnight and touched her. *Bullocks, I'm a real prat.* My cousins were still shouting for me, but I wasn't listening. I had to find her. *Where did she go?* She'd just been right in front of me but her long dark hair and black clothing was hiding her within the darkness.

Come on, where is — there! I spotted her at the very edge of the forest, near the Anchor and the Royal Cemetery. *Stellan, you stupid sod!*

I cursed and sprinted after her as fast as I could.

"Stellan?" Weston shouted again.

But I couldn't answer him, all of my concentration was on *her.* I had to catch her. I had to — I choked on a gasp as a shadow jumped out beside her. My heart leapt up into my throat.

Ladarious.

No.

NO.

I started to scream for her, but I didn't know her name, so I slammed my mouth shut before Ladarious realized I was there. I dug my heels in and pushed my legs harder and faster, but I seemed to be running through quicksand. Ladarious, the enemy of the crown, the parasite of our realm, a monster of all monsters, grinned and strolled toward her.

She was in the light of the streetlamps now. I saw the bright sparkle of her purple eyes and the flush in her cheeks as she spun in circles. She was scared and panicked and I'd already failed her because I wasn't going to make it in time. Ladarious was already there.

I watched in horror as his long legs stepped out of the shadows toward her. The golden glow of the lamps made his bald head shimmer like he polished it every hour. She still hadn't noticed him standing there, but I couldn't blame her. I knew all she was seeing was the lack of New York City.

Electricity pulsed in the air beside me. *Weston!* My heart flared with hope that he was close to her, but a second later he leapt out from between a set of trees a few feet away from me.

"Stellan? Mate?" He shouted as he ran toward me.

Shylock was right beside him, towering over our cousin. His sharp blue eyes scanned over me without missing a step. "What's wrong?"

"It's her, it's her, it's her!" I pointed to my left arm then pointed straight ahead of me. "It's HER!"

"WHAT?" Weston shouted.

That bright, sinister orange magic I knew far too well flashed up ahead and my stomach turned and tightened. I wasn't going to make it. I was too far. He was too close. She didn't know who he was or what he would do. She didn't know how to fight him and his horrific magic. I had to do something. *Anything.*

Ladarious chuckled and rubbed his palms together, then spread his arms wide and dove for her.

NO!

I flung my hands out in front of me and my silver magic filled the air.

FIVE

ELLIE

PLEASE WAKE UP. Please wake up. Right now.

I squeezed my eyes shut and took a deep breath...then opened my eyes — and screamed.

A massive man with tattoos covering his bald head and big bloodshot blue eyes stood towering in front of me. I stumbled away from him, but my legs were not getting with the program.

"Well, aren't you a pretty thing," he said with a wide grin and a chuckle that made my stomach roll.

No, no, no. I spun on my toes and leapt away but big, calloused hands gripped my elbows and yanked me back around to face him. He grabbed my other arm and lifted me off the ground. My feet dangled and I squirmed to fight against his pinching grip. I screamed as loud as I could and kicked my legs. That same bright, neon purple light flashed and the hard-packed ground exploded between us. The man's eyes widened as wind slammed into my chest and threw me backwards into the air. I crashed into the dirt and pain laced through my body.

The man leapt for me and I scrambled back on my hands. A stone slab the size of my body dropped out of the sky, blocking his path. I climbed to my feet and took off running. I had no idea what the hell was going on but I couldn't stay there. I had to get to that glass room. My answers *had* to be there. But when I looked up ahead my pulse quickened.

Oh God, is that it? Is that where I came out of? It can't be. It's too far away!

Loud, rumbling laughter echoed behind me and sent a cold chill down my spine.

I glanced over my shoulder and found the man holding his stomach and laughing like a biker gang version of Santa Claus. He *skipped* forward to follow me and waved his hands. Orange light flashed from his palms. I gasped and spun back around — and slid to a stop.

The glass room was gone.

GONE.

I blinked and rubbed my eyes, then looked again. Nothing.

Instead of a glass room and vintage streetlamps all I saw was the shore of the ocean with ten-foot waves crashing onto the sand in front of me. *No. No, this isn't right. This wasn't here before. This can't be real. None of this can be real. Oh, God, am I really lying in a ditch somewhere in the park tripping?*

I shoved both hands into my hair and tugged.

CHANDELLE LAVAUN & MEGAN MONTERO

Wake up, wake up, WAKE UP.

Snap out of it, Ellie.

"Nowhere to run, poppet," the man drawled. His voice was a low hiss tainted with a thick English accent. And it was much closer than it had been before.

I spun back around and choked on a scream. Everything around me changed. I was on a narrow cliff of a snow-covered mountain. Pebbles and chunks of earth crumbled under my toes and tumbled down the mountain. I leapt back and the man's laughter echoed through the mountains. A wild tremor ripped through my body. Tears pooled in my eyes.

Orange light flashed again and then I was standing in the middle of a desert, my feet sinking deep into the burning sand. Fear like I'd never experienced grabbed hold of my heart and squeezed like a boa constrictor. I choked and gasped for air.

Sand flew up in the air and the black night sky shimmered with silver glitter. The air pulsed and then *he* appeared out of thin air. Stellan. He appeared like a meteor, shooting across this terrifying desert right for me.

NO. Please. I jumped and spun around but there was nowhere to go. Everywhere I looked were rolling hills of golden sand and black sky. A strangled cry left my lips. The air pulsed and turned hot. I turned back and he was still coming for me. His face was a mask of fury. His green eyes shined like a panther's in the dark and I was his prey.

Oh, God. What are they? Some sick team?

What did he do to me?

My arms and legs trembled. My pulse raced so fast black dots swarmed my vision and dizziness assaulted me. He was almost there, only a few feet away. I had nothing to fight him off with. It was just sand everywhere. I bent down and gripped two fistfuls of it in my palms, then turned and threw it right at his face.

The sky rolled and cracked over my head. Lightning flashed and struck the ground by my feet. I screamed and lunged to the side. Stellan dodged the scorched piece of desert and dove for me, but another bolt slammed into the ground inches in front of him. He gasped and flung his body back to avoid being hit. Lightning struck again, and again, and again. Stellan was surrounded, trapped in place.

"YOU!" The bald tatted guy growled, but I couldn't tell if he meant me or Stellan.

Out of nowhere, sharp pain shot through my ears and into my skull.. I hissed and gripped my head. My legs gave out. I staggered, trying to keep myself upright, when something slammed into the side of me. I caught a glimpse of a pale, thin arm wrapped around my waist and then I was being dragged across the sand. I didn't even have time to scream or panic. The pain in my head vanished but it left an achy throb in its place. I squeezed my eyes shut and cried out in fear.

My back hit something hard and I gasped.

My eyes flew open before I told them to and my breath left me in a rush. The desert was *gone.* The ocean was gone. That snow-covered mountain was gone. Cold gray stones lined the ground under my feet and the wall behind my back. I was in some circular shaped structure that had big gaps in the curved wall to let air rush through. I looked up and saw a sky blacker than a bottle of paint. Lightning flashed over my head like a spiderweb.

I gripped my chest and felt my own pulse pounding against my palm.

Something moved in my peripheral vision. I jumped and scurried back —

"I won't hurt you," the young woman in front of me said. She held her palms up in front of her and didn't make a move toward me. Her brown eyes were warm and kind. "I'm sorry I kind of tackled you there, I had to move fast."

I opened my mouth then shut it. Tears stung my eyes.

She cocked her head to the side and her dark brown hair fell over her shoulders. "Are you all right?" Her voice was even warmer than her eyes and something about the delicacy of her British accent calmed my frantic nerves.

Am I all right? NO. No, I am not all right.

But I couldn't get my mouth to work so I shook my head. Unable to stop myself, my gaze flickered to the edge of the stone wall beside me. I peeked around and spotted the bald man growling and pacing up and down the length of a black iron fence.

"This is the Royal Cemetery." The girl stood tall by my side and her voice hardened. "He can't get us in here."

SIX

ELLIE

"W-who are you?"

The girl turned and looked down at me. "Why don't you sit—"

"Who are you? Where am I? Who are those guys? What is this place? Why can't he get us here?" I knew I sounded crazy and was firing questions at her without giving her time to answer, but I was helpless to stop it. "Where the hell is Columbus Circle? Why are you helping me – wait, *are* you helping me? Or was this a trap I fell for? Girls can be monsters, too. Who are you? What is—"

"Stop," she said in a soft tone that sounded like a cat's purr. She held her palms up in surrender. "Sit down."

My back slid down the cold stone wall until my ass hit more cold stone. I kept my eyes on her the whole way down. I didn't want to sit and calm down. I wanted to freak out and get some answers, but when she spoke my body listened. Not in a sexual way, more like she'd used some kind of sorcery to take control of my body. Maybe it was just the softness of her accent.

The girl crouched down in front of me – then she actually *smiled*, like a friendly one that I wanted to instinctively return. "Deep breath in, then we'll get things sorted."

I nodded. Now that I was sitting, I realized how hard my heart was beating and how tight the muscles in my legs felt. I licked my lips then did as she asked and took a deep breath. Then another. And then one more but I wasn't going to calm down until I got answers.

She must've noticed, too, because she chuckled softly. "First off …*I* am Melanie Christin, and I will not hurt you. And you do have the right of it, girls can be monsters too, but I am not one of them. I hope to prove you can trust me soon."

"Melanie…" I heard myself whisper as I nodded.

"Yes. What is your name?" Her British accent was light and gentle as she spoke.

For a horrifying moment my mind was blank. But then I shook myself and it came back. "Eloise Sutton, my friends call me Ellie."

Melanie smiled and held her hand out for me to shake it. "Very well, Eloise, may *I* call you Ellie?"

I bit my lip and eyed her outstretched hand. My immediate reaction was to say yes, of course. But she was giving me a choice and I didn't want to make it lightly even if my gut told me I could trust her. I had no proof yet. I shook her hand. "I think that stands to be seen."

Melanie grinned and took her hand back. "Good. You're a thinker. Blind faith is a lot to ask of a person, isn't it?"

Despite everything, I chuckled. "Yes, indeed."

Orange lights flashed and reflected off the stone walls. I flinched. Melanie cursed.

My stomach tightened into knots. "W-who is t-that? The bald guy with the tattoos on his head?"

"A nightmare with two feet, and a complete nutter."

I must've made a face because she turned away from the space between the walls and looked back to me. She grimaced. "His name is Ladarious, and he's as vile of a monster as it gets. He's a tyrant. A parasite. A dark soul who enjoys his crimes. Eloise, you must stay away from him at all costs."

"O-okay, so what…we wait here for the police to arrest him?"

"*Arrest him?* No, Eloise, this is not a matter of arresting him. He's…he's…how do I put this…" She looked down at my body then up to my head and narrowed her eyes. "Are you dressed as Catwoman?"

I blinked and nodded. "What? Yes, I am, but why does—"

"Okay, okay right…nerdy human Earth girl, right. Okay—"

"*Earth girl? Are we not on Earth?*"

"We'll get back to that. You need to hear me on Ladarious."

I made a strangled groan I'd never heard before. "*Get*

back to Earth? What the hell does that mean? Where am I? No, no I need to go home right now. How do I get back?"

I started to get up but she leaned forward and gripped my elbows tight, holding me down. "You can't go back right now. Not with Ladarious out there—"

"*WHY?* Who the hell is this dude? Let's just sneak out while he's—"

"*There's no sneaking, Eloise!*" She shook her head wildly and her eyes sparkled in a way that made my pulse skip in fear. "If you leave this cemetery, he will kill you. Tonight. Right away, without mercy or compassion, and without missing his chance to enjoy your body the way he wants to first."

I gasped.

She nodded. "You heard right. Ladarious is a Lex Luther. A Sauron. A Lord Voldemort."

I shook my head. "But that's comic book stuff. Movies. Fiction—"

"What did he make you see?" She dropped my arms then pointed to where we'd come from. "Out there, you were panicked. Frozen in fear. I saw your eyes. I saw your reactions. *What did you see?*"

My heart thundered in my chest, shaking my bones. My lips were dry and cracking. "I- I – I saw the ocean...then a snowy mountain cliff...then a desert—"

"*None of that was real, Eloise.*" She sank down onto her knees in front of me, her brown eyes pleading for me to believe her. "I did not choose those fictional references for dramatic effect. Ladarious has gifts— horrible, terrifying gifts. He can make you see whatever he wants you to see. Look between these tombs and you'll see. Outside this cemetery is the forest and the lands of the palace. He *made* you see those other things to scare you. To make you stop running so he could capture you."

My eyes widened. A cold chill slid down my spine and I shivered. "*He* did that?"

She nodded. "He is evil and the most dangerous person you have ever met. He wants to overthrow the throne, not because they're corrupt and deserve it, but for *himself.* And he will kill anyone who gets in his way slowly and painfully with a smile on his face. There is no remorse. He is the hero of the story he created in his mind and he will stop at nothing until he gets it."

I swallowed through the ball of nerves climbing up my throat. "So...so...so he's...*Hitler*?"

She sighed and her shoulders dropped. "*YES.* Now do you see what I'm saying? He catches us, we're dead. Understand?" She leaned forward. "I don't say this to give you a fright, I say this to teach you. Respect the fear you feel for him and stay away."

"Okay, okay, okay....so who is *that*? I know his name is Stellan but what the hell is he doing here?" I pointed in the other direction, to where he hid under a tree branch.

Melanie followed my point, then smiled and sighed. "Oh, *that* is Prince Stellan. He's a good guy and would never hurt you. In fact, he's the main reason we got away just now."

"Right. Sure. Ok. Prince." I pushed my hair back and nodded. "And where the hell am I?

SEVEN

ELLIE

"Let's circle back to the Earth question now, please? Because that's kind of important and the only thing I really care about right now."

"Yes, I understand how this could be frightening—"

"*Frightening?*" I shouted and my cheeks warmed. "You're acting like I'm not on Earth! That is not frightening that is spine-chillingly, bloodcurdlingly terrifying!"

"I know."

"Are you telling me I'm not on Earth anymore?"

"No...technically you are still on Earth. Sort of."

"*Sort of?*"

Lightning flashed and cracked across the black sky.

She glanced up as thunder rolled over our heads, then frowned and tucked her brown hair behind her pale ears. "This is rather complicated and difficult to comprehend upon first learning. It took me years to come to grips with it myself. We are still technically on Earth but not in the same way you're used to. The place you come from, the world you lived in—"

"You mean New York City?"

She nodded. "Yes. New York City, and the rest of the Earth that you know of, is known as First Realm—"

"I'm sorry, did you say *FIRST? Realm?? How many realms are there?*"

"There are five realms in total—"

"*WHAT?*" I shook my head. Hot tears stung my eyes as fear sank its nasty fangs into me. I tried to get up. I had to get out of here. This had to be a dream. More lightning spread across the sky like a neon spiderweb.

"You're not dreaming, Eloise."

I scrubbed my face with my hands and sucked in a few ragged breaths. "You're telling me there are *realms*? What the hell is a realm? And how are we both on Earth and not? You're not making any sense!"

"All right…think of Earth, the planet, as a glass of water, okay?"

I bit my lip and nodded as my mind rattled like a volcano about to blow.

"Again, this is a loose, *loose* explanation that is definitely not scientifically accurate but it's the easiest way to understand how the realms work." She eyed me until I nodded again. Then she licked her lips. "Right, so Earth is a glass of water…each of the five realms is an ice cube in that glass."

I opened my mouth then shut it. I blinked and shook my head. "Ice cubes."

"Ice cubes. Now, First Realm—"

"Where I'm from?"

"Yes, where you grew up is First Realm…it's as it sounds, the *first* realm. It was the *only* realm for millions of years before the other realms were created – but we're not going to talk about that right now. All you need to know tonight is that each realm is a place for different species to live."

"Different. Species."

"Yes. First Realm is the realm for humans." She took a deep breath. "This realm you're in now is Second Realm, the land of mages."

I blinked and shook my head. "Mages?"

"Yes, mages."

"As in…you're not *human*?"

She opened her mouth then closed it and shrugged. "Obviously, we're a little bit human. Look at me? We look like humans."

"*But you're not*," my stomach turned and rolled. I threw my hands out to steady myself. "You're not a human. She's not human. Not. Human. It's fine. I'm okay. This is totally normal."

"*Eloise…*"

"Gimme a minute here, I'm freaking out!" I shouted and jumped to my feet. "She's not human. They're not human. Mages. Not Earth, oh God, what is even happening?"

My legs gave out and gravity took over. I stumbled over my own feet then tripped and slammed into one of the tall stone slabs. I hissed as pain shot through my arm and shoulder. My mind was burning a mile a minute. I couldn't keep up. Everything looked like Earth – *like the first ice cube.*

Ice cubes.

God.

The lightning flashing and striking the ground looked the same. The thunder roaring and shaking the ground sounded and felt the same. The smell of rain and burning wood, it was all the same.

But everything wasn't the same. This wasn't Columbus Circle, in the middle of New York City. It wasn't this dark or this quiet anywhere, even in Central Park. And we certainly didn't have flying debris. All around us were flying pebbles and rocks, long tree branches and broken stones with pointed edges.

I leaned against the cold, rough stone and peaked around the edge. The bald guy, *Ladarious,* prowled up and down the black iron fence like a tiger in a zoo. He snarled and stalked us, his eyes sharp and glowing. A cloud of orange wrapped around his balled fists. He threw his arm forward, launching that power toward us. I flinched back waiting for the visions to take me once more. His orange magic exploded into a hard barrier inches before it smacked into the stone wall surrounding us. It shot up and away from us and I sucked in a breath of relief. He really couldn't get to us in here. The muscles in his arms flexed tight as he roared. He glanced over and his gaze met mine. His lips pulled back in a nasty snarl and then he *grinned.* I didn't hear the words he shouted at me, but the hand gestures were vile and vulgar enough. I shuddered as a cold chill slithered down my spine.

Then I remembered the purple light I'd seen when I punched that Prince dude and then again when Ladarious picked me up.

"Mages...so like...magic." I licked my lips and swallowed down the fear climbing up my throat. "Like witches and wizards. Like Harry Potter and shit?"

Melanie leaned against the next stone, that stood a few feet over. She peaked around the edge then turned away and looked to me. "Essentially, yes."

Yes. Damn.

I nodded like this wasn't the craziest thing I'd ever heard. Like my heart wasn't pounding and my hands weren't trembling. "So, what, you about to pull a wand out or something to fight him off?"

Melanie smiled then tried to cover her mouth, but I'd seen it already.

My stomach dropped. "Oh, God...*are you?*"

She bit her lip then reached inside her coat...and pulled out a long wooden wand. It was very plain with only a few rings carved into the top of the smooth dark wood. "I *do* have a wand, it's true."

My eyes widened. I stood there frozen, just staring at her magical object.

But then she put it back inside her coat pocket. "Unfortunately, it won't do us any good right now."

"What? Why not?" I waved my hand toward Ladarious,

who was still stalking the cemetery. "*Stupefy* some shit! *Leviosa* his ass out of here."

She chuckled and shook her head. "Trust me, I've tried before. Our magic doesn't work like that and even if it did, Ladarious's little army out there would —"

"*Army?*" I glanced around the stone again and frowned. "Where?"

"You see behind him, at the edge of the shadows?" Melanie pointed. "The lot of them are dressed in black and blending in with the night. That's what they do."

My heart sank. I *hadn't* seen them. But now that she pointed them out, I couldn't *not* see them. Had to be dozens. We were outnumbered. Easy. I wanted to run, to flee, to find my way home and never leave my house again. But my gut was telling me to trust Melanie.

"Where is this Prince Stellan at anyway?" I gestured toward the men waiting to pounce on us and the debris flying through the air. "Where is he?"

"There." Melanie pointed to a large tree straight out from where we were, beyond the line of trees. "He's there, up on the branch in the tree. His two cousins, the Dukes, are closer to the bottom."

I scrubbed my face with my hands and groaned. "Why is he *there*? Why isn't he trying to help us?"

"He is. Everything you see flying through the air is *him.*" A smile pulled at her lips but she fought it. "He has telekinesis. All of *this* is him trying to help us."

I frowned. "Why would he help me? I'm a perfect stranger and I punched him in the face."

"You punched him in the face?" Her brown eyebrows shot to the clouds. She chuckled but I must've made a face because as soon as she saw me, she stopped. "Well, Eloise, that should tell you something about his character."

I opened my mouth and then the air around me pulsed with electricity. Something whistled then shot across the sky like a rocket. I gasped and leapt back. But Melanie jumped forward and caught it in her hands. Then she turned toward me and lifted her hands out, showing me the red brick that she'd caught.

"It's from Prince Stellan," she said softly.

On the top, carved into the stone, it said in elegant script. *He can't get in there. He'll leave with sunrise to avoid the Royal Guard.*

Melanie sighed and put the brick on the stone floor. When she straightened, she looked to me with sad eyes. "We'll have to hunker here tonight. You're looking knackered anyways."

Knackered? Is that a nice way of saying I look like shit? "Hunker? *Here?*"

I looked to the ground and spun in a circle. The stones were cold and the wind was bitterly sharp. There were no blankets or pillows, and there was barely any protection from the outside. From Ladarious.

"What about...what about...about..." I groaned and pointed to Stellan. *"Him."*

Melanie winked. "That's why we can't leave. In the morning, the Royal Guard will know we're here. And more importantly, they'll know Ladarious is out here. They'll come rushing right out."

The Royal Guard.

PRINCE Stellan.

I shook my head. "I don't understand. How is Prince Stellan safe out there but we wouldn't be? And why can't we call for this Royal Guard *now?*"

"Well, Prince Stellan, and the Dukes, are hiding in a tree on Palace grounds. Ladarious is not foolish enough to attack him there. Unfortunately I could not get *you* over there, so we had to settle for *this.* But it's at least protected by spells that are keeping us safe." She exhaled a rough breath. "The Royal Guard…the only way they'd come out at this time of night is if there's an attack. Ladarious isn't technically attacking us right now."

My stomach rolled. This was all nuts. Crazy talk. I was not in some other realm. I was still in *my* ice cube. Though in my heart I knew I wasn't. I knew Melanie was telling the truth, even if I couldn't wrap my head around it. She'd saved me, protected me. I had to trust her. My only other options were the bald tattoo guy screaming at me or the pretty boy I kissed and punched.

I'd trust a girl over them any day.

Besides, even Prince Stellan told us to stay put. His note on the brick said the Royal Guard would come in the morning. We just had to wait it out. Once they got here, they'd realize I wasn't supposed to be here and they'd help me get home. I just had to be patient.

Melanie sat down on the ground then stretched her arms. "Come on, Eloise. You need to rest. Sit down."

My body obeyed in an instant. *Wait.* I frowned. "Did you *make* me do that just now?"

"I just softly recommended it." She had the grace to blush. "Please, Eloise. I know you have to be terrified, but your energy is weak right now. I can feel it. Rest before you collapse."

I groaned and leaned back against the stone. "You're a witch."

"A mage," she corrected softly. "But yes."

"Because this is the realm for mages? Everyone here is one besides me?"

"Yes, everyone in Second Realm is a mage."

I shook my head. This was all too much. "What are the other realms for?"

"The Fae reside in the Third Realm. The Vampires in the Fourth…and shifters are in the Fifth." I must've made a face because she smiled and shook her head. "Eloise, I promise I will answer your questions tomorrow. But you need to sleep now."

My breath left me in a rush. "You might as well mind control me into sleep because there's no way in hell my brain is shutting down voluntarily."

She chuckled. "I like you."

I opened my mouth to say something sassy back…when everything went black.

EIGHT

ELLIE

I KNOW I'm no Jason Momoa..." Ravi gestured to his stomach where he had one ab instead of the eighteen Momoa had. "But I've been begging you to let us do Justice League since the movie came out. Aquaman is finally cool. All of this naturally tanned skin is finally paying off. Thank you, India!"

The doors opened behind him. Nickel smiled and stepped forward. "Let's go, Ravi."

The wind ripping up 61st street was bitter. Ice-cold air slammed into my face, prickling like glass shards against my bare skin. I shivered and zipped my jacket closed.

We stopped at the corner of 61st Street and Central Park West as cars and cabs sped by in a noisy blur. I looked over to my right where a good-looking guy with skin even darker than Nickel's stood in a pristine white suit. He had massive white angel wings hanging off his back and I knew he had to have spent a ton of money on them because they looked legit. He stood *there double fisting tacos - actually, he had at least two in each hand. I grinned.*

And then I saw the guys he was talking to and I recognized that chiseled, scruffy jawline instantly. Stellan? What? How? I frowned and glanced back at the building then spotted a red exit sign. He must have taken the stairs. I turned back to him and found his gaze locked on me.

I gasped and my stomach tightened into knots. My pulse fluttered. He was stupidly gorgeous, his sandy blond hair and bright green eyes glistened in the neon lights of the buildings around us.

I needed to look away, but I couldn't. I was locked in a trance. My breathing grew tight. I licked my lips.

"Eloise, wake up."

I shot straight up with my heart lodged in my throat and Prince Stellan's face plastered on the backs of my eyelids. *It was a dream. Just a dream.* I rubbed my eyes then scrubbed my whole face. I didn't want to be awake yet. I wanted to go right back to sleep and have a *peaceful* dream. The way my heart raced blood through my veins, the heavy thumping was the only sound I could hear. It echoed around me. It was a little chillier than I liked my room to be, so I reached for my blanket without opening my eyes – if I opened them, I'd lose all my sleepiness.

But then my hand hit cold, hard stone and my heart stopped.

No, no, no, no, no.

"Eloise," Melanie's soft British accent was a rude wake up call.

I cringed and squeezed my eyes shut. *This can't be real. Go back to sleep.*

"Eloise, it's time to wake."

I took a deep, shaky breath then opened my eyes. My stomach rolled and my pulse took off faster than *The Flash*. It *was* real. Not a dream at all. A living freaking nightmare. Tears stung the backs of my eyes but I refused to let them fall. I swallowed through the hot lump in my throat. "It wasn't a dream."

Melanie crouched down in front of me and sighed. Her soft brown eyes scanned my face, then she frowned. "I'm sorry, 'twas not."

Orange light flashed over our heads. I gasped and sat up on my knees, ready to move. "What's going on?"

"Ladarious." She grimaced. "He's relentless. I fear he won't stop until he has you."

I peeked around the massive gray stone and my eyes widened. "It's still nighttime?"

"Not for much longer." She pointed to my right. "Dawn is upon us."

When I followed her point, I found she was right. Although the sky was a dark navy blue to my left, to my right was a painting of soft oranges, pinks, and golden yellows. In between, the sky was lightening to a beautiful pale blue. I looked around...and sighed. It wasn't nearly as terrifying as it seemed last night. It had been pitch black with moving shadows and eerie nothingness. There just hadn't been any lights to help me *see*.

But now that I could...it wasn't so bad at all.

We were in the middle of a cemetery with a black iron gate surrounding it. There were tombstones around the edges that grew bigger and more ornate as they got closer to where we hid. To my right and left were small stone and brick mausoleums with flowers around them. Everything seemed to be placed in a specific layout and it made me want to fly over it all to see the design from above. Whatever it was, these tall stones we were hiding in were the focal point. There were five stones that towered at least twenty feet into the sky. Now that I had a little bit of light, I saw that the stones behind me had to be six feet deep.

"The kings are buried here," Melanie said softly.

I jumped, forgetting she was there for a second. Then her words registered. "The kings? Oh, right. *Prince* Stellan. So there's a king and queen. Right. Totally with you."

She smirked and pointed to the biggest rows of mausoleums. "Those are for the queens. The tombs get smaller with each position. So the princes and the princesses are slightly smaller, then the tombstones are for the dukes and the like."

I frowned. That felt a little...*off.* I opened my mouth to voice this opinion when I spotted that small building with the glass walls. I gasped and pointed to it. "That's it. That's where I came out of!"

Excitement and hope flared inside of me. I scurried across to the bigger stones and looked around them at the glass building – and the lush forest behind it. The one I'd thought was Central Park. I smiled. *That's how I get home.*

"Not right now, you cannot."

"What? Why not?" I spun around to glare at Melanie. "I came in through there, I should be able to *leave* through there."

She narrowed her brown eyes at me, then they widened. "Oh, of course." She pulled her wand out of her brown coat and waved it around. "*Now* look."

I frowned. Everything looked the same. But she pointed behind me, so I turned back — and choked on a gasp. My jaw dropped and my heart sank farther. Sure, that building was still there, along with the park. A moment ago, I'd seen green grass and lush forest. Then, as if she'd cleared a hazy picture, it all faded away. Now, I saw only the dozens of men strapped with swords and daggers. They each wore menacing snarls and held sinister, pointy wands in their hands.

Then I saw *him.* Ladarious.

My pulse quickened and I gripped the stone for support.

"Ladarious was projecting an empty, peaceful land. Because he wants you to walk out there alone and unexpecting."

I groaned.

"Eloise, I know you want to get home and you're not wrong on where to go to get there…" she grabbed my elbow and pulled me back to lean against the stone out of sight. "But you will not make it there alive if you go now. There are things you don't understand. Things I can't yet explain to you, for we do not have the time."

"But…"

She shook her head. "But nothing. If you go to that building now you risk unleashing dark magic on First Realm, and a war like you've never known will follow."

My stomach sank and bile rose in my throat. "Are you – are you saying I can't ever go home?"

"I'm saying to please trust me. I'm saying I will get you home when it is safe to do so."

I didn't want to wait. I didn't want to trust her. But she had saved my life and then kept me alive while I slept. And I couldn't argue against what I saw with my own eyes...nor could I deny the magic he'd used on me already. If he got into First Realm — I shuddered at the thought. I'd seen enough Marvel movies to know how that went down, except we didn't have the Avengers to save us. My nerdy friends and I were smart, but we weren't Tony Stark and Bruce Banner smart.

Even if they wouldn't admit it.

Just thinking about my friends made my heart hurt. They had to be terrified. I'd disappeared. Nickel had to be beside herself. I pulled out my cellphone—

"Those don't work here."

I gasped. "*What?*"

She shook her head. "No sodding technology like in First Realm. It's bloody trying at times, but everything here is run by magic. Which makes it a little better. We are not as advanced as the humans in some regards. You might as well turn that off and save your battery."

I narrowed my eyes on her. "You talk like you've been to First Realm...."

"I have, but that is a story for another day—"

"Why?" I huffed and pushed my hair back. "You ask me to trust you, blind faith and all that, yet you haven't given me the same respect."

Her eyes widened...then she nodded. "You do have a point. I am sorry." She moved closer until there was only a foot between us, then she whispered. "I have spent time in First Realm but no one, and I mean *no one*, from Second Realm can know that. It is my biggest secret and if anyone finds out I will be killed instantly."

I swallowed. "Y-you're not being dramatic?"

"No. We are on Palace grounds, just being in here is illegal but to go in *there*?" She pointed to the glass-walled building. "Means for execution by the King and Queen themselves. I know. I know you have questions, but it is not safe here to speak another word on it. All right?"

"All right," I whispered back. She had given me her secret, putting her trust in me as well. "Thank you for trusting me with that."

She smiled. "Thank you for trusting me to keep you safe, Eloise."

"You can call me Ellie."

Her grin widened. "Ellie." She nodded.

"So...what now? We wait for the Royal Guard?" I frowned. "Wait, if it's illegal to be in here then why would the Royal Guard help us?"

Melanie's face darkened. Her eyes turned colder and sharper than the stones we leaned on. Gone was the sweet, soft girl. In her place was a dangerous, furious warrior and

I suddenly wanted to know her other secrets. "They won't help us. They're the most dangerous people in our world. They'll kill their own child for some silk gowns."

I gasped. *What? Who are these people?*

She reached out and squeezed my shoulders. "Ellie, listen to me, Prince Stellan is the *only* royal you can trust. Only him. No one else. You understand?"

I nodded as fear resurfaced with a vengeance.

"Good. Now, sit here and do not move. Stay hidden—"

"Wait, *where are you going?*"

"To get help, but I cannot do it from in here. I'll be right back."

And then she was gone, just like that. *Doesn't she know when people say that in movies they never come back? That's how you get killed.* I knew this wasn't a movie but it sure felt like it. Magic wasn't real. Mages were fictional. Yet I couldn't deny what I'd seen already.

Just breathe, Ellie. She'll be right back. He can't get you in here.

That's what Prince Stellan said.

But what if he lied? What if he's mad I punched him and —no, Melanie was adamant in his trustworthiness.

The air around me sparkled and flashed like bright silver glitter. I sucked in a breath and tried to blend in with the stone pillar at my back. My heart stopped.

The glitter brightened and thickened, then moved together.

Light flashed — and then a person stood in its place.

I gasped and tried to back away, but I was already up

against the stone. Like in a dream, I tried to move but my body was frozen in place. Locked in fear. Time seemed to slow down.

It was a man. He smelled like crisp fallen leaves. I knew that scent. My stomach fluttered. He was crouched down but I knew by the length of his legs that he'd be tall when he stood. His shoulders were broad and his skin tanned like he was out in the sun a lot.

And then he picked his head up and big, soft, lime green eyes met mine.

My breath left me in a rush, and I sank back against the stone.

Prince Stellan.

He reached up and pushed his dirty blond hair back off his forehead. His nose had a little cut on the bridge with dried blood caked on it. His eyes shined bright and his smile was brighter. "I do believe we've already met."

God. That accent. Everyone knew a good accent added at least four hot points – and Prince Stellan didn't need any more. If ten was the highest hot rank, then the prince was born at least a twenty. The accent just made his beauty almost cruel. The cut I'd given him from punching him in the nose didn't even hurt his looks. He looked like a younger, grittier Brad Pitt... but bigger.

Like Brad Pitt's younger, hotter, bigger brother who definitely played in the NFL or something. Everything about him screamed trouble. Danger. I felt brick walls going up around my heart just looking at his beautiful face.

He arched one eyebrow and I gasped. *Shit. He was talking to me. Real smooth, Ellie.*

I opened my mouth to respond...but completely forgot what he'd said. I wasn't sure I'd even heard it around all that accented heaven. "Um...uh...what?"

He chuckled and it made my heart flutter. "I said, I do believe we've already met."

"Oh. *OH.*" Heat exploded in my cheeks. "I punched you."

"Yes, yes you did." If he didn't stop smirking like that, I was going to die from asphyxiation. "You also kissed me if I recall correctly."

I knew I needed to say something. That was how conversations worked. One person spoke, the other responded. But with his eyes on me...my brain just melted.

"If you're wondering why I didn't do..." he gestured around himself "*that* last night, it's because there's a delay when I come back through from First Realm before that'll start working again. Rubbish, really, but true nonetheless."

"Uh huh...." I nodded.

Things were happening inside my body that I'd never felt before, never experienced before. I didn't know how to explain it to myself...but I felt like I was drowning in a river of fire *and liked it.* I opened my mouth then shut it. I forgot words. My tongue was paralyzed. The pressure in my chest felt like a rhino was sitting on me, pushing me into the ground. I couldn't move. I couldn't breathe. He needed to go away before Melanie shipped a body bag back to my parents.

Finally, he looked away and I sucked in a deep, ragged breath.

He cleared his throat. "Where is Melanie?"

I swallowed and pointed to my left. My hand trembled and I hated that he had this kind of effect on me. "S-she said – b-be right b-back."

He nodded and kept his eyes on where I'd pointed.

The sky was lightening by the second.

Something whistled through the air like a rocket. I jumped up and spun toward the sound just as red smoke burst in the sky. "What is that?"

The red smoke swirled and moved until it took the shape of a red circle with a red spider inside of it.

"The Rebellion," Prince Stellan said with a growl.

His voice was like velvet and honey. Both smooth and rough. I was so lost to the sound of it that it took me a minute to process the words he'd said. *The Rebellion.*

He nodded. "It's them."

My eyes widened. I glanced over to his gorgeous profile. *Rebellion against the King?* Melanie had said the prince could be trusted but that didn't mean he approved of a rebellion that was fighting his family. His monarchy. If he was a prince, then he was potentially heir to the throne.

"They're your only chance at getting out of here alive."

Orange light flashed all around us. Men shouted and screamed. Ladarious's voice sent a shiver down my spine and I instinctively moved *closer* to Prince Stellan. Something exploded in the distance and the ground trembled. My pulse quickened as horror set in.

The Rebellion was attacking Ladarious's clan.

And we were stuck right in the middle of it.

"Ellie, it's time to —" Melanie suddenly gasped from right behind us. She bowed her head a little. *"Prince Stellan."*

He jumped to his feet and nodded at her. "You have to go. Now. The Guard is almost here and you can't be here with her when they arrive."

"We won't be," Melanie said in a rush as she unbuttoned her coat. Once it was off, she leapt forward and wrapped it around my shoulders. "Here, wear mine for now. You can't be seen in First Realm clothing—"

"How do you know about that?" Prince Stellan hissed and turned razor sharp eyes on her.

"Now is not the time to discuss old legends." She grabbed me by the arm and pulled me to my feet. "The Rebellion is waiting just outside the cemetery for us."

"Good. But we're not finished discussing this." He twirled his wrists and that glittery silver light coiled around his hands. "I'll cover you. *GO.*"

NINE

ELLIE

THREE OPPOSING forces were about to clash, and I was in the middle of it all.

The Rebellion, The Royal Guard, and Ladarious' forces. All of them sounded terrifying to me. Melanie motioned for me to follow her and we both crept toward the edge of the iron fence. Ladarious paced like a tiger in a cage, ready to pounce at any moment. Melanie and Stellan kept insisting he couldn't get to me in here, but we all knew eventually I'd have to come out... *and what then?* I still didn't understand how his magic worked or what he could do to me, and the not knowing was crippling. My heart raced in my chest as we waited on the edge of safety and danger.

On the hill, up to my right, the sounds of the Rebellion echoed in the forest. Loud explosions sounded and the ground shook beneath my feet. Ladarious rounded the corner of the cemetery and pointed up toward the Rebellion forces. His men rushed in that direction.

Behind us a flood of mages in purple waistcoats and matching trousers came running over the meadow toward the fray. They held their wands high and at the ready, weapons strapped to their bodies. Beams of magic fired toward Lardarious' forces. Chunks of earth shot into the air, dirt and pebbles rained down on us.

Melanie grabbed my hand. "Get ready to run."

"I'll cover your backs." Stellan started to back away.

"Wait…" I took a step toward him. *What am I doing?* I barely knew him, but I didn't want him to leave. Not yet. But I had no idea what was going on in my head. And now he was staring at me, waiting for me to finish my sentence. I shook my head and cleared my throat. "T-thanks."

He nodded once with a sexy little smirk. Power shimmered around his hands and an asteroid shower worth of boulders shot off the ground and flew toward Ladarious' clan.

Ladarious glared at me and held his hand up, his lip snarled back. Orange magic sparkled from his palms as he held my gaze. He couldn't touch me here, but I got the message loud and clear. I took a step back.

A dark chuckle passed his lips. "Soon," he mouthed.

As the Rebellion drew nearer, Ladarious turned his attention toward the forest as mages streamed out dressed like warriors, like a gritty militia weighed down with weapons. None of them matched like an army. They threw their wands up and arrows flew from the thick treetops behind them. The Royal Guard held their wands up and magical shields shimmered over their bodies. The arrows smacked into them, each one a sharp thunk against a hollow barrel.

The Rebellion seized the moment and charged forward, emerging from the forest in dozens and attacking Laradious' army. Lights flashed and the ground rumbled under their wake. Pieces of the earth were upheaved and thrown like balls across the field. The Royal Guard splintered in half as they fought off the Rebellion and Ladarious' army.

Melanie pointed toward the forest the Rebellion had just emerged from. "We need to get through there."

"Are you shitting me?" The armies blocked the way, the raging skirmish rocked the world around us, and she wanted us to go through them to get there?

"I shit you not." She nodded toward the forest, then seemed miles away. "Come now, best foot forward."

Stellan kept the boulders flying just enough to distract the dueling sides. "I'll keep them busy. Go now."

I began to step forward, ready to run. "But wait? What about you? How will you get away?"

The corner of his lip pulled up in a half smile and then he vanished. A second later, he reappeared fifteen feet away. He glanced over his shoulder to me and nodded his head. "Go now!"

"We do not belong here, Ellie. The Royal Guard will arrest us if we stay." She pulled on my arm. "Time to go."

I hesitated. "Okay...right...got it..."

I gave Stellan one last glance. There was something

about the way his hair fell into his face and the way he smiled, like even in the chaos of the moment nothing could phase him. I turned away from him and ran behind Melanie. Her coat was a bit long for me so it kept catching on the tall grass as we sprinted, but I couldn't stop.

A large man ran into our path. He stopped dead and pointed his wand just over our heads. His eyes widened and his arm flinched back as if he'd fired a shotgun. I ducked down and looked over my shoulder just at the blast hit one of Ladarious' men square in the chest, sending him flying back. He gave us a single nod and took off running.

Melanie tugged me into a sprint behind her. My heart thundered in my chest as my boots slipped over the dew-covered grass. A boulder the size of a car flew right at my head, I dove to the ground and mud slashed up over the side of my face. I scrambled back to my feet, ignoring the burn in my muscles.

Melanie surged forward. "Come o—"

Her words were cut off as a mage in a long black cloak leapt out in front of her from behind a tree and lifted her off the ground by her elbows. His beady yellow eyes flashed with excitement. Her legs dangled for a second. A scream ripped up my throat and lightning flashed. A bolt struck just beside us. The ground exploded. Melanie and I flew back a couple of feet and landed on our backs. The man went flying even further as dirt and rocks rained down on us.

She was on her feet in the blink of an eye and dragging me back up. "Keep going."

75

The forest was only a few more yards away, we just had to make it there alive. *I think...I hope.* I raced toward it, hoping the trees would give us the cover we needed. The war raged on around us, magic firing in all directions like a broken rainbow. I leapt over craters in the ground and ducked under flying rocks. I pulled the cloak in tighter over my face to shield my eyes from particles of dirt flying around.

Melanie flicked her wand and a tree trunk flew over our heads. Silver magic wrapped around the tree, propelling it forward like a boulder of death.

Melanie waved me forward. "Follow it."

It bounced and rolled, knocking anything in its path to the ground. I pumped my arms and sprinted after it, trying to keep up. The tree slammed into the dense line of trees at the edge of the forest. I scrambled around it and ducked down. Melanie fell in beside me and leaned her back up against the hard, scratchy bark. Her chest heaved with panting breaths.

I pressed my hands to the trunk and leaned up next to her. Screams filled the air and shots of magic rained in all different directions. The smell of burning grass invaded my nose. Ladarious marched out into the middle of it all with not a care in the world. Sunlight reflected off of his bald head, making those tattoos look even darker and more sinister. He held his hands out to his sides and orange magic blew up like a mushroom cloud over the battlefield.

The opposing forces stood motionless. They dropped

their hands down to their sides. His power hit them like a hammer, rendering them sightless. *Is that what I looked like when he infiltrated my mind?* The Royal Guard and Rebellion both sat like ducks ripe for the picking.

Ladarious chuckled. "Spread out. Find the girl."

I'm gonna throw up. My hands shook as paralyzing panic flooded my body. This was a manhunt and I was the man. Ladarious' army fired shots of magic at their blinded opponents, knocking them to the ground or sending them flying off in directions.

"Bring her to me. Now." His voice demanded in a scratchy growl.

"Oi, wank stain!" Stellan popped out from behind one of the gravestones and waved his hands.

I wanted to jump up and help him. To tell him to run and not risk his life because of me. My muscles tightened as I was about to rise. Melanie's hand slammed down on my shoulder, holding me in place.

"Don't do it. He knows what he faces." She shook her head. "Be ready to run."

Silver magic wound around Stellan's hands just as Ladarious let his orange magic flow. A huge crater flew up out of the ground and right at Ladarious. He spun out of the way and laughed. A smaller disc-like rock shot through the air and smacked Ladarious in the back of his head, knocking him to the ground. The hold he had on the other troops dropped. The fighting broke into a frenzy once the Royal Guard and Rebellion forces regained their senses.

"Now!" Melanie jumped to her feet and ran into the shadows of the woods.

With barely a glance at Stellan, I turned and followed her. Under the canopy of trees the air was cool and damp. I sucked in deep gasping breaths. The cloak she'd given me caught on stray branches as I fought my way through the brush. Up ahead, both sides of the forest connected to surround us.

"Into the forest. Go!" Ladarious' voice boomed over the chaos.

My heart hammered in my chest and my lungs burned with every breath I took.

Melanie turned on her heels and lunged for me. She wrapped her hand around my wrist and yanked me forward. "*Keep moving.* This way."

I glanced back and saw at least ten Royal Guards heading straight for us. Black clouds rolled across the sky and the wind kicked up again. Lightning forked above our heads. I was going to die in a world I didn't belong to all because I had to pee. *Damn it!*

"We follow the river to the village, then we'll be okay," Melanie whispered.

I nodded even though that didn't sound too promising. *Okay* wasn't a measurement I wanted to bet my life on, by any means. But I had to trust her, she'd kept me alive this long. I leapt over falling logs and ducked under branches. There was a flash of bright light and the boulder next to me exploded to dust. I ducked away, pumping my arms harder. The forest began to thin out ahead. I could see light shining in.

Melanie darted to the left and I scrambled to follow. I had no idea where we were going as we dove between two overgrown cypress trees, slid under low hanging tree limbs, and jumped over one massive broken tree trunk. I wondered how many times she'd run through here like this. There was no way she was figuring this out as we were running. Just as I thought the forest was going to swallow us whole, we leapt around a pine tree…and onto an empty dirt road. My steps faltered and my jaw dropped. *Where the hell am I?*

Melanie grabbed my arm and yanked me down to a crouch beside her. "Slow down, stay low, and pull your hood up."

I pulled the hood of her cloak up over my head and tightened it around my waist.

Just in front of us was the beginning of a small town. A town straight out of the Victorian era. I was so far from New York it made my head spin. Dust kicked up as town folk rode their horse-drawn carriages down a road lined with two-story buildings. The sidewalks were full of people dressed in simple cotton clothing as they passed by the shops on the first floor. Above them, windows were framed with ivy and little buckets of flowers that hung from the windows.

I huddled into the cloak. My *Catwoman* costume screamed *alien* and the last thing I wanted to do was draw attention to myself. These women all wore long dresses like Melanie's, with corset bodices that barely dropped low enough to show any cleavage. My skin-tight, ripped up jeans were wild enough, but my crop top didn't even cover my whole chest – it had three little straps that went across my sternum. There was a whole shit ton of skin showing.

What am I even doing here? This isn't where I belong.

Melanie glanced over her shoulder and cursed. She grabbed my hand and yanked me around a corner. "Royal Guards. Walk normal and stay close to me."

My stomach turned. *Walk normal. Walk. Normal.*

What is normal? Short steps? Fast steps?

"Head down," she hissed and grabbed a stray basket from a cart on the street, then handed it to me. "Come on."

I ducked my head, letting my hair fall into my face to hopefully hide me. We fell into step and she turned us down another small pathway that ran back behind the buildings of the main street. Part of me wanted to enjoy the beauty of this little town, but the bigger part of me needed to remember this wasn't a movie. This wasn't a comic book. This wasn't a damn dream. This was real. I was really in some other realm. I couldn't let myself enjoy this, not even for a second. I had to stay on alert. I had to find my way home.

Everything was so wrong. So, *so* wrong.

"We're nearly there, we'll be safe soon," Melanie whispered and peeked over her shoulder. "I think we've lost them."

"Kinda hard to tell who's on our side and who isn't," I

grumbled, looking over my shoulder. I didn't even know what I was looking for. Or who.

Two pillars rose up on either side of the dirt road in front of us. They were wide and sturdy. Small stone balls sat on top of each. Ivy vines wound around them in a tangled mess of dead leaves. Melanie glanced around, then grabbed a handful of the ivy and yanked it to the side. There, painted on one of those stony pillars, was the same symbol I'd seen in the sky earlier. A red circle with a red spider in the middle of it.

I heard Stellan's deep, velvety voice in my head saying, *The Rebellion.*

My heart fluttered. "This is…this is…*the Rebellion?*"

"We'll be safe here," Melanie said quietly but sharply, ignoring my question. She dragged me between the pillars and the air pulsed around her.

I froze and pointed to her. "What was that?"

"This is a sanctuary for people who need it. Anyone with the intent of doing harm cannot pass through *that,*" she said and gestured around her. She waved me forward. "Please, Ellie. You've come this far. Just walk through."

Right. This isn't weird at all. I sucked in a deep breath and blew it back out, then took a step forward. The air shimmered around me and I felt it beat against my skin, like walking through a warm waterfall. Once I was on the other side, my jaw dropped. What I'd just seen was *gone.*

Now, a beautiful old house with large windows and a faded stone and brick exterior stood before us. That same ivy from the pillars covered almost every inch of the building, like it was part of the structure. The roof ran straight from one end to the other, with sets of windows running across the first and second floor. Four round columns connected the flat stones on the ground to the half-moon roof that stood over the front door.

"What is this place?" I heard myself whisper.

Melanie sighed and her lips curved. "Home."

TEN

ELLIE

HOME? I would give anything to be home right now. To be in *my* bed with my big fluffy blanket and mushy pillow. But I wasn't. I was stuck in a nightmare without an end in sight. My heart sank. I sucked in a deep breath to try and calm my frayed nerves as best as I could. The sky finally started to clear, and the sun shinned down on us as we approached the sanctuary.

"What kind of sanctuary is this?"

"It's a home for displaced women and children." Melanie strolled up to the front door and gave three quick knocks. Then she stepped to the side and smiled at me. "They don't turn away those in need..." She grabbed the doorknob and gave it a quick twist, then shoved it open. "In you go."

"Are we supposed to just walk in like this?" I hesitated.

She looked me up and down. "I'd say we're bloody

needing some help right about now. So in we go. Not to worry, I know the owner…and I live here."

I stepped into the doorway and froze. There in front of me was a set of stairs leading up to the second floor. A dozen black cats lounged on those steps, covering them like a furry carpet. Their golden gazes all landed on me and I suddenly wanted out of this *Catwoman* costume, worrying that I might've insulted them in some way. I pulled the ears from my head and shoved them into my back pocket. The moment they were out of sight, the cats went back to lounging.

"Right, come along." Melanie waved for me to follow her down a narrow hallway.

A door creaked open to my right and I couldn't help but peek through. There was a single table with a group of women sitting round it. The table was bare of any food, yet they all sat so still, just waiting. Then another woman walked in from a swinging door on the side of the room, she held her wand up and steaming dishes of food soared through the door to gently land on the table for the others.

"Ellie? Are you coming?" Melanie's words jarred me from staring in wonder.

I wanted to walk through the door and pull up a chair. Not to eat their food, but to see what else would happen.

"Yeah, right behind you." I left the magical floating food and followed her.

To my left was a smaller library with the door sitting wide open. I froze in the doorway, staring at the small quiet room. Dark wooden shelves lined the perimeter of the room and a steaming cup of tea sat untouched on a round table in the center of the room. I tilted my head inside, searching for a sign that anyone was there. No one. It was completely empty, yet there was a stack of books sitting in the middle of a small table. Like someone had taken them all out for a research project. One by one the books floated across the room and slid into place on the shelves. Off to the side sat an oversized chair where a bin of laundry was quietly folding itself. The shirts rose up into the air, folded in on themselves, and landed in a neat pile back in the basket.

This place was something else. There was magic all around yet it didn't feel like some opulent castle. Melanie was right, it felt like home. The walls were an aged pastel teal that gave a welcome feeling. The hardwood floors creaked under my feet with every step I took. Two small children in plain brown cotton dresses ran past us with their little wands passing a ball back and forth.

"Don't let it hit the ground!" The taller girl called out.

"I won't." The smaller one's eyes widened as she flicked her wand and it froze mid-air and then went sailing back.

I pressed myself up against the wall and out of their way. But this didn't seem like anything new to Melanie, she simply stepped around them and kept on going. Once they passed, I hurried to catch up. There, at the end of the hall, dozens of papers floated up near the ceiling. They whizzed in and out of the double doors on the right. It looked like the old parchment I'd seen at museums, complete with the brown scrolling writing. As I got closer, I couldn't stop myself from reaching my hand up and letting my fingers brush over the soft paper.

They spun around my hand and down my arm. Puffs of wind drifted over my skin and I smiled. This was the coolest shit I'd ever seen. That magic-filled battle earlier had been incredible to see yet terrifying, but this…it was… everything. I didn't risk grabbing one but as soon as those double doors opened the whirl of papers left me and filed into the room where a group of people gathered around a single table. They all had their eyes trained on a map in front of them, while the floating papers just hovered above each of them, waiting to be snagged.

Melanie stepped to my side. "I rather fancy the fly notes. Not as quick as a text message but more beautiful."

I nodded. "Yes, it's like they're dancing."

She tapped my arm and crooked her finger. "Moving on."

I wanted to stand here and let this world just go on around me. I suspected if I sat still enough, more would begin to happen and I could witness it. I was torn between following her and waiting for more.

She chuckled. "Fine, I'll show you something better."

That got my feet moving. "Something better?"

She glanced at me over her shoulder and smiled. "Yes." She turned left down another hallway and stopped just before another door. With one hand she pushed it wide open, and my jaw dropped.

It was the kitchen but so much more than that. At the back of the room an oversized fireplace blazed with flames that danced over the bottom of a huge black cauldron. Bubbles fizzed over the side and steam drifted up from it. A large wooden spoon stirred the liquid inside, yet no one was holding it.

"Potions?" I pointed toward it.

"Soup." Melanie giggled. "Even mages have to eat now and then."

I almost felt silly for asking, but how was I supposed to know? The water in a copper farmhouse style sink began to run, and the dishes stacked on the counter all ducked themselves under the faucet. Soapy bubbles flowed over the side as the scrub brush worked each one clean. Once the dish was spotless, it spun around, drying itself, and then found its place in a stack among the other clean dishes on the other side of the sink.

"I wish I could do magic like that. It'd make home life a lot easier."

"Brilliant, isn't it?" She tapped my hand and nodded down the hall. "Onward."

Just as I was about to step away a cupboard flew open and two brooms jumped out. Each dashed around the room, sweeping the floor and tidying up. *Roomba my ass.* I turned and walked with Melanie in comfortable silence. For the first time since I got here, I felt like I could breathe. Like maybe this world of magic wasn't so destructive and full of people like Ladarious.

Melanie stopped at the last door on the right and pushed it open, then motioned for me to walk through.

It was a very simple room with two single beds that

were pushed into the corners against the far wall. The blankets were thin and made of a light beige material. Across from the beds, on the wall to my right, sat two identical wardrobes. The cream-colored paint was chipped and faded in some places, giving it that antique feel that people in New York paid hundreds for. Directly across from the door was a single window that latched at the center and would open outward if I chose. It wasn't like my room back home, with the walls covered in posters of my favorite comics. The walls were bare here and still held that pastel teal color.

I stepped in the room and Melanie hurried in behind me. She let the door fall shut behind her. "We have to get you changed. You cannot be seen like that."

"That makes sense, what do you have in mind?" This little revealing cat costume wouldn't do for the modest way the women dressed. I walked over to the bed nearest me then slid her heavy cloak off and gently laid it across the foot of the bed. I tugged on the sleeves of my leather jacket then pulled my arms out and laid it next to the cloak. As I straightened, I spotted something dark covering almost my entire forearm. I gasped and held my arms out. "What the hell?"

"What's happened?" Melanie moved in close to me and I held my arm out toward her.

There on my forearm was a cluster of geometric shapes all connected together. At the center of it was large circle, with a halfmoons above and below it. Four triangles poked out from each side, making the shape of a diamond. Floral swirls danced around and through the main shape with extra dots and lines throughout. The dark ink stood out against my pale skin. Except I didn't have any tattoos. "What is this?"

Her eyes widened as she stared down at it but then she shook herself and licked her lips. "It's…um…well it's a sign that you've been touched by dark magic."

"*Dark magic?*" My pulse quickened. *What does that even mean? How can she be so calm about it?* I ran my finger over it, but it didn't hurt in the least. "What do you *mean* it's dark magic? You can't just drop that all nonchalantly."

Melanie took a deep breath, then sighed and her shoulders dropped. She pushed her dark hair over her shoulders. "It means you've been exposed to violent magic, and violent magic leaves a mark. A scar, so to speak."

"A *scar?*" I waved my arm around. "This does not look like a damn scar, Melanie. Scars aren't pretty! How am I supposed to hide this? What do I tell my – *oh my god.* My mom is gonna kill me. Would your mom kill you over this?"

She chuckled but there was a strange haunted expression in her brown eyes. "Indeed, she would. And I do see your point. We can cover it with a glamour spell prior to returning to First Realm."

I groaned and tugged on my wild hair. "Why are you so calm about this? It's a violent magic scar! If it's no big deal, then where's yours?"

She held her arms out, but they were bare. "As you see, I do not. But many people do, and everyone's scars manifest

CHANDELLE LAVAUN & MEGAN MONTERO

differently, so theirs won't look the same as yours. Maren, the woman who runs this shelter, has one. But...if I may... do not inquire about them should you see them. People do not like to speak of their battle scars."

A light knock came from the door and Melanie stepped around the bed in front of me. "Who's there?"

The door eased open and a young woman only a few years older than me stepped through. She was petite with brown hair that fell in loose waves down to her shoulders. Her chocolate brown eyes widened at the sight of me.

She jumped into the room and closed the door behind her. "I saw you rush in here—"

"Maren, this is Eloise. Eloise this is Maren." Melanie smiled and stepped away from me. "As I was just saying, she runs the shelter here but also lets it serve as a base for the Rebellion. This world owes her a lot."

Maren narrowed her dark eyes on me then she turned to Melanie. "Did you steal a royal?"

I gasped. "*Me?* A royal?"

Maren arched one eyebrow and pointed to me. "Your makeup."

"No, Maren, of course I didn't." Melanie sighed. "I saved her from Ladarious last night. He's after her."

"Ladari— you know what?" Maren shook her head and held up her hands. "I really don't want to know. Just...make her blend. *Quickly.*"

Melanie pulled her wand out and smiled. "On it."

A bell rang from out in the hallway. Maren turned toward the door. "Who could that be?" She opened the door. "Eloise, a pleasure. Glad you're safe now. We'll get better acquainted soon."

"Yes, a...uh...thank you." I wanted to sound like I belonged here. Like I could blend in. But I knew my New York accent wasn't doing anything to help with that. Maren gave me a tight-lipped smile as she let the door fall shut behind her.

Melanie turned toward me with her wand ready to go. "Hold very still."

I just saw her use that thing to launch a guy across a field and now she wanted to point it at my face? *No thank you*. I backed away from her. "What are you doing?"

"You've heard of a makeover?" She wagged her eyebrows at me. "Well this, my dear, is a make *under*."

Butterflies fluttered in my stomach. I'd seen magic do so many destructive things. But then I reminded myself of all the wonderful little things I'd seen in the shelter and how comfortable it made me feel. I sucked in a breath. "You're not gonna cut my hair off like in Ragnarök, right? He was totally hot but I'm not about the chopping off my hair."

"I promise I will not chop your hair off." Melanie smiled. "Arms out."

I held my arms out to my sides and sucked in a breath. The air shimmered at the tip of her wand and I felt the clothing on my body shift and change. My crop top stretched down and over my arms. It lowered to cover my stomach yet still maintained the tightness of a corset. Gone were my black jeans, in their place a flowing skirt fell from my hips to the floor. The light material felt cool and soft against my skin. When I glanced down, my clothing matched the people I'd seen. The neckline dipped lower across my chest, giving the barest peek at the cleavage the corset caused. My clothing went from black cat costume to a light purple, Victorian era peasant dress with loose sleeves that cinched at my wrist.

"Looking good." Melanie pointed her wand at my nose. "Now just the face. Make-up off."

A blast of cold wind puffed in my eyes and I squeaked. Purple magic erupted, filling the room. My heart went into overdrive. "Oh God, how did he find me?"

"What?" Melanie spun in a circle. "Who?"

I pressed myself back up against the wall, trying to fight the ball of nerve in my stomach. "Ladarious, that purple magic. I saw it when he tried to grab me."

"I can assure you he isn't here." Melanie looked so calm as she smiled at me. "I give you my word."

"I saw it!" I shouted and dove toward the window to look for him.

"Ellie, Ladarious is not here nor is that from him. Now, come away from the window."

I spun and narrowed my eyes on her. "Then where did it come from?" I glanced toward the window and the door, hoping to find some kind of explanation.

"Ellie, look at your hands." She waved her wand toward me. "Go on. Look."

I held my hands up and gasped. Vibrant violet smoke

coiled around my fingers and slithered up my arms. It clung to my palms like a glove. *"WHAT?"*

"It came from *you.*"

"What? No. *How?*"

"Yes."

"Are you saying…" I swallowed hard and stumbled back until I slammed into the wall again. My pulse raced out of control as I stared down at the impossible on my hands. "Are…you…are you saying…. I'm a…a…a…*mage?*"

The door flew open and Maren hurried into the room. She narrowed her eyes at Melanie and slammed the door closed behind her. Her face was flushed and frazzled. She lowered her voice to a hiss, "Prince Stellan and the Dukes are here…he's asking for *you,* Melanie. Why?"

Melanie opened her mouth then shut it. She raced to the door, then paused and looked back at me. "Ellie, stay here, okay? I'll be right back."

ELEVEN

STELLAN

"STELLAN, MATE," Weston said with a heavy sigh as he turned away from the window. His normally playful sapphire eyes were serious. "Are you sure it's a good idea to be here?"

"It's not." Shylock yanked the curtains closed, drenching the small library in darkness. "We should not be here right after an incident with Ladarious, especially not when both the Rebellion *and* the Royal Guard were involved."

I waved my hand and let my magic flow over the lantern on the table in the middle of the room. My silvery magic wound around the switch on the side, making it twist until the flame rose high enough to bathe the room in warm light. "Listen—"

"No, you listen." Pale, powdery blue smoke erupted beside me and then light filled the room. Weston stood with his hand stretched out toward the lantern on the wall, giving us more light. "Going into First Realm is the highlight of my existence. I won't have it go balls-up because you've decided to recklessly risk it—"

"Or the Rebellion." Shylock had his arms crossed over his chest and his light blue eyes narrowed at me. The flickering light cast a shadow of him against the wall that was nearly as tall as his six-foot-five stature and just as lanky. Strands of his wild black hair fell across his forehead in a disheveled mess. "But as you are the one who set the rules for our presence here, I assume you have a reason for bringing us here now."

"You mean *besides* the girl from First Realm who is suddenly somehow in Second Realm, despite the fact that she is not a Royal, and the fact that she has purple magic and destroyed half the palace garden with her lightning?" I put my hands on my hips. "You mean besides all that?"

Weston opened his mouth then shut it. He cursed. "I forgot that bloody part."

"I did not." Shylock arched one black eyebrow at me. "However, that to me is more reason to stay away. You have your discreet methods for communicating with Maren. You could have used such avenues for a few days until things calmed down. Or at least until Ladarious and the Royal Guard weren't watching. Why are we here when you know it is a risky move that could expose our part within the Rebellion?"

"Because of *this*," I growled and pushed my black coat sleeve up to my elbow, revealing the intricate black markings on the inside of my forearm that went nearly all the way to my elbow. "*This.*"

"I don't—" Weston's eyes widened. *"Mistakes were made."*

Shylock's jaw dropped. "That's what she said right before she snogged you."

"And right before she entered Second Realm." I pushed my sleeve back down and started pacing the length of the book-lined wall. My stomach tightened and turned with every step. I still couldn't believe this was happening. I'd found my soulmate, after all these years. I stopped and turned to my cousins, my best friends. "How could I not come here? Put aside her apparent magic, her sudden entrance into Second Realm, and her attack from Ladarious...she's my *soulmate*. The one we all assumed had *died*. How do I not come right here?"

Shylock let out a long, deep breath and shook his head. "No wonder we couldn't find her all these years...she was in First Realm."

Weston scratched the back of his head. "But how did she get there? She's not a Royal."

I cracked my knuckles as my mind spun. "Exactly why we're here, lads."

Weston narrowed his eyes. "Are we sure she's not a Royal? Someone's lost daughter? There's some shady people in our family. Hell, old Baron Reginald would've sold his own child for a night with a courtier."

Shylock eyed me and pursed his lips, tapping his finger on his pointy chin. "Is there something else you have yet to tell us, Stellan?"

There were certain secrets only the Crowned family knew of, secrets my sister taught me while hidden away in a closet so our parents wouldn't hear us. Secrets our parents hadn't wanted *us* to know. I remembered those moments like they were happening now, cramped in a dark crawlspace with candles in our hands and that old dusty journal she'd found. She'd always insisted that I tell no one, not even my two best friends. And I'd upheld that promise I made to her…but now that *she*, my soulmate, was here, there were things that were going to happen, things that would require their assistance for sure. But I couldn't bring myself to tell them. Yet. At least not *here.* And not without getting a good look at the journal again. I hadn't seen it since Savina died. My sister's room had become a shrine no one could enter.

And now I know. The journal wasn't a story of fantasy and fiction.

I was only at the shelter because I had to see her. My soulmate. I couldn't believe it. My soulmate mark appeared when I was only a year old, which meant she was only a year younger than me. But my whole life we hadn't been able to find her. My parents assumed she had died. I'd started to believe that too. *But she hadn't. She's alive and she's HERE.*

The library door flew open and Melanie hurried inside, closing it quickly behind her. When she spun back around her brown eyes were fiercely sharp and focused right on me. Her dark brown hair was tied haphazardly behind her head and her long gray dress was thick with mud on the bottom. She glanced to the Dukes before turning back to me, then she pulled a plain wand from her dress pocket and pressed the tip to the door. Puffs of light flashed from the tip of it, coating the room, and I heard the door lock. She lifted her wand then flicked and swirled it around – the air pulsed along the walls of the room. *Did she just soundproof this room?*

I smiled. I liked this Melanie Christin woman. She worked closely with Maren, both for the shelter and the Rebellion, and she was fierce. I always wondered what my sister would have thought of her. I suspected she would've liked her as much as I did.

Melanie hurried across the library then stopped right in front of me. She bowed, *not* a curtsey, but when she stood her eyes were laser sharp and hot. "Your Highness, if I may, what are you doing here?"

"I need to see her," I said before I could stop myself. Usually I had more tact than this. But after believing my soulmate was dead my whole life and finally finding out she was alive…I couldn't stay away. Not now…not ever. I had to know her. I could not wait.

Melanie scowled so low her eyebrows dropped over her eyes. "Are you sure that's a good idea after last night? I assure you I have it under control."

I pushed my sleeve back up and raised my arm so she couldn't miss my soulmate mark. My pulse raced with urgency. Somewhere hidden in this house was my fated one, every fiber in my body felt it. Like a pulsing energy I couldn't deny. "I assure you, you don't."

Melanie narrowed her dark eyes on it but there was no element of surprise in her expression. Just calculation.

My heart fluttered. "You saw it." And not the English words, but the actual Second Realm version of my soulmate mark. The one with the geometric pattern that matched my own. I yearned to know what it looked like against her pale skin. If she fancied it the same way I did. What would it look like next to mine?

"Indeed, I saw it but a moment ago." Melanie cocked her head to the side and tapped her lip with her pointer finger. "Question, your Highness, do humans in First Realm have soulmates like we do?"

"Um…" What was she playing at? I blinked and shook my head. "Uh, no, they don't believe in that."

"Exactly." She moved closer and crossed her arms over her chest. "Tell her and she's bloody likely to lose it. There's enough on her plate already. Perhaps give it just a bit longer. Let her adjust. She's had enough of a fright already."

I opened my mouth then closed it and groaned. She had a point. This was my soulmate and I wanted to tell her. To know how she felt about it. I'd been searching for her my whole life, yet she'd only known me a moment. Would she feel the same excitement and mystery? Or would it mean nothing to her? If it meant nothing…I'd be gutted. Or maybe it would frighten her? *"Bugger me. Shite."*

"She's right. You can't tell her." Shylock steepled his hands in front of his face. "Though, courting her might be the right of it. Let her fall for you before she knows."

Weston slapped my arm and wagged his eyebrows. "Yeah, dude, you're charming AF."

CHANDELLE LAVAUN & MEGAN MONTERO

"Dude?" I narrowed my eyes at him. "You spend too much time in First Realm."

"And she's spent *all* her time in First Realm, *amiright?*" Weston leaned back against the mahogany table and shrugged. "You're gonna need that knowledge, mate."

I pushed my hands through my hair and yanked at the strands. My heart screamed for me to tell her. But in my head, I knew waiting was the best fit. Give it some time, then tell her. It'd be bloody murder waiting, but if it helped her adjust, then I would do it. *"Fine."*

"This sounds like a better plan," Melanie said calmly.

I couldn't truly argue with Melanie's point, it was far too valid. In First Realm they thought of soulmates as fantasy, pure fiction—

"Wait one blasted second," I half-yelled and spun on her. "How do *you* know about First Realm? And don't even think about lying."

Peasants didn't know about the realms. Hell, not even all the court knew about it. So how was it that Melanie, a peasant rebel, knew so much? The realms were hidden for a reason. This wasn't something that could get out.

Her eyes went cold and her voice dropped. "Do you remember your dear old cousin Baron Reginald?"

I gasped. My stomach turned and bile rose in my throat. I didn't even need her to say a single thing else, I already knew. My cousin, the Baron, Reginald was my grandfather's cousin and before he passed last year, he'd been the most vile, disgusting man I'd ever known.

She must have seen the recognition in my face because

she just shrugged one shoulder. "I've found, in my experience, that men in power love to exert said power while...overpowering defenseless women."

I felt sick.

"He talked. Especially when intoxicated," she mock-whispered.

"I'm sorry to hear that." If Reginald wasn't dead already, I'd see to it that he was. I sighed and shook my head. "Did you...tell anyone about it?"

Melanie arched one eyebrow. "And bring the royal family down on me? I'm with the Rebellion, your Highness, and we know what happens to those who speak out. We will never forget what happened to your sister."

I ground my teeth together. The sharp pain of loss shot through my chest. Even now, it felt like it happened yesterday. It'd been six years, yet I still could not get away from my sister's death. It haunted me at every turn. It was the reason I devoted everything I could to the Rebellion on her behalf. Savina had been more of a mother to me than my own mum. I mourned her loss every day of my life. Even now, to speak of her burned agony down into the pit of my soul.

Even with her warning about my sister, something didn't sit right. Melanie was not supposed to know about First Realm in any capacity. Neither should've Reginald. It made me wonder exactly how much she knew. And how much was she keeping from me? This strange tingling sensation in my gut told me she knew more.

I met her gaze and held it. "What the bloody hell else did he tell you?"

She waved my words away. "That is hardly the pressing matter at the moment, though I do swear to tell you the truth at some point. And, I'll also admit to knowing that her purple magic means something important."

My heart stopped. *No, no way did Reginald tell her THAT.* "You're not supposed to know that."

"Yet I do." Melanie glanced to my cousins then back to me, her brown eyes laser sharp. "I have not wished to play all my cards yet but now you have to make a decision."

"Me?"

"Yes...you can either punish me for being told something I shouldn't have been told. Something I didn't ask to be told, even though the man who told me is dead already and nothing can be done about it....or....you can realize that you have an unexpected ally who can help you help the realm."

I frowned. "What are you suggesting?"

"She has an important job to do, but she's not ready. She has to be trained." Her gaze was so steady, so calm.

Shylock stood up straight. "What's she on about?"

I squeezed his shoulder, silencing him, then turned back to Melanie. "Then I'll train her. I'm her soulmate and I have the most similar magic to her."

She folded her hands in front of her and nodded. "And what will the whispers say when Prince Stellan is seen at the women's shelter frequently? Do you think your presence here would draw the right kind of attention?"

I cursed and placed my hands on my hips. My feet itched to move, to pace the room so I could think better, but I needed to stay strong in front of this woman who knew too much. My insides warred with each other, logic and desire battling for victory. I *wanted* to be there for my soulmate during her greatest time of need. But I had to play it smart. Exposing the Rebellion would hurt everyone, especially my soulmate. If I were a peasant, this wouldn't be a problem. No one would think twice of my presence here. Except I was of royal blood so my being here was a danger to everyone, even myself.

"Mate?" Weston glanced between Melanie and me with his eyebrows arched. "What's goin' on?"

"Codswallop," I grumbled.

"Give me a couple days. I'll get her started." She gestured to me. "Then we'll arrange for you to train her, but in a way that does not compromise the work you've done for the shelter. Work we need you to continue doing."

For my people, for the memory of my sister, and for my soulmate, I would do this. I would fight every instinct I had that drove me toward her. I would do it to keep them all safe. "Fine. You've got two days. I'll send word on where to meet me and when." I started for the door then stopped. "One last thing."

"Yes, your highness?" Melanie's eyes widened.

"Tell me, what is her name?" My heart hammered in my chest as I held my breath waiting.

Melanie gave me a small smile. "Her name is—"

There was a quick, soft knock on the door. We all

jumped and spun toward it. Melanie cursed and pulled her wand out of her skirt pocket, then flicked it toward the door. There was a click and then she turned the handle. The door swung wide open – my breath left me in a rush. It was *her.*

Over Melanie's shoulder I saw those brilliant violet eyes and the cascading midnight hair.

Melanie cursed as she grabbed her by the wrist and dragged her inside.

My heart fluttered then seemed to stop completely. My mouth went dry. I felt parched, like I hadn't had a drink in days. It was strange to be so affected by someone whose name I still did not know. But it was *her.* My soulmate... standing right in front of me. Her long light purple skirt swirled as she hurried inside the library. The dark corset made her waist look small enough to wrap my hands all the way around and forced what had to be an inappropriate amount of cleavage *up.* I licked my lips and swallowed to relieve the dryness in my throat.

Get a grip, mate.

"I thought I told you to stay in my room," Melanie hissed and slammed the door shut again, locking it with her wand once more.

"You did, but well...you said this was a safe place, so I figured I was safe to come here to you...and..." she turned away from Melanie and those violet eyes met mine.

My breath left me in a rush all over again. She looked different without the heavy dark eye makeup and bright red lips, but she didn't need all of *that*. She was breath-taking in her natural beauty.

"I realized I wanted to thank Prince Stellan myself for saving my life. For helping us get away." She took a step toward me, her eyes never leaving mine. Her cheeks flushed a deep rosy pink. "So…thank you."

My chest tightened. My lungs screamed in protest for the air I wasn't breathing. I smiled and bowed my head. "You are so very welcome."

She bit her bottom lip and stuck her hand out between us. "We didn't officially meet. I'm Eloise Sutton."

I put my hand in hers and electricity shot up my arm. Heat exploded inside of me like I'd swallowed fire. I cleared my throat. "Stellan Wentworth."

"I believe there's a *prince* missing there?" She arched one dark eyebrow and smirked.

I shrugged to try and cover up the giddiness I felt inside at her hand *still* in mine. *I don't want you to think of me as a prince.* But instead, I said, "felt awkward to say, no?"

"Well, *Prince* Stellan. I really appreciate your assistance and thank you for checking on us now."

Let go of her hand now, bloke. "My pleasure."

"Mate, no," Weston pretend-whispered in my ear and smacked my arm. "You're supposed to kiss her the second she walks in the door."

TWELVE

ELLIE

"You're supposed to kiss her the second she walks in the door."

Prince Stellan's face turned bright red and his lime green eyes widened. The muscle in his jaw flexed. His grip on my hand tightened.

"Well done, cousin. This moment called for a dash of awkwardness," the tall Duke with the messy black hair said in a polished accent as he rolled his bright blue eyes. "I'm positive the girl feels comfortable now. Perhaps you'd like to objectify her change of wardrobe?"

"Yes, and I'm sure being referred to as *the girl* immediately after telling us her name makes her feel right at home, *cousin.*" The other Duke rolled his dark blue eyes right back, but *he* was grinning like a kid on Christmas morning. I didn't know if Stellan was directly related to them but these two definitely shared the same gene pool. He turned back to me and smacked Stellan's arm, forcing our hands to drop. "Oi, you're supposed to let go after two seconds. Perhaps you need a refresher on your people skills, mate."

Stellan's face turned as red as an apple and it was absolutely adorable. His eyes never left mine as he stood there frozen.

I chuckled and looked to the playful duke, holding my hand out to him. "I'm Eloise." *Really?* I NEVER went by Eloise, it just felt wrong to say my nickname to royalty.

"Duke Weston Wentworth," he said proudly as he shook my hand – but only for two seconds. "I don't feel awkward saying my title at all."

"Is it because you're only a duke and not a prince?"

The tall duke in the corner threw his head back and laughed. Stellan covered his mouth with his hand but I saw him chuckle.

"*Ellie,*" Melanie hissed behind me.

Weston narrowed his eyes at me then grinned wider than he had before. He glanced to Stellan and pointed at me. "See, Second Realm just doesn't make girls like that, and it's a damn shame. I like her."

The tall duke strolled over then held his hand out to me. "Shylock Wentworth, also a duke. I do apologize for my cousin here, he about worships everyone in First Realm. We're contemplating sending him there permanently."

I pursed my lips. "That might be dangerous...for the girls of New York."

Weston snapped his fingers. "Oi, what was with that

kiss at the party? Why the bottle? I tried to watch but I think I missed something."

"Oh that's called *spin the bottle*. It's a party game." I shrugged and tried not to look at Stellan. "You just spin the bottle and kiss whoever it lands on."

"I know what I want for my birthday."

I giggled. Stellan and Shylock both closed their eyes and shook their heads.

"Are all three of you related?"

Stellan opened his eyes and smiled. "We are. Our fathers are brothers."

I nodded and eyed the dukes. "Shylock and Weston... like Sherlock and Watson."

Shylock scowled and cocked his head to the side.

"*Damn my leg!*" Weston shouted.

I snorted.

"*Oh,*" Shylock's eyes brightened. "I am not offended by this."

"Well, it's nice to meet you, too," I said with a chuckle. "And thank you both for your help as well, it did not go unnoticed."

They both bowed their heads.

I turned back to Stellan and hated the way my pulse skipped beats every time I made eye contact. "I can't believe how lucky I got to have all of you there right at the moment I needed help."

Stellan's cheeks flushed. "Of all the parties to choose..." his eyes darkened and I wondered if he was thinking about that kiss as much as I was.

Yeah, except he's a prince and you're not even from here. It's a lost cause. Get over it.

"Also…um…sorry for…uh…ya know…" For some ungodly reason I swung my fist to re-enact what I'd done, as if once wasn't enough. "…for punching you. Before. In the park." *SHUT UP, Ellie.*

Stellan's smile turned sideways and mischievous. "Don't be. The error was all mine. I should never have snuck up on you like that, let alone touched you without your permission. I'm afraid I was just so surprised by your presence that I handled it poorly. I do apologize."

I felt my lips curve up at the ends. "Thank you, I appreciate that. You are forgiven. I hope I didn't hurt you."

He laughed and rubbed his jaw. "Oh, it hurt. You have excellent form and delivery."

If my face wasn't on fire before then it was scorching now. "My father will be very pleased to hear that."

"If you ever get the chance, please don't hesitate to show Ladarious the same welcome." He grinned and it looked downright wicked. "I would pay to see the look on his face."

"Your Highness." Melanie stepped up beside me and glared at him. "Dare I say, let us not encourage close proximity to that vile rat."

He grimaced but when he looked to me his eyes twinkled. "Yes, let's stay out of his reach."

Shylock cleared his throat. "Speaking of, lads, I do believe we've been here too long. Time to get moving."

Stellan sighed then nodded. His eyes were warm as he

looked over my face. "It was a pleasure to meet you, Eloise, but I'm afraid he is right."

"Ellie. You can call me Ellie." My cheeks burned like a forest fire. I bowed to him then scurried backward to the door. I looked up and smiled. "I hope to see you again sometime."

Melanie pulled her wand out and flicked it toward the door. It clicked and then she pulled it open. "Go on back to my room. I'll return shortly."

I nodded then glanced back at his beautiful face one last time. "Bye."

Without another word or response, I jumped into the hallway and sprinted back to Melanie's room with my heart in my throat. Melanie had been fairly adamant about me staying in her room and remaining unseen…but I'd *had* to see him. I had not been able to stop myself. Not with *him.* And I was glad I'd gone, even if my heart was a mess for it.

Ten minutes later, I'd paced the length of the room a dozen times with my heart in my throat and my stomach in knots. My thoughts were a blur, moving a thousand miles per minute…and I wasn't going to have any finger-nails soon if I didn't stop chewing them. Purple magic lingered in the air around me and I wasn't even sure when it came out. I pulled at the bottom of the corset, trying to get my boobs not to strangle me. Or maybe it was the magic that kept flying out of me that sent me into a panic attack where I couldn't breathe? *No, I'm fine. This is fine, everything is fine.*

What the hell was I doing in another realm? *A freaking REALM!* I glanced down at myself. It'd all been such a whirlwind until this point. I slept on the ground in a cemetery, lived through the battle of the three armies, hid in a strange magic house that I somehow loved, and stood here wearing clothing that I was pretty sure set back the women's movement by like three centuries. Physically I was okay, exhausted but okay…maybe…no, definitely not.

I was not okay. This was all…*not okay.*

When I'd been with Stellan in that library, all of my nerves had vanished, but they returned tenfold now that he was gone. And I didn't like one bit that a boy was having this much effect on me.

My hands shook with nerves. Little puffs of purple smoke came out. I ran them down the front of my dress. "Stop it. Damn it."

I didn't want to be here. I needed to go back home. Nickel and the rest of my friends would be losing their shit by now, not to mention my parents. I couldn't imagine what was going through their minds. I had to go home. That battle had to be done by now, or at least everyone should've been in hiding. If I could just get back into that building I could go home and pretend that none of this ever happened. Just as I reached for the door it flew open and Melanie walked inside.

She glanced down at my outstretched hand. "Going somewhere?"

I wrung my hands together. "I can't stay here. If I could just get home…"

"You can't go home, Ellie." She walked over to the bed and sat on the edge of it.

"But I have to. My parents will be worried…my friends." I turned and paced. "Ladarious is after me and all kinds of weird things keep happening. If I go home, maybe it'll stop…"

Melanie patted the bed beside her. "Perhaps you should sit. You'll wear yourself out."

I turned and sat on the bed next to her. "Please Melanie, if I could just get there, I know it'll all go away."

She wrinkled her nose. "What exactly do you think will go away?"

My dress fanned out over my legs, and I gathered a piece of it between my fingers. "Before you left… you said…you know…that the magic was mine. And I thought that if it came out in this realm then maybe, I don't know, it would just go back if I went back to *my* realm."

Realms! I was talking about freaking realms here. What if I went home and this all went away? It might work.

Melanie gave me a soft smile as she shook her head. "It doesn't work like that, Ellie. You're a mage. Just like me, just like Stellan. Once your magic is awakened, it will not go away."

"I'm sorry…did you just say that I'm a mage?"

She arched one eyebrow. "Yes. Hence the magic coming out of you."

"I'm a mage."

"Yes."

"No."

"Yes."

"No."

"Yes."

"Shut. Up."

"I can, but it won't change a thing."

I shook my head. *"NO. No, no. Can't be. WHAT?"*

"Yes. I assure you it's true. You are a mage."

I bit my bottom lip. "No...no, I'm not..."

She nodded and smiled. "Yes, you are."

"No."

"Yes."

"Can't be."

"Yet it is." She shrugged as though it was that simple. "We can continue this game as long as you'd like, but I assure you the answer will remain a resounding yes."

I bit my bottom lip and eyed her for a long second, but she wasn't twitching or fidgeting like she was lying. I wanted to believe her. Hell, I spent my entire life reading comic books about magical and supernatural people. I'd just been dressed as *Catwoman*. After all the comics I'd read and all the things I'd dreamed of, this was something I never saw coming. But also, I'd seen what happened with Ladarious and Prince Stellan. I saw the Rebellion, the Royal Guard, and Ladarious's men. There really was no other way to explain it.

But still.

I narrowed my eyes. "Prove it."

"Okay." She glanced around the room. "Stand up."

I rose to my feet and held my hands out to my sides. "What next?"

"Close your eyes."

I sighed. It felt stupid standing in my room with my eyes closed waiting for something to happen, for some kind of magic to erupt out of me. I wiggled my fingers at my sides waiting for something to happen. Anything to happen. "This is silly."

"Ellie!" She yelled so loud my eyes flashed wide.

An object came flying at my face so fast I flinched back. I threw my hands up and bright purple smoke shot out of my palms. Whatever she'd thrown exploded into pieces right in front of my face. The tinkering sound of sharp glass pieces filled my ears and I narrowed my eyes at her.

"What if that hit me in the face?"

"It would only have hurt for a second." She stood across from me with her wand at her side. So casual, so relaxed, like my whole world hadn't just changed. "You wanted proof, didn't you?"

My breath left me in a rush and I sagged down onto the bed.

"Now, it's important to note that there are three types of magic a person could have. The Royals have wandless magic, like Prince Stellan and how he didn't need a wand to use his telekinesis." She held out her wand so I could see. "Peasants, such as myself and the rest of our society, have wand magic. We *must* have a wand to access and use our magic. Then there are the unfortunate individuals who are for some reason born without magic at all."

"Squibs," I heard myself whisper.

Melanie gave a small smile. "Precisely, though we don't call them that. And those people wind up servants to the Royals and their Court."

I looked down at my hands and the purple smoke still coiled around my fingers – and gasped. I sat up straight. "*Wait*, are you saying this is a Rapunzel situation and I'm some lost princess?"

Melanie frowned. "I don't think that is what I'm saying, no."

My chest tightened. "But-but-but I just did that without a wand."

She opened her mouth then shut it. She sighed and sat in the chair across from me. "You have magic like the Royals, yes, but I do not know how that came to be."

I whined. "Well why don't we just ask the Royals?"

Her face fell and her eyes turned cold. "If the Royals find out you exist with your type of magic, they will kill you on the spot. They are cruel, heartless monsters who will do anything just to keep their throne."

I gasped.

She nodded, but her face was pale. "Do you understand what I'm saying, Ellie? You cannot trust the Royals."

"Even Stellan?"

Her face softened. "No, as I said before, Prince Stellan is the only one to be trusted. And you better be sure to call him *Prince* Stellan around other people or it will get you attention you cannot afford."

"And the Dukes?"

"They are on our side, but it's safest if you assume Prince Stellan is the *only* one you can trust."

I swallowed roughly. "Got it. But like...um...maybe I should just go home, and no one will have to know I'm here?"

"It's too late for that, but also, you can't go home yet."

I groaned and hung my head. "Why not? You promised me last night you'd get me home."

"And I will." She leaned forward with her elbows on her knees. "You don't know the world you stumbled into, Eloise. You have to trust me."

"You have to help me out here, Melanie. I'm scared." I gestured around the room and at my purple smoke magic. "This is all terrifying and overwhelming. You can't even tell me *how* I have this magic or why I was in First Realm and not here."

She held her palms up and smiled. "I know you want those answers, and I'm going to help you find them...but we're going to need Prince Stellan's help on that."

"Why would a prince help me?" I sighed. I was a stranger to this world, and he was royalty.

"Prince Stellan is the only hope we have for the future and he knows it. His parents rule the kingdom with an iron fist. They care not for the suffering of their people who starve in the streets while they feast each night. The Royal Guard are their tools for maintaining control over the realm and they do so by any means necessary."

"That's awful." I shook my head. "Then why doesn't the

Rebellion team up with Ladarious? You know, unseat the Royals and be done with it?"

"Have you seen him?"

"Good point." I nodded as my mind whirled with all the information that she'd given me. The magic and the layers of this world. I froze. "You said that only Royals could do magic without a wand."

She nodded. "I did."

"But then...why does Ladarious have the magic of the royals? Is he related to Stellan?" Because that was so not cool. It was bad enough that his parents were selfish jerks, but to add Ladarious to that would be a straight up family curse.

"Ladarious isn't a Royal."

"But then why…"

"Why does he have the magic of the Royals?" She sat back in the chair and let her hand lay on the armrests. "Because long ago, when the royal family was being chosen, there were two Wentworth brothers...one was chosen as king and the other was to be a prince. However, that prince felt slighted and wronged. He felt he should have been king and tried to take the throne. He was over-powered and lost the battle, but his bloodline still fights for the honor they claimed to have been robbed of. That line brought us Ladarious...Ladarious thinks he's the rightful heir and will stop at nothing to get what he wants."

Thinking back to his bald tattooed head, his evil laughter, and the way he attacked with such determined venom in his veins made me shiver. When he was in my mind, I felt the evil running off of him. I shivered. "I wouldn't want him ruling either."

"You and I see that, but make no mistake, he's got a following. The people are tired of being repressed by a royal family who cares very little for them. This gives power to a very dangerous man. A man who has no problem killing anything or anyone who stands in his way."

I ran my hands over my arms, trying to rub away my goosebumps. "Yes, I see that."

"He wants you, Ellie, and if he gets to you before you're ready..." She shook her head. "I shudder to think of the possibilities."

"But if I go back home then he won't be able to get me." I was grasping at straws. The more I listened the more I knew I might be stuck here. Yet I still had to try.

"Last night, you were lucky you ran out of the portal when you did. But on a normal day, you'd have to make it through the forest where Ladarious lingers along with his men. They sit and wait for the time to attack the Royals. And if he caught you, well, killing you would be the best scenario. If that's not enough, you'd have to get onto the Palace grounds to get to the portal. And those grounds are heavily guarded by the Royal Guard and if they caught you then they too would kill you. Not to mention, once you reach the portal, how would get through?"

I held my hand out stopping her. "I get it. I try to go home, I die. Awesome."

"It's not so bad as all that. Once you learn to control

your magic, I will do everything in my power to get you home." She gave me a half smile that did not comfort me in any way.

I wanted to go home but I had to learn so I didn't end up dead. If I didn't know any better, I'd say I was in my own comic.

"I can control it...I think." I sat up straighter and held my head up. If this was my power, then I should be able to do just that.

Melanie flicked her wand, forcing a burst of air and light to smack into me. I squeaked and threw my hand up to block it. Purple magic shot from my hands and the pillows on the bed exploded. Feathers rained down like snow in the room. She arched her eyebrow at me and pursed her lips.

I blew a feather off my lips. "I see your point. Cheap shot, but touché." I grimaced. "Okay, so if I learn to control my magic, you'll bring me back home to First Realm and we can find out what the hell I am?"

"Yes."

I exhaled a deep breath. "Okay. Okay. Right. I can do that. How do I do that?"

She smirked. "I'm going to teach you some basics of magic and then when you're ready, and when it's safe, Prince Stellan is going to train you."

My heart fluttered and memories of his minty taste assailed me. *He's going to train me?*

"And remember, absolutely *no one* knows the other realms exist so you must not tell anyone." She met my eye, giving me a deadly serious look. "It is life or death if they find out."

"Besides Prince Stellan and the dukes."

Though the party was only last night it seemed like a lifetime ago. A lifetime between when I kissed him and standing here now learning about the world of mages. Why, even in the face of all this, could I not stop thinking of him? Yes, his power was great, but his lips were even better. I licked my lips, missing his minty flavor on my tongue.

"Yes, Prince Stellan, Duke Weston, and Duke Shylock. Only the Royals are privy to this information."

I frowned. That didn't make any sense. "But *you* know."

Her face fell. "And I'll be killed for it if they find out."

I shuddered. "Then your secret is safe with me."

THIRTEEN

ELLIE

"So what now?" I sighed and flopped back on the bed, which was surprisingly soft. "What do I do now? Where do I go? Where do I hide out?"

"*Here*, Ellie. That's why I brought you here. This women's shelter was made for reasons not unsimilar to this." She gestured around her room. "I think it would be best if you shared my room with me. I'd hate to leave you alone in a foreign realm."

Relief hit me like a tsunami. "That's…yeah. Thank you. I'd like to stay with you."

"Right. That's done then." She rubbed her hands together. "But we have to get you some other clothes so it's not super suspicious."

I gasped and sat up straight. "Clothes?"

"Yes, *clothes*. As in garments to cover your body?" She chuckled and shook her head as she headed toward the door.

I frowned and looked down at the clothes I had on. "But can't we just use magic? Like you already did?"

"*I* can, but *you* cannot." She waved for me to join her. "Besides, those clothes did not just appear out of thin air. They were in my wardrobe and I used magic to change you into them."

"*Oh.*" I frowned. That was less cool. *Less cool? Wow, someone adjusted fast.* I shook myself and hopped off the bed. "Okay. I'm following you, Obi."

She paused with her hand on the door handle. "Remember, no pop culture references."

"Right. Got it." I mock saluted her.

"All right, follow me and stay close." She pulled the door open and led the way down the hallway.

We passed the library where Prince Stellan and the Dukes had been and I wondered just how far they'd gotten. And where did he go? What was he doing now? Melanie opened a door at the far end of the hallway that opened to a wooden staircase. She waved for me to follow then began her descent. Lanterns hung every few feet, with golden flames flickering inside that seemed to glow brighter as we moved by them. I kept waiting for the stairs to creak under us, but they were completely silent.

When we got to the bottom, there were three doors to choose from. All of them unmarked and identical. But Melanie didn't even pause. She went right for the door on the left, yanking it open and charging inside. My steps faltered. My jaw dropped. This tunnel was made of rock, like they'd torn into the earth itself. Those same lanterns from the wooden stairwell hung from the roof of the tunnel in both directions. I glanced over my shoulder and found dark nothingness behind us.

I shivered then turned and skipped to catch up to Melanie. "Where are we?"

"The Rebellion made these tunnels after Princess Savina's death to help us get around town unseen." She glanced sideways at me as we walked. "And no, we don't have one that'll bring us to the portal."

"I wasn't going to ask that." *Okay, maybe I was.* "Where else do they lead?"

"A few important places around town, but we're always working to make more." She pointed down the tunnel ahead of us. "That way takes you into the heart of a village with a lot of children. Behind us, it leads to a dodgier end of town."

"And the other two doors?"

"That's a lesson for another day." She stopped and pointed her wand at the stone wall. Light flashed and then a door appeared, like she'd wiped the dust away. She opened the door, revealing another set of wooden stairs. "For Megelle Lane, which is the only place to shop, we have to make half of the trip on street level. We couldn't risk the courtiers finding this."

My eyes widened. "So we're going out like...in public?"

"Yes." She pursed her lips and eyed me. "Where we're going...there are eyes everywhere. You must blend, your life depends on it. *Our* lives depend on it. This is not Times Square or Fifth Avenue, you understand?"

My pulse quickened but I nodded. "I'm just not going to speak at all. If someone talks to me, tell them I lost my voice or something."

She grinned. "That's brilliant. Come on then, Silent Bob."

I threw my head back and laughed, then hurried up the steps after her. After about fifty steps, she stopped and pointed her wand at the stone wall again. Just like before, a wooden door appeared in front of us. She looked to me and nodded once, then pushed the door open. Bright light filled the stairwell. I hissed and shielded my eyes. Melanie grabbed my wrist and yanked me through the doorway... into darkness.

I frowned and opened my eyes. We were in an alley of some kind. Brick buildings stood on both sides of us, blocking out the bright sunlight. The air was thick with the stench of garbage and human pee. I was a New Yorker, I knew that smell all too well. I took a step back and four rats the size of my foot jumped out from behind a door. I stomped my foot and yelled, they squealed and sprinted away from me.

Melanie chuckled. "Such a New Yorker."

"I take that as a compliment." I shrugged but then her words registered. "Wait, how well do you know New York? What's your story?"

"One for another day," she said softly and in a rush as she grabbed my wrist and dragged me down the alley toward the opening. "Let us not linger in these parts."

I glanced over my shoulder to see if anyone was behind

us and discovered the alley hit a dead-end. In the far corner, a person lay in a crumbled heap on the ground. Their clothes were tattered and stained, their hair ragged and knotted. I only realized it was a person by the bloody scratches on their arms and the way they rocked back and forth.

"There's nothing you can do for him," Melanie whispered and tugged my arm.

I knew that. After all, I *was* a New Yorker. Homeless people were not a new thing to me, but there was something about his posture that hurt my heart to look at. Melanie practically dragged me down the alley and around the corner before I forced myself to snap out of it. This wasn't my home. This wasn't my realm. I needed to follow her lead. Their problems weren't my problems.

But as we walked down the sidewalk my heart sank. The street was probably once a thriving beacon of social activity...now it was falling apart. The brick and stone buildings were literally crumbling from the top. Pieces of the walls littered the sidewalk. The windows were either smashed or boarded over. The shop and restaurant signs were covered in dust and dirt, most of them even broken in half. The street itself was rough and had more holes than swiss cheese.

"Watch your step."

I jumped and looked down just as I was about to step into what I could only assume was a puddle of blood. I didn't want to know. I didn't ask. That was the New Yorker way. You just kept going.

But when we got to the intersection at the last decrepit brick building, I glanced to my right and my feet stopped. I gasped. The paved road that went to the right looked like it'd been smashed or blown up. Beyond it, the road was a rock-filled dirt path. Tree trunks shot up from the ground on either side of the dirt road, except there wasn't a single leaf on any of them. The trees were a dull grayish brown. It was like their souls had been sucked right out of them. The ground was an ashy gray as well, no grass in sight.

Up ahead a little ways, there were brown tents popped up in rows, huddled close together. They were dusty and stained and it looked like one deep breath would knock them all down. Ropes hung between the tents and the dead tree stumps had clothes hanging from them. Movement in my peripheral vision had me look to my left – my jaw dropped. A group of people of varying ages stood near a large wooden barrel with stricken faces. None of them wore shoes and their clothes were barely hanging together. Their arms were thin, too thin, like they hadn't eaten in weeks. An older man bent down and picked up a little boy then lifted him to the top of the barrel. The little boy cupped his grimy hands into the barrel and scooped up a handful of water that looked as filthy as he was.

"Ellie, we need to keep moving—"

"What happened here?"

"The Royals," Melanie growled beside me. "They take everything for themselves and leave us with nothing."

"They're starving…they don't even have clean water—"

"*I know.* This is what the Rebellion is fighting for." She

sighed and shook her head. "We do everything we can but it's not nearly enough. There's no fresh water we have access to. The only river is illegal to drink or fish from, punishable by death from the Crown."

Rage filled my lungs with fire. *"What?"*

But Melanie just shook her head sadly. Her dark eyes were weary and angry at the same time. She grabbed my arm and pulled me along. "We have to focus, Ellie."

I followed her down a wide set of stairs made of red brick. "But they need help…"

"We cannot fight each battle. We must focus on the war." She glanced up at me over her shoulder, her brown hair flying in the warm breeze. "This is bigger than you could ever imagine, Ellie. Trust me when I say we're doing every single thing we can."

It didn't feel right to just accept something so awful, but what was I to do? I didn't even belong to this realm. I looked back, but the staircase blocked my view of the people. "O-okay, but what — *whoa. What is this?*"

In front of us was a visual I was not prepared for, not after that little hike through misery.

The red brick street was bright and not missing even a chunk. The sidewalks were clean and clear. Across the street, a black iron gate stretched left and right with lush green trees lined up alongside it. Melanie gripped my hand tighter and dragged me through the gate opening.

I meant to keep up with her pace but my steps faltered. My jaw dropped. We were inside some kind of restaurant and it was bustling with activity. There were wooden tables in every direction and each one was filled with people. All of them dressed to the nines in fancy gowns and lavish hats, some of the women even wore white silk gloves up to their elbows.

"*Ellie,*" Melanie hissed.

I looked up just as a stack of white plates flew past me. I gasped and blinked. *Wait, what?* My eyes widened. Old fashioned wooden brooms swept the red brick floor *on their own.* Glass pitchers carrying different colored liquids floated through the air, stopping at tables and filling cups up like someone was pouring them.

Plates and bowls overflowing with food flew from the building in the back to the tables before sitting themselves down in front of the waiting customers. There were women in black dresses walking to and from the tables. Notebooks hovered closely behind them with wands scribbling down words like Rita Skeeter's magic quill.

"What is this place…"

"The Café of Megelle Lane." Her voice thick with disgust.

"Look at all the magic…" I blinked and spun around, trying to take it all in.

This was something right out of a fantasy, like one of my comic books come to life. *Is this real-life right now?* I looked down at my hands —

"Don't even think about it." Melanie grabbed my hands and pulled me forward. The restaurant passed by us in a blur, but when we walked under a massive canopy of trees, she slowed us to a normal pace. "No one can see your magic, Ellie. *No one.*"

Your magic.

I have magic.

I still couldn't believe that I had magic, even though Melanie had already proved it. I was a mage but my mind couldn't come to grips with that knowledge. *I'm a mage. I have magic. I can do magic like this.* The thought had me grinning as we passed through another black iron gate, down a few steps, and out from under the leafy canopy— my jaw dropped. Again. I was going to be sore if I didn't control my face.

But it was just…beautiful.

The steps led us right to another street, a wide red brick street that could have fit at least three lanes of cars back home. Trees lined the sidewalks every few feet, their leaves a bright green and full of life. Each side of the street was filled with shop after shop, each one looking equally pristine as the next. The glass windows glistened in the afternoon sunlight. Signs were full of vibrant color. The walls of the shops were a sharp, spotless white.

"This is Megelle Lane." Melanie sighed and gestured around us. "It is separated into two sections: the Court and the peasants."

My stomach turned. "Say what now?"

She arched one eyebrow. "You heard me. These first few blocks are the shops for the Royals and their Court, and the occasional splurging. It is basically unheard of for a peasant to step foot in one of their shops, let alone purchase something."

I scoffed. "Yet we're allowed to walk through?"

Melanie chuckled but it was not a humorous tone. "Well yes, how else can they show off their riches and torture us? How better to put us in our place?"

I balled my hands into fists. "That's...that's barbaric. This is the twenty-first century—"

"*Ah,* for you perhaps." Melanie winked playfully. "Time has not progressed the same way here."

"Why not?" I asked as a woman in a white silk gown scowled and wrinkled her nose at us as we passed by.

Melanie shrugged. "For the same reason our people are starving to death in their tent homes."

My heart sank and my stomach tightened into knots. I didn't understand how people could be like that to other people. It was so wrong. I'd learned about cultures like this in my history classes, but it was different to be experiencing it first-hand.

I clenched my teeth together to stop myself from speaking more. I could not be trusted to behave myself when I felt like this. Instead, I glanced around at this fancy ass street and scowled. Through the glass windows I spotted a never-ending array of lavish gowns and men's suits – or whatever those were called. Every New Yorker knew how to spot expensive clothing through a window, there was just something about the shimmer of the fabric and the light reflecting off leather shoes that screamed *you can't afford me.* But it was also the emptiness of the stores that told the story. For some reason, the more expensive the store the less people who were inside. Apparently, this carried over into other realms and not just New York.

The whole thing was beautiful and posh, yet it felt so...*cold.*

Melanie sighed. "Finally. I hate that walk."

I frowned and turned to follow her gaze – my eyes widened. In front of us, cutting a straight line across the fancy street, was a wall of vibrant green leaves. "What...is that?"

Melanie hooked her arm around mine then led me up to the leafy wall. With her wand in hand, she flicked her wrist and the leaves slithered away, leaving an opening just big enough for the two of us. My breath left me in a rush, and it made Melanie chuckle. We stepped through the opening...and into a maze. Green hedges stood tall off the ground, lining up at different angles to create a pathway. As we walked, the hedges moved.

"It's a little trick of our own," Melanie said with an evil chuckle. "This maze will not let anyone through who harbors ill will toward the peasants. For us, we just walk and the walls will move around us."

"Amazing..." I heard myself whisper. "It's so...pretty."

But as I said it, I knew something was off. Sure the hedges were made of green leaves and there were flowers sprouting all over them...but the colors were *off.* They weren't vibrant. It was like looking at an old painting that needed to be dusted off and refreshed.

"This used to be gorgeous...one day...one day it will be again."

I started to turn toward her when the hedges opened up in front of us and golden sunlight shined down. I stopped dead in my tracks, frozen like a statue. The sight before me was absolutely nothing like what we'd just seen.

There was life and activity *everywhere.*

We stood in the middle of a cobblestone street that had definitely seen better times. The stones were worn and broken. The trees that lined these sidewalks were just as dead as the ones we'd seen before getting to Megelle Lane. Except each and every lifeless trunk had ribbons and scarves wrapped around them. Symbols I recognized but couldn't place were burned into the flaking trunks. I didn't know how I knew this, but I knew they were some kind of tribute to the life lost.

There were people everywhere...walking, standing around talking, sitting at tables together and laughing. Children darted back and forth across the street, giggling and flicking their wands at each other. They may have been barefoot and in clothing that were either too small or falling apart, but their smiles were brighter than anything I'd seen before.

I grinned.

"*This* is peasant lane, our own private little heaven." Melanie took a deep breath then exhaled. "The court wouldn't dare belittle themselves by going through our maze, so they have no idea what's on our side. We want to keep it that way."

"I can't believe this..." I blinked and glanced around. "The walk here was…"

"Destitute? Yes. They come here to get away."

As we walked down the middle of the street, I felt like I was back in New York. There seemed to be a bit of everything and I couldn't get enough of it. I was going to have whiplash from swinging my head back and forth to see it all.

There were stores for clothing where the dresses in the window *moved,* like they were modeling themselves off. A seamstress shop on the right had its windows wide open. Inside, I saw a plump little woman that reminded me of the fairies from Sleeping Beauty. Scissors, needles, pins, and measuring tape floated in the air around her, following as she walked through her store.

"Margarite! Your shoes are all finished!"

I turned to the left to where an older man with glasses sliding down his nose waved his hand in the air. Behind him, the shop window was lined with shoes that all looked beaten up. The sign read *shoe repair* and I smiled. The Court stores didn't have a single repair shop. Next door to that was a store to buy shoes – I stopped and peered through the window. Shoes floated in the air. A woman plucked one and a red box flew straight toward her.

"This is amazing." I shook my head and skipped forward. I wanted to see *more.*

A few women who looked about my mom's age crossed in front of us. They all smiled and waved.

"Good afternoon!"

"Hi, Melanie!"

"I love your dress!"

"They're all so friendly…" I said, glancing left and right, back and forth. There was too much to see. A wand shop I was dying to go in. A shop full of crystals. Another shop with plants hanging from the ceiling. Each store was bustling with activity, I felt like I was shopping in Soho with Nickel on a Saturday afternoon.

Everywhere I turned there was magic…and black cats.

What's with the black cats?

"Mommy, I want ice cream!" A little girl cried as she charged by me, a woman chasing her and laughing.

I watched them run off to the right to where an old-fashioned looking ice cream parlor sat on the corner. There was even a giant ice cream cone sculpture by the front door. Through the open windows I heard nothing but laughter. The sweet smells of ice cream wafted through the air and my mouth watered.

The front door opened and a horde of children poured out, bouncing and giggling. Their eyes were all bright and their smiles wider. Their ice cream cones were already starting to melt down the cones and onto their hands but none of them seemed to mind.

I looked up just as Stellan walked out the door with a massive ice cream cone in his hand. His blond hair glistened a bright gold in the afternoon sunshine. His light lime green eyes sparkled like stars in a black sky as he smiled down at the children. "All right, did everyone get one? It's hot out today, we've got to stay cool."

Oh my God.

He didn't.

He did.

My chest tightened and my breath left me in a rush. I actually swayed on my feet. Stellan looked up and our eyes met. A huge grin spread across his face that sent heat rushing to my cheeks. He reached down and handed his ice cream cone to a little boy sitting with crutches leaning against his table and a cast on his foot. I swooned. I actually *swooned.* I had never believed it was a real, physical thing…but it was.

And then his gaze found mine again and my heart did that familiar flutter. He waved to someone – I couldn't tear my eyes off of him to see who. As he stepped away from the children and into the street, I bit down on my cheek to stop myself from squealing out loud. He strolled over, looking devilishly handsome in his black ruffly silk shirt and black trousers. There was something so light and intoxicating in the ease of his smile and skip in his step as he strolled toward us that had my pulse beating wilder than a taxi cab in Friday night rush hour traffic.

Oh God. He's coming over. Be cool. Be cool. You're good. Be cool.

He stopped right in front of me and his smile widened. "Eloise." His voice was warm and rough, and it took everything inside of me to not think about that minty way he tasted.

I bit my lip as my pulse did crazy things. "Ellie, call me Ellie."

His grin curved sideways and he tipped his head. *"Ellie."*

I stared up at him with my heart caught in my throat and he *stared back.*

Melanie cleared her throat. "Hello to you, too —"

"Melanie! Melanie!" A little girl screamed from suddenly right behind him. She reached out and grabbed Melanie's hand and dragged her toward the ice cream parlor. "Come on, Melanie!"

I watched Melanie's back as she was pulled away, wanting to make sure she didn't get too far from me, but I felt the heat of Stellan's gaze on my face the whole time. I took a deep breath and tried to brace myself. It was a useless attempt. When my eyes found his again the wind was knocked right back out of me. I swayed on my feet, *again*, and prayed he hadn't noticed.

"Ellie," he said my name softly, like a purr, and it sent my pulse into overdrive.

My cheeks warmed. "Prince Stellan."

"Please, call me Stellan?"

"Stellan," my voice was barely more than a whisper.

He took a step forward and the tips of his boots touched mine. Butterflies danced in my stomach. I licked my lips and his pale eyes tracked the movement. Every single inch of me yearned to touch him…to run my fingers through his hair…to fist his shirt and drag his lips down to mine. I could do it. I'd done it before, at the party. Being this close to him was like standing in Central Park in autumn.

I pushed up on my tiptoes to kiss him just as a group of

young girls walked by us, giggling his name. He glanced over at them and nodded his head, giving them a tight-lipped but friendly smile and reality came crashing back down around me. *What am I doing? I was just about to KISS him. In the middle of town.* I cursed and looked around at all the dozens of people who would've played witness to my little slipup. I cursed and shook myself, trying to break free of the daze he put me in.

His green gaze swung back to me and I watched them light up for me in a way they hadn't for those other girls. I hated how much I liked that. His smile was wickedly dangerous and his one shoulder shrug threatened to bring me right back down to a puddle of swoon at his feet.

I looked up at him with my breath caught in my throat. "Should you be standing so close to me?"

He frowned. "Am I bothering you?"

Not in the way you think. I shook my head. "You're a prince, I am... a peasant."

He leaned forward and his golden hair fell into his face. His eyes twinkled. "You're more than that."

My heart fluttered. *Don't look at me like that. My brain can't handle it.* I licked my lips and peeled my eyes away from him before I crumbled. "But still, people might see. Might talk."

He stepped *closer*. His feet were now *under* the hem of my long skirt. The heat and electricity rolling off of his body sent goosebumps across my skin. "I don't believe you answered my question," he rumbled real low.

My heart fluttered. "W-what was that?"

"Am I bothering you..." he dipped his head down and our faces were mere inches apart. "Being this close?"

I shook my head and felt my crumbled brain rattle around. "N-n-o."

Someone cleared their throat and we jumped apart.

Melanie stood just behind Stellan with her hands on her hips and her eyebrows arched. She was watching him closely as she walked back to my side and hooked her arm around mine. "C'mon, Ellie, let's get you sorted before curfew."

I flinched. "*Curfew?*"

Melanie's brown eyes darkened. "Yes. The Royals do not allow for us to be out at night."

I looked to Stellan.

He shrugged but his cheeks flushed. "Not my crown, not my rule. I assure you."

I frowned. "Will it be your crown one day?"

A haunted shadow passed over his pale eyes and his face fell. "Unfortunately, yes. Ladies, enjoy your shopping. Good night." Without another word or glance at me, he turned and rushed away.

Wait. I turned to Melanie. "What did I say?"

Her face fell. "The crown is passed to the eldest Wentworth child of the reigning monarch, whether that be male or female...his sister Savina should have been Queen."

I opened my mouth then closed it. *Shit.* "I...I... shit. I didn't mean to offend him."

Melanie smiled sadly. "I don't believe you did. Everyone knows her death still destroys him, he makes no secret of it. When he first started helping the Rebellion, he talked about her nonstop."

My heart hurt for him. "How long ago did she die?"

"Six years."

"Wow." I gripped my chest like I could somehow help his heart by holding my own. I wanted to chase after him and hug him. "He grieves her that hard still...he must have loved her very much."

Melanie nodded but then she shook herself and smiled. "Come, the curfew is serious and we have shopping to do."

FOURTEEN

ELLIE

"ALL I'M SAYING IS that when Harry went shopping with Hagrid he came home with a snowy white owl." My arms were full of books and bags of things Melanie thought I'd need.

"I'll tell you what, next time you decide to visit our realm *and stay,* we'll go get you your own pet." She reached for the door and twisted the knob. "We can't have you getting a pet attached to you if you're not going to be here for it. Plus, you can't take it with you. Animals in First Realm are very different than those in ours."

I staggered through the door behind her, struggling to hold all my supplies. "I'll take that deal."

Melanie paused just inside the foyer. "Wait, did you just call me Hagrid?"

"Ah, you caught that one?" I laughed. "You've got to see the parallel though."

She shrugged. "I like to think of myself more as a Newt Scamander than a Hagrid, but I can't say I'm offended."

I followed her down the hallway back toward our room. The sound of voices drifted out from the sitting room to my right. I paused at the doorway. Maren stood at the back of the room with her wand in hand. A group of small children sat on the round carpet in front of her. She glided around the room with a smile on her lips. Her soft brown hair brushed over her shoulders as she bent down to adjust the way a little girl held her wand.

When she stood, she pushed her shirt sleeves up to her elbows and my gaze landed on the black interlocking triangles on her left forearm. My breath caught in my throat. Melanie had said Maren had a similar mark as mine, but I hadn't seen it yet. Though it was similar in style, it looked entirely different. Mine had circles, diamonds, flowers, and vines whereas hers was just a bunch of triangles. It was strange to think these were from dark magic when they were so pretty. Maren didn't seem to mind showing hers off, either.

"Now let's talk about our magic and how it flows through the body." Maren held her wand and waved it over herself. She used the tip to point to her head and motion downward to her toes.

The circle of kids each sat on the edge of the carpet with their legs crossed. All eyes were on Maren and I could see why. She had a light about her, an aura of wisdom and peace. There was something about her that made me want to sit and listen, to follow her anywhere.

Maren paused in the middle of the room and a smile played on her lips. "Now, who can tell me, what is the first part of us we should let go of when trying to unleash our magic?"

A little girl with wisps of her dark curls sticking out from the bun on the top of her head raised her hand. Her tiny fingers wiggled excitedly as she waved her hand back and forth. "Me, me, me."

Maren pressed her wand over her lips and lowered her voice, "If we call out, how will we hear each other."

The little girl smacked her other hand over her mouth yet kept on waving.

Maren fought to hide a smile but failed. She pointed with her wand toward her. "Okay, Angelica, tell me what you think."

Angelica lowered her hand and straightened out her dress. She sat up straighter and smiled. "The first part you have to release is the inner lock. The one that sits on your tummy and holds you all in."

"Very good." Maren pressed her fist over her stomach and held it there. "There is a dam here that helps control the flow of our magic. If we unlock it, the magic flows like water. Now what happens if we lock it back up. All together."

The entire class called out together. "The magic stops."

"Very good." She raised her arms, motioning for them all to stand.

Her students all shot to their feet and bounced excitedly. They couldn't have been more than six years old. Some of them swayed back and forth while swinging their arms the way that all small children did. *Somethings weren't so different after all.*

"Wands up." Maren motioned for them to raise their arms. As soon as they all raised their wands, Maren grabbed a pillow off the table against the wall and threw it up into the air. The air shimmered around her wand and the pillow exploded. Feathers rained down on her students. "Keep the feathers off the floors dears."

"You wanna join them, don't you?" Melanie whispered with a chuckle.

I grinned and nodded. "I would already be in there if you would've let me buy a wand."

Melanie rolled her eyes. "I'll tell you the same thing I did about a pet."

I pouted playfully. "Fine."

The children giggled as they summoned their magic and the air moved around them. The feathers floated up and down like deflating balloons being hit around the room. The children scattered in all different directions. Their eyes blazed with happiness as they giggled and chased the feathers with their wands held high.

"If only I had them to clean up the mess in my room." I laughed under my breath. "They make it look like so much fun."

"It is fun." Melanie never took her eyes off the classroom. "It's the way it should be anyways."

Watching the joy of those kids made me realize there were so many things to embrace about this world. The magic, the wonder, the creatures. I wanted to know it all. For the first time, my heart fluttered with excitement. This could be the beginning of my own story. A story I had a chance to write myself. This world was dangerous and chaotic, but it was also beautiful and full of wonder. *Maybe I should be a part of it and embrace this side of myself.*

Melanie turned to me and laughed. "Now you're seeing it, aren't you?"

I nodded. "I am."

"You could really be something, Ellie. Are you ready to learn?"

"I'm ready." The knots that'd been tight in my chest since I arrived in this realm began to loosen.

"Then follow me." She crooked her finger at me as she turned down the hallways and headed toward the back of the house.

With my bags in hand I lumbered down the hall, past the kitchen, the library where I'd introduced myself to Stellan for the first time, and the Rebellion meeting room. We turned and headed down another hall that would lead back to our room. Melanie held the door open for me and I passed through quickly.

I dropped my packages onto the chair and turned toward her. I was ready to learn, to help the people in this realm. They may not have asked for me, but now that I was here, I wanted to do all that I could for them. The way that Stellan did.

"Melanie, can I ask you a question."

"Of course, always." She closed the door.

"Why is it that Stellan is the only Royal we can trust? Why is he the only one to help? And why does he keep it such a secret?"

Her face fell and she sagged onto her bed. "You have to know Stellan is nothing like his parents. He sees the way his people suffer and he wants to make a difference the way a monarch should."

"Yes, but it seems so personal to him." I sat down next to her. "He's risking an awful lot to be part of the Rebellion when he could, I don't know, try to convince his family to do more?"

Melanie let out a heavy sigh that sounded like it hurt. "It's because of his sister, Savina. Stellan was only twelve when she died and she was…they were…very close. A thing like that leaves a scar."

I knew his sister had died but I hadn't learned anything about it yet. "How did she die?"

"There's some debate on that." She glared at the wall and balled her fists. Her voice was tight and dripping with rage. "Savina was the people's princess. She fought for them, against her own family. She spoke out on behalf of the people and the people loved her. But then…six years ago…" she shuddered.

"It's okay, you don't have to talk about it."

"Yes. I do." She turned to look at me. "Back then the Rebellion was a scattered, unfocused group. Unorganized. But they had all the passion needed. Ladarious was just as much a problem then as he is now. That was one of the Rebellion's earliest complaints – that the Crown was doing nothing to eliminate the beast."

I leaned forward, literally on the edge of my seat.

"It was a horrible day." She closed her eyes and cringed, her arms were wrapped tight around herself. "There was one infirmary – a hospital – that was small, but healthcare was free. Anyone who went got the help they needed, no matter their age or illness. The healers who worked there were some of the nicest, most kind-hearted people. The neighborhood around the infirmary protected them, helped them. Cared for them. Lots of children and elderly lived there. Ladarious attacked mercilessly. He took out the neighborhood from the outside, burning his way to the center. By the time the Rebellion could get there, the infirmary was the last building standing. Everyone was trapped inside."

Bile rose in my throat. I didn't need her to finish, I knew where this story was going. Yet I didn't stop her.

She shook her head. "Savina got there...she tried so hard. She almost did it, almost saved them, but then the Royal Guard arrived fashionably late as usual. For a few brief moments there was chaos, with the fire and the smoke and the screaming...and in those moments...Savina was murdered."

I gasped.

"There's debate over how it happened. Was it an accident, a rebound or misaimed shot by a Rebellion member, or was it Ladarious and his men?" She fisted handfuls of the blanket on her bed. "The official statement from the palace was that it was an accident. They use it to tell the Rebellion not to arm themselves, to leave the fighting to the Royal Guard."

"But the Rebellion got stronger…"

Melanie grinned. "In spite of them, yes. In revenge, yes. After Savina's death, Maren took control of the Rebellion. Made it what it is today. She still runs everything. It was all her—"

"I find that so hard to believe. I mean, obviously I believe you but…" I shrugged. "Maren seems so soft and tender…kind and compassionate. She doesn't fit the role of Rebellion leader."

"Ah, yes…well…" Melanie cleared her throat. "For Maren, it became personal."

I frowned. "Why?"

"Savina was Maren's soulmate."

I gasped. Again. I pressed my hand to my chest and felt my heart pounding against my ribs. "Oh no. Love will make a person do things they never imagined, or so I'm told."

"It's more than just *love*, Ellie." She glanced sideways at me. "Soulmates are a real thing in Second Realm. Two souls that are fated and bound together by the Heavens for all eternity. Losing your soulmate is losing the biggest part of yourself."

Soulmates are real? Whoa. Of all the things I'd learned so far, that might have been the biggest pill to swallow…but in a good way. Then I realized what she'd just said. *Oh, Maren.* A piece of my heart broke for her and for Savina, the princess I would never meet. "Did the king and queen not approve of their daughter being with another girl?"

"The crown's official statement is that they have nothing against same-sex couples. It's legal to marry and everything." She rolled her brown eyes. "But it's not acceptable for *their* children. Savina was heir to the throne. She was to be queen. Her parents did not approve of having two queens. They were adamant that she had to marry a male so that there would be a king, and then to procreate to keep their line going."

"That's ridiculous. She still could've had children—"

"It didn't matter to them…and now she's gone."

"So Maren is doing this for her."

"Yes, and no. The Rebellion was already happening, with Maren at the helm but in a slightly different context. Savina's death solidified the movement. The Rebellion honors her. You know their symbol? The one you saw in the sky this morning?"

I nodded. "The red circle with the red spider inside of it?"

"Savina was known as the Red Widow."

"Bad ass. But why?"

"Her magic was red in color, like yours is purple? But also because of her magic, which was telepathic pain, is basically the same as what red widow spider venom does."

My breath left me in a rush. "Wow. And they use it for

the symbol of the entire Rebellion. What a slap in the face to the Royals. Poor Stellan, it must kill him."

"When Stellan was fourteen, two years after her death, he started coming around. Talking to Maren and the Rebellion." She smiled. "He wanted to finish what his sister started. He said he would do it for her because it was the right thing to do. That he would be the king she'd never get the chance to be."

"That's pretty amazing."

I knew he was special, right from the moment I wandered into this realm. The more I learned about him the more wonderful he got. Now my heart hurt for him. It made me want to stick around and fight by his side, even though this wasn't my fight.

Melanie motioned around the room. "All of this is because of him. The shelter, the food on the table, the funding for all our missions. It's all Stellan. And he does it in secret."

"How does he do it without his parents finding out?"

"Oh, he's creative. He takes stuff from the palace and sells it, then gives us the money." A wicked grin spread across her face. "What most people don't know is that he sells this stuff in First Realm. He brings stuff from there as well."

"Wow. That's awesome. It must be amazing to be able to make a difference like that."

"Indeed. That's what we're all trying to do here." She rose to her feet. "Now that I've given you the story on us and our prince, are you ready to learn some magic?"

CHANDELLE LAVAUN & MEGAN MONTERO

My pulse quickened in my veins. I jumped to my feet. "Okay, Yoda, I'm ready to learn your ways."

She rolled her eyes. "Really, Ellie, I hardly resemble a small green goblin-like creature. First a giant now a goblin. Whatever am I to do with you?"

"Teach me. I'm ready." I held my hands out to my sides and wiggled my fingers. Nothing came out, no purple smoke, no magic. I held my hand in front of my face. "Hmmm."

"You have to remember what Maren said." She took her wand out of her pocket, then she pointed to her midsection. "There is a door inside all of us. It's locked up tight in your chest. Below your heart and above your stomach. It is there, deep in the pit of your soul where it is stored."

I pressed my hand just where she said, right over my diaphragm. "Here?"

"Precisely." She smacked her wand against her stomach. "Now you must breathe with it. Picture it in your mind like opening a door and release that knot. The one you've been carrying for years but couldn't place why or how."

All my life I thought everyone felt that way. Like there was a weight on their chest that couldn't be explained or denied. Perhaps because it'd been there my whole life, I thought it was normal to feel this unexplained pressure. I sucked in a deep breath and blew it out slowly. Again I took another breath, following Melanie's guidance. That knot deep in the pit of my stomach began to loosen and I felt the power course through my veins. My heart sped up and I sucked in a gasping breath.

Melanie shook her head. "No, don't let the panic lock you up. Keep breathing. Find that calm and let it go."

I fought to control the rush of power through my body. *Deep breath in, Ellie*. I opened my hands and let that knot deep in the pit of my stomach go. Purple smoke seeped from my palms. I wiggled my fingers in wonder as my power tangled around them.

"Good. You're doing it." Melanie smiled. "Now, let's see if you're as good as the kids."

She pointed to the mess of feathers from the pillow I blew up before. "What can you do with that mess?"

I held my other hand out and let the power flow. Purple smoke covered my bed and the feathers lifted up off the blanket. They floated it the air with the light wind my power created, each of them floating around each other. It reminded me of snow falling at night in Central Park, where the white flakes would twirl and fall in slow motion against the high-rise skyline.

"Ellie, control." Melanie chided.

I shook away the thoughts of home and stopped the feathers from spinning like a tornado. Instead I turned my focus on breathing, on relaxing into my power. I stemmed the flow of my magic and held the feathers there, floating.

"Excellent. Now try to tone it back little by little." She giggled. "Preferably so they fall in a pile we won't have to clean up."

The knot in my stomach, the one that held my power back, tightened and guided the feathers toward the corner of the room. As I pulled my power back into myself, the feathers all drifted to the ground. I smiled and that knot holding my magic back suddenly disappeared. In its place I felt only a small dam that I could open and close at will…in theory.

I turned toward Melanie. "What should we do next?"

"Next?" She glanced out of the window. "We go bigger."

FIFTEEN

ELLIE

"When you said go bigger, I didn't think this big." We stood in the middle of the forest with two boulders sitting in front of me.

The trees towered over us, casting our tiny clearing in dark shadows. Hints of the early evening sun peeked through the dead trees. Though there was only a slight crisp in the air, the forest looked like it was full winter. Pine needles crunched under my feet and the trees were bare of any leaves. The water in the small stream off to my left was low and barely flowed over the stony riverbed.

Melanie stood before both of the boulders and spread her arms wide. "Jedi training time."

"I love when you talk nerdy to me." I shifted from one foot to the other, eyeing the rocks like they were the Empire State Building and I the little ant who could not lift it. "You want me to move those?"

One of the boulders was much bigger than the other

but both were equally intimidating. I'd moved a couple feathers and now I was supposed to move boulders. *How'd I go from a light walk through the park to maxing out on CrossFit boulder lifting?* The two were very different things. I crossed my arms over my chest and shook my head. A little wind wasn't going to do it. I needed like hurricane force winds, a tornado, maybe a freaking sharknado so a great white would lift that shit up for me. Because as far as I could see those things probably hadn't budged in hundreds of years.

Melanie's smile faltered. "Don't think I don't see the look on your face, Eloise. You can master this."

"Listen, I don't have a wand to swish and flick to move that shit. I just did a tiny bit of feathers. How do I go from that to—" I motion to the boulder, "—this?"

Melanie held her wand out and looked at it. "Swish and what?"

I shook my head. "Never mind. Look all I'm saying is I'm not Magneto. All I can do is make some wind blow around"

"It's more than that." Melanie walked around the clearing. Her gray skirt brushed the ground with each step she took. Rays of the sun shined on her dark brown hair. She brushed the loose strands out of her face then turned to look at me. "With feathers, you move the wind around them. With solid matter, you must focus and use your power to go through it. The important part is realizing you aren't going around the object, you're going through it."

"Through it?" Images of me charging full force and

smacking into it like some kind of bad cartoon filled my head. "Riiiighhhttt, through it. Got it."

I held my hand up and focused on letting that knot deep in the pit of my stomach loosen just enough to let my power flow. Purple magic flowed from my palms and drifted over the ground toward the boulders.

Melanie held up her hands and jumped out in front of me. "Wait! Stop for just a second."

I started and fought to pull my power back in. "You ever heard the saying don't jump in front of a moving train?"

"Yes." She chuckled.

"Okay, well, me?" I pointed to myself. "Moving, runaway train here. Proceed with extreme caution."

"I wasn't worried." She chuckled and held up her wand. "I have talents all my own."

I raised my eyebrows at her. "So why'd you stop me?"

"Your magic is altogether different than wand magic, so I have to make sure we don't draw any unwanted attention. You know, runaway train and all."

She walked to the edge of the clearing and held up her wand. The air around the tip of it moved with a hazy shimmering effect. Foggy light expanded out from the tip of her wand and expanded over the small clearing. At first it went around us like a cylinder, then once the beginning of the circle touched the end, her power shot up and around us, creating a huge dome. I walked to the edge of the dome and placed my hand against it. The magic gave around my fingers like I was trying to push through a piece of thick plastic.

I held up my fingers and wiggled them. There wasn't anything on them, yet I felt the lingering magic on my skin. "Well that's interesting."

"Think of it as a clean-up tarp. Nothing in and nothing out." Melanie turned back toward the boulders. "Now, I'm completely out of the way. Let's see what you've got."

I moved back to my place in the little clearing across from the two boulders. I held my hands loose at my sides and wiggled my fingers. My magic answered the call. The more I used my power the easier it became to let it free. I lifted my hands then threw them forward and let go of everything I had. Purple magic surged at the boulders. I held my breath, waiting for them to shoot backward into the barrier around us. All it did was make a ditch of dirt blow around it...and nothing else.

"Damn, really?" I shook my hands and groaned.

Melanie waved her hand through the dust cloud I'd created. "Perhaps we need to start with something smaller and work our way up?"

"Yes. Let's."

She grabbed a rock about the size of her fist and placed it on the ground ten feet in front of me. "Okay, move that one. And remember, through the rock. Not around."

I hesitated. I wanted to succeed with everything I had. But what if I didn't? What if I wasn't good at this? I was human, or I was yesterday. Today I was a mage. "Um, okay I'll try."

Melanie lowered her voice, "Do or do not. There is no try."

I froze. "Did we just become best friends?"

She winked.

It'd been a long night for me, and the day even longer. But standing here with her, learning my magic, her jokes made me feel lighter. Like trying and failing wasn't such a big deal as long as I kept on going. *Okay, Ellie, through the rock.*

With everything I had I unfurled my magic and let it flow from my palms. Purple power filled my vision, and all I saw was that rock. It was in my way. I had to be more stubborn than it. I was Ellie, I could out stubborn the best of them. I thrust my hands forward and shot my power right at it. The rock shot up from the ground in a blur and flew at the barrier like a bullet.

I jumped up off the ground. "Yes, I did it!"

The boundary gave way to the rock then it stopped, pulling it back like a sling shot. My eyes widened and the rock hurled back toward me. I squeaked and ducked, covering my head as the damn thing soared over and smacked into the tree trunk behind me. The bark cracked and fell to the ground along with the pile of brown pine needles below it.

Melanie wrapped her arms around her midsection and laughed. "Well, that's one way to accomplish things."

SIXTEEN

STELLAN

She was amazing, completely amazing. I hunkered down behind a fallen tree trunk, just sitting there watching. I knew I told Melanie I'd give her two days but honestly how could one be expected to stay away from their soulmate for two whole days? So here I was watching from afar as she learned things I should've been teaching her. Even though Melanie was doing a fine job of it...so far. But I was here just in case a moment arose where she might need me. I leaned up against the cool rough bark of the tree behind me and settled in.

Shylock jumped over the back of a fallen log and slid down next to me. "What have we here?"

Where one was the other would follow. Weston slid in on my other side. His clothes scraped against the rough bark and sent pieces of it flying in my direction. "A besotted prince watching his object of bloody affection."

"Bit stalkerish, no?" Shylock smiled and ran his hand through the thick waves of hair on the top of his head.

"Oh, sod off." I sunk down lower and watched as her magic filled the protected area and she moved a rock the size of a basket from one end of the clearing to the other. She learned at a remarkable rate. Even after having to dive to the ground a couple times, the control was astounding.

"Did you hear that, Shylock?" Weston chuckled and plucked a stick from the ground. He poked it into the tree in front of us, digging at the dead bark. "I reckon we nicked a vein on that one, mate."

"And I suspect you're about to make it worse." He sounded bored, but that was typical for him.

I ground my teeth together and said nothing.

"So I think to myself...self, what's crawled up Stellan's arsehole and rotted itself there? He's got himself a beauty of a soulmate. What more could a lad ask for?" Weston tapped the side of his head. "Then Shylock pointed it out to me. What was it that you said?"

He sighed. "Her magic was purple. A Royal color."

I held my breath. "What of it?"

They were dangerously close to a theory I'd been holding onto since the night I saw Ellie. It was a secret not even my parents wanted me to know. Yet here she was with her purple magic, moving boulders around like they were twigs with more control than the best of mages.

Shylock steepled his fingers and pressed them to his lips. "You're neglecting to tell us something. Which quite...displeasing."

"Right you are. So, Stellan, out with it." Weston chucked the stick a few feet away.

The girls froze and looked in our direction. I grabbed Weston's arm and dragged him down behind the log and out of sight. "Are you bloody daft? What if they saw us?"

Shylock didn't duck down at all. "I find this behavior rather odd. Isn't it, Weston?"

"Oh, very odd indeed. Why would a prince of the realm be hiding from a wee thing with purple magic? Could it be because she herself is a Royal?" He wrinkled is nose and shook his head. "Not my cup of tea but Royals are known to pair off with their own."

"Yet I must warn you against such things." Shylock looked down at me with grave, piercing blue eyes. "Genetically, it's abhorrent."

I held my breath waiting for the girl to get back to work.

Melanie's eye bore into mine for a split second before she turned back to Ellie. Clearly, she could see through my cloaking spell, but Ellie couldn't. "Probably just some wild animal being nosy."

Ellie gave her a single nod then started back up with her practice. "Like this?"

I wanted to go out there and tell her she was doing well. But I'd promised two days and I was a man of my word. I would wait, or at least until I was given reason not to. Besides, my cousins wouldn't let this go. They were like a dog with a bone, staring at me until I cracked. The last thing I needed was for Ellie to play witness to this charade.

In truth, I was surprised Shylock even went along with something like this. My guess was he was annoyed that I was keeping something from him and he knew Weston was more likely to ruffle my feathers until I broke.

I shook my head. I couldn't break this time. "All right, enough. She's not a bloody Royal."

"Then explain the colored magic." Shylock pointed to Ellie as she picked up three smaller stones and stacked them one on top of each other. "Because first of all, she has wandless magic. Only Royals have that. Secondly, the color purple is a Royal color. No other mage has ever had *purple* magic, not even a Royal. This is something and I know you know."

"I have a theory, but it's only a theory." I picked up a dried pine needle and broke it in half.

"We're all ears, mate." Weston offered. "Because I'd rather she wasn't some distant cousin of ours."

Just tell them enough to satisfy them. "There's a legend that told of a mage that would come to our realm and save it."

The legend of the Stone Keeper. It was a story I heard only from Savina in secrecy. As a child I'd assumed it was merely that. A story. A legend meant for fun and maybe a bit of false hope. But as I grew older and Savina grew more intense on the matter, I realized this was no legend but a prophecy. That old journal she'd found gave us details that Ellie was fitting. It was her. She was the one who would bring the life back to our world. I didn't know how or why, but I knew it in my gut. Because everything about Ellie was bright and alive. Our world needed her...I needed her.

Shylock shook his head. "I've heard of no such legend and I have committed every book in the Royal library to memory. You couldn't possibly be correct on this."

"Even to me it seems a bit far-fetched. One person to save us all?" Weston shook his head. "Not bloody likely."

"It wasn't in any book in the library. This was a leather-bound journal Savina found."

At the mention of my sister their eyes widened. I didn't speak of her often but when I did it still drew the sharp ache of loss from my chest. They knew it, I knew it, yet here I was bringing her up here and now.

Shylock licked his lips. "Then we must find this journal."

Melanie's voice carried on the air. "The damn animals are noisy tonight. I wonder what they're on about?"

Ellie paused and frowned. "Are we in their space? Do we need to move?"

"No." Melanie shook her head. "They're probably just curious about what we're doing."

Shit. I hit the both of them and pressed my finger to my lips. I didn't want Ellie to know I was spying on her. It was not the way I wanted to start things off between us. No, I wanted her to trust me. If that was going to happen, then she damn well couldn't catch me spying.

Melanie smirked in my direction then turned back toward Ellie. "One last one." She pointed to the biggest boulder in the clearing. "You lift that one and we will take a break."

"What if I don't want to take a break?" Ellie countered.

"Every mage needs to give their powers a break. Especially a new one." Melanie redoubled her effort. "Now up it goes."

Ellie turned her attention back to the boulder. Her brows furrowed in concentration as her magic flowed from her hands. "Through the boulder."

The boulder rose up off the ground and hovered there for a long moment. That kind of feat took so much power and focus. Yet my perfect soulmate did it within hours of her first lesson. The boulder wavered and then cracked in half. The two large pieces crashed to the ground, causing it to vibrate under my feet. Ellie swayed on her feet and dropped to her knees, then she tipped forward onto her hands. Her breaths heaved in her chest and a sheen of sweat covered her forehead. I shot to my feet about to hurdle the log and run to her aid, but Melanie was there. I hesitated, stuck between running to her and keeping my word to Melanie.

She hurried to Ellie's side and dropped down beside her. "Are you all right?"

Ellie gave a lazy nod. "I think so."

"Okay, that is enough for one day or you won't have any energy to use tomorrow. Rule one for mages, do not deplete all your power at once unless in a life or death situation. And this is decidedly not life or death."

From across the clearing I heard Ellie's stomach growl. She could barely hold her head up. I took a step forward, but Melanie shot me a look and shook her head. She turned back to Ellie and wrapped her arm around her waist. She helped Ellie stagger to her feet. "Come on, let's have dinner."

The two of them stumbled their way toward the shelter. Melanie's protective barrier dropped as soon as they left. Shylock marched out from behind the logs, headed toward the boulder. I followed behind him with Weston hot on my heels. It was amazing. I'd never seen power like that. Yet here I was wanting to go to her, to make sure she was okay. It took everything in me to stay away. I kicked at one of the rocks she'd been training with. It tumbled across the clearing and smacked into the broken boulder.

Shylock ran his hand over the smooth flat side where Ellie had split it wide. "We need to get that journal."

We did. He was right. I needed more information on the legend of the Stone Keeper. The prophecy was coming true before our eyes, but I knew my parents wouldn't do anything about it. Otherwise they would've told me. The secrecy told me all I needed to know...I was on my own on this. I wished more than anything that Savina could be here to help. She'd know what to do. But she wasn't here, which meant I had to get in her old room and get that journal.

"There's one problem. It's locked in my sister's room." I put my hands on my hips.

"The one room in the castle that is heavily guarded day and night?" Weston's eyes widened. "I can't believe it. You'd have to be bloody daft to try and get in there."

"It's the only way I can figure this out for sure." I looked to Shylock. "What are your thoughts?"

He narrowed his eyes. "There's no way all three of us could get in there together."

Weston turned to me. "What does that mean?"

"So I go alone. Won't be the first time I've stolen from the palace. I've yet to be caught."

"Shite, Stellan." He shook his head and chuckled. "*Yet* is a key word there."

I rubbed my hands together. "Excellent. So you're in then?"

SEVENTEEN

ELLIE

WE WALKED into the main dining room and I felt like death on my feet. The table was crowded with women and small children who occupied the shelter. Though the food hadn't been served yet, the smell of baking breads, roasted chicken, and something sweet like cake hung on the air. My stomach growled in response to the heady aroma of the rich food. I couldn't remember the last time I'd eaten. It might've been a slice of pizza at the party the night before. It felt so long ago even though it was less than a day.

Maren walked through the doorway with a plate of rolls in her hand. Steam drifted up from the plate as she waved for us to come in. "Tuck in, don't be shy."

Good thing Melanie kept her arm wrapped around me as she helped me to the table. If it wasn't for her, I might've fallen over. For some reason, in my mind when a super-hero got superpowers they had an endless supply to give. But as I slipped onto a wooden bench on the side of the table, exhaustion sucked me down. It was like all my strength had been leeched out and now I had nothing left.

Melanie hovered over the small child sitting next to me. "May I sit next to you?"

I recognized the small girl from the class Maren had taught earlier. She smiled and nodded up at Melanie. "Yes, please, Miss Melanie."

Melanie wrapped her hands around the little girl's waist and slid her further down the bench. She giggled as she went, and I tried to smile along with her, but I felt glued to the bench.

"Think of your body like an engine." Melanie leaned in and whispered, obviously seeing my struggle. "You need more fuel. From now on we'll have to take care that you eat much more."

I nodded to her, or at least I tried. My head may not have moved. I didn't think eating would make me feel any better. Sleep would. I needed a shit ton of sleep. Suddenly, dinner didn't feel as important as the bed calling my name from upstairs. Maren placed the rolls down in front of me with a bowl of butter right next to it. My mouth watered, yet I hesitated to grab one. No one else had moved and I didn't want to be rude. I folded my hands in my lap and held them there, never taking my eyes off the steamy pile of carb loaded goodness.

"Go on then, have at it." Maren waved for me to start and I wasn't going to question it.

I reached out and snatched a roll. It was warm in my hands and my stomach tightened the second the smell of it hit my nose. I grabbed the knife from right next to the empty plate in front of me and cut through the bread. I quickly spread the butter over it and watched as it melted into the hot inside. I licked my lips and glanced up and froze. No one else was digging into the bread like I was. I held it poised for a bite.

Then I leaned in closer to Melanie. "Did I do something wrong?"

She shook her head. "Whenever someone new joins the shelter their first meal here is always started by them. It's kind of like a welcome to the family."

"In that case." I shoved a big chunk of the roll into my mouth and moaned around the deliciousness.

Everyone chuckled.

Maren grinned from the head of the table. "Welcome to our newest resident, Eloise."

I waved at the table full of strangers. "Ellie, please."

Maren held up her wand. "And now…dinner."

The air shimmered around the tip of her wand and the kitchen door flew wide open. Dishes of all shapes, sizes, and colors marched into the room. I glanced around, hoping there'd be a dancing candle stick, preferably one who could sing and dance. But there wasn't. I hummed the tune to *Be our guest* to myself as the plates drifted down toward the table one by one. They landed gracefully, like my humming was helping them with their presentation. Plate after plate laid over the table, each dish more delicious than the other. Right in front of me was a big plate of mashed potatoes and I was ready to dig in.

"Looks wonderful, doesn't it?" Melanie smiled next to me.

I sucked in a deep breath, letting all the aromas hit me. It was like Thanksgiving dinner back home. I nodded to her. "I love magic."

She chuckled. "Yes, me too." She pointed her wand at a plate across the table and a spoonful of carrots floated toward her and tipped over onto her plate. The room suddenly grew darker. I glanced out the window to my left and saw that the sun had set since we came in. Something moved out of the corner of my eye. When I looked, a little giggle slipped out of my mouth. Candles floated up above our heads, each one lit themselves like stars in the night sky as they lifted in the air.

I sighed. "I really love magic," I mumbled under my breath.

If I hadn't been starving, I would've sat there all night watching these wonderful mages fill their plates with the feast. Spoonfuls of food floated overhead, dishes rotated around the table, and not one person had to stand or reach for anything. I grabbed my fork and dug in. The warm flavors filled my mouth and I sighed with relief. With each delicious bite my energy seemed to come back. *Guess I better eat more. A lot more.*

A smaller, fragile looking woman sat to my left. She didn't speak a word, she simply grabbed things as they passed her while going around the table. Though she said nothing, she kept giving me sideways glances.

I gave her my best warm smile. "Hello, I'm Ellie."

"Hi." She grabbed the cup in front of her with two hands and held it to her face. She drank deeply like it was the first and last meal she'd ever had. The bowl of rolls slid by her and she pounced on it, grabbing three at once. She shoved a whole roll into her mouth like a hamster saving food for later.

Melanie leaned around me and looked at her with a warm smile. "There's plenty to go around, Lisa. No one is going to stop you from eating."

She didn't say a word, but her face turned red as she nodded.

Just then a pepper shaker stopped in front of my face.

The little girl on the other side of Melanie tipped forward holding her tiny wand. "Would you like pepper, Ellie?"

She'd been doing this for all of the people sitting at the table and I wanted to indulge her practice just as much as everyone else. I was, after all, in the same place she was when it came to just learning my magic. I waved to my plate. "Sure."

The pepper shaker wavered back and forth. A blast of pepper shot right at my nose. I flinched back and shook my head. My eyes watered and I rubbed my hand over my nose. A wild giggle slipped up my throat. I probably wouldn't have done much better.

"Oh no, honey. Put your wand down." The little girl's mother chided her then turned back to me. "Are you all right?"

I nodded. It didn't hurt and I was fine, except for the tickle in my nose. "I'm fi—"

The sneeze hit me like a tsunami. I let it loose and a gust of wind blew from my body right at the mashed potatoes. They exploded out of the bowl and flew in all different directions, covering me, the walls, and everyone else in potatoey goodness. The room fell completely silent and I felt a rush of heat flood my cheeks.

I grabbed a glob of the potatoes off my cheek and slopped it back onto my plate. "Dammit."

There was a collective gasp and then bursts of laughter filled the room. Melanie pulled a particularly bad clump from the side of her neck and flicked it back onto her own plate. Her face turned bright red as her whole body rocked with laughter. *Great. My first mage dinner and I bathed the room in potatoes.* I shook my head and found my own lips pulling up into a smile and my own laughter mixing in with theirs.

I wiped my eyes. "I am so sorry—"

A blaring alarm filled the room so loud the glass windows rattled and the ground rumbled. The flames of the candles all flared to life like huge torches. Everyone shot to their feet, leaving the meal on the table like an afterthought. They rushed from the room out into the foyer.

I jumped up beside Melanie. "What's happening?"

"The Rebellion is needed." Her face grew deadly serious as she ran out into the foyer.

"Needed where?"

CHANDELLE LAVAUN & MEGAN MONTERO

I ran behind her, but she didn't stop until she was outside and standing with the rest of the crowd. I froze and followed their gazes as they looked to the sky. A bright red spider hung in the sky. I'd seen that the night before. It was a call to arms. A war cry for the people. They didn't move, only looked at it, and then a bright orange ring started at one end of the spider and moved around it until it fully connected. They all gasped.

Melanie stepped out in front of them all. "Only the strongest come along, you know who you are. The rest of you stay here and prepare."

"Prepare for what?" My eyes widened.

"The casualties of war." She took a step back from me. "Stay here, Ellie."

"What does it mean?" I started to follow her.

"Red circle, the Rebellion needs back up. Purple, the Royal Guard needs handling. But orange—" She shook her head, "—the most dangerous of them all…"

"Ladarious." His name was a growl on my lips. That man, that thing, was really pissing me off. I stepped up beside her. "I'm coming."

"You're not ready." She continued marching forward.

"I'm strong and I'm coming." Nothing was going to stop me. Sure, he terrified me. I'd never seen anything like him, not even among the other mages. I had no real idea what I was doing but there was no way in hell I was staying behind. My magic flared to life in my chest. It was a battle cry I felt deep in my bones. "I'm coming."

EIGHTEEN

ELLIE

FLAMES FLICKERED against the night sky, blocking out the stars. My eyes widened as I watched the smoke billow up from the center of town. Screams of the innocent filled my ears and my magic answered their cry. I felt it unfurl in the pit of my stomach and sizzle through my veins, ready for me to use at any moment. The smell of burning embers filled my nose and I followed the Rebellion as we passed that black iron gate at the opening of Megelle Lane.

Melanie pointed off to her right. "Five of you this way."

Then she pointed to her left. "Five that way. The rest of you with me."

People rushed by, running in the opposite direction of the burning fires. Children clung to their mothers while hiding their tear stained faces. Fear hung heavy in the air. I felt it in my bones. It crawled over my skin and made me shiver.

"Why would Ladarious attack like this?" I glanced

around at the shards of glass shattered on the ground. The fancy magic-filled café I'd seen earlier today was in shambles, debris everywhere.

"He's raiding for food and riches for his men," Melanie growled.

I froze for a second, letting it sink in. How could a man raid people who already had so little? "Bastard."

"Indeed." Melanie's lips pressed into a hard line. She pumped her arms as she began to run in the direction of the towering flames.

I followed closely behind her. The sound of crashing and screaming filled my ears and all I could see was red. How could such a monster attack the people he wished to rule? As we made our way down Megelle Lane a group of women ran by me, followed by three men in black cloaks. The smiles on their faces sent a cold shiver down my spine and made my stomach turn. I planted my feet and threw my arms out. A gust of wind blew my hair back from my face as I fired it toward the men. It smashed into them, sending them flying off their feet. They sailed back through the air and slammed into a shop window behind them. The glass shattered and silence followed for a brief moment.

"Well done." Melanie gave me a nod of approval.

Yet the others seemed surprised by my show of power. Before they could question it, Stellan emerged from the shadows. His silver magic rolled out in front of him like fog rolling over the ground. Sheer menace sizzled in the air around him.

He moved to my side and whispered, "Just do what you want. They'll think it's me. We don't want you to blow your cover just yet, do we?"

I nodded up at him. "Got it."

Together we turned toward a swarm of black cloaked figures that filled the small area across from us. Tension hung heavy in the air as Melanie and I stood with Stellan and only three other mages at our sides. I didn't know where the rest of the Rebellion was, but I heard the sounds of fighting in the distance. Ladarious' men held their wands at the ready. The air around them shimmered, and I didn't know what to do… but I was going to do something.

Stellan raised his hands at his sides and the shards of glass that laid on the ground rose up to hover in the air. They floated in front of us like a deadly glittery veil. The cloaked man at the center of the line of mages flicked his wrist and a shot of magic went right for Stellan. My heart jumped up into my throat and my power erupted in a panic. A huge chunk of the cobblestone street rose up in front of him. The ball of magic slammed into the top of the cobblestone and light exploded like fireworks, dust rained down on us. My jaw dropped. *Oh shit, did I do that?* I looked to Stellan but he was untouched. I sighed with relief and the cobblestone crashed back down into the hole I'd made.

Stellan arched an eyebrow at me but said nothing. Instead he flicked his fingers and the glass shards shot through the air like bullets toward the cloaked men. One pointed his wand at the glass and a clear shield went up. The glass smacked into it and fell to the ground like salt from a shaker. Stellan growled low in his throat and the debris around us spun like a tornado through the street. Rocks and bricks smacked into the line of mages, forcing them to take a step back.

The ground rumbled under my feet and I shifted, feeling the magic in the air. It rolled toward us in a sinister wave that left me feeling cold and nervous. The first battle I saw, I hid. Now I wouldn't hide. I would help in any way I could.

"My, my, my what have we got here." Ladarious' voice carried on the wind. It sent a chill down my spine.

I glanced from side to side, trying to find him. One moment I was standing in the middle of the courtier section of Megelle Lane, the next everything was gone. I hovered on the edge of a cliff with the wind at my back. Far below me jagged rocks shot out of the black water. The sea was furious, slamming waves into the rocks and spraying up into my face. I held my arms out at my sides, trying to hold my balance. My breath caught on a scream and my arms flailed.

"He cannot get to you." Stellan's voice rang out of the raging sea.

I gasped and looked around in a panic, but he was nowhere in sight. "Stellan?"

"Eloise," His voice was low and lulling, a whisper in the wind. "Ellie, come back to me."

My heart raced in my chest, but I dared not budge. A single inch and I would be lost to the waves and rocks below. I pressed my lips together to stop from screaming as the wind at my back grew stronger, pushing into me.

"Ellie, hear my voice." Stellan demanded right beside me, but I couldn't see him. "It's his magic, nothing more. Break through it."

It's his magic, nothing more. A sharp pain exploded behind my eyes and I felt myself sucked back from it. I shook my head and felt my hand wrap around something strong and firm. The vision receded and I blinked my eyes open. Pain remained in the back of my eyes and in my temples. But I was back on the cobblestone path with Stellan beside me. My hand was wrapped around his wrist. I sucked in a heaving breath and steadied myself.

Ladarious smirked at me, his face twisted in a snarl. "Enjoy your trip?"

I ground my teeth together and called on everything I had. Rocks lifted up off the ground. I hurled them forward, right into Ladarious' line of men. They toppled over like bowling pins, rolling backwards head over heels. Melanie's story about Ladarious destroying that whole village and the infirmary filled my mind and I screamed with glorious rage. My magic buzzed in my hands. I flexed my fingers and threw anything that wasn't attached to the Earth. His men shouted and sprinted *away* from me.

Orange magic poured into the air. I turned and spotted Ladarious with his hands out, his orange magic slithering across the ground. It seeped toward us and I took a small step back. Stellan tugged me behind him and threw his powers out. Silver and orange crashed together like two rising tides. They forced each other straight up into the sky, like skyscrapers back home.

"I will have her," Ladarious hissed and pointed at my chest.

"Not today," Stellan growled.

Have me? Who the hell does he think he is? I wasn't a possession or something to be owned. Something in me snapped. Rage boiled and I couldn't stand it anymore. I'd been scared, cold, tired, and beaten up by my own powers. Not to mention trapped in a world I didn't know existed and unable to go home because of him.

Lightning forked out over the sky like spider webs. The wind kicked up, blowing my hair back out of my face, and sending my dress flying behind me like a cape. The ground shook under my feet. I curled my hand into a fist and the earth rolled out from me in a sharp wave. Ladarious squatted down then leapt over it. His toe caught on the edge of my rock wave and tumbled forward. As the wave slammed into his line of mages, they fell to the ground. Their wide-eyed gazes all landed on me. Both from the Rebellion and Ladarious' forces.

Melanie ran to my side and shoved me toward Stellan. "Get her out of here. Take the tunnels."

He wrapped his hand around my wrist and tugged me to the side. "This way."

I planted my feet. "No. I want to help."

He whirled around. "You've helped them enough. Any more attention and you'll bring the lot of them down on us all."

NINETEEN

ELLIE

I FOLLOWED SO close behind Stellan that his autumn-y scent enveloped me. At the end of the alley he pulled me to the right and dragged me down a silent sleepy street. He motioned for me to press myself up against the wall of the building beside us. My heart hammered in my chest as I flattened behind him.

The hard brick scratched at my skin. "We should've stayed."

He glanced at me over his shoulder and narrowed his pale green eyes before turning away. His voice was a low hiss, "And have the rest of the realm hunting you down?"

"Why would they hunt me?"

Before he even answered, he grabbed my arm and yanked me down to the ground where we hid behind a group of wooden barrels. The sound of rushing footsteps hurried by and we sat there for a long moment surrounded in silence. Electricity sizzled between us. I crept closer to him. I couldn't have stopped myself even if I tried. Something about him made me want to be closer. No— need to be closer..

He leaned in so close I could feel the heat of his body rolling off of him. His lips hovered just an inch away from my ear. His breath tickled the skin on my neck, sending goosebumps over my skin. "Because I'm afraid you've got something everyone wants."

When his bright eyes met mine my stomach did a little flip flop. I wanted to ask if that included him. If I had something he wanted. Because even though we were just getting to know each other, there was something about him that I wanted.

I lowered my voice to match his whispered tone, "And what exactly is it that you want?"

His lips curved into a sinful smirk and his eyes blazed. "So many things."

He wound his fingers with mine and my pulse jumped at the brush of his skin. He urged me to my feet, and I fell into step with him as we ran headlong down a dark alley. Two men in dark cloaks jumped out at the end of the road. Stellan froze in his tracks. He dropped my hand and it felt like he'd taken all the warmth with him. I opened my stance, ready to use my power however I needed. Stellan would not take them on by himself.

Stellan tilted his head to the side and eyed the two. A slight smirk slid across his face and he flicked his wrist. The two men sailed back and slammed into the side of a building. With a sickening crunch, they fell to the ground in a heap. Stellan didn't even look at me when he wrapped his hand back around mine and tugged me into a run. I pumped my arms and matched his pace. We sprinted by the two men. They were lying in a tangle of unconscious limbs. There was so much power in that one little flick.

Stellan arched his back and yanked me backward a split second before a blast of magic soared in front of us. My eyes widened and I felt the heat of the blast on my face. He turned to the side and threw his arm out toward the mage a few feet away. The dirt under the mage's feet erupted, spraying gravel into his face. He staggered back, scrubbing at his eyes.

Shouts came from behind us and he looked over his shoulder then back to me. "Time to go."

The sound of rushing footsteps filled my ears as we ran even more. It felt like Ladarious' men were on every street looting and causing madness. Two more cloaked mages stopped before us with their wands held high. A group of Rebellion members sprinted in front of us, blocking Ladarious' men. I recognized them by the Red Widow symbol on the cuff of their sleeves. Stellan swung his arm out and barrels on the sides of the street flew into the two men, knocking them sideways. He tugged me away before the Rebellion even knew what happened.

Fires burned around the city. People scattered in the streets, running away from the evil mages. Since the second I got here I felt like this was some twisted Middle Earth, battle of the five armies bullshit. All I needed now was a money-grubbing dragon, cold hearted elves, and a couple greedy dwarves. I wrapped my other hand tightly around the skirts of my dress and pulled them up so I could run easier.

Adrenaline rushed through my veins. I sucked in deep breaths. We came to a stop in front of a random wall on the outskirts of the town. I frowned and glanced around, checking to make sure we weren't followed. Stellan brushed aside a large patch of ivy hanging on the wall. A small red widow spider with a circle around it was painted on the bricks where the vines had once been. Stellan placed his hand over it and the hard, stone wall shimmered and disappeared. Like an illusion dropping right in front of me. A dark black hole greeted us and I moved a little closer to Stellan.

"This will take us back to the shelter." He stepped into the darkness.

I knew it would take me back, yet I froze for a moment. I didn't make a habit of walking into dark holes. I swallowed down my nerves and followed behind Stellan. "Right behind you."

The chaos of the streets disappeared in the darkness of the tunnels. The sounds of panic were now muffled by the hard-packed stones around us. My steps crunched on the gravel under my shoes. "We should go back."

"No, we shouldn't." The tunnel descended into pitch blackness and all I could do was follow the sound of his deep smooth voice.

Stellan whispered some words I couldn't make out, then a small flame danced in the center of his palm. He held it out to his side like a torch and it illuminated the area around us. It bathed him in warm light. It glinted off of his sandy hair and reflected in those mesmerizing light green eyes of his. Without saying a word, he held his hand out toward me and tossed the little flaming light up into the air. It hovered beside me, flickering in the dank tunnel. He whispered the low words once more and another flame illuminated in his palm. He tossed it up and it too hovered just near his face.

"Aren't we supposed to help?" I followed behind him as he led me farther down the tunnel.

"We did." Though his words were few, I still felt a thrill every time I heard his British accent.

"It wasn't enough." I climbed over a long snaking vine. "I can help more."

"You helped." He didn't turn back to look at me.

Is he trying to maintain a distance from me? Or am I the only one attracted here?

"But you're the prince surely there is more to be done." Guilt riddled my insides. If I hadn't been there tonight, Stellan might very well still be out defending his people.

He stopped dead in his tracks and spun around to face me. "I *am* doing more."

"By walking me home?" I couldn't keep the accusing tone out of my voice.

"You're important." He took a step toward me and raised his hand like he wanted to brush a stray lock of hair from my face. He curled his fingers into his palm and dropped his hand to his side.

"I am not that important." I rolled my eyes.

"You are." His voice was so low I almost didn't hear him.

Before I could say anything, he turned away and continued crunching down the tunnel. My cheeks heated and my heart did little flip flops. I didn't know how he could say I was important to him. He barely knew me. But somehow, I felt the same. Like I was connected to him in a way I couldn't describe. I didn't know how to respond to him, so I remained silent.

The further we walked, the denser the vines grew. It was so different than the one I'd traveled earlier with Melanie. I brushed my fingers over the oversized heart shaped leaves. They were cool to the touch, with a waxy feel. At the center of a group of them sat a pod of petals folded and twisted in on itself.

"Beautiful." I whispered.

Stellan stiffened and halted in his steps. He held his hand out and the flame closest to him extinguished. He fell into dark shadows. My little flame was like a candle in a great hall, it barely gave off enough light to brighten the path in front of us.

Stellan motioned to the flame. "Let it go out."

"But I didn't do it, you did."

His lip pulled up in a half smirk. "Trust me."

I sucked in a deep breath and focused my power on the flickering flame. A slight wind burst around me and the flame went out, leaving us in complete darkness. "Why did we—"

His finger brushed over my lip, silencing me. "Wait."

When had he gotten so close? Why did that one little touch do so much to my insides? What were we waiting for? I hadn't heard anyone coming, nor even a hint of a sound. And then it happened. A single soft silvery light lit up just a few feet away. Then another and another. The flowers were opening. One by one, those petals peeled away from their tight cocoon and blossomed before my eyes. They glowed like diamonds in the dark. I opened my hand to brush over the delicate glowing petals and for a moment I thought this was what it would be like to float among the stars. To see these beautiful beacons in a sea of blackness. And there Stellan stood among them all. He didn't look at the flowers, instead his eyes never left my face. My cheeks heated and I stood marveling at this hidden gem.

"What are they?"

He shrugged. "Night Realm Flora. They only bloom at night in the darkness of the cave."

I bent down and sniffed in their light sweet scent. This place was magical, even in the darkest of places there was light. "Thank you."

"What for?" He crouched down beside me and touched a petal.

"I don't think I've ever seen anything so beautiful." My gaze bore into his and I was transfixed. The silvery light illuminated his skin in a warm, moon struck blue tint that made his eyes even more vivid.

"I have." He leaned in toward me.

185

I licked my lips, wanting his mouth on mine. We'd only shared one kiss, but I still dreamt of his minty flavor on my tongue and the way I knew his lips would fit mine perfectly. They would be firm yet soft. I wanted it. I wanted it more than I wanted air to breathe. I wrapped my hand in his shirt, ready to pull him closer. He was nearly there. My eyes fluttered shut.

"I saw them go down there!" A deep voice called.

Stellan shifted his stance. He turned and brought me down to the ground with him where we laid in the cover of the thick vines. The flowers closed all at once and we lay in darkness. A dim light moved at the end of the tunnel.

Stellan's lips brushed against my ear. "Shhh."

At that second, I didn't care who was following us. All I could think about was his lips against my skin. I nodded my head and held my breath. Not in fear, but because if I got one whiff of his minty breath, I was going to yank his mouth to mine, danger be damned.

"Christopher!" That same deep voice shouted in the distance. "I found him! Ladarious is out this door here! C'mon!"

There were heavy, quick footsteps like someone was running...and then the light at the end of the tunnel moved from view and the flowers once again started to bloom.

Stellan was pressed up against my side. The heat of his body seeped into me and I wanted to stay laying among the flowers with him. He sucked in a deep breath. "We better be going. They were Rebellion fighters, but we're better off avoiding them as well."

No! Bastards. If I ever found out who ruined this moment, I was gonna throw a boulder at their heads. "Yeah, you're right."

He slowly rose to his feet then offered me his hand. Without hesitating I took it and let him pull me up. My body pressed against his. He took a small step back. His eyes roamed down my arm to where our hands were intertwined. "Best get you back now."

I know you're right, but I want to stay with you.

TWENTY

STELLAN

ELOISE WAS safe back at the shelter with Melanie and the others. Ladarious had been stopped, but for how much longer? And how much longer could I keep her from discovering the truth? She was too cunning to go on without an explanation. Even now I wondered if we could keep her in the realm for any period of time. Would it be safe for her? Would it be safe for us? Ladarious wasn't the only power in this realm we had to worry about. As I walked through the dark, quiet hallways of the castle, I wondered how Ellie might fit into this life.

There was only one thing that might offer the answers we needed. The journal. My sister used to read it to me as a child and now I needed it more than ever. There was something in there that'd stuck with me. As I tiptoed my way through the castle, my anticipation built.

Moonlight peeked in through the slotted windowpanes

that lined the walls of the empty hallway, throwing pale light on the thick, plum-colored carpets. Though this was my home, this was not a place I traveled to often. Two guards walked down the hall toward me. Their purple uniforms gave me pause. But as they approached, they both stepped out of my way and pressed themselves against the walls on either side. They slammed their fists over their hearts in a salute.

Nothing to see here, lads. I inclined my head at them. "Stanford. Herbert." I greeted them by name.

"Your Highness," they replied like trained robots.

This was a song and dance we'd done every day for my entire life. I knew their first names and they knew me as *Prince Stellan.* A title I both loved and hated. Yet that was the extent of our knowledge of each other. As a boy I'd tried to get to know our guards but my parents put a stop to it as quickly as it started.

There was so much more I could be doing for my people, and now with Ellie by my side I could. My soul-mate was the one, I just knew it. And with this journal, she would soon know it too. I glanced over my shoulder. The guards had already turned and continued down the other hall, leaving me to do what I came here for.

Just up ahead on my left sat a single door. It was made of thick white oak and had carvings of the Night Realm Flora etched into it. The same flower as the one in the tunnel that my Ellie found so beautiful. Even now, while I placed my hand on the carvings, my thoughts returned to her and how the sparkling silver had glistened in her midnight hair.

As I reached for the gold, glinting doorknob, I felt the magical enchantment my parents had put on the room long ago. It was thick against the palm of my hand. Any other mage who dared to approach would feel it too. It was like placing your hand on cold sludgy mud. My power seeped back from my fingertips and curled into my stomach. It would be useless here. I couldn't just use my telekinesis to simply have the book fly out toward me. If I wanted it, I was going to have to do it the old-fashioned way. Smash and grab.

The hinges creaked as I twisted the knob and shoved the heavy door inward. The only light coming into the room was from the hallway behind me. It'd been six years since I'd stepped foot into this room. The spell had preserved it perfectly. Nothing had changed since the last time I was in here with my sister. It felt like yesterday. Crippling grief filled my chest. I felt heavy and paralyzed by it. The pain suffocated me. I was drowning in it.

"Stellan." My name came out sharp, like the crack of a whip.

My back stiffened and I forced a smile as I turned and found her standing in the doorway. "Mother."

"What are you doing?" She glanced at me, then rose up on her toes to look over my shoulder. Her sharp green eyes were only a few shades darker than my own. Her long blond hair was pulled tight and braided intricately. A glittering crown sat perched among all the braids. Heavy jewels hung from her neck and wrists. Even at this time of night, she was picture perfect.

"I was just looking." *Lame excuse.*

"For what exactly?" She showed no emotion behind those eyes. Never had. My mother hadn't loved, or hated, or cried, or felt. She was cold as ice right down to her core. It showed in the smooth skin around her mouth and eyes. Any other person her age would at least have smile lines of some sort. But not her. As young as she looked, she could've been Savina's sister. They were so alike in height and build. Both long and willowy, with breathtaking features.

"It'd been so long. I just wanted to remember her." Not a lie, but not the truth either. I remembered my sister every day. The pain of her loss still burned deep in the pit of my stomach.

Just then my father strolled up beside her. Whereas Savina looked like my mother, I held most of my father's looks. He too had sandy blond hair, though instead of falling into his eyes like mine, his was cut short and combed tight to his head. He puffed up his chest and narrowed his eyes at me. We stood the same height, eye to eye.

"Why would you do such a thing?" His accusing tone gave me pause.

I frowned. She was my family too. I should've been allowed in this shrine. I should've been allowed to attend the funeral. "I don't know, father. Perhaps I miss her."

Again, not a lie. They stood there, still as statues,

showing the same amount of emotion a hard slab of rock would.

My father cleared his throat. "You know how your mother feels about this room."

I looked down at her impassive icy face. *No, I really don't.* "She was my family too. Don't I have a right to be here?"

"Not at this hour, dear." My mother shook her head. "Off to bed with you."

Spoken to like I was some kind of child. At eighteen years old, I was considered an adult in First Realm. But here the opinions that mattered were *theirs*. Part of me wanted to defend my right to be in her room, but the bigger part of me knew I had to play my part. The journal was too important to risk. I would have to return once they weren't looking. I walked toward the door and they both took a step back. Just enough to let me exit the room but not enough to respect me in any way. I stopped just outside, right in front of them, and let the door fall shut behind me.

Their faces held no expression. Just empty coldness. Perhaps the slight edge of annoyance at the atrocity of my behavior. I wanted to argue. I wanted to rail at them. But when they showed no emotion whatsoever, I didn't know how to argue with that. I didn't understand their coldness when they clearly cared about the condition of this shrine to her.

"Very well." I couldn't stifle the growl in my throat.

It's fine, I'll just go to my room for a while then come back.

"Ah, what do we have here?"

I straightened at the voice of my father's advisor coming from down the hall. *Wilbur Stamford.* My stomach tightened into knots. *Shite.* I clenched my teeth as his stupid little heeled shoes clacked against the stone floor. The entire palace was lined with carpets that ran the middle of the hall, yet he insisted on walking along the edge so that his steps would echo. Because he wanted people to hear him coming and run in fear. He was a right plonker, that one.

"My apologies, Wilbur, we were unavoidably detained," my father said, like he hadn't been referring to his own son.

"I had wondered what the delay was, Your Majesty, but was only concerned something had happened." Wilbur stopped beside my father, standing just behind him like he was his shadow.

The shadow. That was what Savina and I had nicknamed him as children. The memory made me smirk.

Wilbur narrowed his beady eyes on me. "Your Highness, everything all right?"

I wanted to snap back with all the sarcasm and sass in the world but that wouldn't help me get back into Savina's room. Every time I got mouthy with Wilbur, he had me watched and followed. That was not something I could afford at a time like this. I looked down at his old pointy nose and his puffy white hair that he always wore combed back and imagined having the chance to punch him in the face. *That* made me actually smile.

"I have myself handled, Wilbur." I shrugged. "Just a trip down memory lane for a moment."

He adjusted the collar of the black silk waistcoat that he thought made him look important, when really it only looked like a child playing dress up in his father's closet. He smiled, but I saw the irritation in his eyes. "Ah, yes, well perhaps trips down memory lane can occur when the king isn't needed for strategy meetings."

I frowned. "Strategy meetings? At this hour?" They usually held those in the morning, as an excuse to stuff their faces with biscuits and tea.

"Yes, we're brainstorming creative ideas to eliminate the Rebellion." Wilbur arched one eyebrow. "Don't you worry, you'll get your orders with the rest of the Guard."

I nodded, because that was my role to play.

Wilbur turned to my father. "Your Majesty?"

My father gave him a curt nod but then looked to me. "Do remember this is not a playhouse, Stellan."

"I'll endeavor to do so. If you'll excuse me, I hate to keep you any longer, Father."

At that, I held my head high and turned away from them. There was no hope of returning later this evening, which meant I'd failed my mission for the night. Disappointment riddled my chest and sat heavy in my stomach. There'd be no moving around the palace without Wilbur watching. It wasn't worth the risk.

But I *would* return another time. I needed that book for

Ellie, I needed it for the realm, but most of all I needed it to remind me of all that Savina believed in. It was my turn, my job, to discover the truth of all this so that I could finish what I knew my sister had started...and what Ellie had only just begun.

TWENTY-ONE

ELLIE

My arms pinwheeled as I flew through the air. I landed flat on my ass, my back slamming into the ground. Again. Dirt scratched my forearms. If I hadn't been wearing a dress, my legs and back would've been ripped all to hell. The thick fabric wrapped around my legs, tangling me up each time I fell. Sweat gathered on the back of my neck. I would've given anything to be wearing shorts and a tank top, or even leggings. Anything but this dress.

Melanie hovered over me, blocking out the early morning sun. Her face was shadowed so I couldn't gauge her reaction at all.

I placed my hand on my forehead to shield my eyes. Frustration filled my body. I wanted to stop, if only for a moment. "What am I doing wrong?"

Melanie offered me her hand. "Nothing, it just takes time."

"We don't have time." I took her hand and she pulled me

to my feet. I dusted my hands off and ran them down the front of my dress, then shoved the wild stands of my hair out of my face. "I can't stay here forever."

Even if I wanted to stay to explore my powers, I just couldn't. My family would be worried, and my friends would be flipping out. Yet the thought of leaving felt...*wrong*. A flash of Stellan's sexy smirk lit in my mind and a slow ache spread in my chest.

Melanie gazed out at the surrounding forest. "You've got to give me just a bit more time. There is nothing more important than learning your magic."

I shifted and kicked at a rock on the ground. It was important. Hell, I wanted to learn all there was to learn about this world and my own magic. But with each passing hour I became more torn. *Home or here?*

Melanie shook her head. "Patience is a virtue."

I sighed. "Virtues are overrated."

"Come now, things were going so well only a little while ago." Her face lit with a smile. She motioned toward a larger boulder sitting at the end of the clearing. The same boulder I'd learned to move yesterday. "See if you can split it."

"Split it? It's solid stone." I shook my head. "Impossible."

"For me, yes. For you?" She grinned. "No."

I arched an eyebrow at her. "You were just trying to teach me how to curve my power over wind. And now you want me to cut through rock."

She shrugged. "You need to make your power sharp and strong, like a blade."

I opened my stance and narrowed my eyes at the boulder. "Like a blade." I repeated as I let my power flow through my body. The dam that'd once been in the center of my stomach was gone and I felt my magic just waiting at the ready for me to call upon it.

With both hands I threw my magic at the boulder like my life depended on it. I let everything go. My frustrations at feeling trapped, my fear of this new world, fear of the new power I had, my desire for a prince I couldn't have… everything shot out of me and slammed into that boulder.

The boulder groaned and I waited for something. It looked normal and whole, like maybe I'd just — the boulder groaned again and then a dark line split through the middle of it. Half of the giant rock slid to the ground a split second before the other followed. My eyes widened. I took a small step back. When I looked down at my hands, purple magic coiled around my fingers like snakes. *"Holy shit." Whoa. I did that. That was ME. If I could do that...what else could I do?*

"Indeed." Melanie clapped. "Now, you can push your wind and you can use it like a blade…but can you spin it?"

"Spin it?"

She held one finger up and twirled it in a circle. "Like a twister."

My eyes widened. *"OH.* Shit. Okay, um…sure…why not…"

I held my hand out in front of me and visualized what I wanted. I'd never seen a tornado in real life. We didn't get those in Manhattan. But I'd seen Storm in X-Men make plenty of them, not to mention that classic movie with Helen Hunt. I knew what they were supposed to look like. *Twister, twister, twister. If Storm can do it, why can't I?*

I took a deep breath then forced my magic from my hands, imagining it curving into a cylinder. Dust kicked up in front of me. My power gathered the dirt and dead leaves off the ground, sucking it up like a vacuum cleaner. It spun around and around, filling the little clearing with whipping winds and debris. I held my hands out to revel in the power coursing through my veins. The last training session had nearly knocked me out. But this time I felt like a well of unending magic was there at my fingertips. My hair whipped around my face and my lips pulled up in a smile.

Melanie held her hand out in front of her. "Okay, Ellie, that's enough."

Enough? No, it wasn't nearly enough. I wanted more, I wanted to push myself to see what else I could do.

"Ellie! You have to stop it now or someone will see." She shouted over the howling wind.

I groaned. "Okay." I reached deep inside of myself, trying to stem the flow of it all. To shut if off the way a sink could. But I couldn't. I fought to curl the power into myself but it was trying to suck me in with the leaves.

Melanie staggered backward. Her skirt wrapped around her body, her hair flew into her face. Branches snapped off the trees surrounding us. "Any time now, Eloise."

"I'm trying!" My heart raced. I felt my power raging out of control. Then the wind whipped around and picked up those two pieces of boulder like they were loose sheets of paper. They whirled around the clearing and panic flooded my body. My hands shook. Melanie fought to get to me but the wind kept her back. Dirt stung my face as it smacked into me.

One half of the boulder soared toward me. I ducked down as it sailed right over my head, severing the tree in half and crashing to a halt in the forest behind me. Melanie was sprawled on the ground fifteen feet away with the other half of the boulder imbedded in the ground right beside her legs. Two inches and she would've been crushed.

My feet lifted up off the ground and I was flung backward by the raging wind. I glanced at Melanie but she too was caught in my twister of magic. My back smacked into a tree and I slid to the ground, pain shot through my body. Black dots swam in my vision and the world spun. My twister wobbled then broke apart and the air calmed once more.

I slumped down, sucking in deep breaths. I let my head hit the ground and gazed up at the sky. *That was close.*

Melanie's face filled my vision. "Are you all right?"

I pursed my lips and shrugged. "That's debatable."

She grinned. "Good. Again."

I staggered to my feet and narrowed my eyes at her. "Are you insane. I almost killed us both."

"I couldn't agree more." That smooth velvety voice glided over my skin, sending goosebumps all over me.

I gasped and froze.

Stellan strolled into the clearing with his hands in his pockets and a smile on his face. The sun caught in his sandy blond hair and glinted in his lime colored eyes. His pants clung to his trim waist and encased his muscular thighs. Today's shirt was a pristine, crisp white that made his skin look even more tan. It was the same billowy style, with loose long sleeves that cinched at the wrist. The collar had a lace-up detail that he'd left untied and made him look like a sexy pirate. I licked my lips and fidgeted. Here he was looking like some kind of Greek God and I was a beat-up mess covered in dirt and twigs.

"Stellan...hi." I tried not to sound so happy to see him... I failed.

"Prince Stellan." Melanie gave him a quick bow. "I'm surprised to see you here. I thought our bargain was two days."

"Two days for what?" I looked back and forth between the two of them.

"I have things well in hand." Her voice was hard and her eyes even harder.

Stellan motioned to the destruction I'd caused in the clearing and how disheveled we both looked. His lips pulled up in a wicked smirk. "Clearly, you don't."

TWENTY-TWO

ELLIE

"I THINK I've got it from here."

"Your Highness, my two days aren't up yet." She spoke through thinned lips.

Clearly, they'd come to some kind of arrangement pertaining to me, yet neither of them clued me in on it. I was being kept in the dark and I didn't like it. "How about one of you tells me what's going on?"

"Prince Stellan agreed to give me two days to train you." Melanie turned and met my eyes. "My two days aren't up yet."

"Two days? TWO? Two days seems like a lofty goal." I didn't understand how either of them thought I'd get control of my magic in two days. Forty-eight hours. Hell, even Peter Parker stuck himself to his own ceiling a time or two. Thor didn't even know *he* was the thunder and not his hammer. I put my hands on my hips and shook my head. "Really? Two days."

"It is lofty." Melanie nodded in agreement. She turned pointed eyes to Stellan. "Which is why I think I deserve at least that."

Stellan held his hands up and sighed. "I come in peace. I'm not trying to undermine your efforts, Melanie. I had every intention of giving you the agreed upon two days, but I felt the need to watch."

My eyes widened. "To *watch?*"

He shrugged and pointed to some trees behind him. "From a distance, yes."

"Until now." Melanie crossed her arms over her chest and scowled.

"Until she almost leveled a forest *and* the both of you." He shoved his hands back into his pockets. "Ellie has wandless magic. As good of a teacher as you may be, Melanie, her magic requires guidance from someone who also has wandless magic. And given Ladarious' intent to capture her, I figured I'd step in now."

Melanie's chocolate brown eyes flared. She opened her mouth, then closed it just as quickly. "Damn it. Ellie, I had wanted to get you more of a baseline before he started training you but he's made valid points."

I frowned. "Sooo....?"

She gestured to him. "He's going to train you now."

I turned to look at him and butterflies danced in my stomach. I could think of a lot more things I wanted from him. But magic lessons? I wasn't entirely sure about that. This guy had a realm to rule, a Rebellion to support, and most of all I didn't want to embarrass the hell out of myself with my rookie moves. I'd nearly decapitated myself and crushed Melanie.

"What if I hurt you?" I bit my bottom lip.

His eyes bore into mine and he leaned a little closer. "Do you want to hurt me?"

I shook my head. *Never.* "No, not intentionally."

"There you have it."

"But...but—"

"Ellie." He ducked down to meet my eyes. "I won't let you hurt me, or anyone else. That's why I'm going to train you instead of Melanie."

I nodded and looked over to her. "Are you staying?"

"If Prince Stellan is going to train you then I think it's best if I go back and make sure no one spots you two out here." Melanie glanced from me to Stellan. "I'll reinforce the barrier just in case things spin out of control."

He nodded at her. She smiled and turned away from us. Her skirt billowed out and swished around her with every step she took. Soon she was completely out of sight, disappearing in the forest. And then I was completely alone with Stellan. My stomach twisted like this was a first date. Which was ridiculous. Sure there was an inexplicable attraction between the two of us, but was there more? I didn't know. I didn't even know if I wanted there to be more.

Stellan turned that devastating smile on me and slowly strolled in a small circle. "Your strength is growing."

Holy hell, that accent did things to my insides and sent shivers over my skin. I held very still, not wanting him to know the effect he had on me. I stared up into his eyes. *Do you feel this too? Tell me I'm not alone in this.*

Wait, shit, he was talking. What did he just say? Oh right. "I think so. Maybe?"

"You are. Definitely. So here's what I'm thinking…" He strolled away from me toward the other side of the clearing. "We'll start with your wind, since you're used to it. Then we'll move on to lightning."

My jaw dropped. "What do you mean lightning?"

His lips pulled up in a cocky smile that made me want to kiss him all the more.

"Didn't you notice it before? The purple lightning." He wagged his eyebrows. "It'd never been seen in this realm before you arrived."

"Wait, wait, wait." I held my hands up as my mind reeled. I did remember the lightning, it was there in every fight — *oh my GOD.* "Hold up, are you telling me…wait… you're saying…dude, am I Thor?"

He scowled hard. "And Thor is?"

"God of thunder? Norse mythology?"

He pursed his lips. "So this thunder lord, he's famous where you're from?"

"*God of thunder* and yes, very." I acted out Thor wielding his hammer. "I know I don't need a wand, but can I have a hammer? Like a big one."

He cocked his head to the side. "Would you like a talking raccoon sidekick as well?"

I froze. *He did not just speak Marvel to me.* The accent gave him ten extra hot points, but talking Marvel to me…

infinite amount of hot points. My heart fluttered. "You know Marvel? You know who Thor is?"

"Yeah, I've seen every Marvel movie. I know who Thor is, I was just messin' with you. End Game killed me. Haven't been able to watch a Marvel movie since." He shook his head. "Tony didn't need to die."

I gasped and threw my hands up. "THANK YOU! It's all Star Lord's fault. Because punching a dude in the face who could kill worlds would make sense when they had the freaking gauntlet one inch from coming off of his hand. A freaking inch, he had to all bitch up and ruin EVERY-THING. And why the hell does he get Gamora back when we don't get to have Tony? It's bullshit! Bullshit."

Stellan grinned so wide his cheeks dimpled. He leaned back against the chunk of boulder and crossed his arms over his chest, waiting for me to finish my tirade. But I wasn't even close to being done.

I held my hands an inch apart. "*This close* and the whole thing wouldn't have happened. If Star Lord had just done his damn job like *everyone else was* they would've won in Infinity Wars, but nooooooo, idiot ass strikes again and in a complete act of idiocy ends up letting the big bad kill half of life on earth. Five years of that crap all because he couldn't be smart enough to see the bigger picture the way Tony did! Where was *his* punishment? It's HIS fault they all died. Tony. Black Widow. Vision. LOKI. Should I even continue? His fault. He ruined everything. But yeah, lemme just punch freaking Thanos in the face right when we're about to win like a damn idiot."

He threw his head back and laughed. "That was a lovely tirade of rage."

"I'm right though."

"Absolutely."

The fangirl inside me receded. I was pleased he agreed with me. If he hadn't, it could've been the first loss of hot points. I dropped my arms to my sides and sighed. "Good, glad that's out of the way."

"So, lord of thunder." He teased. "Are you ready?"

I shrugged. "I'll do the best I can without a hammer."

"Good." He held his hands out to his sides and silver magic poured from him. Two logs broke from a fallen tree close by. They were shaped like discs and floated up. He hopped on top of them. They dipped for a moment then rose up off the ground. He floated toward me.

He crooked his finger at me. "Come on then."

"How?" I wanted to float up with him, to be in the air, free.

"You have the power of wind...control it." He shrugged and I felt his power surround me.

"I just nearly killed myself and I was on the ground. You want me to get up there with you?" I shook my head and took a small step back.

"Ellie, confidence." His voice was a low purr. "You're in your head. Let your instincts take over."

Am I too much in my head? I'd focused just as Melanie had said, yet I'd failed. *Maybe I should try it his way.* I wanted to join him, to have fun with my magic. I held my hands out to my sides and let the dam in my stomach loose.

Purple magic seeped from my hands and the wind kicked up around me. It twisted around and I shoved my hands down toward my feet, concentrating my power there. Dust kicked up and my feet lifted off the ground. I wavered for a moment, teetering back and forth, trying to catch my balance.

"Get out of your head, Eloise." My name was a purr on his lips.

I forced my eyes up to meet his. He hovered closer to me, his power completely under his own control. I was unsteady but still I rose to meet him in the air. There we stood at least five feet off the ground. Hovering. Flying. Excitement rushed through me and the wind surged. This was better than a freaking comic book, better than any Marvel movie. I was my own freaking superhero. My heart soared, energy coursed through my body.

Stellan smirked at me. "Better than moving rocks?"

"Way better." I held my arms out to my sides and closed my eyes. I let the heat of the sun warm my skin as the breeze from my magic cooled it. The air was fresh and warm in my lungs. I'd never felt so free in all my life.

All too soon my body shook from side to side and I floundered in the air. Stellan soared in closer to me and suddenly his arm was wrapped around my waist. He pulled me toward him and I let him hold me flush against his body. He smelled like fallen leaves and crisp autumn air and I wanted to bury my face in the crook of his neck and stay there. I barely stifled the urge when we touched back down to the ground.

Except I didn't move but neither did he. We stood there with his arms wrapped tightly around me and my hands on his chest. If I went up on my toes, I could press my lips to his. He was right there, I could do it. Yet something held me back.

"Maybe next time don't let go so completely." He chuckled and the vibration of his laughter rumbled against my chest.

I wanted to reach up and brush those stray strands of hair from his eyes. He cupped my cheek and leaned down toward me. My toes curled, my stomach turned to knots, my hands shook with excitement. I'd wanted him to kiss me since the night we'd met. The air crackled around us, pulsing with electricity that matched my rampant heartbeat.

Lightning flashed bright and hot, striking the top of a tree only twenty feet away. It cracked clean in half. Dead branches crashed down, making the ground shake under our feet. A large piece of a branch soared right at us. I threw my hands up to push it away with my magic but Stellan was *faster.* A blast of silver power erupted in my peripheral vision and the branch disintegrated into dust.

I groaned and walked away from him. "I'm so sorry."

He frowned. "What for?"

"For, I don't know, blowing shit up?" I motioned to the downed tree and destruction.

"Well." He turned to face me. "Now we know how to bring the lightning."

"How?"

He strode toward me and ran the backs of his fingers across my jaw. "Your emotions."

My cheeks heated. That was damn embarrassing. How was a girl supposed to hide any secrets when her magic gave her away? "Oh."

"Oh, indeed." His eyes darkened. "So, I think we should test this theory. Don't you?"

"Test it how?" I narrowed my eyes at him. Was it fair for him to know exactly how I felt and for me to have no clue at all what he was thinking or feeling? Did he like me? Sure, but was it as intense for him as it was for me? I had no idea. And what girl wanted to lay it all out there in front of her crush only to be blind when it came to him? Definitely not this girl.

"I can see your hesitation." He pursed his lips. "Just think, what would Thor do in this exact moment?"

"Eat guac and refuse to face any of that deep crap." Visions of fat Thor filled my mind and I couldn't hold back a chuckle.

"Hmmm…" He purred as he moved around me and ran his fingers down my arm. "Touché."

Though I had on a dress with long sleeves, I felt the gentle skim of his fingertips through the soft cotton material. A shiver ran down my spine and the air charged with electricity. I held my hand up at my side and it sparked bright purple. My eyes widened.

"I like this very much," he whispered from right behind me and I felt his breath tickle the back of my neck.

A tiny bolt shot from my fingers into the ground. Dirt exploded up just ten feet away from us.

I gasped. My face was on fire. "I think this is cheating. Who are you, Loki?"

His lips pressed to the skin on my neck and a jolt shot through me. A bolt of lightning rained down from the sky, hitting even closer to us. Yet he didn't flinch away, didn't move. Just kept pressing light kisses to my throat. My head fell back of its own accord, giving him more room to move, to kiss. Everything in me was on fire and I wanted more of it.

Another bolt and I turned to face him. "Is this supposed to be helping me or distracting me?"

"Both." He didn't smile, didn't tease.

Like the strike of a snake he reached out and grabbed me by the back of my neck and dragged my mouth to his. Our lips crashed together. Fire exploded between us and I wanted more of it. My lips parted and our tongues wound together. His fingers splayed over my lower back, burning through my dress. I fisted his shirt and pulled his body tighter against mine.

Bolts of lightning rained down around us, striking the ground in quick succession. Stellan hesitantly pulled away. His fingers still dug into my back and held me there. He pressed his forehead to mine and our breaths mingled together.

He closed his eyes for a second. "Now use it and control it."

Use it? How the hell was I supposed to use it? I backed

away from him. *Use it, Ellie. Use it.* I moved to the middle of the small clearing and held my hands out. I let that fire I felt for him flow through my body and focused on where I wanted it to strike. A bolt dropped down from the sky and struck to my right. I felt the energy sizzle across my skin like static cling during winter. Another bolt landed to my left and I felt my hair standing on end. I didn't care, this was power, this was how my magic needed to feel. Stellan moved toward me just as I called upon another bolt.

I held my hand out. "No!"

Lightning struck where he'd just been standing. The ground shot up and chunks of rock flew in all different directions. A resounding boom echoed off the deadened forest around me. My throat closed on a scream. *Where is he?* One second he was standing there, the next he was gone. Had my lightning disintegrated him to nothing. My knees shook. Sweat gathered on the back of my neck and ran down my spine. I was going to vomit, right here and right now.

"Well, lord of thunder. That was interesting." He stepped up beside me from out of nowhere.

I spun on my heels about to throw up on his shoes. *Don't throw up, don't throw up.* "Oh god, I thought I killed you!"

He shook his head. "Not that easy to kill."

"H-how did you?" My words failed me. Adrenaline spiked through my body the moment I thought I'd hurt him. Now it seeped from my system, leaving a trail of exhaustion behind it. I tackled him, wrapping my arms around his waist. "Damn it, I thought...don't do that to me."

He took my face in his hands, tipping my head back so our eyes met. "I'm sorry, that part was not intentional." Then he leaned down and pressed his lips to mine once more.

I sighed into him but he pulled back too soon. He brushed hair back out of my face.

"How did you — wait." I frowned. *How could I forget?* "You can teleport."

He nodded.

"How? How do you do that?"

His lips quirked in a sad smile. "Savina taught me."

My heart sank. I didn't know if I was supposed to tell him that I knew of his sister and her story. Would he think I gossiped about him? Would that get Melanie in trouble if he knew she'd told me? I didn't know. "Oh...is that your...girlfriend?" I knew it wasn't, but I hadn't known what else to say.

"No, Savina was my sister." He gazed down at me and I could see the sadness around his eyes and the way his brows furrowed.

I swallowed. It felt wrong to lie to him completely, so I nodded. "Oh, that was her name. I...I heard about what happened to her. I'm so sorry."

"Thank you." His smile was long gone. "She was the one who thought I'd be able to do it, so she'd been working with me on that trick, but I hadn't achieved it before she died. I was twelve."

"You have now, though." I reached up and brushed a strand of hair from his face. "I think she would've been proud of you."

"You think?" He whispered.

I nodded up at him. "Yeah."

He stared at me for a few long moments before he let out a deep sigh and nodded. He shifted from one foot to the other and blew out a breath. "Let's go one more time then take a break."

I nodded up at him, though I felt tired down to my bones. My magic was almost empty. I felt it weakening deep inside me. But I looked up at his face and saw how he was trying to pull his emotions back in check. I could do one more, for him, to help him shake this moment off. Except I didn't want a repeat of last time, so I moved away from him. *Just one more.*

The cloudless sky suddenly cracked with lightning and it fired down at me. *Shit shit shit.* I threw my hand out and it slammed into my palm. Hot energy shot through my body and threw me backward. I tumbled in midair then crashed into something. Big, warm hands gripped my hips but I'd been moving too fast. Momentum sent us both sliding across the ground. When we stopped, I looked up to find Stellan with his arms wrapped around me once more.

He sucked in a sharp heaving breath. "Are you okay?"

My eyes dipped with exhaustion. "Did I just...did I just get struck by lightning?"

"Yes, thunder lord...you did. Willingly, too." He sat up and moved me to his side. Once he was on his feet, he bent down and helped me to mine. He threw my arm over his shoulder and took most of my body weight. I suspected that if he wanted to carry me, he could.

But I wanted to walk. "God of Thunder status here I come."

"I think you need a rest." He swept my legs out from under me and lifted me up against his chest.

I yawned. "No, I don't."

I wanted him to stay, needed him to stay. There were so many things I had to learn about him. I needed to know everything. Yet my body fought to drag me under, to force me to take the sleep I so desperately needed. My head rolled and landed on his shoulder.

"Rest, Ellie. I'll be here when you wake."

Each step he took was like being rocked to sleep. My eyes drifted shut and the exhaustion of using too much of my power took me. "You better be…"

TWENTY-THREE

STELLAN

THE ROOM WAS STILL and silent but for the sound of Ellie's steady breathing. Outside the doors, I heard the daily shuffle of life going on. The Rebellion and the women who took shelter here were going about their business. The most powerful mage to ever walk this world slept in a bed only a few feet away from them all. I ran my fingers through the silky strands of her wild hair. It'd all come loose from the bun she'd wound it in. Those midnight locks spread over her pillow in thick dark waves. Her eyelashes fanned out over her creamy cheeks as she drew in deep soft breaths.

Just sitting in the bed next to her, letting my fingers drift through the ends of her hair, was so soothing to me. Like all the pressure I felt to save this world somehow wasn't so all-consuming when I had her with me like this. I leaned back against the headboard and let my head rest on it. Ellie flopped onto her side and draped her arm over my hips, tucking her face into my side. She was like a kitten, stretching and seeking comfort in her sleep. I froze, not wanting to stir her.

My soulmate was wrapped around me and I could hardly believe it. For years I thought she was dead, so to have her laying here with her ocean scent surrounding me…it was a dream. And with it came a kind of peace I had never experienced.

The door creaked open and I sat there unsure of what to do. Melanie peeked around the door and raised her eyebrows at me. She crooked her finger, signaling for me to leave Ellie to follow her. But I didn't want to leave this moment. I shook my head. She pressed her lips in a thin line and narrowed her eyes at me. She pointed at me then out toward the door with jerky, insistent motions. Like I didn't have a choice in the matter. I sighed and rolled my eyes, then mouthed the word *fine*. As gently as I could manage, I lifted Ellie's arm from my waist and slid out of the side of the bed. The warmth of her little body left me all too soon.

"Stellan?" Her words were slow and sleepy. Was she dreaming or just waking up?

"Shh, rest." I whispered, then ran my fingers over her cheek and smoothed the hair back from her face. Soon she was snuggled into her pillows and fell into steady even breaths.

Once she was comfortable, I walked out into the hallways to face Melanie. "Yes?"

"What are you doing?" She hissed under her breath. "I don't recall cuddling as part of the plan."

"I'm improvising." I glared at her. Yes, Melanie was helping me more than I could even say. But when it came to my soulmate there were some instincts that couldn't be denied. Holding her while she slept seemed to fall into that category. Especially when she asked me to.

Melanie crooked her finger at me. "Come on, we need to talk some place private."

I hesitated, reluctant to leave Ellie alone in such a depleted state. Her magic was drained. It put her into such a deep sleep it left her vulnerable.

"She'll be safe here."

"Sure." This realm was turbulent and violent. It didn't take a genius to know no one was safe. The death of my sister proved that.

Melanie led us through the house to the library. I walked into the room and halted. She wrung her hands as she paced from the windows at one end of the room all the way to the book stacks at the other. Stacks of books were strewn across the table. One by one they drifted up and put themselves back into place. She moved by them, holding her wand up. Little beads of shimmering light came out the tip and drifted over the walls in the room. I'd seen this spell before. She was soundproofing it so no one would hear a word that was uttered between us. She'd done the same thing the last time we'd been in here.

Once the spell was complete, Melanie whirled around to face me. Her skirt billowed out around her and swished around her legs. "She's not going unnoticed. The lightning on a perfectly cloudless day."

"I thought we had a barrier spell up for training." I narrowed my eyes.

"There is a barrier spell. I did it myself. But she's simply too powerful. We're running out of time." I must've made a face because she narrowed her eyes at me. "You're not the only one with ears on the street. Nor were you the only one there when she came through the portal. Ladarious saw her and he wants her. He's seen her power."

"Before, you implied that you knew of something I once thought was the deepest secret in the realm. Was I wrong to think so?" I held my breath. I thought she knew, but the words hadn't been spoken out loud.

"The Stone Keeper?" She whispered.

I nodded gravely. "My sister had a journal, one she'd found in the palace. I think it can give us the details we've been looking for."

She took a step toward me and her deep brown eyes were grave. "Then we need that book."

"Savina's room is heavily guarded. My parents, cold as they may be, keep it like a shrine to her." I shook my head and moved to lean up against one of the bookshelves.

"Oh." Her eyebrows shot up. "Do they?"

"Yes, and the bloody book is there. There's a spell protecting the room, so I can't even use my magic to pull it out. I have to physically walk in and take it." I curled my hand into a fist at my side. "I know where it is too. We never moved it. We always kept it in the same place. I just need to be able to get there. I tried already and was caught."

"Sounds like what you need is a distraction." She crossed her arms over her chest and let a slow smile spread across her face. "Just so happens I have an idea."

For some reason I didn't like that smile *or* the mischief that flashed in her eyes. "Let's hear it."

"What if we could get the Royal Guard to come away from their post?"

I shrugged. "In theory that'd be a perfect distraction."

"Then let's make it a reality." She nodded as if this would be so easy.

"How?" If she had a way to give me the time I needed, then I was bloody well taking it. "And what about Eloise?"

"She'll stay here, of course. Where it's safe. And as for the distraction." She held up her finger. "Just a moment."

Melanie turned and opened the door to the library. She waved for someone to join us. I didn't know if I liked anyone else knowing what we were up to. Rumors in this realm spread like wildfire. Maren walked into the room with her hands folded in front of her. Her tousled brown hair brushed at her shoulders. Her deep brown eyes were rimmed with worry.

Melanie let the door fall shut behind her and Maren turned to face me. "Prince Stellan." She gave me a quick bow. "How may I help?"

"We need a distraction." Melanie blurted out. It wasn't subtle but definitely to the point.

"I don't follow." Maren wrung her hands together.

"Prince Stellan has to retrieve something from the castle that is guarded. If the Rebellion could create a distraction long enough for him to grab it, then it would really help the realm and the Rebellion." Melanie was so animated as she spoke.

"What kind of distraction?" Maren's brows furrowed and I felt apprehension roll off of her in cold waves. Maren was never a fan of starting battles, not after Savina died. This woman was supposed to be my family, my other sister. The soulmate to my sibling. She'd felt like that once, now she was almost a stranger.

Melanie cleared her throat and licked her lips before answering. "We want you to attack the castle."

"Wait, what?" Maren's eyes shot wide. "You want the Rebellion to attack the palace without telling me why?"

Ballsy, very ballsy. And I liked it. This would be exactly what we needed to give me the time to retrieve the journal. "I like it."

Maren held her hands up and shook her head. "You are asking a lot of the Rebellion. Putting their lives in danger for something I don't even know about. Prince Stellan, of course we appreciate all your support, but this could go horribly wrong, or worse, could be a trap."

I moved away from the bookcases and stood up straight. There was no way that I would lead the Rebellion into a trap. And it bothered me that she might think so. "I think I have proved my allegiance by now. I need you to trust me. I need you to help me."

Melanie met Maren's eye. "We owe him that much."

Maren sighed and nodded. "Fine. But this needs to be a quick fight. We need to get in and back out quickly."

I rubbed my hands together and excitement flooded my body. The castle had never been attacked before. I didn't want anyone to get hurt but this would give me the time that I needed and maybe the warning shots to wake my parents the hell up. "Exactly. I only need a few minutes once the fight starts."

Maren pointed toward Melanie. "Okay. Mel, this part is more your alley. How do you want to do this?"

Melanie gave a dark humorless chuckle. "Prince Stellan, you have fifteen minutes to get home, then the Rebellion will be at your doorstep."

"And you're sure Eloise will stay here?" I couldn't risk her being there, not even for a minute. Her powers were so new, she was still learning, and if anyone saw her it would mean her death.

Melanie nodded up at me. "I promise she won't be there. I've got this. You just be ready when the time comes."

I curled my hands into fists at my sides and felt the power within me stir. "I'll be ready."

TWENTY-FOUR

STELLAN

THE THICK CARPET cushioned every step I took as I walked from one end of my room to the other. The cold stone walls seemed to keep out the heat that plagued the realm. They were a dreary sort of light gray that matched a storm covered sky. It wasn't original as they were the traditional color of the Royals. Across from the entrance of my room was a set of double doors that led to a half-moon shaped balcony overlooking the front of the castle. It would give me a perfect view of what was about to happen.

I glanced at the grandfather clock on the wall. *Two minutes.* I had exactly two minutes until the Rebellion came knocking on our door. And then only fifteen to collect the journal I needed. Was it wrong to attack my childhood home? Probably. Did I care? Not in the slightest. This was for my people, my realm, and my soulmate.

To my right sat my king-sized bed. I moved to sit on it, but the second my arse plopped down on the thick comforter I popped right back up. I smoothed my hands through my hair and tugged at the strands. My magic hummed through my veins with my racing pulse. This had to work. The answers I needed—no, that *we* needed— were in that book. I was sure of it. In the distance, I heard the first sounds of the Rebellion. A loud crash came from just below my window. And my lips curved into a smile.

I hurried to my balcony just in time to see Melanie leading a group of mages toward the castle. She held her wand high and fired a blast of magic that hit the ground just outside the palace walls. The ground exploded, chunks of grass and dirt flew up the side of the castle, smearing the pristine walls with muck and filth.

"Mother will love that." I muttered before I turned away from the chaos and headed into the castle.

The sound of rushing footsteps echoed through my door as the Royal Guard hurried toward the commotion. Once the silence came, I slipped out of my room and into the hallway. The place was like a museum, complete with suits of armor lining the walls. Sunlight peeked through the high windows, lighting the way toward Savina's room. The outside of the castle rocked and the sound of a battle ensued. I wanted to be there, to help, but I couldn't. My family couldn't know I aided The Rebellion.

Particles of dust drifted down from the high beams that ran the length of the vaulted ceilings. Another loud explosion and the floor vibrated under my feet. This chaos felt like more than a distraction. *How far is Melanie going to take this?* A couple more hits like that and the castle doors would burst wide open. I wanted to run out to see the extent of the damage of what they were doing but I couldn't. My sole focus had to be the journal.

I turned the corner and rushed by three guards running for the stairs in the opposite direction. I recognized two of the three as the ones who stood outside Savina's room. At the end of the hall I slowed my pace and pressed myself up against the wall. Just around the corner stood Savina's room. I inched toward the corner and peeked around it, checking to see that the corridor was empty.

Not a soul in sight. This time I wouldn't hesitate to open that damn door and go right in. Last time I'd paused, letting my emotions and my grief for her get the best of me. This time, I wouldn't. I ran toward the ornate wooden door and grabbed the knob. With the hard twist of my wrist, the latch gave and I jabbed my shoulder into the door.

It flew open and I hurried inside, slamming it closed behind me. The sounds of the skirmish faded to a faint cry. White. The walls were so white in this room. It was the only room in the palace that held a color other than the sad gray. An oversized chandelier hung from the ceiling. Its crystals gave off rainbows that wavered over the room as the rays of the sun peeked in from the window. My room was bigger, but hers was more beautiful. This room was a harsh reminder of what my mother wanted Savina to be and of everything she wasn't.

Her bed was large and covered with a fluffy white blanket. A dozen pillows were stacked on the bed...all for show.

And wasn't that just the way. Everything with my family was for show. The one thing they couldn't hide was the lingering scent of leather in the room. My mother preferred light, soft scents like vanilla or lavender. But my sister was a badass and always smelled of leather, though I'd never discovered why.

I wanted to stand here and take in the room. But I couldn't. Others were counting on me, on my ability to do this for our realm. I darted over to the other side of the bed. In the far corner of the room the wall was smooth and flat, but I remembered there was a secret door there.

I placed my hand against it and whispered the words she'd taught me so long ago. "Bound by blood of mine own hand, reveal to me which I have banned."

There, at the bottom of the wall, a three-foot by three-foot panel appeared. The thick glamour dropped from the space. The panel popped out slightly and the smell of wooden planks filled my nose. *This is it.* This was the place Savina had showed me all those years ago. The same exact place she'd found the journal as a child. I dropped to my knees and crawled into the small deep tunnel. When I was younger, I used to play in this hidden cave. Now my shoulders barely fit through the door. The light wooden planks groaned and wobbled under my weight. My heart hammered so loud in my chest that it filled my ears. I reached forward to the spot where we hid that damn journal. I used to be able to fit my hand in the hole to pull the wooden plank free, now barely two fingers fit there.

I shoved them in and yanked at the wood. It popped

free and a puff of dust smacked me in the face. My fingers brushed over the worn leather binding of the journal and I snatched it. I crawled backward out of the tunnel as quickly as I could, while keeping that damn journal tight in my grasp. The second I was free I popped to my feet and opened the pages, *just* to be sure I had the right one before I left. But It was exactly as I remembered, with the thick browning parchment and the scrawling handwriting. I wanted to stand there and read it all, but I was running out of time. I shoved the book behind my back, letting the waistband of my pants hold it tight to my body. I straightened my coat to smooth over the journal.

My magic flowed through my fingers as I held it over the panel once more. "Bound by blood of mine own hand. Conceal for me which I have banned."

The panel melted back into place. The perfect pristine white wall was once again exactly how my mother wanted it. With no time to spare, I ran for the door, silently vowing that this would not be the last time I visited her room. Somehow just being here made me feel closer to her. Like her things could give me the littlest piece of her that I'd lost way too soon.

As I twisted the doorknob, I gave it one last look. It wasn't decorated for Savina, but it was how I remembered her. I glanced out the door, checking to make sure no one was coming. The hall was empty. I stepped out and quickly closed the door behind me. With the journal pressed to my back, all I had to do now was make it back to my room and shoot the all clear signal off my balcony. The Rebellion would retreat, and I would have exactly what I needed. With rushed steps I walked down the hall and turned the corner to head toward my quarters.

I slammed into someone. Our bodies collided like two trains, except mine was still standing while the other crashed to the floor. I gasped. My eyes widened. *"Father?"*

He laid on the ground, flat on his back. "Stellan." He extended his hand out toward me.

I quickly grabbed it and hauled him back to his feet. "My apologies, Father. Are you all right?"

"Quite." He brushed his hand down the thick purple robe he wore, straightening it out. He cleared his throat. "Where are you headed in such a hurry?"

"Back to my chambers."

Just then I heard the clacking of heeled shoes walking on stone and then Wilbur rounded the corner. He strolled up beside my father, always the shadow. He ran his hand down the front of his black suit coat and pursed his lips. "We are under attack, Prince Stellan. Do you not care for your future throne?"

The daft wanker was always sticking his nose where it didn't belong. I glared at him. "I do."

"Perhaps you'd like to help." This man reached too high. He was an advisor, not a Royal family member. Too often he forgot that fact.

My father nodded at Wilbur. "Quite right. We are under attack, your people need you. The guards need you." He placed both of his hands on my shoulders and spun me around to face the stairs. "Help them, Son. Your fighting days end only when my life does. Go."

He was too easily swayed by that man. It made my skin crawl.

"As you wish. Are you coming?" I motioned to Wilbur. "Surely you're not scared, are you?"

He tugged at the sleeves of his coat and lifted his chin. "I think I best serve here."

"Not surprising. And you, Father? Will you be joining?"

This was not part of the plan. I wasn't supposed to join the fight against the Rebellion. I was supposed to signal their retreat.

He cleared his throat. "Of course not. I must command from here."

Good thing he was behind me and couldn't see my eyes rolling. "Yes, Father."

"Fight bravely, my boy." His voice was deep and gruff.

I didn't bother replying. What could I say? Coward? Lazy? Terrible ruler. He would hear none of it. Instead I walked down the stairs and through the foyer. What I wouldn't give to knock down those suits of armor, or to remove the portraits on the walls of pompous family members, or to even rip up this stupid purple carpet. But it wasn't in my power...yet.

I shoved through the front doors and hurried to join the line of guards facing off against Melanie's wild attack. When she saw me her eyes widened. I returned her wide-eyed gaze. This wasn't part of the plan but Melanie and I both knew if I didn't keep up the appearance of being part of the Royals then this was all for nothing.

She pointed her wand toward my chest. "Charge!"

Our forces collided. The Royal Guard was a swarm of purple against the peasant-looking Rebellion. Battle cries rang out and my heart slammed in my chest. This wasn't supposed to happen. Magic fired in all different direction. Flashes of every color filled the area in front of the castle and magic flowed to my hands.

Melanie strode up to me and pointed her wand at my chest. "Duck."

I tilted my body to the side and ducked as she fired a shot over my head. "Hold on." Silver magic flew from my hands as I lifted her up off the ground and flung her back. At the last second, I pulled back on my power and she landed only a few feet away from me.

Her feet dug into the ground as she slid to a halt. "Right!"

I leaned back just as a nasty curse flew right by my face. I regained my balance only to see Melanie was in her own spot of trouble. "Left."

She jumped to the left and I fired a shot that barely missed her torso but smacked into the guard standing behind her about to attack. He flew back into another group of guards. I hissed in a fake breath like I hadn't meant to hit my own men. Melanie pointed at me and fired a bright flash of white light. She took her time telegraphing her move before she made it. I spun to the right and dodged it.

We circled each other and I stepped in closer to her. "My father shoved me out here just as I was heading back to my quarters."

Her eyes lit and she fired another ball of magic at me. This one hit me square in the chest, I sucked in a sharp breath waiting for pain to come, but it didn't. I pressed my hand to my chest and staggered back like it did. I returned the same shot and smacked her in the shoulder.

Melanie staggered to the right, coming closer. "Did you get it?"

I pressed my lips together and gave her a tight nod.

Her lips twitched like she was about to smile. "Then we must go." She lifted her wand to send the retreat signal I was supposed to send, then froze.

I glanced around to see Ellie running into the fray. A swarm of pebbles spun around her and her hair blew all around her face. She flung her hands forward and the pebbles pelted the Royal Guards closest to her. She took them down with one foul shot.

"I thought you said you got this?" I snapped at Melanie.

"Clearly, I don't got this. She's stubborn." She cursed and lowered her arm. "I'll get her to retreat with us."

The hairs on the back of my neck stood up the way they did when I knew my father was around. I glanced up toward the balcony where he stood gazing over the skirmish. His calculating green eyes flared with interest. He pointed down at Ellie just as the ground exploded before her, sending some of our guards flying. He grabbed the guard closest to him and yanked him over to the edge, motioning to Ellie.

Bloody sodding son of a bitch. I started toward her to get her out of here before he got a glimpse of her purple magic when a battle cry came from just beyond the trees surrounding the grounds of the castle. *No, it can't be.*

Black cloaked figures sprinted into the chaos with their wands held at the ready and their cloaks billowing around their bodies. The first wave of them smacked into our skirmish like a tsunami. *Shit, shit, shit.* This whole thing was going straight to hell. I needed backup and I needed it now. I lifted my hand and used my magic to scribble the symbol the Dukes and I used to call upon each other when we were children.

With my silvery magic I drew a line straight down then crossed it with a symbol that resembled the letter Z. I smacked my hand over it, and it exploded beneath my touch. I sent it to my cousins, telling them to come as quickly as possible. I turned to go for Ellie and then I saw *him* step out from the shadows of the trees. My breath caught in my throat and I pumped my arms, sprinting toward her.

Ladarious stared, his eyes were locked on only one thing...Eloise.

TWENTY-FIVE

ELLIE

MAGIC PULSED through my veins and shot from my hands. Pebbles swarmed around me like angry bees. I flung my hand out, letting my magic spill from my hands. They wanted me to stay hidden away, like some kind of coward, while they fought. Not for one second would I shy away from this. Not while Stellan and Melanie were out here risking their necks for me and for the realm. I was here for a reason dammit. No comic book hero ever hid in their shelter while others fought their battles.

A rush of black cloaks smashed into the Royal Guards and the Rebellion. Someone slammed into my shoulder and I tumbled forward onto my hands. I staggered to my feet and lightning forked out over the sky.

Stellan rushed to my side and threw his arm around my waist. He yanked me back just as one of Ladarious' men shot a flaming ball of magic from the tip of his wand. The ball smacked into a guard and his entire body went up in flames. Just as quickly, the guard next to him hosed him down with water. The man stood, smoking and charred, but he was alive.

"Thanks for that." I leaned back against Stellan.

"What are you doing here?" He growled.

I stepped away from him. "I'm here to help."

"This isn't your fight." His eyes blazed.

"The hell it's not."

Another one of Ladarious' men reached for my arm. I spun away from him but his nails raked across my forearm. With my other hand I summoned my wind. A single rock the size of my fist flew up from the ground and smacked him like a rocket. He dropped to the ground, clutching at his face.

Just then the Dukes appeared at Stellan's sides. The three of them moved through the wave of Ladarious' men like they were hacking through overgrown bushes with machetes. Black cloaked figures ran away from them, screaming and crying as sage colored magic seeped out from Shylock. He had a roguish grin as people dropped to their knees. His tousled hair fell over his forehead and bounced with each of his movements. Weston chuckled among the chaos. His movements weren't big or overly flourished. When he used his power his deep blue eyes flared with excitement. Just a simple touch here and there. The poke of a finger, the brush of a hand, and a pile of bodies lay scattered around him. The second his hand brushed them they'd fall to the ground as if they'd been tasered.

Stellan was at the center of all three of them. They fought back to back like this was nothing new to them. They were fierce and anyone who even dared to come near me was either thrown back or dropped like a rock. A heavy magical presence slithered over my skin like toxic sludge. I knew that feeling. It made the hairs on the back of my neck stand on edge. I whirled around, searching him out. That toxic man I was beginning to know as my enemy. By the time my eyes landed on his bald tattooed head, it was too late.

Ladarious had Stellan in his sights. He stood with a ball of electrified, flaming magic in his hand. His blue eyes met mine and he smiled. The bastard actually smiled. When he glanced from me to Stellan and back again I knew his plan. He was going to take out Stellan to get to me. Because right now I was untouchable with Stellan and his friends helping me.

I pumped my arms, running for Stellan.

But it was too late. Ladarious let go of that ball of electrified fire and sent it soaring right at him like a rocket. My magic rolled with me and hurried to the forefront. Purple exploded out of me. The people standing closest to me flew off their feet from my wind. A boulder shot up from the ground right in front of Stellan. He staggered back as the blast fired right into the boulder. Ladarious' magic reflected off the stone and headed straight at me. I whirled to the side to get out of the way.

Burning hot pain exploded in my side. My knees gave out as the electrified power sizzled through my muscles.

The air left my lungs in a rush and I clutched my side. My skin burned and ached, and I struggled to catch my breath. The battle raged on around me but I heard Stellan's roar of anger.

Two sets of arms seized me, one around my hips and the other around my shoulders. I didn't have the strength to fight them off. Pain like I'd never known thrummed through my body, making the world around me grow hazy. They shoved me forward, dragging me across the battlefield. I twisted in their arms and dropped to the ground.

"No, Miss, be still. We're taking you to the tunnels." A light male voice said from just beside my ear.

"We'll get you back to the shelter." A woman with a childlike voice said from my other side.

When I glanced up, I recognized her from the other night's dinner. Though we hadn't spoken, I'd seen her from across the table. I leaned into her, letting her guide me away from the open field and under the canopy of trees. My steps were halted and stumbling as we hurried through the underbrush of the forest. Their breaths heaved in my ears as leaves crackled under our feet.

We came to a stop deep in the forest. The sounds of the battle were a faint echo. The man, a smaller guy with a wide brimmed hat and brown cloak, glanced around us. I followed his gaze.

"I don't think we were followed." His accent was more common than Stellan's regal British.

"Best get her out of here." The woman motioned to a large tree.

The man reached up and pressed his hand to a knot in the tree. The center of the trunk slid to the side like the opening of a door. The woman guided me forward, helping me step over the roots of the tree and into the trunk. It was dimly lit and smelled of earth. The air was cool and damp.

The man walked in behind us and we started to move down the tunnel. "This'll take us back to the shelter."

I straightened my stance. They couldn't leave the battle for me. The Rebellion was suffering, and they needed every wand they could get. I stepped away from them and put on a bravado I didn't feel. "You must go back."

"But, Miss, you're hurt." The man motioned to my side.

I didn't want to look down at it. Sometimes it was better not knowing how bad things really were. Judging by how much it hurt and the warm liquid seeping over my hand, it was very bad indeed. "I can make it on my own. The Rebellion needs you."

They shared a glance then turned back to me. They hesitated only a moment before the woman placed her hand on my arm. "You're sure?"

No. I pressed my lips together and nodded. "I am."

Without another word they turned away from me and ran back toward the entrance to the tunnel. Light flooded the dark cave when they opened the door, but it went out just as fast when they left me. I sucked in a heaving breath and let my knees give out. My whole body quaked. I rolled to my back, leaning up against the hard-packed dirt of the walls. I eased my hand away from my side. Blood covered my fingers and seeped into the side of my dress. The charred material stuck to my exposed skin. I couldn't tell how bad the damage was, but it felt like death shooting into my side.

I let my head fall back against the cool side. I groaned and let my body sag further. If I just rested here a moment, then I could gather my strength to move once more. The world swam around me. Then that bright light shined in the dim tunnel once more and I knew the entrance had been opened.

I tried to raise my hand to wave them off. "I said leave me."

"Not bloody likely." Stellan growled, suddenly on his knees beside me. He looked down and his eyes widened at the injury on my side. His hands fluttered over me for a moment like he didn't know if he should touch me or not. "You took this…for me?"

I would've taken much more for him. I shrugged and pain shot through me. I winced. "I couldn't let you die."

He cupped my face in his hands and pressed his lips to mine. Taking my mouth in a fierce kiss. A different kind of fire burned through my veins and I wanted to reach for him, to wrap my hands in his hair and tug him closer. But I couldn't. My body wouldn't let me. It was finished faster than it started.

He pulled back and gazed into my eyes. "Don't ever do that again."

"I make no promises." If his life was in danger I would do it again…in a heartbeat.

He placed his arm around my back and lifted me to my

feet. The world spun and I swayed on my feet. He pulled me closer to his side. "I can carry you."

"No, if you just help me a bit, I can do this." I shook my head. Damsel in distress was not in my vocabulary, and though I was injured, I refused to be one now.

He pressed his lips to my temple, brushing a kiss there. "Come on then. Let's get you out of here."

TWENTY-SIX

ELLIE

THE DOOR FLEW open and slammed into the wall with a loud whack. As we made our way through the tunnels, I felt myself becoming weaker by the moment. My body went cold. The pain still shot through my limbs, leaving a throbbing, gaping mess. Stellan laid me out on the bed. The pillows felt so good under my head, and the mattress was soft and inviting under my back. My eyes fluttered and Stellan snapped his fingers.

"No bloody sleeping." His face was pale and his eyes kept darting around. His hand fluttered over my side again, like he was swatting at bees in a panic. "I have to get your dress off."

"So *that's* what this was about?" I winced in agony. "There were easier ways to get my dress off, *Your Highness.*"

He froze and gave me a blank stare. "Are you joking, now of all times?"

"It's all I've got." I moved to sit up so he could help me

with the ties of the corset and gasped. Searing hot pain shot through my side and I fell back on the bed with black dots swarming my eyes.

He bent over me and tugged on the ripped edges of my dress bodice. "I'll do my best not to look."

I arched my eyebrow at him. But he'd already averted his gaze. He flexed his arms then pulled. The bodice of my dress tore like tissue paper, taking the material under my dress with it. I shivered and goosebumps spread across my skin despite the sultry air. It wasn't every day a hot guy ripped you out of your dress. This silly, stupid crush of mine was the only thing keeping me sane as the pain raged inside me.

Stellan *still* didn't turn to look at me. He cleared his throat. "Is the wound visible?"

I glanced down at my side. "Yes."

"And the rest of you?" He whispered.

"Yep, that too." I slipped my arms from the sleeves and lay there in my torn dress, bare from the waist up.

"Bloody hell, I'd like to check your wound. Can you – can you cover yourself?"

Despite everything, that made me smile. Here I was, burned and bleeding, and he wanted to be prince charming. It was actually really adorable. I tried to pull a corner of the blanket across my chest to cover my breasts, but I didn't have the strength. The effort to get my sleeves off had drained me. My limbs felt heavy. *Come on, you can do it.* I curled my fingers to grip the blanket then pulled my arm up with everything I had left.

My arm rose...and the blanket slipped right out of my grip. *Screw the blanket.* I threw my arm over and let it land right across my bare chest. I couldn't see from where I was, but it felt like the important bits were covered. I sighed. "Okay. Done."

He turned to face me and his eyes widened. His gaze dropped to my chest and stayed there. He licked his lips. "Thought you were going to cover more."

A warm breeze swept through the room. I felt it brush over the sides and bottoms of my breasts. *Ah. That explains the face.* "The blanket deserted me in my time of need. Gimme a sec, we'll host a rematch."

"No." He shook himself then bent down low over my wound to examine it. "I mean, it's okay. Save your strength, I'll just...I can't believe you took this hit for me."

I looked him dead in the eye. "That hit was heading straight for your chest. You wouldn't have survived something like that."

"Likely not." He walked over to the door and opened it, then stuck his hand out. Silvery magic drifted in from the opening and when he brought his hand back there was a black vial clasped within his fingers. He looked at the vial, grunted, and extended his hand once more into the hall.

"What are you doing?" I eyed the dark gothic vial in his hands.

"I need the right potions to heal you."

"Heal me? I thought I was in for some stitches." Looking at the rivers of blood slowly seeping from the wound on my side, I knew it was at least stitches worthy. I'd been injured enough times as a kid to know that.

"Stitches." He scoffed. Strands of his sandy blond hair fell into his eyes. "Barbaric. Your realm is advanced in a lot of ways, but in this we far surpass you."

"Oh...oh good." I sagged with relief. I didn't relish the idea of getting stitches in my side and definitely not in a different realm.

When he pulled his hand back inside he held two more vials, one a dark crimson and one a bright white. "This should do it."

"Do your worst."

He held up the first vial. The dark black gothic one with a twisted silver cork. He uncorked it. "Sorry for this."

"Wait. Can't we count down?"

"Right. One...two..." He dumped the clear liquid over my side.

It burned and hissed. White bubbles fizzed over my skin like hydrogen peroxide, except this burned so much deeper. I ground my teeth together. "What the hell happened to three?" I screamed through clenched teeth, but it came out more like a growl.

"Better this way." His face was pale, nearly green. He opened the dark crimson bottle.

"Don't you dare." My side still burned from the stinging. "What the hell is that?"

"The last one was to clean the wound. This one is to remove whatever spell he used to do that to you." He held it over my side. "Take a deep breath."

I sucked in a breath as a thick glopping liquid poured out of it. It was the color of maple syrup and felt just as sticky when it hit my skin. This one didn't burn or hurt. It was cool and soothing like aloe vera gel on a deep sun burn. The tension in my muscles eased and I sighed.

The corner of his lip twitched. "Better?"

"Mmmmhmmm." I nodded up at him.

He wagged the last bottle at me. It was a simple white bottle with no writing and a plain cork. With little effort he popped the cork from the bottle and held it above me. His eyes followed the little drops. One by one they fell to my skin and ran over my side. This wasn't burning peroxide or soothing aloe syrup, it was an oil that was cool against my skin.

"Okay, um, so I have to...uh..." he wiggled his fingers "massage this in to complete the healing, okay?"

"There were easier ways to give me a massage, *Your Highness.*"

His cheeks flushed bright pink.

"You're cute when you blush."

He arched one eyebrow. "You're cute when you taunt."

I tried to smile but lacked the energy. I thought at least a smirk came out. "Go ahead, do your worst."

He chuckled and shook his head, his face still flushed. He sat the vial down and rolled his shirt sleeves up. When he pressed his hand to my side and began rubbing the oil into my skin, I felt myself start to heal. I looked down and the open wound steadily closed with each brush of his fingers over my skin. I watched the serious look on his face, loving the adorable way his eyebrows scrunched up as he concentrated. His fingers were hot against me, yet goosebumps covered my body. My pulse thundered through my veins and I had the horrifying suspicion he could feel the way he affected me. And then his eyes met mine and it was like someone hit the fire alarm. My whole system lit up.

In a panic, I looked down at his hands, but instead my gaze landed on a mark on his left forearm. It was made of simple, clean lines. Three circles with triangles sticking out around it, with flowers and vines. It was totally and utterly familiar…because it was identical to *mine.*

The only other person I remembered seeing one on was Maren, but hers looked nothing like mine or Stellan's. *But how? I must be imagining things, right?* We couldn't possibly have the same mark. I knew Melanie told me not to ask anyone about the marks, but I couldn't help myself. I had to ask. Had to know.

"Your mark matches mine."

His eyes flared for a second. His hands froze on my body. "It does."

"Why?"

"Umm…" he wouldn't look at me. "What do you know about these?"

"Melanie told me they were a type of scar from dark, violent magic."

His expression didn't falter, it stayed locked as an emotionless stare. He lifted the edge of the blanket up and over my chest. "So then there's an answer, why ask me?"

With the blanket now covering my body, I lifted my arm up to where we could both see it. "Because she also told me not to ask anyone about it, which sounded suspicious then and certainly does now. And because of the look on your face…and the fact that we match."

"Um…well…" he cleared his throat and focused his eyes on his fingers as he continued to massage my skin. "They're…it's…I mean, it *is* a magical mark—"

I pressed my fingers to his mouth. "I'm gonna put a stop to that little brain fart right now. Don't you dare speak another word if it's going to be anything other than the truth."

He sighed. "*Ellie,*" he whispered against my fingers.

"Please, Stellan. I can handle lies from other people, but not *you.*" I lowered my fingers. "Not you."

He groaned and ran a hand over his face.

"What is the mark really, Stellan? I promise if you tell me I won't be angry, whatever it is."

"That's hardly fair to you." He smirked. "You don't even know what you're promising not to be angry about."

I stared at him.

He held his left arm up next to mine so that our marks were side by side They were even more identical than I had realized. His eyes seemed to glisten as he stared at them. It made my heart flutter in weird ways.

"This mark does not mean dark magic, nor is it a scar," he said in a low, soft voice. His eyes seemed to trace the lines on our arms. "This mark means that we're soulmates."

I gasped. "*WHAT?*"

His cheeks flushed. "We are soulmates."

"We're…" I looked to our arms with their matching marks, then back to him. "Soulmates?"

"Yes."

I narrowed my eyes at him. "If this is some kind of joke or prank—"

"It's not. You're my soulmate for real, for eternity." He watched me closely and he held very still, looking for some kind of reaction, I was sure of it.

"You're my soulmate?" I shouted. I didn't know if I was more shocked or thrilled at the idea of being bound to him.

"Yes." He nodded simply. I still didn't know if he even took a breath. Was he holding it this whole time, waiting to see what I'd do?

"Oh my GOD. Oh no, oh shit. You're serious?" This couldn't be happening. This was the kind of thing you saw in fairytales or books. This wasn't something in real life.

"I'm afraid so."

My heart pounded in my chest. This explained so much. Why I was drawn to him, why I missed him when he wasn't near, and why I wanted him more than anything else. "H-how? How is this possible? How does it work? Oh my God. I have a soulmate."

He licked his lips and lowered his arm. "We were marked for each other the very day you were born."

"Me?"

"The marks show up the moment the youngest of the two is born." He traced his fingertips over my skin, making me shiver. "I am a year older than you, so for that whole year it was blank. But then you were born and this mark appeared."

My jaw dropped. "You've had *this* since you were one? Since I was born?"

He nodded.

"*What?*" I tried to sit up but sharp pain shot through me. "But no...no I didn't have it then, I only just got it—

"Normally, yes, you should have been born with it. Granted," he shrugged "I suspect you've had it all along, but it was blocked from sight to protect you since you were in First Realm. Then when you walked through the portal, it awoke your magic and your soulmate mark."

"So if I go back to First Realm right now, everyone will see this?"

"Um, no. It's different there. In First Realm, instead of seeing this image the soulmate marks show us our first words to each other." A wide grin spread across his face and his eyes sparkled. "The words on my arm read *Mistakes were made.*"

I gasped. "That *is* the first thing I said to you, right before I kissed you."

He chuckled. "And next time you're in First Realm and look down at your arm you'll see my first words to you – which I believe were *what the bloody hell.*"

If I had been standing, I would've fallen down. "You knew this whole time."

"For years I've been going to First Realm with the Dukes, and we always wonder what *mistakes were made* would mean in the proper context, from the right girl. And now here you are."

My eyes widened. This was a lot to take in. "So you're saying that I have been destined for you since the day I was born? Because you're my soulmate?"

"Yes. And I for you." Stellan suddenly gripped my hand in his and met my eyes. "I would have looked for you if I had known, but my family thought you were dead and therefore, so did I. When I was a kid, they'd scoured all the realm to find her, to find you, then insisted she must have died."

I narrowed my eyes at him. "Why didn't you tell me the truth?"

"I wanted to, I did. That's why I followed you to the shelter. Remember when we officially met in the library?" He waited until I nodded then continued. "My plan was to tell you until Melanie and the Dukes pointed out that soulmates aren't a real thing in First Realm. They thought it would have scared you and I realized I agreed."

"Scared me? To have a soulmate?" *How could THAT scare me?*

He shrugged. "You've gotten used to our realm now, to magic. But at first, you were freaked out. I didn't want you to think you had no free will. I didn't want you to think I expected anything from you without your permission...I just...I wanted you to meet me without knowing that I was already yours. I wanted you to like me on your own."

My heart soared with so much happiness it almost hurt. This boy went to great lengths to protect me in every single possible way. I shook my head, not sure how to form words after that.

"Please don't be upset with Melanie. She lied because she had to...she had to keep you safe and it is against the rules for me as a prince to marry anyone who isn't a Royal or courtier. My parents, and entire family, would object."

I sucked in a breath. I wanted this down to my bones. But did he? "Do *you* object?"

His eyes softened and a light smile played on his lips. He brought my hand to his mouth and kissed the back of it, then ran his cheek against my fingers. "No. Not to you. Not ever."

It explained so much, and why I always felt like I wanted him and that I could trust him. Before I knew what I was doing I wrapped my hand around the back of his neck and pulled him down to me. Our lips crashed together and Stellan spread out in the bed next to me. Yes, I only had a blanket covering my chest, and I didn't care. He was mine and I was his. Everything about us was right. This wasn't some fling. This was more. It was a deep connection that destiny set for us. Two people from different realms meant to be together. I opened my mouth and let my tongue twine with his. I pressed my body up against him and the muscles in his body shot tight. I wanted him, more than anything I needed him.

I'd saved his life and he'd healed me. We'd found each other through space, time and different worlds. If this wasn't right, I didn't know what was. Gone was the stinging pain, in its place was the deep burning I felt for him. He ran his hands over my lower back and pressed his body to mine. He was flush up against me with only a blanket between us. Heat rushed and bloomed in my lower stomach and I wanted more of him. When his fingers pressed into my side, I winced ever so slightly and hissed in a breath. I was healed but it was tender to the touch.

Stellan pulled back from me and looked down. His lips were swollen and damp from our kiss. "Are you all right?"

"Yes." I leaned into him for more.

He leaned back. "We should – you need to heal."

"No." I pulled his lips back down to mine and my toes curled just as his minty flavor assailed me. I wanted to drop the blanket to bare my body to him and let him take it however he wanted.

The door flew open and slammed against the wall and then I heard Melanie grumble, "No. Ew. Gross. Can we not do that in a shared room? My *eyes.*"

Stellan cursed and scrambled to his feet. His loose, flowy black shirt was unbuttoned almost all the way down. He wiped his mouth with the back of his hand. "Melanie…"

"Just gross." Melanie scowled and shook her head. "Please, just not in our bedroom?"

Stellan cleared his throat and shuffled from one foot to the other. "Yes. I apologize."

A light knock came from the door and Melanie turned toward the opening. Stellan turned to face me and smiled. "Later."

Was it a threat or a promise? He moved around the room and stepped in front of the door. "Who is it?"

"Maren." The reply came from behind Melanie.

Stellan stepped aside and gestured for them both to come in. Maren strolled into my room wearing fighting gear. A streak of dirt ran across her tan cheek and her hair was a tangled mess around her face. A deep scratch ran just above her eyebrow. She walked toward me holding a tray with a steaming bowl, a glass of water, and some utensils.

"I saw Ellie was gravely injured. I brought some healing soup to ease her." Maren's voice was deep and raspy, yet her words were kind. I felt guilty for wanting her to leave. Stellan motioned for her to come further into the room.

She hesitated just inside the door, glancing from me to Stellan and back again. "I didn't mean to interrupt."

"You're not." I lied. What was I going to do? Call her out on it. *Yes, Maren and Melanie, you're a pantie saver, a pleasure popper, a freaking beaver dam, a box jock.* I laid back on the bed and sighed. "Thank you."

Stellan straightened his clothing and smoothed his hair back. "If you'll just excuse me."

I sighed. *And there goes my thirst quencher.*

TWENTY-SEVEN

ELLIE

I CURLED on my side and gazed out the window, watching as the moon rose high into the air. A group of crows gathered, sleeping just outside my window. Somehow, I found their presence comforting. My thoughts lingered on Stellan, the fact that he was my soulmate, the battles I'd seen in just days, and the reason for them all...*me*.

At first, I was thrilled to learn of our connection, but the longer I laid here the longer I latched on to one resounding thought. My presence here was endangering him. Ladarious wouldn't have attacked him that first night had my magic not been visible. Nor would he have attacked the Royal Guard if I hadn't been there. If that hit I took for Stellan had actually touched him, he wouldn't have survived it. I'd been gravely injured and that was after the shot had lost some of its power from hitting a boulder.

Not to mention the constant danger Melanie and the Rebellion were in just from me merely being here. I kicked my legs over the side of the bed and rose to my feet. In the few days that I'd been here I'd grown attached to these people. Especially to Stellan. Our soul-deep connection hammered at me to keep him safe the only way I knew how. I crossed to the wardrobe across from the bed and pulled out one of the dresses Melanie and I had got on Megelle Lane. I quickly laced up the undergarments and pulled a dark gray dress over my head. The sleeves billowed around my arms and cinched in at my elbows. The skirt fell down over my legs and brushed just at the top of my shoes. Lastly, I grabbed a dark plum cloak that would blend in with the night.

The rest I would leave to the shelter. It was time to leave this place, to keep them all safe. Stellan, Melanie, and the people living at the shelter. As quietly as I could manage, I opened my bedroom door. The latch didn't creek as it clicked open and the door swung aside. The shelter was still this time of night. The occupants upstairs all slept soundlessly. Down the hall, some of the boards creaked under my feet. I kept on moving. There was movement and voices in the dining room. I slowed my pace and peeked into the room.

My heart hammered in my chest as I spotted Melanie sitting with her back to the door, other women sitting in a half moon circle next to her. They spoke in urgent, hushed tones that I couldn't make out. Had I been staying, my curiosity would've gotten the better of me and I would've stopped to listen. But I wasn't staying, I was leaving, going home to protect them all. In my realm there was no danger from Ladarious, and if I was lucky, Stellan would come to see me there. Lots of people did long distance.

Long distance like New York and Florida, not different worlds.

I wanted to cry at the thought of not being with him. But the thought of losing him was far worse than not having him. I pulled my cloak in around myself and darted to the door by the entrance. Thankfully the door didn't make a sound as I snuck out. My pulse raced in my veins and my stomach twisted the farther I walked away from the shelter. Gravel crunched under my feet and the cool night air seeped into my body through the cloak. Or was that the chill at the thought of leaving Stellan behind? Thankfully the moon was bright enough to light the way back to the portal.

"Going somewhere?" His deep, smooth voice ran over my skin and halted me in my tracks.

I curled my hand into a fist at my side to help strengthen my resolve against him. But when I turned, I felt a piece of my heart break at the sight of him. He stood a few feet behind me, dressed in the same all black outfit he'd been wearing, but his hair was more disheveled than I'd ever seen. Every single part of me wanted to run to him, to feel his arms around me, yet I somehow remained in place. His green eyes glowed in the light of the moon and I felt every bit the prey to his predator. Except there was a brokenness in his gaze that turned my heart cold.

I didn't wait for him to speak. I knew his words would hurt. "I'm leaving. It's not safe for any of you if I stay here."

"You can't leave." The muscle in his jaw ticked.

"Stellan, *I have to.*" I took a step toward him then hesitated. I lowered my voice. "I can't let anything happen to you."

"*But it already is happening to me,*" he said in a rush, his cheeks flushing even in the dark.

I shook my head as tears stung my eyes. "If I go home, you'll be safer."

"No, I won't." He took a hesitant step toward me. "Things are happening here, Ellie. Things my people need and only you can do."

I scoffed but it came out like a strangled cry. "You're just as powerful as I am. If not more so. They don't need me. They need you...alive. And as long as I'm here and Ladarious is after me, you're all in danger."

"That's not true—"

"Yes, it —

"*Eloise, you're the Stone Keeper and I believe you're here to save us all.*"

I threw my hands up. "I don't even know what that means."

"I know that. *I know.* And I'm sorry that I haven't explained it to you. I...I didn't have all the information, I still don't." He closed the distance between us. "But it's time that you know. Please, just give me a chance to explain."

I put my hands on my hips and pursed my lips. "I'm listening."

"Not here." He grabbed my hand and wrapped his fingers with mine.

Stellan tugged me back toward the house. I had to quicken my pace just to keep up with him. We flew through the door and it smacked into the wall. He wasn't even trying to be quiet. He hastened me down the hall then led me through the door to the library. He pushed me in front of him and stood blocking the doorway.

"What are you doing?" I demanded.

He held one finger up, signaling me to hold on, then he extended his other hand out. Tendrils of his silver magic wound around his fingers and the sound of something crashing through the house toward us echoed down the hall with a very distinct string of curses.

A moment later Melanie sailed through the door. Literally flying with her feet up off the ground. She landed on her feet and shoved her hair out of her face. Her cheeks were pink with annoyance. She narrowed her eyes at Stellan. *Did you just do that?"*

He shrugged. "Desperate times, desperate measures. I can move stuff."

"I do not constitute as *stuff.*" When she turned to me her eyes roamed over my traveling outfit. "What's going on?"

"She was trying to leave." Stellan pointed an accusing finger at me.

Melanie's eyes shot wide. "What, why?"

"It's time to tell her." Stellan pulled an old leather-bound book from behind his back and let it drop to the table in front of him. "Melanie, soundproof, if you will."

Melanie pulled her wand from a hidden pocket in her dress and pointed it toward the wall. Little puffs of light flowed from it and smacked into bookshelves. They shimmered over the ceiling, floor, and all four walls. When every inch of the room was covered, her magic faded.

"There. Done."

"No one can hear what I'm about to tell you. It would send the realm into chaos." Stellan met my eyes. "Do you understand?"

"Not in the slightest." I shook my head. "But I will keep whatever you're about to say to myself."

Melanie leaned over the table and ran her fingers along the leather journal.

Stellan motioned to the journal. "This is George Wentworth's journal. He was my great grandfather's brother. My family thought him dead, but I think his disappearance had so much more behind it."

"Is this why you were attacking the castle?" I ran my hand over the soft worn journal.

He nodded up at me. "Exactly and look at this."

When he flipped the cover open, my eyes roamed over the cream color parchment and the scrolling lettering. Stellan cleared his throat and read the first sentence, "*Our realm is dying. Today the water ran brown and the Flora has begun to wither and die at the outskirts of our world. We have errored, and the world suffers.*"

Chills ran down my spine, and not from the weather. His words were dire and showed a deep sadness and regret. "I don't understand how this has anything to do with me."

Stellan held the book out to me. "It's all here in the book. It explains everything."

Melanie's eyes narrowed. "Everything?"

Stellan sighed and ran a hand through his hair. "Well, okay, not *everything*. But enough to make her see what's really going on."

I took the book and thumbed through the pages. "Let me take a look."

"Look at the last page." Stellan pointed to the back of the journal, knowing the pages like he'd poured over them for hours.

I flipped to the back of the book. I licked my lips and began to read, "*Today I learned the truth of our fate. Our realm will die without our Stone. My brother will not divulge this information, as I am only learning through my own sneakiness in overhearing his private discussions with his wife. The Stones will return to us through the birth of a child, marked at the instant life begins. They will carry the Stone within their eyes.*"

Stellan stepped in closer to me and ran the back of his finger down my temple. "Violet eyes like our realm."

My breath hitched. Was the journal really referring to me? I continued reading, "*Only this person will be able to retrieve our Stone and save our realm. This person is the Stone Keeper. It is unsure what their magical abilities will be or what they can do, but they will have our violet magic.*"

"Magic like yours, Eloise." Melanie stepped in closer. "Do you see?"

How could this be? How could I be the one they were waiting for. I let my eyes fall back to finish the page. "*This*

Stone Keeper must seek the Angel for guidance. Today I return to our bastard realm to try and correct our mistakes. I will seek the Creation Stone and return it to First Realm as that is the first step in saving us. The Angel has locked the realm down, no one in and no one out. However, my brother insists he can get me through. And I must try, for I am the one who brought this to life. I leave this journal here in case I do not return. If you find this...find the Stone Keeper. They are our only hope."

I shook my head. "I don't understand, how is this realm locked down if we all got through?"

"He wasn't talking about this one, he was talking about another realm...one he only refers to as *bastard realm*. I don't know what that means exactly but he does give instructions in here on how to travel to and around this bastard realm." Stellan turned to Melanie. "Does any of this make sense to you?"

Melanie sighed. "That realm isn't our concern at the moment. We need to save ours first. And to do that we need to talk to the Angel."

I let out a sigh but it sounded more like the scream of a dying animal. They both watched me with wide eyes. "So you're saying I'm this Stone Keeper. That my purple eyes and purple magic are the indicators. Okay, okay, okay. Cool, cool, cool, cool, cool."

"Ellie—"

"Oh my God, I don't know what scares me more...that I'm this Stone Keeper or that I actually believe it." I ran my hands through my long, wild hair. Part of me wanted to fight this, to insist they were wrong and they had the wrong girl. But even I couldn't deny the evidence. "You're sure about this?"

"This is why Ladarious wants you so badly," Stellan said softly. "This is why we've tried to keep you hidden."

"Ellie, only a Royal can use the portal to and from First Realm." Melanie leaned forward to catch my eyes. "You walked through by yourself without even knowing it. That alone is proof that you are the Stone Keeper."

Stellan eyed her. "But you've been —"

"We've already discussed that." Melanie shuddered. "Baron Reginald had his…tastes. This isn't about me."

Stellan sighed and turned back to me. He reached out and put his hands on top of mine. "We are ninety-nine percent sure we're right…but there's only one way to find out. We have to talk to the Angel. Let's go talk to him, or her, and find out."

"And if I'm not this Stone Keeper?"

Stellan's face fell. "Then he'll tell us who you *are* and you can decide to go home if you'd like."

My stomach turned. My heart hurt watching him. "A-and if I *am* this Stone Keeper?"

He gave me a small smile. "Then together we save Second Realm."

"We'll help you, Ellie. We won't leave you alone in this."

I set the book back down on the table and rubbed my temples. "Do you guys know an Angel? Because I sure as shit don't."

They shared a look, then Stellan gave me a half smirk.

"Looks like your wish is about to come true. The only Angel I know is in First Realm."

My heart raced. "Then that's where we need to go."

"Yeah, but how?" Melanie grimaced. "We need a plan."

"The glass room, right? The one I came out of?"

Melanie nodded. "Yes, the glass room...*in the palace.*"

Stellan turned away from me and paced the length of the room. "There's a small window of time to get to the portal unnoticed when no one is paying attention. It is a very narrow amount of time. We won't have any room for error. But it should be enough to get us through without the Royal Guard or Ladarious noticing."

"Okay, when is it? What do we do?"

"Just before dawn. Once the sun is fully risen our window will be gone, but if we can get there it should work." He stopped and put his hands on his hips. "I can get us there. I know the exact paths to take. The Dukes and I usually go through at this time."

Excitement ran through my body. I was going to get to go home. "Okay, where do I meet you? Or are you going to pick me up here?"

Melanie chuckled. "I think Stellan needs to stay here."

TWENTY-EIGHT

ELLIE

LYING in my bed and listening to Stellan's sighs was torture. Melanie's breaths were deep and even. A pile of fuzzy black cats laid at the foot of her bed. I couldn't even tell how many there were. They didn't seem to bother her because the second her head hit the pillow she was out cold. Yet there I was wide awake. I was going home in the morning. *My* home. First Realm. New York. And I was excited, I really was...but all I could think about was Stellan and how he was only a few feet away.

He'd caught me leaving him here and I still didn't know how he felt about it. The wooden floor groaned as he flipped over. I was all too aware of him. His every move, every sigh, his heady autumn scent. I licked my lips, wanting a taste of his minty flavor.

I leaned up on my elbow and looked over the side of my bed to the floor. A prince sleeping on a hardwood floor, yet he hadn't complained or objected for a single second. One day, he would make an amazing king. He laid there shirt-less, with one hand behind his head. The moonlight streamed in from the window and seemed to kiss every bit of his skin the way I wanted to. His sandy hair fell back from the chiseled edges of his face. His eyes seemed to glow in the moonlight, and I wanted to reach out and run my fingers over the hard ridges of his stomach.

I glanced at my small bed, then to him and how big he was. "You should come up here and join me."

Silence.

"Stellan?"

He sighed. "I heard you."

"Then come up here?"

"I'm thinking."

I rolled my eyes. "What is there to think about?"

He sat up and arched one eyebrow at me. "Really?"

My cheeks warmed but I shook them off. "Still better than that floor. C'mon, I can't let my soulmate sleep on the floor when I have a perfectly good bed here."

He rested his arms across his knees and watched me. "You sure you want me to?"

I slid back against the wall and raised my blanket in invitation. "Yes, absolutely."

He popped to his feet and grabbed the single pillow Melanie had given him. The muscles of his stomach flexed with each move he made. By day he was proper prince, by night he looked like a bad ass Adonis with his low hanging pants that revealed his perfectly cut V shaped muscles that pointed in such a tempting direction. He shoved his hair out of his face and then spread himself out in the bed next to me. It dipped under his weight and I found my entire body pressed up against his.

I rested my hand on his stomach.

He placed warm fingers over mine. "You were leaving."

"I know."

He squinted his eyes and a flash of hurt crossed his face. His voice was barely a whisper, "After everything I told you. You made it look so easy just to go."

I shook my head. "It was the hardest thing I'd ever decided to do. But I had to."

"Ellie, the only way to keep each other safe is to stay together. Do you see that now?" He tilted his head to face me fully. The pillow curved under his cheek as he gazed at me.

"I do now." I pressed my fingers to his stomach. "I didn't mean to hurt you. Protecting you was one of my main reasons for going."

"Things like this can't be fought. We are destined to be together." He said so simply. Like our marks just decided we should be together without so much as a conversation about it.

He may have grown up thinking this was how it was, but I needed more than a tattoo on my arm.

"Are we together?"

Great, Ellie, have the determine the relationship conversation now. I wanted to smack myself in the forehead. In my experience the quickest way to make a guy run was to ask him to determine the relationship.

"Depends."

"On?" I held my breath waiting for his answer.

"On whether or not you're going to try and leave me again." His fingers pressed into mine, holding them there.

I shook my head. "It was impulsive. And I could only leave to keep you safe. I won't do it again."

"Then, Miss Eloise Sutton." He said my name so formally. "Will you be mine?"

My heart did a little flip flop in my chest and I couldn't stop from smiling. "I will."

He gave me that breathtaking smile. "This pleases me."

He turned to face me, and I slid my leg up over his hip, pulling him closer. He cupped the back of my neck and pulled me to him for a fierce kiss. This wasn't the gentle kiss that he'd given me before. No, this was powerful. His lips parted and he dipped his tongue into my mouth. I wound my arm around his back, digging my nails into his skin as I pulled him in for more. Suddenly, my cotton night gown felt like too much between us.

Melanie stirred in her sleep and we broke apart. I threw my arm out and let my magic go. I'd seen Melanie do this in the library. A soundless wall flew from my fingertips between my bed and Melanie's.

Stellan's eyes widened. "How'd you learn how to do that?"

"I watched Mel do it." Then I let more of my power go and soft purple clouds surrounded us, giving us the privacy we needed.

"Sound and sight proof. Very nice." He pressed his forehead to mine and his fingers slid up and over my leg. He grabbed my backside and pulled me against him.

His hips ground into mine and I sighed at the feel of him. His fingers slid higher over my stomach and I arched into his touch. Stellan pressed his mouth to side of my neck and I threw my head back, giving him the room to lick, nip, and kiss his way from my jaw down to my shoulder.

He groaned and pulled back to look down at me. "We can't. Not here, not like this. I can't."

"We're doing something very dangerous in the morning." I threaded my fingers through his hair. "I just want to be with you tonight like this."

He sighed and pressed his forehead to mine. "But nothing more than this."

"Nothing more." I pulled his mouth toward mine. "Now focus, give me your tongue back."

TWENTY-NINE

ELLIE

THE SMELL of early morning dew seeped down into the tunnel from the earth outside. Fog clung to the bottom where we walked, swirling around our feet as we moved. A small flame hovered in the air ahead of us. Stellan clutched my hand tight in his. We didn't speak a word. The two of us were about to try and sneak into a part of the palace that was forbidden for anyone to enter. This was different than all the times Stellan snuck in with the Dukes. It was hard to believe only yesterday I laid injured in this same tunnel. So much had changed since then.

Stellan stopped just at the end of the tunnel. "You stick to me like glue."

I nodded up at him. "Okay."

He dragged me to him and pressed his lips to mine while cupping the back of my neck. It was a quick, punishing kiss that branded me as his, the same as he'd done the night before. He pulled back and gave me a single nod then pressed his hand to the entrance to the tunnel. It slid to the side and rays of the rising sun peeked down through the trees. I didn't know why the land around the castle still lived while the rest of the realm was dying. After reading the journal, I could see the evidence in what was happening. The unusual heat, the dying vegetation, and even the dark brown river. It all pointed in that direction. But now we would save it, Stellan and I. *And Melanie.*

We moved through the forest around the outskirts of the castle. Leaves crunched under our feet but not loud enough to draw attention. Through the dense shrubs I could see the dark, looming exterior of the castle. It stood stark against the rising sun and blue skies. When I'd first gotten here it seemed so far away from where I hid in that cemetery from Ladarious. Now the distance didn't feel as immense. Especially as we made our way around the small cemetery.

Stellan pointed to a wing of the castle that jutted out from the main part of the castle. I recognized the glass wall instantly. That was where I'd come out of. The roof sloped on both sides and little spikes rose up from the apex of it.

He lowered his voice. "That's where we need to be. There are two entrances to the portal room, one from inside the castle. There's always a guard there. The other is at the end of the wing, through those glass doors. That's the one we're going for."

"Will it be guarded?" I was nervous, I'd never broken into a palace before.

"It might very well be. But we've got do this."

Stellan stopped behind a huge flowery tree and glanced out over the property. The entire wing seemed to be made of glass on both sides. Even from here I could see there wasn't a single piece of furniture inside either. There were stairs inside, that much I remembered. Stellan ducked down and waved me forward, signaling for me to move closer with him. We crouched in behind some bushes and he pointed toward the roof where two guards were perched.

"If we keep to the gardens, they won't see us. Especially behind the hedge over there."

He pointed toward a wall of very tall thick bushes that rose up from the ground like great big green boxes. Then he turned his attention to two more guards patrolling the garden. "They aren't usually there this early in the morning, but I suspect the little skirmish last night put my parents on edge."

"What do you want to do with them?"

He shrugged. "Either knock them out or contain them."

"Got it."

Stellan stepped out from the brush and sprinted across the way. He pressed himself up against the hedge wall. I held my breath waiting for someone to notice him. But all was silent and still. He waved for me to follow. I stepped out and pumped my arms, running to get to him. When I reached the hedge I nearly slammed into his body. His arms wrapped around me and he pulled me to his side. He pressed his finger over his lips, pointing toward the castle.

Behind the hedge I heard something rustle, then a

sharp, overly proper voice broke the morning stillness. "You there. Come."

Stellan splayed his hand over my stomach and pressed me back. He mouthed the name. "*Wilbur.*"

"Sir," The guard answered. I heard their footsteps from just on the other side of the hedge.

"Have you seen any Rebellion members since last night?" Wilbur snapped.

"No, sir." The guard answered.

Wilbur lowered his voice. "If you do, it is your job to do what must be done. The world is better off without trash like that here. Do we understand each other?"

Stellan's hand curled into a fist as the guard answered. "Yes, sir."

"No survivors," Wilbur barked, then their footsteps moved away from each other.

Stellan quaked beside me, his cheeks flushed with anger. He took a step in the opposite direction of the castle and I pressed my hand to his chest. I wanted him to throttle Wilbur as much as the next person, but we had a mission and now wasn't the time. His nostrils flared but he shook himself and turned for the castle. I followed close behind him, trying not to make a sound as my heart thundered in my chest and my lungs burned for breath.

Just then the other guard turned the corner. His eyes widened and he pointed his wand right at Stellan. My magic flared and I forced it into the ground. Jagged rocks shot from the dirt, one knocked the wand away and the others all rose up around his legs, holding him in place like cement pillars. He opened his mouth to scream and Stellan was there.

He shoved his hand over the man's mouth and whispered, "Sleep."

His body slumped forward but was still held up by my rocks.

"How'd you do that?"

"Shylock tried to teach me. It's the only thing I picked up from him." He grabbed my hand. "Now we run for it."

I fell into step with him as we wound our way through the garden. We turned around fountains and hopped over bushes. Rose thorns grabbed my clothing and pulled at me. We still didn't stop. I could see the glass walls. The sun glinted off of it. We were only a few feet away. The air in my lungs burned and I prayed no alarms would go off. Stellan hurried to the glass doors and pushed them open. He stepped to the side waiting for me. I vaulted through the doorway then slid to a stop.

How did I not realize right away? I'd come out of this room a mere three days ago. I'd come up and not really thought anything of the fact that this room with glass walls and white marble floors was empty of all furniture...or the fact that it looked absolutely nothing like the Upper West Side.

Stellan yanked the glass door closed behind us, slowing it down at the last second so it wouldn't slam. It closed with a faint click. I couldn't believe I thought I was still in New York when I was here. Stellan took my hand and led me down a flight of stairs made of that gray stone, a detail I somehow missed when I came through. Adrenaline rushed through my veins as we hurried down the steps and into a dark, dimly lit hallway.

Memories of that night flashed in my mind. I remembered thinking a light bulb had gone out, when really the low lighting was from the candle flames in the lamps. I shook my head. *Oh, Ellie. Where was your head that night? So unlike you.*

"All right. We did it. We're here."

I turned to follow his gaze and frowned. We'd stopped in front of a mirror.

Stellan glanced over our shoulders. "We're alone. There's no one behind us. If we move quickly, we just might make it through the portal and back into First Realm."

I nodded. My heart pounded like thunder in my veins, drowning out any other sounds. "Okay, where's the portal? How much farther?'

He gave me that cocky sideways grin that I loved and hated and pointed in front of us. "This is it."

"*What?*" I hissed. "This? It looks like a mirror…?"

The mirror was intricate and gorgeous, standing at least eight feet tall. The thick edges shimmered a glossy gold with a dark, antiqued border.

"That's kind of the point, love," he whispered and gave me a wink.

I looked back to the mirror and my pulse quickened. Adrenaline rushed through my body. I had no reason not to trust Stellan. He'd proved his loyalty enough times. And he was my soulmate. Hurting me would hurt him. There was no one in this entire multi-realm world I could trust as much as *him.*

But it was hard to believe *this* was a portal to another realm.

"Love?"

"It looks like the *Mirror of Erised* from Harry Potter," I heard myself whisper.

"It's not that far off, now is it?" His soft chuckle calmed my racing nerves a tad. He reached down and took my hand in his, then brought my fingers up to his lips. "Let's step through together."

My heart fluttered as electricity shot up my arm. I reached up and took his hand so that his was cradled between both of mine. My fingers trembled with nervousness and excitement, though he didn't seem to notice or mind. I nodded. "Together."

His smile widened and I felt my lips curve up to match his. *Together.* Despite everything, all the chaos, danger, and confusion, finding him was like finding a four-leaf clover in a concrete jungle. Never would I have ever imagined that finding my actual soulmate would be more amazing than finding out I was a mage, but as I stared up into his eyes, I knew he was the only thing that actually mattered.

I pushed up on my tip toes just as his lips crashed down onto mine.

For a moment, we were lost to each other.

But he pulled away far, far too soon. I groaned and leaned into him.

"Perhaps let's get through the portal first?"

I cursed and shook myself. "Right. Yup. Totally. How do we do it?"

He lifted his left hand, the one I wasn't gripping with both of mine, and pressed it flat to the mirror. The gold family sigil ring on his middle finger glistened under the candlelight beside the mirror. The gold band was thick and had symbols etched into the sides. The top had a massive amethyst with so many facets the color sparkled vibrantly. A gold *W* sat on top of the stone.

W for Wentworth. A ring for kings...one day he'll be king.

One day he'll be king...of Second Realm.

And I live in First Realm.

A horrible, sickening feeling came over me. Somehow I hadn't stopped to think about it until just this moment. Perhaps it was leaving this realm that made it dawn on me. *How is this going to work? How are we going to be together?* Stellan was going to be king of Second Realm soon, potentially very soon if the Rebellion had anything to say about that. *What does that mean for us?*

Before I could even think of voicing this new but very real concern, bright white light flashed from inside the mirror. Stellan squeezed my hand and stepped forward *into* the light. I practically leapt forward so that we walked through the portal together. A wall of ice-cold air washed over me like I'd stepped outside into a blizzard.

The light vanished as my foot hit the ground in front of me.

I blinked and looked around and frowned. We stood in

the middle of a bank of mirrored elevators — I gasped. "I remember this...I was here."

"Yes, you were," Stellan said with a chuckle as I slipped away from him. "How did you find your way here, anyways? I've been dying to know."

I spun in a slow circle, shaking my head. I couldn't believe it. "My friends were heading into Central Park, but I had to pee, so I ran inside here to find a bathroom. The line was like a mile long upstairs. I went down a level and found the bathroom there. Then got a little lost on my way back up...and wound up here—"

Here. HERE. We just came through the portal. I'm in New York.

I'M IN NEW YORK.

I'M HOME.

I gasped, hiked up my skirt, and sprinted down the hall. Stellan shouted behind me, but I was lost to the moment. I flew around the corner to my right, retracing my steps the night my life went to hell. My pulse thundered in my ears as I climbed the stairs up to the main level then ran by the bathroom that was now empty. There wasn't a single person in the hallway besides us, which was good because by the time I reached the lobby of the Emerald my cheeks were burning from the grin plastered on my face.

But I saw it. New York. I felt its energy radiating through the glass front doors. I was almost there. Part of me hadn't thought this moment would ever happen, that I'd ever make it back home. As I pushed through the doors and sped out onto the sidewalk, a little squeal slipped up my throat.

The sun was only *just* rising, the sky still clinging to the rosy hues of dawn, but New York City was already bustling with life. Men and women in business suits hurried up and down the sidewalk around me, carrying briefcases and screaming into cellphones in their ears. People in exercise clothes jogged around them. Bicycles flew by, dancing along the curb. Yellow cabs raced down Central Park West, heading towards Time Square like their lives depended on it. Horns and police sirens wailed from every direction.

The ground rumbled under my feet a split second before hot air shot up through the metal grates in the cement as the subway passed beneath us. I giggled and moved to the edge of the sidewalk. The heavy flow of cars was the only thing stopping me from sprinting right into Central Park. I stopped and took a deep breath. The smell of car mufflers, garbage, and the hot dog stand across the street mixed together in an aroma that could only be described as *New York City.*

I'm home.

I'm HOME.

I threw my arms out to the side and spun in a circle, squealing like a little girl at a Taylor Swift concert. *I'm home. I'm home. I'm home!*

"Ellie?"

At the sound of Stellan's voice, I turned and found him watching me with wide eyes that sparkled with amusement. I grinned and tackled him, throwing my arms around his neck. He stumbled back a few steps, but his arms wrapped tightly around my waist. I felt each of his fingertips press into my hips. I pulled my head back then pressed my lips to his.

He sighed against my mouth and his breath mixed with mine. Our lips crashed together and heat bloomed all over my body. At that exact second my heart might've exploded. I was home and in his arms. The world melted away until it was just the two of us. There was only him, the way he held me, and his flavor on my lips. My fingers pressed into his shoulders, urging him on for more. He chuckled against my lips.

My feet hit the ground and then he pulled back. "Well…" he shook his head and chuckled, his cheeks flushed a deep pink.

I giggled and bit my bottom lip. My face was on fire but my heart was soaring. I felt giddy, like a kid on Christmas morning. For some ungodly reason, I reached up and ruffled his hair then jumped back and threw my arms out to my sides. I sighed and smiled. *"I'm home."*

His expression darkened for a second, but it was gone before I could inspect it. A wide smile took its place. "Remind me to bring you home more often then."

"*God,* I love New York. Don't you? This place is just so…so…" I shook my head and gestured around us. "So…*perfect.*"

"You're not wrong about that," he said with a smile. But then he took my hands in his and his expression grew serious. "We need to get to Araqiel."

"Right. Yes. Game face is on. Ready to do this shit. 'Cause I've got questions. Wait, Araqiel? Is that the Angel's name?"

"That's his name."

"Oh, cool name." I let him take me by the hand and lead me back toward the Emerald when a gust of cool wind rushed by me carrying the most heavenly sent ever. *Coffee.* I pulled him to a stop. "Wait. Wait, wait. I need coffee."

He frowned. "What?"

"Coffee." I pointed to my left, to a local-owned coffee shop. "Coffee. I need it. Now. I'm going through withdrawals. I have to have it."

"Okay, we'll get you a cup after—"

"No, *now.*" I dragged him toward the corner, my gaze locked on the prize. "If you want my brain to function for this conversation, then you need to get me coffee first."

Stellan laughed behind me. "Such a New Yorker." But he'd stopped trying to resist.

I was so pumped for coffee, real New York coffee, and *not* tea, that I raced right across the street like I was playing frogger. Stellan cursed and threw his hand out. Cars slammed on their brakes. I shook my head. *Such a tourist. We had plenty of time.* But apparently only New Yorkers were game with jaywalking.

By the time we got to the glass door of the coffee shop, I was bouncing on my feet. I yanked that door open so fast and just inhaled the heavy scent inside. It was super early, right at sunrise, so the shop wasn't quite packed yet. It would be any minute, but for now there was only about a dozen or so people inside – which for New York was nothing.

I dropped Stellan's hand and pushed my way to the front.

The barista girl looked to be about my age. She looked down at my dress and arched one eyebrow, but that was the biggest reaction a New Yorker would really give to someone dressed weird. She turned to me. "What can I get you?"

"Give me a venti caramel macchiato with six shots of espresso." I tugged on Stellan's sleeve. "You want anything?"

"No, th—" He gasped and pointed toward the street. "Araqiel! He just left the Emerald. I need to catch him."

"Oh, shit—"

"Don't move." He gripped my shoulders and met my eyes. "Don't move."

Before I could respond, he turned and sprinted out the door and onto Central Park West. My pulse quickened as he disappeared into the crowded sidewalk. Which was ridiculous. This was New York. My home. My apartment was only twenty blocks from here. Yet I still had a mini panic attack as he walked away from me.

I took a step forward to bail on my order and follow him when he emerged from the crowd. Relief washed through me and I sighed. He stood across the street, on the corner next to the hot dog stand, looking every bit the Disney prince in his Victorian style clothing. He was standing there talking to an insanely tall guy with gorgeous black skin and a bald head. He wore all white — *wait. No.*

Those are WINGS. The guy had huge white wings that glistened like freshly fallen snow in the rising sunlight. And then it hit me. I'd seen this guy before. Saturday night, right before I ran inside the Emerald to pee, I'd seen Stellan talking to a guy dressed as an angel...the angel had been double fisting two tacos in each hand. I remembered it vividly. The world spun around me.

Holy shit. The taco angel guy is Araqiel? He was right there that night and I missed him.

I blinked and shook my head. Life was so surreal lately.

"Miss?" The girl cleared her throat. "*Miss?*"

I jumped and spun back around. "Yes?"

She arched both eyebrows. "You didn't pay."

I cursed and rushed back to the counter. Luckily, I'd been prepared and shoved my debit card in my bra- *corset.* I wiped it on my dress then held it out to the girl. "Here, sorry. Name's Ellie."

"Thanks." She handed my card back. "Just a minute."

I nodded then turned back to watch Stellan and Araqiel, only for my gaze to land on a second angel. This one looked younger, though that was probably just from a distance since he was an angel and probably ancient. But he looked no older than twenty-five, at most. *HE is an angel?* If he didn't have white wings hanging off his back, I never would have believed it. With his midnight black hair and pretty porcelain skin, he looked like sin incarnate.

More specifically *lust.* If I looked up *brooding* in the dictionary, this guy's picture would be next to it.

"Eloise," a woman shouted from behind me.

I started to turn, but I'd told them Ellie. And I wanted to keep my eyes on Stellan, even though this was First Realm. He wasn't in danger here. There wasn't a single human being here that could hurt him, he'd just use his magic. But apparently my stupid heart couldn't accept that.

"Eloise?" the woman shouted again, this time a bit softer and closer. "Eloise Sutton?"

A cold chill ran down my spine. I stood straight and slowly turned to face a woman my mom's age wearing a coffee stained apron. The girl who'd taken my order stood right beside her, looking anxious as hell. They both were staring right at me. Still, I had to be sure, so I pointed to my chest and arched my eyebrow. They nodded and waved me over.

What the hell? I frowned and walked over. "How do you know my name?"

The green-eyed woman, whose name tag said Jocelyn, threw her red hair over her shoulder then dug into her white apron. She pulled out a folded-up piece of paper and handed it to me with shaking fingers.

The girl, Clarissa, who was clearly this woman's daughter as they looked alike, smiled at me and nodded. "Go ahead. Look."

I stared at them for a long second, unsure what the hell this was about. But there was something in the eagerness in their eyes that made me need to look. I frowned and carefully unfolded the white piece of paper — I gasped.

My heart stopped. My body turned to ice.

My face was staring back up at me.

My face. Mine. The words *MISSING* were etched in bold black letters above my picture. My stomach tightened and turned. Bile rose in my throat. My name and a description of what I looked like was written under the picture. Along with the fact that I was last seen on this street corner Saturday night.

Shit, shit, shit. I felt my blood rush out of my face and the world spun. I was a missing person. I knew that, or I should have known that. Of course my friends and family would be terrified and looking for me.

"W-wh-what's t-t-today?" I heard myself stutter.

Clarissa leaned forward and whispered, "it's Tuesday morning, the twenty-ninth. You've been missing three days."

I sighed with relief and steadied myself against the counter. I knew it had only been three days in Second Realm, but it wasn't until that very moment that I wondered whether time worked the same way. The fact that it did made me feel infinitely better. Three days wasn't that long.

Jocelyn reached out and grabbed my hand. "We called the cops already. Just stay here and that guy can't hurt you anymore."

Wait, what?

A chill slithered down my spine. *That guy. Stellan. She*

means Stellan. They told the cops Stellan took me. I spun around then sprinted out the door, cursing under my breath. I had to get to him. We had to get out of here. Surely the angels could help us.

I just had to get to them first. The sidewalk was shoulder-to-shoulder full with people, everyone waiting for the crosswalk. I cursed and shoved my shoulders into people's sides, but there were too many of them. I wasn't making enough progress. We were all packed in like sardines. *C'mon, c'mon, c'mon. Move, move, move.* Police sirens wailed from nearby. I wasn't going to make it.

"MOVE," I screamed, and a burst of purple smoke exploded out of me.

Everyone within a few feet radius of me flew back a couple feet.

I cursed, but I couldn't change it now. Instead I raced to the edge of the sidewalk and looked up and shouted, *"Stellan!"*

His head snapped up and our eyes met.

Red and blue lights flashed in my face as two white sedans slammed on its brakes in front of me. Four doors flew open in the blink of an eye and uniformed officers raced toward me. I cursed and tried to back away but the crowd had re-formed behind me, blocking me in place.

"Eloise Sutton?" The closest cop said, with a hand on the gun strapped to his hip.

Shit, shit, shit, what do I do? I glanced over to Stellan and my heart sank. He was alone. The angels were gone. I cursed and tore my eyes off of him so the cops wouldn't see who I was looking at. The cops surrounded me. Their voices all blended together as they drilled me with questions. I wasn't in trouble, *I* was the missing person...but Jocelyn had reported Stellan. If they saw him, they would arrest him and I wasn't sure how I would get him out of that. The truth wasn't an option. No, I had to do something. I had to protect him. They couldn't arrest a person they couldn't find.

I saw Stellan in my peripheral vision as he started to cross the street. My heart skipped. My magic tingled in my fingers. I held my arms down by my sides and kept my gaze locked on the police officers fussing over me...then I subtly flicked my fingers and Stellan slid backwards across the sidewalk. He slammed into the short wall that ran alongside Central Park, then flipped *over* it.

"Eloise?" The older cop right in front of me said with a smile. He ducked his eyes to meet mine then gestured toward the open door of his squad car behind him. "I said we need you to come down to the station with us."

THIRTY

ELLIE

"Miss Sutton, you have to talk to us."

I looked up at the middle-aged detective with a thick mustache and a mustard-stained tie and frowned. "I…am?"

He sighed and sat down on the edge of his desk. We were in the middle of the precinct, with all of New York's craziness raging around us. The room wasn't big enough for the amount of activity. It was difficult to even tell who was a cop and who was a criminal.

Officer – actually, I had no idea what his name was – shook his head and shoved his hands in his pants pockets. "You may be talking to us but you're not talking to us. Do you understand?"

I did. "No."

"Can you tell me what happened?"

Yes. "No."

He narrowed his brown eyes at me, but they weren't unfriendly. "You don't know what happened?"

I did. "No."

He scowled and pulled a chair up, then sat down in front of me so we were face to face. "Are you okay? Are you having memory problems?"

I thought about lying and saying yes but it just sounded exhausting. "No."

"Are you sure?"

I arched one eyebrow at him. "Test me."

"What's your name?"

"Eloise Sutton."

"Age?"

"Seventeen."

"Address?"

"1412 West 82nd Street."

"Parents' names."

"Teddy and Penelope Sutton. They're painters."

"Best friend's name?"

"Nicole Walsh," I said with a smile. "But I call her Nickel."

He pursed his lips and grabbed a stack of papers off his desk. His dark eyes scanned them. "Your other friends?"

"Lao Liu, Sherman Colper, Hewie Wolitzer, Ravi Kapoor, Bernadita Martinez, and Andy Freeman." I wrung my hands together and glanced at the clock on the wall. It'd already been an hour. *Where are you, Stellan?* "Would you like to know their birthdays and zodiac signs?"

The detective chuckled and leaned forward to put his elbows on his knees. "Miss Sutton, you do know that you're not in trouble...right?"

I arched both of my eyebrows. "Then why am I here?"

"When a seventeen-year-old girl goes missing for three days, there are going to be questions…" he cracked his knuckles and nodded to someone off to my right. Then he turned his eyes back to me. "Tell me about the boy—"

"What boy?"

"The woman from the coffee shop who called us said you came in the shop with a guy." He held his hand out to his side and a uniformed officer handed him a coffee as he walked by. "She also said this guy ordered you not to move before he went outside…did he…take you Saturday night?"

You have no idea. My stomach tightened into knots. *Where are you, Stellan?*

"Eloise?"

I sighed and scrubbed my face with my hands. "Call me Ellie," I said before I could stop myself. Eloise just put me on edge.

The detective let out half a laugh then took a sip of his coffee. "Okay, Ellie. Tell me about him. If he hurt you or threatened you in any way—"

"No. God no." I leaned back in my metal seat. "He's my…he's my good friend. He didn't kidnap me. Nobody did."

"So…" he twirled his coffee cup around in front of him. "You ran off with him? Perhaps your parents don't approve?"

"No, *no.* My parents don't—," *wait, what if my parents don't approve of him?* I shook myself. "It's not like that. I

288

wasn't kidnapped. I didn't run away. It's all a misunderstanding."

"And this outfit…the woman claimed the guy with you was also dressed strangely."

I gave him a blank stare. "We were LARPing."

His eyebrows scrunched together and dropped low over his eyes. "Larping?"

"Live Action Role Playing. Google it. It's a real thing. It's like Dungeons and Dragons in real life." When he just continued to stare at me like I'd grown another eyeball, I rolled my eyes. "I'm a nerd, detective. Surely one of my nerdy friends pointed that out in your search for me."

"Okay, okay. So you were…*larping*. That's where you were?"

Metaphorically speaking, sure. I hadn't ever actually LARPed before. It was on my bucket list, but this detective sure as hell didn't know anything about it. "Yes. My *friend* needed a last-minute teammate so I went with him after a party Saturday night. I'd texted my parents before I left but I'm guessing that text never sent – of course if you'd let me call my parents, I could ask them."

This detective wasn't buying it, which I had to admit was kind of nice since I was lying my ass off. If I *had* been in trouble, it would've been nice to know someone was seeing through my lies. But right now, I needed him to let me go.

"Where is your cellphone? Maybe I can see why it didn't send?"

I forced a laugh. "Detective, I'm a Zoomer—"

"Zoomer?"

"Gen Z'er?" I waited for him to nod. "I highly doubt you know more about my smart phone than I do. We both know you're looking to catch me in a lie, but it won't happen. Besides, I don't have it on me. The truth is, I left with my friend last minute to go to a LARPing event and didn't realize my parents didn't get the text saying where I went."

He pursed his lips. "Where is this guy now?"

"Why so you can harass him next? He's innocent." I tugged at the hem of my sleeves. "I don't know. He went to talk to a friend while I was attempting to get coffee and then you guys busted in and dragged me away."

He opened his mouth and shut it. Then he huffed and pushed to his feet. "Sure, kiddo. Hang tight, I'll be right back."

I started to protest but he was fast. He was out of sight before I could take a deep breath. *Damn it.* I needed to get out of here and find Stellan, then go to Araqiel. I needed to get my answers. And I very much needed to have words with my parents. But none of that could happen with me trapped in a police precinct.

Think, Ellie. Think.

My magic rushed to my palms, begging me to call on it. Part of me wanted to, to just unleash it and let it handle this mess. I was still a rookie with my magic but there had to be a way to use it to get me out of here...except I had no idea what that might be. I groaned and looked down at my hands. Melanie would know what to do. Stellan would've already escaped.

Thinking about Stellan stung my heart. I was worried about him, even though I knew he was fine. This wasn't his first time in First Realm and he had an insane amount of power. Still... I was still worried about him nonetheless.

I reached down and pushed my right shirt sleeve up — and gasped. My eyes widened. The black markings on my left forearm that marked me as Stellan's soulmate were *gone.* My arm was a clean slate – *no, wait. What is that?* I forced my sleeve up more and my jaw dropped. The geometric shapes had been replaced by a single line of text. I frowned and raised my arm to look closer.

What the bloody hell was written in an elegant, old English scroll.

Stellan said my soulmate mark would change once we were back in First Realm, but I couldn't picture it. Now a smile played on my lips as Tyler's party came crashing back down around me. I remembered that spin the bottle and how I'd stormed over and kissed Stellan...and then he'd said *what the bloody hell.* It was only days ago yet so much had happened since then.

"Eloise Sutton?"

I jumped and glanced over my shoulder. "Yes?"

A detective I hadn't met before smiled at me. "Your parents are here."

THIRTY-ONE

ELLIE

"Your parents are here."

I gasped and sat up straight. "Where?"

But then the elevator doors opened at the far side of the room and I saw them. They rushed off the elevator and into the precinct, their faces stricken and pale. Their gazes scanned the room, left and right and back again in a panic. My heart caught in my throat. *Mom. Dad.* Tears stung my eyes. So much had happened since I last saw them...I hadn't realized how much I missed them until they were in front of me. I meant to call out for them, to let them know I was there and okay, but I was frozen.

Mom had one hand gripped around Dad's elbow and the other cupping her very pregnant belly. Her hazel eyes bounced around faster than a pinball. The hand on her belly was trembling so hard I could actually see it shake from across the room. Her shoulder-length dirty blonde hair was tied in pigtails just under her ears. There were more paint stains on her khaki green oversized overalls than usual, and I wondered what she'd been painting to keep her mind occupied.

I looked over to my dad and smiled. His black, thick-rimmed glasses were missing one arm and sitting lopsided on his face. His gray eyes were wide and crazed. His dark hair that matched mine was disheveled and sticking up in every direction. The green shirt he wore was definitely inside out and his socks weren't matching.

They looked exactly like they always did, like nothing had changed. But then again, *I* was the one who'd changed. Not them.

My mom's gaze swept over the room and landed on me. She gasped and let out a little scream. *"ELLIE."*

Dad's eyes widened and he hurried after her. "Penelope, don't *run.*"

She swatted at his *helpful* hands and growled. Dad's attention locked in on her darting through the precinct, but I couldn't blame him. She was eight months pregnant, running was a terrible idea. Granted, it was honestly more of a waddle.

When she was about five feet away her panicked expression turned hot and angry and she balled her hands in fists at her sides. *"Eloise Elizabeth Sutton, where have you been,"* she screamed, sounding every bit like Mrs. Weasley.

Everyone within a twenty-foot radius turned and stared.

"Who took her?" Dad shouted to the entire precinct. The harsh edge in his voice was so foreign to me that it sent my

pulse flying. *Dad,* who *never* raised his voice or got angry, looked like Bruce Banner about to Hulk out. "Who was it? Where are they?"

"Mom…Dad, no one took me. It was…I got lost…" I jumped to my feet and held my hands up. "I can explain later, but I'm okay."

"You got lost?" The detective grumbled beside me, then fired question after question in rapid fire.

My parents swerved around a desk and three officers stopped right in front of me. Their angry gazes moved down to my body and their faces paled.

Dad scowled so hard his glasses slid down his nose. *"What?"*

Mom's jaw dropped but then her hazel eyes met mine and hers watered. *"No,"* she whispered and shook her head.

I frowned and looked down at myself, wondering what could have caused their reactions. But all I saw was my cream-colored dress from Second Realm – I gasped and looked up to meet my mom's eyes again. I turned to Dad and he was staring at my dress like it was a snake about to bite him. My stomach sank. *You know. You KNOW.* My heart fluttered. They knew where I'd been. They had to. They took one look at my outfit and their entire demeanor went from worried parents to…*terrified.*

Because they know.

They know I've been in Second Realm.

Wait…they know about Second Realm? How? No, they must be thinking something else.

"Mr. and Mrs. Sutton," the detective said with a gravelly

voice. "Thanks for coming so quickly. If you'll have a seat, we just have some questions—"

"No," Mom said without taking her eyes off of me. She reached into her back pocket and *pulled out a wand.* She didn't flinch or fluster, she just flicked her wand toward the detective and the air shimmered in front of her. "Thank you for finding our daughter, detective. There was no foul play, she was simply lost. She is free to go without further questions."

I gasped. *What the bloody hell?*

The detective stood straight and scratched his mustache. He cleared his throat. "You're very welcome. Maybe put a GPS tracker on her from now on. Have a nice day."

Then he, and every other cop within a ten foot range of us, turned and *left.*

My heart was pounding against my chest. *"Mom —"*

"Not here." Dad grabbed my elbow gently and pulled me forward. "Outside."

Mom nodded once then took my other elbow with her shaking hands. They both held my arms as they escorted me back outside. I opened my mouth to speak but there was something in their expressions that stopped me. I'd seen faces like that before...from the Rebellion. They wore the faces of soldiers marching into battle and it sent chills down my spine.

None of us spoke as they led me outside and to the street.

Dad kept glancing down at me and shaking his head. He

was mumbling something but not loud enough for me to hear. "Get us a cab, dear."

Mom stepped out into the street and threw her hand up in the air the way all New Yorkers did when hailing a cab – except she held her brown wand between her fingers. Light flashed from the tip as she twirled it around.

A cab slammed on its brakes right in front of her even though its light wasn't on. This cab driver wasn't working, yet he stopped anyway.

"Dad, I—"

"Get in the cab, love," he ordered softly and gave me a little push while looking to Mom. "Dear, you first?"

Mom whirled on him with both eyebrows arched. "Really? *I'm* going to slide with *this* belly?"

Dad cursed but he leapt forward and slid inside the cab. Mom basically shoved me inside after him. I'd just caught my balance when Mom climbed in after me and closed the door.

The cab driver spun in his seat. "Sorry, folks, I'm off duty —"

"The Emerald, Central Park West," Mom said calmly with her wand pointed right at him. "As quickly as possible, please. We tip nicely."

The driver's face went blank. "You got it, lady." Then he spun back around and flew into traffic.

"*MOM—*"

She put her hand over my mouth and touched her wand to the plexiglass that separated us from the driver. Light flashed and it turned to actual solid glass with a foggy tint. She sighed and leaned back against the leather seat, dropping her hand from my mouth. "Okay, now it's safe to talk."

"*WHAT?*"

"Eloise, dear—"

"*WHAT THE HELL JUST HAPPENED? Oh my God. OH MY GOD.*" I looked back and forth between them and Mom's wand. "You used magic. You have a wand. YOU HAVE A WAND. Oh my God. What the hell? What's happening?"

"Ellie, we can explain—"

"OH, *now* you can explain, Dad? NOW? Not, I don't know, before I accidentally walked into another realm and almost *died?*" I shook my head and tugged on my hair.

All of my confusion and fear over the last few days rushed to the surface. I felt like a volcano about to explode. Anything not bolted down in the back of the cab rose up to hover in the air. Napkins and candy wrappers whirled around us, smacking into the windows. The glass my mother made solid between us and the driver vibrated with my rage.

"How could you not tell me? How could you LIE to me? Oh my god, are you even my parents? Did you steal me from some poor mage in Second Realm?"

"NO. Ellie, no." Mom took my hand and squeezed. "You are our biological daughter. We are your parents in every way."

"*THEN WHY DID YOU LIE TO ME?* And don't you dare pretend like you didn't. You know where I was, I saw your reaction to my dress and I obviously saw that wand and the magic you just used. ANSWER ME."

Dad sighed and pinched the bridge of his nose. "We didn't want to – we didn't have a choice."

"Bullshit. You expect me to believe that?" Spiderweb-like cracks forked out over the glass.

"It's the truth, Ellie." Dad looked defeated and sad. "We were not allowed to tell you until...until..."

"Until *what?*"

"Ellie." Mom squeezed my hand, bringing my eyes to her. "Your father and I are mages. We were born in Second Realm. We lived there our whole lives. But when you were born, the angel Araqiel came to us and told us that you were the Stone Keeper. That you were the key piece to the realm's survival."

My heart stopped. "What?"

"We hadn't known anything about it...we were peasants."

I nodded. "Wand magic means peasants," I heard myself say.

She smiled encouragingly. "Araqiel told us that you had to leave. You had to be moved to First Realm for safe keeping. There was nothing we could do. He said we could either go with you, leaving Second Realm forever...or he would take you and we would never see you again."

"We obviously chose you," Dad said softly. "Without hesitation."

"But Araqiel ordered us not to tell you anything. He'd said the ramifications would be dire if we did. Our job was to protect you at all costs then to bring you to him when the time came." Mom sighed and licked her lips. "Apparently, that time is now."

"None of this makes sense. I understand none of it — wait, the Emerald. You said The Emerald. You're bringing me to Araqiel now?"

They nodded.

"That's where I was when the cops grabbed me. I was on my way to see him."

"I really thought this was going to happen differently. Calmly." My mother rubbed her round belly. "I thought we'd have time to prepare. I even had a little speech memorized."

"You can give her the speech now, dear."

"No. It's too late for that. Seventeen years of preparation out the window —" she stopped and narrowed her eyes at me. "Did you say you were on your way to him? How did you even know about him? How did you end up in Second Realm in the first place?"

"You were supposed to be at a house party with Nickel and the others." Dad shook his head and spun his gold wedding ring around his finger. "Do you have any idea how that felt for us? To have Andy and Hewie show up and say they lost you? Do you have any idea what it was like to show up and see cop cars?"

"Are you *serious* right now?" I groaned and balled my fists. Purple smoke billowed from between my fingers. "Do you have any idea what it's like to suddenly find yourself in a different *realm*? Do you have ANY idea what it's like to be told at seventeen that you're a mage with magical powers? Do you have any idea whatsoever what the last three days have been like for me?"

The cab pulled off to the side of the road and stopped. Mom cursed and pressed the tip of her wand to the glass. Light shimmered and then the cracks I'd caused were repaired and it turned back to the normal plexiglass. Dad threw his door open and jumped out while mom tossed two twenty-dollar bills to the cab driver. I wasn't ready to end this conversation. I had questions. There were things to be said. They owed me more of an explanation for lying to me for my entire life.

But I couldn't say anything in front of a human.

Human. What have I become? What's happened to me?

Mom kicked her door open then Dad reached in and pulled her out of the cab. I scurried across the ripped leather backseat then hopped out behind them. I looked up to see where we were and my eyes widened. We were outside The Emerald. I'd come full circle. If I hadn't insisted on getting a damn coffee, Stellan and I — I gasped. *Stellan.*

My parents' arrival had distracted me for a moment, but I still thought my best bet at finding Stellan was Araqiel. I scanned the sidewalk around me and the one that ran along Central Park – the one I'd thrown him over. Stellan was nowhere in sight. My pulse quickened and dread filled my rolling stomach. *Don't freak out yet. He's probably with Araqiel. That's where we were headed.*

"Ellie," Mom hissed as she grabbed my hand and yanked me toward the building.

Dad stood at the front door of The Emerald, waving us on, his gray eyes scanning the street behind us like someone was going to jump out and grab me. The second we caught up to him, he wrapped his arm around Mom's waist and took my elbow with his other hand. They rushed us inside the lobby then made a sharp left turn down a flight of stairs.

"Where are we going?" I hissed as we rounded a corner then slid to a stop at a dead-end. "We're not done talking about this. You still owe me —"

"I know, sweetie. And you're right." Mom squeezed my hand then turned to the blank wall in front of us and pressed the tip of her wand to the solid white paint. Light flashed and the wall split open in half. "Let Araqiel explain things, then we'll be an open book for you. Okay?"

I nodded absently, my gaze zeroed in on the wall that had just opened into an elevator. They ushered me inside and pressed me into the back wall. Dad held his hand to the wall and the doors shut. Mom slammed her wand into a black screen and a big red *A* flashed.

Everything was happening so fast. My mind and emotions were a blur, like someone had thrown me into a blender. I was mad at my parents for lying to me but I just couldn't even fully process that. They were going to answer for their indiscretions…*after* I found Stellan. After I found out this business about a Stone Keeper. I had no idea what that meant, but my parents, Stellan, and Melanie seemed to think I was something special.

The elevator doors opened and I saw him.

At the end of the hall, pacing in front of a set of wooden double doors, was a tall blond boy looking sinfully delicious in all black. He was dressed exactly the same way he'd been this morning when we'd come through the portal, but being separated from him had done something to me.

"*SHIT*," Mom shouted and yanked me backwards.

Stellan spun with wide pale green eyes. The collar of his flowy silk shirt flew open and my gaze latched on the tan skin of his chest. My heart fluttered and then our eyes met and the world stopped. My lips curved. Goosebumps spread across my skin. *Stellan.*

"*King Benedict?*" Dad leapt in front of us and threw his arms out to the side. "*Close the doors, Penn.*"

Mom dove for the wall with her wand outstretched, lights already shimmering from the tip, and my brain snapped into action. The elevator doors slammed shut. *NO.* I threw my hands out and purple smoke shot from my palms. The doors buckled and snapped off. My parents gasped. I leapt out then sprinted down the hall.

Stellan's eyes sparkled. He took a step forward and flexed his fingers, silver magic shot out and coiled around my waist. I heard my mom scream out my name, but I was lost in the heat in Stellan's eyes as my feet slid across the hardwood floors. A foot away from him he dropped his magic and I dove for him. I pushed off the ground and tackled him with my arms wrapped around his neck. The heat of his body burned through our clothes and melted that icy chill I'd been feeling since we were separated.

I squeezed him tight and just inhaled his autumn-y scent.

"*Ellie,*" he sighed softly and gripped my waist. My feet hit the ground and his hands slid down to my hips. He pulled back but our bodies were still touching. He cupped my jaw and pulled my face toward his. His green eyes were sharp as they scanned my face. "Are you okay? Are you all right? Did they hurt you?"

"I'm okay, *I'm okay.*" I put my hands over his and stared into his eyes. My cheeks burned and I knew I was blushing, but I didn't care. "I'm all right. I'm so sorry I threw you."

His answering chuckle took my breath away. He dragged me closer and pressed his lips to my forehead. "Don't be. That was amazing."

I sighed and leaned into his touch. "I had a good teacher."

He groaned and pulled back. The emotion in his eyes made my heart do weird things. He shook his head. "I spent this entire time worrying I hadn't trained you enough and that you'd be in trouble—"

I pushed up on my toes and pressed my lips to his. He sighed against my mouth. His fingers tightened on my jaw. His smell and taste were everywhere, autumn leaves and mint. The combination was dizzying, or maybe that was from his lips brushing against mine. I licked at him once… twice…and then he pulled back with a groan.

His cheeks were flushed pink but his eyes sparkled like stars in the night sky. He rubbed his thumb in circles over my jaw. "How'd you get away?"

"My parents showed up."

His face fell. "Your *parents*?"

"Yeah, we're still here, too," Dad said from behind me.

I gasped and my heart stopped. I'd forgotten they were there…I wouldn't have kissed Stellan like that had I remembered. I'd never, ever kissed a boy in front of my parents. Ever. My stomach tightened into knots. Stellan stared over my shoulder with wide eyes. I pulled Stellan's hands away from my face then glanced behind me. Both my parents stood there with wide eyes and slacked jaws.

I licked my lips and spun around, pressing my back into Stellan's chest. "Mom…*Dad*…this is—"

"*Ellie*, do you know who this is?" Dad hissed and inched closer, like he was about to yank me away from my soulmate. "You can't…they can't—"

"It's okay, Dad. He's on our side—"

"*Our* side?" Mom shrieked, her face paled.

"—he can be trusted." I smiled up at Stellan, ignoring the panicked look on my parents' faces. "This is Stellan Wentworth. And *these* are my parents, Teddy and Penelope Sutton."

Stellan smiled wide and stuck his right hand out, his gold signet ring shimmering in the ceiling lights. "Mr. and Mrs. Sutton, lovely to meet you."

Dad gripped his hand and frowned. "*Prince* Stellan, I presume?"

He shrugged one shoulder. "Yes, but judging by your reaction, I assure you I am not like the Wentworths you knew."

Mom flushed and dropped into a curtsey. "Your Highness."

"Well now, look at that," a loud, booming male voice said from suddenly behind us. When I looked, I found that beautifully dark-skinned angel with a bald head and pristine white wings. He leaned against the doorframe holding a taco in each hand. "She showed up, *with* her parents. I told you not to worry, Your Highness."

Mom nodded once. "Araqiel."

He stepped back and waved us forward. "Come on, we've got lots to talk about."

THIRTY-TWO

ELLIE

"COME IN," Araqiel turned and marched through the double doors, his massive white wings taking up the whole space. "I won't bite…unless you're a taco."

Stellan took my hand in his and squeezed. He winked then pulled me forward. I glanced over my shoulder to my parents and found their gazes locked on our interlocked hands. My stomach tightened into knots. *Shit.* I hadn't told them about him or that he was my soulmate…and they definitely weren't used to me kissing boys.

Did I really just kiss him in front of them?

I'm gonna be in so much trouble.

Araqiel stepped to the side and my jaw dropped. We were inside a beautiful office that was fit more for a celebrity than an angel – not that I had any frame of reference for how angels should live. The first thing I saw was that the back wall was entirely open. A terrace with greenery and a sitting area was just beyond the walls of the room, basking in the sunlight. The floors were made of rich mahogany that shimmered in the patches of sunlight streaming in. In the center of the room, right in front of us, was a white fluffy area rug under an intricately carved wooden coffee table that looked straight out of *Rivendell.* On either side were pristine white couches that somehow lacked a single stain.

But Araqiel didn't sit on them. He walked around and sat behind a large wooden desk. He pointed one taco at a chair in front of him. "Sit. Let's get this going."

Stellan pulled one of the wooden chairs out and scowled. "Um, Araqiel?"

I followed his stare and realized what he'd seen. There were only two chairs for four people.

Araqiel looked up then sighed. He sat one taco down on a plate next to him and snapped his fingers. Two more chairs identical to the others appeared out of nowhere. "Now, shall we?"

Stellan pressed his hand to the small of my back and butterflies danced in my stomach. I licked my lips and tucked my hair behind my ears as I sat down on one of the middle seats. My mother took the one beside me, then Dad claimed the one on the other side of her. I glanced to my left to make sure Stellan was sitting beside me – and he was.

Araqiel shoved half his taco in his mouth and chewed. He rubbed his palms together as he swallowed. "All right, now let's—"

"Who the hell are you?" I heard myself say. The second

the words left my mouth I clenched my teeth tight together. *Shit, I did not just talk to an angel like that.*

Mom hissed my name under her breath. Dad closed his eyes and shook his head.

Stellan chuckled.

Araqiel gave me a sideways grin and pointed to his wings. "These don't give that away?"

I arched one eyebrow at him. "You're an angel. No offense, but that doesn't tell me anything."

"You're not wrong." He grinned and leaned back in his seat. "My name is Araqiel. I am the leader of a group of angels known as the Watchers. We are angels of Heaven sent down here by the Creator to *watch* and oversee all species of life here—"

"The Watchers…?" Mom frowned. "Like from the Book of Enoch?"

"Yes…and no." Araqiel shrugged. "Humans tend to not get the details right and we don't like to correct them. In fact, we tend to enjoy misleading them. But it's in the name of protection—"

A large shadow passed over the room and then a dark object landed on the terrace behind Araqiel. White wings flapped wide in the air, glistening like fresh fallen snow in the morning sunlight. *Another angel?* I craned my neck around Araqiel to watch as this angel sauntered toward us. Judging by their tall height, broad set of shoulders, and muscular arms, I knew it was a man – *or is it male since he's not human?* He stepped into the office and my eyes widened. It was definitely a male, and he was dangerously attractive...and definitely familiar. I'd seen him before, down on the street talking with Stellan.

Except now I had a better look at him. His skin was still porcelain smooth and pale, his eyes a rich, deep sapphire. His midnight black hair was trimmed short on the sides and left longer on top, which he had pushed back away from his face. Everything about this angel was sharp, like the blade of a sword. His gaze, his cheekbones, his jawline...all ready to cut.

I glanced between him and Araqiel and frowned. Araqiel was intimidating as hell. His gaze alone was enough to make me want to run and hide...but Araqiel was dressed head-to-toe in white. Just like his office. This other guy wore a black V-neck t-shirt, black jeans, and black combat boots. Something told me if he could have black wings, he would.

"Ah, yes. This is Zuriel." Araqiel pointed to the angel. "He's my right hand. My strong hand. My enforcer."

Zuriel gave us one nod and nothing else.

I turned my attention back to Araqiel and cleared my throat. "Mr. Araqiel, sir, can you please explain what in the actual hell is going on here? Because I'm one flap of a wing away from losing my damn mind."

Before he could respond, Stellan pulled that leather journal out from behind his back and tossed it onto the table. "This is the journal I've been telling you about, sir. The one my sister found when she was young then shared with me before she died. Is it legitimate?"

Araqiel plucked the journal off his desk and flipped

through the parchment paper, shaking his head. "It's legit, all right." He laughed. "Oh, Georgie boy. You old sneaky shit."

My mom sat up straight and tried to see the book. "Who is George? What is this book?"

Araqiel tossed it back to Stellan. "This is a journal by George Wentworth. You need to hang on to that, you may need information out of it as you go."

"Why? Who was he?" I groaned and pushed my hair back. Where were explanations? I'd traveled to another world and back to see *this* angel and the most I could gather from him was that he liked tacos. "What is all this about?"

"To understand George, I need to take this all the way back. I warn you, this is about to be a lot of information and it's some heavy shit, so buckle up and settle in." He held our stares for a moment, then glanced to Zuriel – who nodded and held his palm out toward the terrace *and glass appeared.* Araqiel nodded then turned to me. "Eloise, by now I assume you're aware of the other species in the other realms, yes?"

I nodded. "Mages. Fae. Vampires. Shifters. And of course humans. They all have their own realms, this one belonging to humans."

"Well, *actually,* there used to only be *one* realm." He gestured around us. "This one."

Stellan sat up straight. "Wait, what?"

Araqiel nodded and grinned. "A long, *long* time ago this realm only had humans in it. Well, and *us.* The Creator cherished the humans and thought they needed protection and guidance, so he sent me—"

"I'm sorry...*you*? Like, as in, actual you? How old are you?" I shook my head. How did someone even begin to understand a person who was here at the beginning of time? It was unfathomable. I couldn't wrap my head around that.

"I'll tell you on my next birthday." Araqiel chuckled. "So anyway, I came down here with a few of my best men and everything was great for a short while. But then one day demons got in – and this is very much the abridged version, you're welcome. When demons arrived it was clear the humans were no match. They were being destroyed. So myself and the other Watchers decided to mix with select humans to create the species of Nephilim. Their sole purpose was to fight demons. But in order to keep things moving smoothly while being balanced, The Creator gave Earth these special stones of power. This worked —"

Zuriel scoffed and rolled his sapphire eyes.

"Until some humans got their hands on these stones... and then brand-new species showed up. All of a sudden we had vampires, faeries, and mages – like yourselves. I won't get into just how that happened, just know it did or we'll be here all damn day." He stopped and waited for us to nod. When we did, he cleared his throat and continued. "Things were a bit rocky but manageable until the fifth century. In year 476, a war broke out between the species—"

"476? That's the start of the Dark Ages," I said before I

could stop myself. Everyone turned to me and my cheeks warmed. "Sorry...nerd alert. Continue."

"Again, you're not wrong. The Dark Ages, as remembered by human history books, were a direct result of the inter-species civil war. I let them fight, since my job at the time was to not interfere unless absolutely necessary...but in year 800, the Nephilim had been entirely wiped out. Extinct. Without the Nephilim to control the other species, the Watchers had to step in."

I leaned forward, my pulse thundering in my veins. "What did you do?"

"The same thing all parents do when their children are fighting...separate them." He shook his head. "Each of the three species, mages, vampires, and Fae, had been created by a certain power stone. So, I took their stone and created separate realms for each of the species. And again, for a while everything was great. The realms were thriving on their own. The existence of First Realm was erased from their memories, leaving only their rulers with the knowledge of First Realm and access back."

"I feel a big *but* coming here," I mumbled.

"*But...*" he pointed to me and winked. "In the year 1820, King Dante Wentworth of the mages, King Cirrus of the Fae, and King Bregan of the vampires got greedy. They didn't like that The Watchers oversaw their realms and made them behave. They didn't like that they weren't permitted to play with humans anymore...so...they came into First Realm and stole the Creation Stone."

"*Oh shit*," I whispered. Here it was, the moment when everything went wrong. I held my breath then blew it out.

Stellan squeezed my hand.

"King Dante gave the Creation Stone to his brother, George Wentworth." Araqiel pointed to the journal in Stellan's hands. "George had earthen magic, which you're familiar with by now."

My cheeks were on *fire*.

But Araqiel kept going. "The three kings wanted a sort of playground for their own debauchery where I wouldn't be able to see them."

Zuriel scoffed again.

Araqiel shrugged. "The three kings brought each of their realms' stones together and had George funnel all of their power through the Creation stone...thus creating a *fifth* realm. I let them play for six months, just to see what they'd do. A test, if you will. One that they failed miserably. As a result of their actions an entire new species was created—"

My jaw dropped. The greed of those three. "The shifters?"

Araqiel nodded. "The shifters, a combination of all of their power. But it didn't stop there. The Fifth Realm is chaos and madness, it lives and breathes on its own. It was dangerous."

"Is that why you closed it?" Stellan asked.

"No." Araqiel leaned forward. "I shut it down because what no one knew was that there was a sixth stone. The

Serenity Stone. It maintained the balance and peace of the world and all its realms. Once it was separated from the Creation Stone, all of the other realms began to die."

I gasped. "George's journal entry…"

"When the other realms began to die, their stones vanished." Araqiel tapped his fingers on his desk and eyed me in a way that sent chills down my spine. "The Creator gave what you'd call a prophecy, saying that when it was time, Stone Keepers would be born and marked as such. These individuals would be born with the power of their stones inside them and they'd be the only people who could save their realms."

Silence.

I felt everyone's eyes turn to me.

Sweat broke out across my forehead and beaded along the back of my neck. *No, no, no.*

But Araqiel was nodding. "You, Eloise Sutton, are the Stone Keeper of Second Realm."

"No…"

"Yes." He tapped his face, next to his eyes. "The Astral Stone for Second Realm is in your eyes and in your magic."

"My magic?" I hissed. I shook my head. "No, no, no."

"The Astral Stone is what gave mages their magic." He pointed to Stellan. "It is why he can move things with his magic. It's why your parents can use wands. And it's why *you* have the power of the elements."

"*Elements?* As in plural?" I shook my head and waved my hands. "You're confused. I don't have magic of elements plural. I have earth, wind, and a little lightning. That's it."

"Yes, and you had those without much effort, did you not?" Araqiel arched one dark eyebrow at me. His hazel eyes were sharp. "You're new to your truth, Eloise. No one else knew to tell you either. You have all the elements in your veins. You simply have to learn to harness them."

My breath left me in a rush. I gripped the armrest of my chair and shook my head. "This is...this is too much. This is crazy. You're telling me that *I* am this special Stone Keeper destined to save the bloody world?"

"Well, at least *your* world, which is Second Realm." He grimaced. "I was ordered to take each Stone Keeper from their realm at birth, as the kings could not be trusted. To protect you, the truth was kept from you."

"*WHY?*" I shrieked and jumped to my feet. I pulled on my hair and stormed away from the desk and started pacing. "Why? Why would you keep this from me? You let me think I was *human* for seventeen years. WHY? How am I supposed to save a realm if I don't even know how to use my magic?"

"Would you rather have grown up with the burden of pressure, knowing one day you'd have to do such a thing?"

I whirled around on him and screamed, "*I don't know!*"

Araqiel leaned back in his chair and steepled his fingers. "I'm sorry, Eloise, the gift of power rarely comes without burden."

"Oh, save me all your Dumbledore bullshit right now," I shouted as I paced manically. "Second Realm is *dying.* I've seen it myself. And somehow, *I* am going to save them? How? HOW?"

"Well, I am here to help you with that—"

"So there are Stone Keepers for the other realms?" I stopped and narrowed my eyes on the ancient angel I had no business disrespecting. "Where are they?"

"I can't tell you that." He shook his head.

I put my hands on my hips to stop from jabbing a finger in his face. "Because you don't know?"

"Because it's my job to keep them safe until they're ready or until it's time. Just like I did with you."

"Oh…right." I cursed and buried my face in my hands.

The smell of autumn leaves washed over me a split second before Stellan's hands wrapped around my wrists and pulled them from my face. His pale green eyes were soft and warm. "Ellie, I know this is a lot. It blew my mind as a child when Savina told me. But it's true, and now we know the full extent of that. This is your destiny."

I looked into his eyes and felt the weight of the world pressing in all around me. "I'm not built for this."

"Oh, love, yes you are." He squeezed my hands and tugged me back toward the chairs. "But you're not alone. I'm going to help you every step of the way."

Hope flared in my chest. I looked over his shoulder to Araqiel. "Is that true? He can help me?"

Araqiel smiled softly and nodded. "You can get help from anyone you trust, and I suspect you're going to need it. But in the end, it will be only your magic that will save Second Realm."

I sighed and plopped back down into my chair. "Damn it."

Araqiel snorted and shook his head. "Well, I'll give you that one."

I shook my head. "So what am I supposed to do now? How do I save the world?"

"You have to return to Second Realm and go to the Anchor Point—"

"Anchor Point?" I hated that this was all on me and I hardly knew anything about this world.

Araqiel sat up straight and folded his hands on his desk in front of him. "The Anchor Point is what it sounds like. The five realms are tethered together by an anchor. This is where the Stones are kept...or used to be."

"And I'm supposed to know where this Anchor Point is?" This was all too damn much.

Araqiel smirked. "As a New Yorker, you pass it often. You've seen the statue in the center of Columbus Circle, have you not?"

I gasped. "*That's* the anchor?"

"Yes." Araqiel glanced to Zuriel, who'd been a silent shadow the whole time, then back to me. "But to save Second Realm, you'll have to go to the Anchor Point *in* Second Realm."

"And I'm supposed to know where that is?"

"No, but lucky for you, your boy toy does." Araqiel looked to Stellan. "Ain't that right, Your Highness?"

I turned to Stellan with my breath caught in my throat.

He grimaced. "I know where it is."

Araqiel clapped his hands. "Excellent. Take Miss Eloise here back to Second Realm and to the Anchor Point. The

Stone Keeper must return to where the Stone belongs to receive instructions. The Stone will be your only real guide."

THIRTY-THREE

ELLIE

Damn it. Damn it. Damn it. Damn it.

"Ellie? Sweetie?"

I jumped at the sound of my mom's voice and looked up. "What?"

We were standing at the end of the hallway, where the magically hidden elevator would appear as soon as one of us called for it. All three of them were watching me. I shifted from one foot to the other. This was all so overwhelming. My body whirled with emotions. Fear and worry took the forefront of my mind. *Would I be enough to save the realm?*

Stellan reached out and tangled his fingers with mine. He ducked his head down to meet my eyes. "We've been talking to you since we left Araqiel's office, love."

"Oh…oh…um…" I shook my head, trying to gain control of my inner turmoil. "Sorry."

"Don't shut me out. Talk to me." He pressed one finger under my chin and tipped my face up. "I'm here."

"Yes, you are, *aren't you?*"

The sharpness in my dad's voice made me jump. When I looked to him, I found him glaring daggers at where Stellan's finger was still pressed to my skin. In that moment, I recounted all the little touches and kisses between Stellan and I since we got here. *Shit.* My stomach tightened into knots. My mom, with one hand on her round belly, was staring at my hand in Stellan's. Dad had his arms crossed over his chest, glancing back and forth.

"*Dad—*"

"Three days." He put his hands on his hips. "*Three* days and…and…and…*this?*"

Stellan dropped his hand from my face and turned toward my dad. He cleared his throat. "Mr. Sutton—"

Dad's face snarled in disgust. "And a *Wentworth—*"

"*DAD,*" I shouted and stepped in front of Stellan like I needed to shield him. He'd protected me from the moment we met and I would do the same for him.

"You don't know what they're like—" He jabbed a finger in Stellan's direction.

"You don't know what *he's* like," I snapped back and balled my hands in fists. I saw my purple smoke coil around my arms in my peripheral vision. "You left Second Realm seventeen years ago. You have no idea who Stellan is or what he's done for the Rebellion."

Mom flinched. "*The Rebellion?*" She looked to Stellan

with wide eyes and a pale face. "There's an actual Rebellion now?"

Stellan stepped beside me but kept his arm wrapped around my waist. "I know who my parents are. I know what they did. I know what they *do.* I may share their name, but I will wear that crown differently. Until I sit on the throne, a wolf in sheep's clothing I must remain."

My parents both just stared at him and I knew they were trying to decide how to proceed. They had never mentioned a single Wentworth my entire life, but I knew enough to understand the bitter taste they would leave. Stellan was not them, nor their legacy. He was a key player for the Rebellion.

But *none* of that actually mattered. Not when it came to me and Stellan. He was mine and I was his. There wasn't a damn thing anyone could do about it. Not even my parents. I wanted their approval…but I didn't need it.

I wanted to make them understand, so I reached across his body and grabbed his left wrist. I pulled his arm out in front of him then yanked his sleeve up. Written in elegant black scroll were the words *Mistakes were made.* I cursed. This would have been easier in Second Realm when our marks were identical. Here in First Realm they were the very first words I'd said to him.

"Ellie?" Mom frowned at me then glanced down at the tattoo on his skin.

"They don't look the same here. Remember?" Stellan said softly, his voice a gentle purr.

I held my own left arm out and pushed my sleeve up.

Sure enough, *'what the bloody hell'* was etched into my skin. My mind replayed the moment when he'd said that, right after I'd kissed him. It had done things to me then. Seeing it on my skin did things to me now.

"Wait. *Wait, wait, wait.*" Mom leapt forward and grabbed both of our outstretched arms with wide hazel eyes. "Your left arms...Ellie?"

My cheeks flushed. My mouth was suddenly dry. I swallowed and licked my lips. "Mom...Dad...Stellan...is my soulmate."

My parents gasped.

Mom swayed on her feet but Dad caught her quick.

"Soulmates...with the prince..." Mom fanned herself. "With the heir to the throne..."

Dad looked like he was going to be sick. "This can't be...you're a peasant, he's a prince. It's not allowed."

"With all due respect, sir, when I'm King *I* will get to make those rules," Stellan said in his calm, deep voice while rubbing circles on my back.

"Are you telling me my daughter will be queen? Is that what you're telling us right now?" Mom groaned and rubbed her round belly. "This is going to send me into labor, I just know it."

My eyes widened. *Me? Queen?* But even as she said it the realization clicked. My soulmate was going to be the king so that meant I would be his queen. Part of me was exhilarated by this...the bigger part of me wanted to run and hide.

Stellan sighed. "Ellie and I have just met, we're moving

at our own pace. Her being the queen to my king would be my preference, yes, but I think you'd agree that is the least of our concerns right now."

"Right." I nodded as my stomach turned. "We need to get back to Second Realm and go—"

"Wait, wait, hold on." Dad gestured between Stellan and me and scowled. "I want to talk about *this* more."

"Yeah, well, I wanted to know the truth behind my entire existence that you kept from me for seventeen years—"

"Ellie, please, we didn't have a choice," My mother pleaded.

"But you have one now, Mother." I shoved past my father, pressed my palm to the blank white wall, and pushed with my magic. Purple smoke billowed out from under my hand. I looked over my shoulder as the elevator doors opened in front of me. "I have a job to do, whether I like it or not. And I'm not going to let the people of Second Realm suffer any longer. We have to go—"

"Wait—"

"*Mother*—"

"What's your plan?" She held up both her palms in surrender. "We'll talk about you two later, at least tell me what your plan is for getting to the Anchor Point?"

"It sits on palace property. I've been there many times. No one will question the prince being out there." Stellan moved to take my hand outside the elevator. "I'll bring her right there."

"Not like that you're not."

Stellan and I both frowned and looked down at ourselves.

Dad sighed. "I don't like this."

But Mom ignored him and pointed to me. "You cannot take her looking like a peasant, she will stand out. And you most definitely cannot take her with these eyes."

Stellan narrowed his eyes. "What are you proposing?"

Mom pulled her wand out of her back pocket and pointed it at my chest. "You need to disguise her."

Light flashed and washed over my body. A warm wave of electricity wrapped around me. My hair whipped around my face. My arms and legs tingled. Cold air swept by. And then the light vanished. I gasped and jumped back.

Stellan's eyes widened. His lips curved into a grin. "*Very* well done, Mrs. Sutton."

She smiled and held her chin high. "Thank you."

Dad leaned in close, holding his broken glasses up. "She's indistinguishable."

I frowned as a cold chill slithered down my spine. They were all just staring at me like I was an animal at the zoo. I looked down at myself and gasped. My cream-colored cotton dress had been replaced by layers of vibrant pink silk that had darker pink velvet embroidery. *Whoa.* I spun and jumped into the elevator, to where the walls were made of mirror.

My breath left me in a rush. The person staring back at me looked nothing like me. Gone was my midnight hair and violet eyes. This person was different, dainty even. She had elegant pale blonde curls that fell to her petite shoulders and big, bright blue eyes that looked too big for a human face. My lips were painted a glossy pink and white silk gloves covered my arms.

I turned and met Stellan's gaze. "Well?"

"Yeah…yeah, this will work." He cleared his throat. "Let's go find this stone."

THIRTY-FOUR

ELLIE

WE STEPPED through the portal and came right back out in front of the grand mirror. It was the same strange room at the end of a wing, shaped in a circle and made of pale gray stones. There still wasn't anything else in the room besides the mirror, but I supposed that made sense, knowing what the mirror was.

I cannot believe I didn't realize I wasn't in Manhattan as soon as I got here.

Stellan jumped in front of me, shielding me with his own body as he scanned around. After a minute of watching, he turned back to me and smiled. "Okay, you're a courtier now. Just don't speak unless you're spoken to. That's standard for courtiers." He held his elbow out and smiled.

I narrowed my eyes. "Shut up and look pretty, really?"

He shrugged. "Not my rules, not my game."

"Once we finish this, we're doing something about

them." His smile faltered and I realized what I'd just said. I'd just suggested eliminating his parents. I cursed. "Stellan, that's not what I meant—"

"I know. I'm hoping once we succeed in this, I may be able to use it as leverage for a change of…scenery." He gave me a small smile and held his elbow out again. "It is customary for a courtier accompanying the prince to take his arm while they walk."

I tried not to smile and failed. I wrapped my arm under his, then rested my hand on the inside of his forearm. "I'm going to ignore the notion that another girl gets to touch you and focus on the excuse for *me* to touch you."

He shook his head but the huge grin on his face was a victory in my book. "Shall we focus, my lady?"

"We shall, Your Highness."

Your Highness. I kept catching myself forgetting that he was a prince. A Royal. The heir to the throne. Maybe it was the way he acted around me or the lack of a crown on his head…or maybe it was my own subconscious wish that he *wasn't.* Stellan would make an amazing king. It was just hard to get behind that when I had no desire to be queen.

Stellan led us straight to the stone staircase, the same one I somehow had run all the way up Saturday night without realizing that something was so very off. At the top, we stepped out into the glass-walled room with white marble floors. I just shook my head and my own cluelessness that first night. It was actually embarrassing. Stellan hurried us over to a glass door to our right, not the same one we'd used on our way in, and pushed it open. He led us through the door and onto a cobblestone path.

The smell of roses slammed into me and it was welcomed in every way.

I must've made a face, because Stellan chuckled and gestured around us. "The palace garden."

Before, when we'd ran through it, I hadn't had time to appreciate how beautiful it was. He went on, telling me about every flower or plant that we passed. None of it was being retained. I was too lost in the rumble of his voice and the cadence of his speech...and my nerves were shot. Now that we were back here, now that Araqiel and my parents weren't hanging around...I knew my time was now. There was no waiting or stalling.

This realm was dying.

These people needed me even if they didn't know it yet.

We walked under a canopy of golden flowers, but they may as well have been dark rain clouds. The pressure of the task ahead loomed over me like a shadow. We turned a corner and strolled down a lane of roses of every color. Stellan was the picture of calm and ease, whereas I was a jumbled ball of mess inside.

I glanced over my shoulders as subtly as possible in case someone was looking but every time I found only garden in our wake. The cobblestone pathways stretched out in an intricate map, weaving around the different plants and elaborate fountains. My stomach turned. The realm was dying, the people were dying, and yet the throne kept a garden as lush as this. Every leaf, every flower was a slap in the face.

This is why you're here, Ellie. You're the Stone Keeper.

Stellan pulled me to a stop and put his hand on top of mine. "Ellie?"

I jumped and looked up to find his pale eyes watching me. My cheeks warmed. "Yes?"

"Are you all right?"

Not really. I smiled. "Yes, why?"

"I've never seen you so quiet."

"You told me not to talk."

He arched one eyebrow. "Ellie."

I sighed and shook my head. "This is all just a lot to take in, okay? I got lost in my own head for a moment."

He squeezed my hand. "That's all right, just don't forget I'm here. You're not alone in this. I'm with you every step of the way."

That made me smile. I wanted to kiss him but there was no knowing if anyone was watching us. So I forced my eyes off him and froze. We stood in front of a massive stone pillar that had to be fifteen feet tall. At least. It reminded me of the Washington Monument. Up at the top there was a crest cut into the stone, but with the sun shining on it I couldn't tell what it was.

I frowned. "What is this?"

"The Anchor Point."

I gasped and eyed the sculpture more clearly. "This is it? Where did the stone go?"

"The other side…" He grabbed the back of my corset,

stopping me in my tracks. "This palace was built *around* this Anchor so the Royals could see the stone from inside the palace. I wanted to give you a moment to prepare yourself."

I leaned to my right – sure enough, dozens of big glass windows had a perfect view of the Anchor…and us. There was nothing to conceal us. "Damn it."

Stellan cursed and rubbed the back of his head. "This is my fault. I wasn't thinking. The last time I was here was in the height of spring and the crepe myrtle trees were thick and full – and blocking the view of the stone spot. I was just wanting us to get moving on this…I didn't *think.* Maybe we should come back late tonight —"

"*What?* No." I frowned and turned to face him. "We're here now, Stellan. And no one has spotted us. We may not get this lucky again. We just need to think of a way to hide us…"

"Anything I can do would be obvious. My parents know I like to walk in the garden, but if they think I'm being sneaky then they'll start asking questions. We don't want that."

"Anything *you* can do…" I spun back around to face the palace and the garden between us. "But what can *I* do?"

He wasn't the only one who had magic. I'd already made my own tornado, moved rocks, and created lightning. Surely there was something I could do or conjure. It wouldn't take much either. Araqiel's words echoed in my mind. I had the power of the elements. All of them. I had no reason to doubt the lead Watcher angel dude.

Okay. Think, brain.

The elements...what can you do?

Fire would only cause a commotion. A flood wouldn't help. I could maybe make it rain but then two people out in the rain would be suspicious. I looked down at my hands as if the answer would be written on my skin. *I moved rocks before but that would be hella suspicious. If I could make the plants bloom like in spring... but elemental magic doesn't mean giving life to something. What other elements are there? Fire, water, earth, air — OH. Air. Okay, okay...all right. Um...*

"Ellie?" Stellan whispered in my ear, his breath caressing the back of my neck.

"I'm thinking. Gimme a sec."

How can air help? It's transparent. Wind is strong but won't hide us. Unless I can pull the clouds from the sky — wait. That's it. That's IT. I walked over to the line of rose bushes just beyond the Anchor Point then dropped to my knees. I bit my lip and pretended to be smelling the flowers. Stellan moved behind me. He didn't say anything but I felt his presence like a warm blanket. I pressed my palms flat to the cobblestones. The hot energy of the earth buzzed against my skin.

My magic sang to life at my fingertips, the barest hint of violet shimmered in the air. I closed my eyes and took a deep breath. My magic was ready to do my bidding, I just had to tell it what to do. I pictured in my mind what I wanted to happen, then pushed with everything inside me. Cold air rushed out of my hands. Stellan gasped behind me. I squeezed my eyes shut and pushed harder. If I looked too soon, I could lose my concentration.

Stellan's hand landed on my shoulder and I jumped. "Okay, that's enough. You can stop."

I pulled my hands off the ground and slowly opened my eyes. A pool of swirling violet smoke curled around my feet but it was already lightening. I stood straight — my jaw dropped. A thick blanket of white fog hovered in the air. It slithered between branches and leaves and clung to the tops of trees. The bright colors of the garden were murky and gray. The palace was still there, but now all I saw was a blurry dark object cutting against the bright blue sky.

Stellan whistled under his breath. "You are amazing."

I grinned as heat rushed to my cheeks. "Thanks. I had a great teacher."

His hands gripped my waist from behind. I felt each of his ten fingertips pressing into my skin as he spun me around to face him. My fog didn't enter the cobblestone circle that the Anchor Point sat in, so there was absolutely nothing blurring the beauty of his face. My heart hurt just looking at him, but it was a good hurt. An overwhelming kind of hurt that told me I may have already been in too deep. He was mine and there was no arguing about it. Our marks said so. I licked my lips and pushed up on my tip toes to kiss him—

"Wait. Just in case someone is looking." He stepped *away* from me, but his eyes were soft and tender. He smirked. "Besides, I'd rather not kiss you while you don't look *like you*."

"What? Oh right." I glanced down at myself. The vibrant pink skirt of my dress reminded me that I was disguised.

He squeezed my hand and nodded his head toward the Anchor Point behind him. "Come, before we're spotted."

Right. Damn it, Ellie. Focus.

Kiss the boy later. Find the stone now.

I cleared my head and shook myself. "Right. On it. Let's see…"

Together, we walked back over to the Anchor, then stopped and stared. I kneeled down on the ground to get a better look at the oval-shaped indention at the base of the Anchor. It was about a foot tall with an intricate border carved into it. In the middle of that was another oval-shape indention about six inches tall, but this one was deep and carved out like something was supposed to be inside of it.

Not something. The Stone. The Astral Stone.

Stellan crouched down beside me. "Araqiel said we'd get instructions from here…but I don't see anything."

"No offense, Cap, but I don't think you're going to." I leaned forward and eyed the hole the Stone went in. There was a hint of purple light lingering within the spot. "Unless you can see this purple-ish haze here?"

Stellan sighed. "I'm worthy enough for the hammer, don't forget," he mumbled.

I grinned and glanced up at him. "Yeah…but you get the little one," I said in my best Thor impersonation.

He arched one eyebrow at me. "All right, Stormbreaker, do *you* see anything?"

"We are *so* doing this cosplay next Comic-con." I turned back to the Anchor as he laughed. "All right…all right…it's got to be here."

He rubbed his hands together and scowled. "Maybe we have to take a stone out of the Anchor itself?"

"No…no, I don't think so." I pursed my lips and leaned back on my heels. "That's not how it would happen in comic books or —"

"This isn't fantasy, Ellie—"

"Isn't it, though?" I arched both eyebrows at him. "Maybe you don't see it because you've known this your whole life but this…*all this*…is something straight out of fandom lore. This whole realm is like Stan Lee and Tolkien had a baby—"

"So what are you gonna do, stroke the Anchor and call it your precious?"

I chuckled. "I am *so* glad Weston made you watch all the First Realm movies because otherwise I don't see how this could've ever worked — *wait.*"

"What?"

"*My precious,*" I whispered. "That's how the ring worked. It looked plain until you touched it…"

I reached out and pressed my palm flat to the Anchor. That soft glowing purple haze swirled over my hand then faded away. A bolt of electricity shot down my arm and into my palm. Light flashed between my hand and the Anchor. My pulse pounded through my body. I felt heat and the movement of energy in my palm. I licked my lips then slowly lifted my hand off the Anchor.

Stellan gasped.

My eyes widened and my heart stopped.

There, written on the wall in the very spot the Astral Stone should have been, was a long passage scrolled in an elegant glowing purple script.

I ran my fingertips over the lines. *"My precious,"* I heard myself whisper.

"Wow." Stellan exhaled roughly. "It's a spell. A *long* spell."

"By Earth and Air, Sea and Fire, Spirit in vine is ever dire..."

"The elements. It's talking about the elements," Stellan said in a rush. *"By the bottle thy cauldron sings, Thy quested spell within the strings* – that means a potion of some kind. It has to."

"But it's a quest, too. Listen…" I tapped on the next lines. *"Find and seek, collect and call, The bouquet of magic First in haul."*

He frowned and cocked his head to the side as he read the rest of it. *"Bound by chaos, essence of youth, A drop of blood from a sharpened tooth. Skin of the dirt by the Fifth's moon night, Winds of the Second coiled and tight. Beware the beckon of charms and flame, To bind the Stone for which you claim."*

For a moment, all I could do was stare. Hearing the spell in Stellan's accent was almost like a lullaby. I could have sat there and listened to him read it over and over. The words sounded like lyrics for a song.

Stellan cursed. "That's heavy. I don't like it."

"What does it all mean?"

He shook his head. "I'm not sure, but we can't sit here and try to figure it out. We need to get out of here, get back to the shelter."

"Okay but there's no way we're going to remember this. Do you have a pen or something?"

He grimaced. "No...but...I know a spell that might help us."

"That would be amazing."

He pressed his big palm to the Anchor, right over the glowing spell lines and narrowed his eyes. Silver smoke coiled around his wrist and between his fingers. *"Written, etched, burned in ink, on my skin these words to link."*

I looked down at his arms and frowned. "Was something supposed to happen? Because I missed it."

He sighed. "It didn't work. Okay, we need something else. Maybe I can summon one of my pens from my room." He half turned and eyed the palace behind us.

"Or maybe..." I copied him and pressed my palm into the Anchor. "How does that spell work?"

He shrugged. "Touch the words you want copied and recite the spell while imagining where on your body you want them. I usually do my right forearm, since my left one is otherwise taken – oh. Right. That spell might only work for the Stone Keeper. Give it a go, Thor."

Right. Give it a go. There's no reason I can't do the same spell. Except, I don't want anyone else to see it...so the forearm isn't idea. But if I put it anywhere else on my body, I won't be able to read it.

I looked to Stellan and an idea came to mind. "Hold still." I reached over and yanked the hem of his black silky shirt out from his pants, then pushed the material up. Tan skin stretched tight over chiseled muscle met my stare.

"Should I be concerned?"

I pressed my palm to his warm skin and tried to ignore the rush of electricity in my body or the way butterflies danced in my stomach. With my other hand, I covered the spell on the Anchor with my right palm. I stared at where I was touching Stellan and recited his same words, *"Written, etched, burned in ink, on my skin these words to link."*

Lights flashed from under both of my palms. Hot energy shot into my hand from the Anchor and traveled through my body, then back down my other arm. The light under my left palm brightened but then there was a flash and it vanished.

With my heart in my throat, I dropped my hand – and gasped. *It worked!* The twelve lines of the spell were written in the same elegant scroll on Stellan's ribcage. The writing was black and not glowing, but they were there. I grinned.

"Brilliant, love." He smirked wickedly at me. "But you hardly needed an excuse to get me shirtless."

Fire exploded in my cheeks. I rolled my eyes. "We needed it somewhere that no one else would see – unless you've got other girls seeing you shirtless?"

"Not voluntarily."

I pushed his shirt back up to check that the spell transcribed correctly.

"Well, seems an odd spot for a shag if you ask me."

We both gasped and spun around – only to find Shylock and Weston standing there wearing shit-eating grins. I sagged with relief and leaned into Stellan.

"At least not if you can't be observational while you're at it to make sure no one is watching or standing behind you." Weston wagged his eyebrows. "But that takes training young Stellan lacks, because he's such a lovely gentleman."

Stellan scrubbed his face with his hands then stood, lifting me up with him. He cursed and shook his head. "Bloody hell, lads."

"Right back at you, mate." Shylock arched one black eyebrow and scanned us over with those sharp blue eyes of his. "What are you doing out here?"

"Um…"

Stellan cursed again. "You remember that thing Melanie and I were discussing before, in the library? That thing I hadn't told you about?"

Shylock narrowed his eyes. "And *still* haven't."

"Well…it's that." He held his hands up to stop them from asking questions. "I promise I will tell you, but it cannot be here."

Shylock pursed his lips and looked to me. "That's all great, lad. But I meant what are you doing here with… whoever this young lady might be?"

I gasped. "Oh shit. Guys, it's me, Ellie."

Weston nodded. "Prove it."

I frowned. "Um…you were a foot away from being the one I kissed Saturday night?"

"HA!" Weston clapped his hands. "That would've been awkward."

"And this disguise has to do with this other thing you're promising to tell us?"

"Yes, Shylock." Stellan wrapped his arm around my shoulders. "Listen, I need to get Ellie back to the shelter. There's a lot to discuss. If you'll just come with us then—"

"I'm afraid that is not possible," Shylock said in a stern, short voice.

Weston's eyes widened. "OH. Shite. You can't walk out of here with her, even in disguise."

Stellan narrowed his green eyes at them. "Why not? What's going on then?"

"Mass hysteria, I'm afraid."

Shylock rolled his eyes at Weston, then turned his attention back to Stellan. "Your parents were, in Weston's such eloquent wording, butt-hurt about the incident here with the Rebellion. They have decided to throw a masquerade ball this evening to assert their strength and dominance to those who oppose their rule."

"A…masquerade ball." Stellan tugged on his hair. "Here? Tonight?"

"Yeah, mate. It's chaos inside the palace. There's people everywhere. It's bloody nuts." Weston used his thumb to point behind him. "And your parents are on the hunt for you."

My stomach sank. I turned to Stellan. "Now what? Your parents know the truth…about everything. We can't risk it."

"I have a plan, if you care to hear it?"

"Thank bloody hell," Stellan said with a sigh. He glanced to me. "Shylock always has brilliant plans. He's the brains of our operation here."

"Well then, go on Mr. Holmes. We're listening."

He smirked then grew serious. "Stellan is going to leave Ellie here with us and return to the palace. He is to go to his parents and help them get the ball ready for this evening. They already have quite the schedule for you, cousin. Weston and I will bide some time with Ellie in the garden so as to not look suspicious and then we will escort her back through the tunnel to the shelter. Ellie will relay to us whatever it is that you just promised to inform us and then we will return to the palace, leaving her with Melanie."

Stellan opened his mouth then shut it. "I hate that plan, but it's the smartest one."

I put my hand on his ribcage, right over where I'd put the spell. "It's all right. We have to do this. They'll keep me safe, and I'm no damsel in distress. Especially not now."

He nodded. "All right, I'll go now—"

"Wait!" He was about to leave with the spell on his body. I didn't remember it enough and I needed to talk to Melanie about it. I pushed his shirt up and slid my hand underneath, then pressed my palm to his skin. "*Written, etched, burned in ink, on my skin these words to link.*"

Light flashed through his shirt and heat laced my palm. When it stopped, I pulled my hand out and found the spell copied onto my palm. I'd forgotten to think of a specific spot, but it didn't matter. I had it. Melanie would know how to make it go away.

I looked up and met Stellan's gaze. "Go. Do what you must to keep your parents happy. I'll talk to Melanie and see what I can figure out about this."

"To the tunnels. Soon." He pointed to the Dukes then squeezed my hand. "Be careful. All of you."

Then he dropped my hand and sprinted off and out of sight.

THIRTY-FIVE

ELLIE

"Wait, what?" Weston's voice rose as he shook his head and wrinkled his nose. "You can't be serious."

Shylock gave him a dead pan face. "She said the realm is dying and—"

"Oh, I know what she bloody well said." Weston pinched the bridge of his nose with his thumb and forefinger.

"Well you did say *what*, implying that you didn't." Shylock grumbled.

Melanie sat at the little table across from me in the library. She glanced from Shylock to Weston and back again. "And you two are supposed to be best friends?"

"I have bad days." Weston snapped as he rose from his chair and started pacing in the small library I now thought of as our meeting place. He stopped dead in the center of the room and threw out his arms. "The thing is dying."

"It's a good thing you soundproofed this place." I mumbled to Melanie. "I think he's just winding up."

"Why do neither of you seem surprised?" Weston motioned to Melanie and Shylock.

Shylock leaned back in the chair and steepled his hands, then pressed his pointer finger to his lips. "I had my suspicions."

"And you didn't think to share with me?" Weston pressed his hand to his chest.

He shrugged. "Proof was needed."

"You know, for someone so brilliant you're bloody daft." Weston dropped back down into his chair. "So this Stone is supposed to save the realm?"

I nodded. "That's what Araqiel said and we just got the spell when you two showed up. But I have no idea what it means."

Melanie sat so calm, the opposite of Weston. "What did the spell say?"

I held my hand in front of my face. "*By Earth and Air, Sea and Fire, Spirit in vine is ever dire. By the bottle, thy cauldron sings, thy quested spell within the strings. Find and seek, collect and call, the bouquet of magic First in haul. Bound by chaos, essence of youth, a drop of blood from a sharpened tooth. Skin of the dirt by the Fifth's moon night, winds of the Second, coiled and tight. Beware the beckon of charms and flame, to bind the Stone for which you claim.*"

Melanie chuckled. "You wrote it on your hand?"

"Well I didn't have a pen and paper handy." I held my hand out showing her. "What do you think it means."

She tilted her head to the side, studying the words. "Well, it's definitely a potion."

"What make you thinks so?" I laid my hand on the middle of the table for them all to see. Shylock turned his head in different directions yet said nothing.

Melanie cleared her throat and ran her finger over one of the lines on my hand. "Well this line here. *By the bottle, thy cauldron sings*, that part screams potion."

Weston folded his hands and put them on the table. "You're going to have to find the ingredients for that potion." He pointed to my hand. "That line there. *Find and seek, collect and call.* Means you're going to have to find shit."

"Well done, cousin." Shylock looked impressed as he nodded toward Weston.

"You're not the only one with a brain inside your head." He snapped back.

"Wait, wait, wait. Hold up. Listen to this line, *By Earth and Air, Sea and Fire, Spirit in vine is ever dire.* It's talking about the elements, which makes sense because Araqiel told me the Stone, *and now me,* create the elements. So what if what we're collecting represent each of the elements?" When I didn't get an answer, I looked up and found the three of them staring at me. "What?"

Melanie grinned and leaned back in her chair. "That is exactly what that means."

"For not being familiar with our world, you do come up with brilliant ideas." Shylock arched an eyebrow at me and nodded with approval.

"Again, she has a bloody brain." Weston sighed. "You don't have to sound so condescending when someone other than you says something smart."

Shylock flashed him a smile. "And yet every time you do, I'm still surprised."

"For someone so smart you would think you would've learned by now. The definition of stupidity is doing the same thing over and over again and expecting different results."

"So like how you continually date vapid courtiers…that might be considered stupidity?" Shylock gave him a direct stare.

"As much as I like seeing you two rip on each other, can we focus?" I tried to get them to stop their staring contest.

Without looking away from Weston, Shylock said, "You'll be traveling to the other realms."

My jaw dropped. "W-what? Why?"

Finally he blinked away from Weston. "The line, *thy quested spell within the strings,* I do believe within the strings is a fancy way of saying within the realms. Then there's the line, *Bound by chaos, essence of youth.* The fae are everything that is chaos and they're immortal. yet they never age. Then *Sharpened tooth*, vampires obviously. And I must say their species fascinates me. How does one survive off of blood?"

"Fangers? Not sure I'd be excited about that visit."

"Do let me know what it's like to get bitten, will you?" Shylock folded his hands. "Now for the next—"

"*What?* How do you figure I'm going to get bit?" My

heart raced. I didn't want anything biting me. Let alone something with fangs.

"Vampires," He said as if that explained it all.

I shook my head. "Yeah, no one is sticking their fangs into me."

"Right. But if they do—"

"Shylock, stop." Weston chided. "Focus."

"Sadly, I fear he is correct. That was my first thought as well. Seems a bit obvious, though I don't see how you'll get blood to put in our potion, but I assume that part will make itself known at the time." Melanie sighed. "But I'm more concerned about the others, Like the next one, *Skin of the dirt by the Fifth's moon night.* The word Fifth is capitalized, which means it's referring to the Fifth Realm. Shifter realm. Skin of the dirt leads me to think of earth, though the *skin* part is concerning given the nature of the species."

"Apparently, you're about to have the adventure of a lifetime." Shylock's gaze looked uncharacteristically wistful. "Shame. I'd love to study the different realms."

Weston snapped his fingers excitedly. "So then *Winds of the Second, coiled and tight...*this means our realm...you need...air...from here? How do you put air into a potion?"

"It can't be a coincidence that Ellie here can control air." Melanie pursed her lips.

Shylock nodded. "Save that one for last and I will think on it. I believe it will be the most difficult."

My mind was spinning. There was too much information to process at once.

Melanie arched one eyebrow. "Really? Not *The bouquet*

of magic First in haul? That's the one I'm concerned over. First Realm is a complicated, messy place and that line could mean anything."

Shylock's eyes flashed. "You're absolutely right. How challenging that one is. I shall work on it as well."

"Umm...lads..." Weston raised his hand then pointed to the last line on my palm. "Is no one bothered by this, *Beware the beckon of charms and flame, to bind the Stone for which you claim?* What the bloody hell does that mean?"

I groaned and ran my hands through my hair. "Guys. *Guys.* You're getting ahead of yourselves. How the hell am I supposed to travel to and from the *other* realms?"

Melanie grimaced. "Trust me, that's what I've been thinking the most on. I wish I had an answer, but I don't know. You have to go back to First Realm and ask Araqiel."

"*We.* Because you're coming with me," I said in a rush. There was no way she wasn't coming. She'd just proved she knew a tremendous amount about this stuff. I needed her. "I won't take no for an answer. This is too important. I'm too new at this. I need you."

She opened her mouth but shut it. Then she nodded. "If you wish me to be there, then I will go. But now we must discuss how we're getting back to the portal."

I already felt better knowing she was going.

Shylock smirked. "Lucky for us, the king and queen have decided to throw a ridiculous ball this evening. Ellie is already in disguise and has been seen at the palace, so all you would need is a good disguise for Melanie... and a proper distraction."

Weston threw his hand up and grinned. "I call dibs on the distraction."

Melanie pulled her wand from a pocket in her dress. She held it up and the tip of it sparked. Her brown hair turned black and her brown eyes changed to a bright blue. "I've always wanted to go to a ball. This face should do the trick."

Shylock grabbed a pen and piece of paper off the desk nearby then scribbled something down. When he was finished, he handed the paper to Melanie. "Your names for this evening will be on the list to get in, Kathryn and Lily Seamour. Just look the part when you arrive and I will handle the rest."

Melanie took the paper and stuffed it in her cleavage. "Perfect. So we're all set then—"

"WAIT!" I cursed as I realized I'd almost forgotten. I held my hand out to her. "Can you take this off of my hand? I don't know how and we can't be having other people see it."

Melanie scowled. "Of course I can, but this is a long spell. The wording is crucial, we need to be able to read it."

I grinned. "Oh, don't worry I put it on Stellan's rib cage."

She arched one now black eyebrow. "Are you telling me that any time we want to see the spell he has to take his shirt off?"

"Yup." I chuckled. I'd have to get him shirtless. It was the best decision I'd made so far. "Brilliant, right?"

"No, definitely not." She sighed, "But it'll do."

She pressed the tip of her wand to my palm and the words started to slowly disappear, like vanishing ink.

Shylock stood and brushed his pants off. "Right, then, so we're ready to go?"

Nerves fluttered in my stomach. "What about Stellan? He doesn't know the plan."

"We may or may not have the opportunity to inform him of the details. If we can safely, we will."

Weston chuckled. "If not, he'll have to just get ready for a wild ride."

THIRTY-SIX

STELLAN

BEING PARTED from Ellie was grueling. It'd only been hours, yet it felt like weeks. So much had happened. It'd shaken her. I was supposed to be with her, not standing here like some pompous ass on parade. But my parents had demanded it. Everything about this situation grated on my nerves. The floods of people surrounding me, the boring string music, the amount of wasteful food being passed around, and this bloody get-up that had been laid out for me...I sighed.

The thick black coat fell from my shoulders all the way down to my knees. The material was cumbersome, with overbearing silver embroidery around my wrists, down the lapels, and over the pockets. Beads of sweat gathered on the back of my neck and rolled under my shirt. I looked like a bloody parading peacock. I tugged at the matching black vest underneath my coat. It was fitted tight to my chest and I wanted nothing more than to tear it off. The three little buttons would pop off so easily. I had things to do. I had to help Ellie. Instead, I stood here in boots polished to a shine I could see myself in. What a waste of time.

Shylock melted from the crowd of courtiers who walked around from the front of the castle to the gardens in the back. He had a statuesque woman with him. Her strawberry blonde hair was piled on top of her head, with large curls hanging down. I ground my teeth together. He wasn't supposed to be shopping for a girlfriend. He brought her to my side, and she gave me a small bow. Her sapphire eyes matched her dress perfectly. Yet they were nearly hidden by a black mask that tied at the back of her head. She too had the customary intricate golden embroidery on her navy blue dress that spoke of money and status. It wound around her sleeves and down the front of her dress.

Her voice was deep and sultry. "Your Highness."

"A pleasure." I said absently as I narrowed my eyes at Shylock. "Cousin."

He wrinkled his nose at me. "Why do you look cross with me?"

I glanced to the woman. "No reason." I had every reason in the world. I wish he wore one of those masks with the elastic around the back so I could pull at it and let it smack in his face. Instead he had the traditional ties, like me and everyone else.

This wasn't Ellie. I felt it in my bones. He was supposed to be watching her, helping her figure out our next step, and here he was dallying about with some woman I'd never seen in my life. Irritation ate at me. "Did you complete the task I asked of you?"

I didn't look him in the eye, didn't turn to face him. My Eloise was out there with one less protector. Not that she needed it. I would just feel better if she had both of my cousins. Just then a tray of food floated by. Crackers with something smeared on them. Shylock grabbed one and held it to his mouth. When he went to take a bite my irritation got the better of me and I swatted it out of his hand.

Shylock looked to the cracker on the floor, then back to me. "Have I offended you in some way?"

"Are you bloody daft?" I sucked in a breath through my teeth. The courtier next to Shylock snickered and covered her mouth in that dainty way, fingers pressed to her lips. I straightened my stance. "Apologies, lady, my cousin forgot something important."

I glanced around at the sea of courtiers, all with their huge dresses, laughing and floating through the gardens without a care in the world. If my parents wanted to give the impression their rule was never stronger, they were succeeding. Among all these people I couldn't find Ellie. I craned my neck and plastered a fake smile on my lips, waving at the stray person here and there.

"Prince Stellan." The woman whispered. "It's me."

"Pardon?" I looked her up and down. "Have we met?"

She leaned in closer and lowered her voice. "Many times. It's me, Melanie."

My eyebrows shot up and I fought to control my features. "Melanie, you look…"

"Different, I know. Ellie insisted I come with you this time." She ran her hands over the dress. "Something, isn't it?"

I nodded. "Quite."

Weston wound his way through a group of women vying for his attention. With a roguish grin, he lifted one woman's hand off his chest as he passed. He walked over to our little group and shifted from one foot to the other. "I don't know what that was."

I pursed my lips. "Don't you?"

He held his hands in surrender. "Nope."

"Is he playing dumb?" Shylock asked Melanie. "He is, isn't he?"

"Yes." She giggled.

I leaned in closer to Weston. "Where's Ellie?"

Weston grabbed one of the cracker things from another tray that floated by. "She was right behind me." He shoved the cracker in his mouth.

"Why does he get to eat and I don't?" Shylock motioned to his snack on the floor.

"Because he did what I asked." I straightened my jacket. "Sort of."

Weston motioned to a breath-taking blonde sauntering her way toward us and I sighed with relief. I'd know that walk anywhere. I'd know the feel of her aura in any disguise. She wore a long black dress that stood stark as midnight against her pale skin. Shining gold embroidery wound around the sleeves across the front of the bodice. The dress was tight to her waist then puffed out like many of the ballgowns here. Curly blonde locks of hair fell down around her neck and face, while the rest was piled on top of her head. A black lace mask ran over her nose and swirled around her eyes. A coy smile played on her lips while she moved toward us.

"Good lord, I don't think he's breathing." Shylock sounded appalled.

Weston went up on his toes to look me in the face. "Nope. Definitely not."

I didn't turn toward him, didn't take my eyes off the beauty in front of me. It wasn't her looks that made her beautiful, it was her soul. I felt it deep in my own. I'd know her anywhere, could feel her in any place. Shylock slapped me in the middle of my back with one quick rap, like I was choking.

"Now I'm glad I didn't eat the bloody things." He hit me again.

I sucked in a sharp breath and batted him away. "I'm fine."

She made her way to our group then grabbed both sides of her dress and gave me a curtsy. "*Prince* Stellan."

Her lips curved into a smile and I did my best to keep up appearances by bowing in return. "My lady."

Shylock leaned down and whispered in my ear. "That's Ellie."

"I bloody well know who she is." *I'd know her anywhere.*

The rest of the group chuckled as I moved to stand

beside her. I wanted to take her hand, to pull her body close to mine, to feel that she was safe with me. But I couldn't. I felt the eyes of my people on me and I had to act as the proper puppet my parents thought they'd raised. "Now that we're all here. What's next?"

Melanie grabbed a flute of sparkling fluid off another tray that glided by soundlessly. "We need to speak with Araqicl. I believe you have to venture to the other realms."

I arched my eyebrow at that. "Interesting."

"Quite." She took a sip of her drink.

I offered my arm to Ellie. "Shall we dance?"

Her eyes widened. "Here? Now?"

"Yes." I glanced around at the courtiers watching our interaction. "Come, Eloise. Surely a little dancing won't hurt."

"Very well." She took my arms and pressed her fingers into it. Her words were low as she hissed, "I'm not a good dancer."

I smiled. "Not to worry. You look lovely."

"I did Loki proud with this disguise." She beamed up at me.

A chuckle escaped my lips and I shook my head. "Even Thor would be fooled."

"I know, right." She looked down at herself and whispered, "I think I prefer leggings over this shit though."

I shook myself, trying to get the image of that out of my head. Instead I focused on guiding her toward the dance area. There in the center of the garden, high above a three-tiered fountain, was the dance floor. I was used to this sight but Ellie's eyes widened like saucers as she reached out and touched the bubbles floating up from the fountain. They were large, and when the candlelight hit them, the bubbles glowed as if filled with glitter. Ellie poked it and it floated away with the others. Her eyes followed it all the way up to where the bubbles collected, forming a moving dance floor.

"Shall we?" I motioned to a larger bubble forming just in front of us.

"Yes." She breathed and grabbed up one side of her dress.

Together we stepped onto the bubble as it caught us. She tilted back and I laid my hand across her lower back, pulling her to face me. This close her ocean scent enveloped me, and I wanted more from her. I held my other hand out to the side. "Take my hand."

I pressed my fingers to her back to pull her closer. She took my hand and rested her other on my shoulder. Her face fell and became very serious. "I'm not kidding. I don't know how."

"Not a problem." As our bubble rose up to the middle of the dance floor, a new song started. It was a delicate orchestra piece with a sensual undertone of yearning. It was fitting for how I felt about her. I pressed my hand to the small of her back and began guiding her around the dance floor. The bubbles rose under our feet with every step we took. They twirled and clung to Ellie's dress like we were moving through champagne bubbles.

She giggled. "This is amazing."

I couldn't agree more. This night was amazing. The candles, the bubbles, her. I would wear this get-up any day of the week if it meant being here with her so she could see something magical worth saving in our realm. We glided effortlessly around the dance floor. Courtiers pointed toward us and whispered to each other. Off to the side, my parents stood side by side, watching me with soft smiles. Playing the doting parents of the only child they had. No one would know by the warm, loving expressions on their faces that they were colder than ice in real life.

Ellie giggled and looked down at herself. I turned away from my family and watched her dress finish turning from the darkest black to a bright pink. All around Courtier's outfits were shifting colors.

"Is that supposed to happen?" She glanced around at the other women

"No." I turned her and found Weston standing at the corner of the dance floor with Melanie next to him. He shot magic across the floor, changing all the colors as he pleased. Beside Melanie stood Shylock, shaking his head with disapproval. He tried to keep up with Weston's rapid fire by changing the dresses back to their original color. It had drawn attention away from us and back onto the others. "Now's the time."

I guided her around the dance floor once more before stopping in front of Weston. "Now?"

Before he could answer me a blast of orange magic fired through the center of the dance floor. The bubbles all exploded at once. Screams echoed in my ears as people plummeted to the ground. My stomach flew up into my throat and my arms pinwheeled for a second before I let my power go and silver magic shot out of me in all different directions. I latched onto Melanie and Ellie, pulling them to my sides. Melanie yanked her wand from inside her dress and fired at the ground beneath us. A large bubble spread over the ground and we hit it with a slap. It dipped under our weight. Weston and Shylock dropped in beside us.

"That was close." Ellie pressed up on her elbow. "We gotta get out of here."

Chaos rained down all around us as more people landed on Melanie's bubble. We were tossed around like popcorn in a pan. Each of us popping up then dropping back down. Shylock lay as stiff as a board with his hands close to his sides while Weston shoved him toward the edge. "Move, you wanker."

Melanie held her wand at the ready as she fought her dress and crawled out over the bubble. "Where did it come from?"

"You saw the orange." I took Ellie's hand and pulled her with me as he fought our way from the cumbersome air bag.

Courtiers were falling like snow onto it, landing and floating back up, making it hard to fight our way out. It was an array of colors and screams. Fabric. So much fabric. The women all looked like bouncing cupcakes. The guards ran out into the gardens and around the bubbles. Closest to the wall, a swarm of black cloaks pushed on the line of Royal Guards. It was purple against the rising black tide.

"Time to go." I slid down the side of the bubble. When my feet hit the ground I turned and pulled Ellie out toward me. Her skirts rode up, exposing her boots and undergarments. When she landed beside me the material dropped down around her with a rustling sound.

"This right here is why superheroes wear pants." She curled her hands into fists.

Melanie dropped down on my other side with her wand pointed at the line of Ladarious' men. A shot of white light fired from the tip and hit one of his followers right in the face. He fell to the ground. Standing just a few feet behind him was Ladarious. His blue eyes sparkled when our gazes met. The candlelight that once looked romantic looked sinister against the dark tattoos on his pale skin.. I took a step toward him, ready to join in with the Royal Guard to hold him back.

Ellie squeezed my hand. "Not now."

I gritted my teeth. How could I leave my people like this? Now, when they needed me. Weston and Shylock ran ahead of me.

Weston called over his shoulder. "We got it."

Ellie started yanking me back toward the wing where the portal was. "You can do more for them by coming now."

I hesitated. Ladarious waved me forward. I wanted nothing more than to face off against him. To burn him to ash. Melanie shoved me in the chest. "We must go. Now. While everyone is distracted."

I growled and turned from him, wanting to tear him apart but knowing if I didn't go my realm would end. Courtiers raced by us in droves, each of them wide eyed and screaming in panic. Chaos rained down. Even the guard had trouble moving through the onslaught. Melanie fisted my jacket, holding onto me to guide her through the stampede. I swung Ellie back beside her. She clutched my hand tightly and I curled my fingers hard around hers. There was no way I was going to let either of them get herded in with the madness. Behind me the sounds of war broke out. Bombs exploded and the ground shook beneath my feet.

Wilbur ran straight at me. "Stellan, you must—"

"I must nothing." I snapped.

I tried to step around him but he blocked my path. There he was with his white puffy hair and pristine suit. Nothing and no one touched him. He barely raised a hand to help anyone. Yet he thought to order me?

I ground my teeth together. "Move."

"I insist that you turn at once." He puffed up his chest.

"You insist?" With my one free hand I flipped my magic toward him. I lifted him up and tossed him overhead toward Ladarious' men. "Do it your damn self."

He landed on the ground and rolled in the dirt just behind the Royal Guard. He rose to his feet and dusted himself off, glaring at me. But I didn't have time for anything else. We had to take advantage of this moment. I hurried Ellie and Melanie through the gardens, winding around plants and fountains. Everywhere I turned there was someone running or hiding. We came upon the wing for the portal. I glanced over my shoulder, eyeing the flashing lights in the distance. Those lights of spells and a skirmish I should be in the middle of.

Ellie dropped my hand and grabbed up the front of her skirt, then leapt through the glass door into the marble terrace. She turned on her heels and gazed out over the scene. Her eyes widened. "I think the line of the Royal Guards just broke."

She was right. The flares of spells being fired moved closer to the castle. Closer to us. I hurried to the staircase then stepped to the side and ushered Ellie and Melanie to go through first. With a last look at my people fighting to hold Ladarious back, I jumped down the stairs before anyone saw. If one courtier or one guard saw, a swarm of people would've come to hide here.

A huge explosion rocked the outside of the castle and we stumbled into the walls as we ran for the portal. I placed my hand on the mirror, ready to take that leap but not wanting to. Another explosion and it sounded like the world was going to drop down on top of us. Just as the portal opened, I wrapped arms around Melanie and Ellie and dove into the abyss.

THIRTY-SEVEN

ELLIE

WE FLEW through the portal and crashed onto the cold hardwood floor in a tangled pile of limbs and curse words. Something heavy laid over my back, pressing me into the ground – or whatever I was on. Silk brushed against my face and then I felt the soft, warm skin of Stellan's bare chest. *Oh, not ground. Stellan. Shit.* But the black hair in my mouth was not mine. I tried to push myself up when a wall of navy-blue satin smacked me in the cheek.

Melanie cursed and groaned from above me and I felt her wiggle against my back. "My hair. Someone's on my bloody hair."

I couldn't see a damn thing with her dress in my face, so I just yanked my arms back against my side. "Better?" I said while spitting her hair out of my mouth.

Cold air washed over my back and the weight vanished. I sighed and collapsed against Stellan's chest. The quick beat of his heart under my ear was more comforting than I could have expected. I just laid there, sucking in deep breaths of his crisp autumn and soap scent.

Stellan groaned and coughed. "Mistakes were made."

I grinned against his skin and pushed up on my hands. Curly blonde hair bounced over my shoulders. His brow was furrowed in pain but those pale green eyes sparkled. "Hey, that's my line."

Melanie cursed. "Bullocks, we forgot to remove our disguises. Here we go."

Before I could move an inch, light flashed around me. Stellan's eyes widened and I felt him freeze under me. But then a wide grin spread across his face. Darkness slid over my peripheral vision then moved all the way down until those blonde curls were gone and my black wavy strands were back – and draped around his face.

"There you are," he whispered up at me.

My cheeks warmed. "You look pretty with dark hair."

His eyebrows twitched and a sly smirk spread across his face as he looked up at me. "Like Shylock pretty or Zuriel pretty?"

I narrowed my eyes. "This feels like a trap."

"If I'm Zuriel pretty with black hair, I may just make the switch."

I snorted and shook my head. "Please don't. I'm not sure my heart, or my body, could handle that level of hotness on you."

"Hmmm…" he pursed his lips. I felt each of his fingertips press into my waist. "Right. May have to let you get used to all *this* first."

Melanie groaned. "Don't make me throw up in this corset, I might break a rib or choke."

Stellan chuckled and lifted his hands up by his shoulders, then flexed his fingers. Silver smoke billowed from his palms and coiled around my body. I rose off of his chest and into the air until I was standing upright with my feet on the ground.

I exhaled and adjusted my corset. "Welcome back to New York."

"Always an interesting experience here." Stellan stood and brushed off his black pants. He glanced back and forth between me and Melanie. "Right, then. Shall we?"

"I hope he's here."

Stellan turned to me. "Why wouldn't he be?"

"Well, I mean, it's like eleven in the evening—"

"Araqiel already knows we're here. Trust me." Stellan pointed behind me.

Melanie eyed the hallway. She was back to her brown eyed, brown haired self, which was comforting. "He's right. Let's get up there before we wake any of the other angels."

Other angels. I chuckled and shook my head as I struggled to catch my breath. We were standing between the bank of mirrored elevators and the portal back to Second Realm. The night hadn't gone entirely to plan, but we'd made it here. I couldn't believe what my life had become basically overnight. It was all so surreal. I kept waiting to wake up.

Stellan pressed his palm to the small of my back and urged me forward. Only then did I realize Melanie had walked to the next hallway. Together we walked over and stopped beside her. She was staring at nothing, with a crazy sort of haunted expression, like she'd just seen a ghost. Her face was pale. Every muscle in her body seemed to be tight and rigid.

I reached out and placed my hand on her arm. "Melanie?"

She jumped, which was entirely unlike her. But then she shook herself and gave me a nod. "After you, Stellan."

He smiled and took my hand, then led us straight down another short hallway that dead-ended a few feet away. I was about to ask what we were doing when he pressed his palm to the white wall and light flashed. The wall split open, revealing that same elevator we'd taken from the lobby with my parents. We hurried inside and the doors closed behind us. There were no buttons inside, the elevator seemed to just know where we were going. Although I assumed there was only one stop on this ride.

I shook my head. "I love magic."

Stellan and Melanie both looked over their shoulders and smiled at me.

"Oh, just a reminder, Thor," Stellan said with a cocky grin and a wink. "No using magic outside of this building."

I pursed my lips. "Is that one of those rules with an asterisk and a disclaimer that lists a bunch of instances where using magic is allowed?"

Melanie threw her hand out and shook her head. "Don't you dare give her any ideas."

"Hey, I was—"

The elevator stopped and the doors opened.

Araqiel stood on the other side dressed in the same all white outfit from this morning and holding three tacos in each hand. His eyes sparkled when he spotted us, his wings even twitched. He gave us a nod jumped into the elevator with us. "Well, well, fancy meetin' you here."

Stellan frowned. "Why are you taking an elevator if you can fly?"

I scoffed. "Fly? With fresh tacos? Amateur hour."

Araqiel grinned and pointed one handful of tacos at me. "You and me are gonna be friends, I see it…but not enough to share these tacos."

I chuckled. "That's okay. I'm still nauseous from our tumble through the portal."

He threw his head back and laughed. "Yeah, I saw that. Bold move. But then, I expect nothing less from Miss Melanie."

Stellan scowled so hard his eyebrows hung low over his eyes. "You know her?"

Araqiel rolled his eyes. "I know everyone. But particularly those who travel to realms they don't belong in."

Melanie shrugged one shoulder.

The elevator stopped again. This time it opened on the top floor, where Araqiel's office was. "Come on, kids. You talk, I eat."

We followed behind him in silence until we got into his office. It looked the same as it did this morning, except there was no sunlight streaming in from the terrace. Instead, the cold air of New York's autumn swept through the room. I shivered and wrapped my arms around myself.

Araqiel settled into the chair behind his big wooden desk, sat his taco feast down, and proceeded to lick each of his fingers clean. He glanced up at me and frowned, then waved one hand in the air and the cold breeze vanished as the opening to the terrace sealed shut with sparkling clear glass. Three chairs appeared in front of us out of nowhere. He shoved an entire taco in his mouth as we sat.

He swallowed then licked his lips. "Have to say, I am very impressed that you've returned here on the same day."

I frowned. "You knew we'd be coming back." It wasn't a question. He definitely knew. Our arrival was not in the least bit of a surprise to him.

Stellan leaned forward. "You knew about the spell?"

Araqiel arched one eyebrow. "It's best for you if you just assume I know everything. Will save us time and headaches. However, I would like to hear from Eloise on what she found anyway."

I nodded and cleared my throat…then launched into the story of what happened at Anchor Point. When I finished, I leaned back in the chair and sighed. "So we have the spell, and after deliberation with Melanie and the Dukes, we think this spell is requiring us to go to the other realms to collect specific ingredients to use in a potion."

Stellan's eyes widened. He hadn't been filled in on *that* part of the plan yet. There simply hadn't been the time or a safe place to do so while at the masquerade ball. Melanie looked uncharacteristically nervous. Not in her face, her eyes were rock steady, but her legs bounced and she kept clasping and unclasping her hands in her lap.

Araqiel sighed and the sound made my stomach turn and tighten into knots. Anything that made an angel sound like *that* sent my anxiety through the roof. "You're right, you do have to go to the other realms."

My breath left me in a rush. Stellan cursed. Melanie just sat there frozen. I realized in that moment I'd been secretly hoping Araqiel would tell us we were wrong and that it was much easier than we suspected.

Araqiel steepled his hands in front of his face. "And you're not gonna like how that works."

I groaned and ran my hands through my hair. "Just tell us. Don't sugar coat it."

He glanced between the three of us then nodded. "The only way to access the other realms is here, right beside the entrance to Second Realm. But *only* a Realm Royal can access the elevators to the other realms. And no, Ellie, that does not include the Stone Keeper."

"So you're saying—"

"Stellan will *have* to accompany you, not that I thought he wouldn't. However, without him you will not be able to get in or out of the other realms."

Stellan rubbed his palms together and nodded. "Okay, so I just access it the same way I do our own?"

"No. Not in the least bit." He balled his hand into a fist and light flashed between his fingers. When it faded, he held his hand out in front of us and opened his fingers. In his palm sat a single simple golden ring, no stone or anything, just a band. "Stellan must wear this ring in order to access the elevators and get in the other realms."

"The one ring to rule them all," I whispered and snatched the ring from his hand. I ran my fingertips over the gold metal. *"My precious."*

"However..." Araqiel waited until we were all looking at him. "The ring only grants you access to each of the other realms once."

There was something in the tone of his voice that sent my pulse flying. "What else? There's something else you're not saying yet."

"The ring only works once per realm. Once in, once out. That's it." He leaned forward and his eyes suddenly looked grave. "And the ring only lasts three days, then it vanishes."

I gasped. "Vanishes? Then what?"

Araqiel grimaced. "If the ring vanishes and you're not in First or Second Realm when it happens, you are stuck there. Forever. Unless a Royal of that realm takes pity on you, which I assure you is not an option you want to plan for."

I cursed and buried my head in my hands.

"So we move fast," Stellan said in a hard voice.

"And we don't look back."

"No pressure." I looked up and sighed, again. With a shudder, I handed the ring to my soulmate. Once he slid it onto his finger, I turned back to Araqiel. "Okay, when does our countdown start?"

"Look at your left hand." Araqiel pointed to my hand. "It already did."

We all looked down at my left hand and gasped. There on the inside of my wrist were four glowing purple numbers – *and they were counting down.* My stomach turned and my heart fluttered.

71:59:56

71:59:55

71:59:54

The office door behind us flew open. We all jumped and spun around just as a young-looking boy with white angel wings rushed inside with wide, panicked eyes. *"Araqiel! Araqiel! Ladarious is in Penn Station!"*

All three of us leapt to our feet.

"WHAT?"

"HOW?"

Araqiel's face turned menacing. His glare icy hot. He looked to us. "We're not allowed to interfere unless you have him detained."

My eyes widened. "But—"

"GO. NOW. Before he destroys Manhattan."

THIRTY-EIGHT

ELLIE

THE SECOND THE subway rolled to a stop at Penn Station I knew we were in big trouble.

The subway platform was unlike anything I'd ever seen before. It was shoulder-to-shoulder crowded, but everyone was pushing and shoving. Every single face in the crowd was panicked and terrified. Their eyes all wide, their faces pale. The subway stopped and the crowd rushed forward before the doors were even open. Dozens of people were thrown against the train itself, their faces smushing up against the glass windows. People on the subway with us cursed and dashed away from the doors, hugging the far walls of the train.

"Why are they all girls? Why so young?" Stellan mumbled with a concerned scowl, his gaze whipping around. "What's happening here? Are you seeing this?"

I hadn't noticed they were all girls. I'd been too busy with their screaming. But I saw now. I looked down at the girls pressed against the subway doors and pounding on the glass and saw their shirts said *Chanegan.* The realization hit me hard.

"Tonight was the Chanegan concert," I heard myself say in a daze. *This is bad. This is really bad.*

"What is a Chanegan?" Stellan hissed.

"A girl group. Pop music. Like The Spice Girls?" I grabbed their arms and dragged them to one side of the doorway. "Stand side to side!"

Stellan looked like he was going to throw up. "What? That'll weaken us. We need to—"

"To listen to a New Yorker on how to get through a crowd like this. Yeah, I thought so, too. Now, get behind me dammit or you'll never get through this!" I pushed my way in front of him, then gripped his hand in mine. I glanced around him to Melanie and saw she'd taken his other hand. I nodded. "Don't let go. Ninja grips, folks. And whatever you do, *do not slow down.* This is the Red Sea and you're Moses. Part it."

Stellan's eyes widened. "I don't know what that means."

I cursed. Of course they wouldn't. The doors started to open and the crowd stuck their hands through the cracks. Their fingers gripped the doors as they tried to force them open faster. It was something out of a zombie movie, but I wasn't allowed to shoot them.

I squared my shoulders and held my head high. I could do this. This was not much different than rush hour on a Friday night. I was a New Yorker. Crowds didn't scare us. We were made for this. I gripped Stellan's hand tighter and focused on the doors that were crawling open like they couldn't handle the attack. "Show weakness and you'll get trampled. Bulldoze anything in your path. Follow my lead. Once we get off the train, we turn and go in a single-file line. Shoulders back, full steam ahead."

Stellan and Melanie both cursed. It was strange to be the one leading them for a change. To be the one not afraid or hesitant. It reminded me that I wasn't weak. I wasn't a coward. I was strong and I could handle anything.

Ladarious picked the wrong city to mess with.

Not on my watch, Satan.

The doors screeched and then flew all the way open. I knew how this went, you hesitate you die – metaphorically speaking, mostly. I leapt out onto the platform and dropped my shoulder to push through the crowd. I'd played hockey, I knew how to cut my way through. Stellan's grip tightened on mine but I didn't dare look back. People were pushing against us from all sides. The screaming echoed off the tile walls and down the long platform. Magic would've made this a million times easier, but there was no way we could risk that kind of exposure.

About ten feet into the crowd, I turned and faced forward and put my game face on. My *get out of my way, I'm a New Yorker* face. The one that got me through rush hour and Times Square. The one that made tourists jump out of my way. I threw my hand out in front of me, using it to slice my path through the crowd. Except there was one major fault in our plan. We should have changed clothes. This stupid ball gown had like a six-foot diameter. Every other second my dress was tugged down as people stepped on it, and I needed both hands so I couldn't pick it up.

I cursed and screamed at the top of my lungs, "*MOVE*."

Only about a dozen people jumped out of my way, but it was enough to get out of the subway platform and to the gates. Women barged the emergency exit gate while others leapt over the turnstiles. Little girls were crying and shrieking. I wanted to stop and help them all but we couldn't. Ladarious had to be stopped and we were the only ones that could do it.

As we pushed through the gate, I glanced over my shoulder to make sure Melanie was still back there. She was. I turned back and looked up ahead. Penn Station was massive, there were a million places Ladarious could've been, but my gut told me he was straight ahead by the Long Island Railroad tracks. Cold, menacing energy blasted down the corridor of fast food restaurants and touristy shops. All of which were closed. People were throwing shoes and purses into the glass windows to break *in*.

There was a staircase to my right that led up to the main level where Amtrak was, but it was at a standstill. People were pushing and shoving to get up the stairs. A middle-aged woman flew back then tumbled down the steps like someone had thrown her. It took everything in me not to stop and help. But I had to focus on Ladarious.

This is what he wanted.

Chaos. Pandemonium. Mass hysteria.

He wanted us to choose between saving innocent

humans and taking him down, but the joke was on him. I was calling his bluff. I was going *for him.* And judging by the fact that every person sprinting past us was looking *behind* them, I knew my gut feeling was right. I reached down without slowing my pace and hiked up my ridiculous dress, balling it in my hand so I wouldn't step on it anymore.

Something roared like a dinosaur up ahead and the ground rumbled under my feet. The whole building shook. Stones and chunks of cement dropped from the ceiling. People screamed and dodged the debris, diving out of the way. I yanked Stellan's arm and dragged them behind a section of the wall that jutted out just as a massive dragon smashed into the pathway. The thing had to be fifty feet tall. Its silver scales looked like pure metal. It threw its wings to the side and swiped out several pillars, sending huge chunks of ceiling to the ground.

"It's not real," Melanie whispered from behind me.

I shook my head. I knew that, I did, but it still looked pretty damn real. If it wasn't for the orange smoke just barely lingering around the dragon's feet, I might've questioned it more. "It's real *to them.* What do we do? How do we erase what they've seen?"

Melanie frowned then pointed her wand up in the air. Light exploded from the tip like an atomic bomb. Little droplets of light fell from the ceiling like glowing rain. Each time a drop hit a person, they stopped running. Their screams halted. They just started acting *normal.* Like nothing had happened.

"That'll only cover the ones *here.* Anyone who has already made it out…" she shuddered.

Stellan grimaced. "We'll have to talk to Araqiel after we handle this tosser."

Something was better than nothing, so I nodded. That would have to do for now. I turned to face forward and my heart stopped.

There he was, in all his hideous glory. He stood at the entrance of the Long Island Railroad waiting area, right where all the train tracks were. The florescent lights above made his bald head glow like a light bulb, blurring out those awful tattoos on his scalp. His light blue eyes sparkled, like this was the most fun he ever had. The sickening grin on his face confirmed it. My stomach turned as he threw his arms out to his side and laughed.

I wanted to fly into battle like Thor at the end of Ragnarök, but I had to remind myself that I wasn't Thor. I still hadn't mastered my power yet, especially lightning. And war was not something I was used to. But the two people I trusted the most *did* know, so I turned to them. "What do we do now? How do we do this?"

Stellan narrowed his eyes on something up ahead. "We need eyes on the land before we move."

I opened my mouth to ask how we did that when he threw his hand out in front of him. Silver magic shimmered from his palm, his pale gaze locked in the distance. I turned to follow his stare and grinned. At the far side of the opening to the waiting area, a sign had fallen to the ground – a sign made out of mirror. I watched as it subtly angled upward until we could see the whole layout of the waiting area around the corner.

It wasn't the easiest to see, but I could just make out the innocent humans huddled on the ground all around him and the ones still fleeing up the escalators.

"I don't see any of his men," Melanie whispered. "I think he came alone."

Stellan smirked. "Not very smart."

"Let's be thankful for that," Melanie hissed.

I leaned toward them. "So what's the plan?"

"I'm going to teleport to the far side of that room and make my presence known. He'll assume you two will be over there with me. The illusion won't last long, but long enough for you two to get in place." Stellan looked to me and pointed straight ahead. "When he turns, I want you to run to the other side and get behind that pole. Melanie, take this side. I don't want him to see you, just in case he doesn't know you're here. Okay?"

Melanie pulled her wand out and nodded.

"And what do we do when we get there?"

The cold look in Stellan's eyes gave me chills. "Kill him." And then he *vanished.*

Kill him. Right. No big deal.

"Ellie, he won't hesitate to kill you and that *is* his goal," Melanie said low and in a rush. "And remember, he's going to make you see things just try and focus on the strongest point of energy and aim at that, that'll be him."

"O-okay."

"Be ready."

Any second Ladarious would see Stellan and I'd have to move, so I grabbed the hem of my long ball gown and fisted it tight. I nodded and rolled to the balls of my feet. My heart pounded against my rib cage like it was trying to smash its way through.

A woman wailed at a high pitch around the corner and I gasped. *This is it.*

Ladarious spun around and even from just his profile I saw his grin widen. He threw his arms out to the side then bent over at the waist in a mock-bow. "Well, well, Your Highness…you're late to the party, I'm afraid."

Except he didn't move, he still stood right in the opening. Right in the path I needed to take to the other side so we could surround him.

"*ELLIE! I got him! Down the escalators!*" Stellan shouted out of eyesight.

Melanie gripped the back of my dress and held me in place. Not that she needed to, I knew he was faking. And it worked. Ladarious stood straight with a wicked glint in his eyes and that stupid grin still plastered on his face. He shoved his thumbs into his waistband and strolled toward Stellan.

The second he was out of sight I leapt into action. I dug my heels in and pushed my legs as hard as they could go to sprint across the opening. When I got to the pole, I slid and dropped to my knees like I was sliding into home base in baseball. Except my feet hit the back hem of my dress and I flipped back on my ass. My skirt flew up over my head and everything went black.

I groaned and cursed as I fought my way through the heavy satin. "This is why women don't wear this bullshit anymore!"

Finally, I saw the light at the end of the tunnel and dove for it, my heavy skirt parted and fell back to where gravity had intended it to be. That wonderful warm, recirculated Penn Station air rushed over me and I sucked it deep into my lungs. I pushed my hair off my face and looked around the pole — and choked on a scream. I slammed my hands over my mouth as my heart stopped.

A massive male lion stood three feet in front of me. I threw my hands up in front of me then froze. This dude was almost as tall as me. His sand colored fur shimmered under the florescent lights in the ceiling. Two massive golden eyes locked on me like I was the first meal it would have in weeks. A deep, ground-rumbling growl slipped between two huge sharply pointed teeth. He took a step forward and my gaze latched onto the claws, each longer than my fingers. My stomach sank.

Every single part of me wanted to run but that was just foolishness. There was no outrunning a damn lion. *Wait. Hold up. Ellie, you're being dumb. There are no lions in New York City.* I peeked over his fluffy multi-colored brown mane and spotted Stellan at the far end of the waiting area at the base of the escalators. Three female lions with chis-eled muscles stood in front of him. Even from behind I could see the drool oozing off their teeth as they snarled at him.

The humans on the escalators were screaming and

crying. They pushed and shoved at each other so hard that no one was making any progress. It was a mad panic that was growing worse. Stellan threw his hand up and the metal from the train track doors flew off their hinges. With a flick of his wrist the metal soared through the air and landed right at the base of the escalators, blocking the humans from everything.

Stellan arched one eyebrow. "Now it's just us, ya tosser."

Ladarious threw his head back and laughed. "You think I don't know your pretty little plum is behind me?"

I looked across to where Melanie was crouched behind a wall. *He doesn't know she's here.* I felt my eyes widen. She arched one eyebrow. I held one hand up and mouthed, *stay hidden.* She nodded. Hope flared in my chest. If he didn't know Melanie was with us, it might give us a leg up. Ladarious was not afraid of me, at least not yet. I hadn't had time to make him fear my magic. But he definitely knew Melanie.

"You're such a child, *Your Highness.*" Ladarious gave a big old belly laugh like a bad Santa Claus impersonator. "That's why you'll never be king."

Bastard. I took a step forward and the lion lunged at me. My heart fluttered. *It's FAKE, Ellie. FAKE!* I threw my hands up and pushed with my magic. Purple smoke shot out and wrapped around the lions, disintegrating them into speckles of light. Two more lions appeared out of nowhere. I knew they weren't real. This was just a product of Ladarious's horrible magic. But logic struggled to win when face-to-face with lions.

In my peripheral vision I saw magic exploding like fireworks in clouds of orange and silver. Pieces of metal and stone darted through the air as Stellan and Ladarious took each other on. But he couldn't fight him alone forever. I had to do something. I was no damsel in distress. I had magic. Real magic. *Strong* magic.

I heard Melanie's words echo through my mind, *focus on the strongest point of energy and aim at that, that'll be him.* So I closed my eyes and let my other senses take over. *THERE. I feel you.* Hot, prickling energy pulsed from across the waiting area on the left. I felt it brush against my fingers and my stomach turned.

My magic rushed to my palms and I didn't hold it back. I pushed out, firing it right where I felt Ladarious's magic. Light flashed behind my eyelids. I opened my eyes and the lions were gone. Ladarious was climbing back to his feet against the far wall. His vile blue-eyed gaze latched onto me and his top lip snarled. He punched the air and a ball of glowing orange magic flew straight at me. I ducked and dove to my left just as it slammed into the pole behind me. Cement and stone exploded like candy out of a piñata.

"That all you got, you little bitch?" Ladarious bellowed and held his arms out to his sides. "Take a deep breath…"

A wave of water rose up from the ground and hit the ceiling. It rolled back and I felt myself being sucked toward it. I widened my stance and held my ground as the tsunami rolled toward me. I felt like Arwen in Lord of the Rings, calling on the power of her people, the river with waves made of horses charging right at me. I summoned my magic into my palms and waited until the wave was almost on me, then fired my magic with everything I had. The wave shot up to the ceiling. Orange light erupted over my head and then golden sand rained down on me in buckets.

I tried to leap out of the way, but the sand weighed my skirt down, pinning me in place. The ground opened up beneath me and I sank down to my hips in the sand. I gasped and thrashed, trying to get myself free, but the more I struggled the faster I sank. The world closed in around me. The sand buried me up to my chest. My heart skipped beats and my hands trembled. He was burying me alive in quicksand. My lungs were already screaming in protest.

"ELLIE!" Stellan shouted, but his voice was muffled. The sand was filling his mouth. *"HELP—"*

He sank beneath the sand and my heart exploded with fear.

"NO!" I screamed and purple smoke blasted out of me in every direction.

The sand disintegrated as my magic hit it. My vision cleared. Stones fell from the ceiling and crashed to the ground around me. The train ticket machines were dented and lopsided. My breath left me in a rush. *Damn it, Ellie. It wasn't real. You know this. Don't let him beat you!*

Orange and silver magic shot left and right in front of me. Their magic slammed into walls and poles, crumbling the building piece by piece. A hard stone formed in my gut. If this fight kept going, Penn Station was going to be destroyed. *Over my dead body. This is MY city.*

I had no idea where Melanie was, but I didn't look. Ladarious had his eyes focused on my soulmate and I was not here to play these games of his. I felt my magic sing through my veins, buzzing with electricity, and I felt myself smile. I curled my fingers and let it fill my palms until my hands were vibrating, then I threw my hands straight out and let it fly. Bright lavender-colored lightning slammed right into Ladarious's spine.

He screamed out, his back arching before he dropped to his knees.

Damn it, not enough power.

He spun on his knees to face me and I shot my lightning at him again. But he threw out his own orange magic and deflected my hit. My lightning ricocheted to the side and *right at Stellan's chest.* But Stellan was faster. He vanished a split second before my magic hit him, reappearing a few feet away.

I cursed and reeled my magic back in.

Ladarious grinned and wagged his eyebrows. "What? Don't want to hit lover boy?"

"You son of a—"

The world went black.

I gasped and froze. *No, no, no.* I blinked, squinted, and tried to widen my eyes. Still nothing but darkness. I rubbed my eyes but there was nothing on me. My pulse skyrocketed. I never thought of myself as afraid of the dark, but this was *black.* There was no difference between my eyes open and closed. A cold chill slithered down my spine.

"*Ellie?*" Stellan shouted, his voice much too far away for my comfort.

"I'm here," I shouted back, my voice echoing.

I spun in a circle, but my feet caught in my skirt and I crashed to the ground. My knees slammed into the floor and pain shot up my thighs. "Stellan, where are you?"

"I haven't moved!" He shouted back. "This isn't real! We just have to fight through it!"

I scrambled back to my feet and sprinted toward the sound of his voice, but my feet were moving faster than my gown. I stepped right on the hem of my skirt and face-planted into the ground. I groaned and pushed back up onto my knees.

"What next, pretty plum?" Ladarious chuckled and I felt his breath brush along the back of my neck. His voice traveled like he was moving, but I still couldn't see a damn thing. "Tell me, doll, what should we make poor Stellan see? How about…"

Stellan roared and I heard metal crash all around me. "*You touch her and—*"

"And what? You can't even find me…"

My stomach rolled. I had a good idea of what he was making Stellan see and it sent a fire through my veins. This was bullshit. It was just magic blinding us…*magic.* But he didn't have the strongest magic around. He wasn't the Stone Keeper, he didn't have the power of the Astral Stone inside him.

I did.

I was stronger.

I took a deep breath and summoned every fiber of magic inside of me. I felt it rushing through my limbs. I felt the pulsing energy begging to be let out. And it'd been so good to me, I didn't see a reason to keep it on a leash. Forget control and restraint. Forget portioning my magic. This was life and death and I'd be damned if it was the latter.

I screamed and pushed my magic out with everything I had. Glowing purple smoke exploded out of me like a volcanic eruption. It poured like lava through the air, lighting up the darkness. I pushed more. I gave it more power. More energy. More of *me.* Purple smoke wrapped around *everything,* painting a black and purple picture. I saw the purple-smoke outline of Stellan on one knee in the far-left corner and Melanie still ducking behind the wall. I saw every curve and corner of Penn Station drenched in violet.

Stellan gasped and his gaze shot over to me. It was purple but it was real. He could see what I saw, and it made my magic sing with pride.

I stood tall with my arms out by my sides and my magic rushing out of me. But I still had more to give. I was just getting started. "This. Ends. Now."

The purple smoke grew brighter by the millisecond. Ladarious frowned and scurried backward. I pushed harder and harder until bright white light flashed from the ground and I saw the tile floor of Penn Station glistening up at me. A wild, wide grin spread across my face. *How 'bout them apples?* The blanket of black from his magic unraveled from the ground up, foot by foot, until it covered only the ceiling.

I shot my lightning into his chest without hesitation. He shrieked and flew head-over-heels into the air then rolled to a stop close to Stellan. Everything seemed to flip into slow motion. I held my breath and froze, waiting for him to finish our enemy off. Stellan vanished then reappeared right beside Ladarious with a piece of metal hovering in the air above his head. The florescent lights sparkled off the ragged edge.

The metal dropped like a guillotine straight towards Ladarious's throat.

I watched, frozen in place.

All of a sudden, Ladarious threw his hand up and orange magic shot out of his palm and pierced through Stellan's chest. The force of the hit lifted him off the ground and tossed him several feet back. Ladarious rolled to the side, missing the slice of the metal, then leapt to his feet. Everything happened too fast, too slow. I was frozen. Stuck. I didn't have a chance to react.

Ladarious moved like a cheetah across the tile, reaching Stellan in the blink of an eye. Stellan threw his hands up *but nothing happened.* His silver magic popped and fizzed between his fingers as Ladarious hauled him to his knees.

"NO!" I charged for them.

Ladarious grinned and pulled a long, shiny silver dagger from inside his boot and pressed the blade to Stellan's throat. He pursed his lips and made a *tsk* noise. "Take another step and I paint the tile with his blood."

THIRTY-NINE

ELLIE

I SLID to a stop with my heart lodged in my throat and my eyes latched onto the blade digging into my soulmate's throat. Beads of bright red blood trickled onto the blade. Fear like I'd never known exploded inside of me.

"*NO!*" I screamed and threw my hands up. Purple smoke coiled around my fingers. "No, no, no!"

Ladarious chuckled. "Tell me, pretty plum, what would you do to save him?"

"Anything," I heard myself say without hesitation.

I knew that probably wasn't the right answer. As the Stone Keeper I had a job to do, a job that was bigger than me. Bigger than my relationship. But with his life slowly leaking onto the blade in front of me, none of that mattered.

"*Ell-ie, d-don't,*" Stellan struggled to say over the blade against his throat.

Tears stung the backs of my eyes. My bottom lip quivered. He won. He'd already bloody won because I wasn't strong enough for this. I wasn't strong enough to watch my soulmate be murdered in front of me and not *try* to save him.

"Anything, really? For *him?*" With his other hand, he fisted Stellan's hair and pulled his head back. More blood beaded against his skin. "Such a waste, pretty plum. Don't bother with your magic. I've paralyzed his, so I can paralyze yours."

I gasped.

"Oh, don't worry. It's only temporary…unless you don't give me what I want."

"*What do you want?*" I shouted through clenched teeth.

Ladarious grinned. "The spell, Stone Keeper. Give it to me and save your lover's throat."

"*NOOO!*" Stellan yelled and thrashed.

Ladarious pressed the blade tighter into his throat. "It's like he *wants* to die. Maybe he wants you to be tortured by the sight of his blood flooding this building?"

"Stellan…p-p-please. Stop," I begged him without any remorse. "We can still win even if he has the spell. But I can't lose you."

Ladarious chuckled. "Pretty Plum has a point, lover boy. You'll still lose, but you'd have a chance. No matter how pathetic it will inevitably be."

No, no, no, no, no. This can't be happening. This can't have come to THIS. I hated that it had come to this. That my weakness would be our demise. I hated that Ladarious had somehow picked up on my feelings for Stellan and was able to use him against me. But I had no choice. There was no world where I didn't choose to save Stellan. I meant what I'd said to him. Even if Ladarious had the spell, it didn't mean we couldn't still win. We could still save the realm. If I lost Stellan…we'd lose. I'd lose.

"So what's it gonna be, plum?" He pressed the blade even tighter to Stellan's throat, making Stellan's face pale. "The spell…or the lover?"

Melanie leapt out from behind the wall and threw her hands out in front of her. Her wand fell to the ground *in pieces*. She screamed and bright red smoke rushed out of her palms. It drowned everything in sight, like a crimson river raging like nothing I'd ever seen. Ladarious' eyes widened with fear *and then it slammed into his chest.* He flew into the air then crashed on his back, sliding along the tile.

Stellan dropped to his knees with a thud. His pale green eyes were wide like saucers and staring at Melanie. His jaw dropped and his face turned sheet white.

"*Noooo,*" Ladarious screamed. He writhed and thrashed around like someone had lit him on fire. "IMPOSSIBLE!"

Melanie sauntered across the waiting area, red smoke billowing all around her. It coiled around the hem of her skirt and moved up, like someone had tugged a loose thread on a spool of yarn. My gaze followed the magic up, watching it change her outfit inch-by-inch.

The navy-blue satin skirt changed to a pale, rose colored chiffon that dragged the floor like water over rocks. The material twinkled like stars in the sky as she walked. Sparkling gold beads covered the entire bodice and sleeves, then stretched across her cleavage and around her neck like lattice. The waist cinched tight and long sleeves slid down her arms. Pale, wavy blonde hair cascaded down her back all the way to swing by her hips.

Ladarious was screaming and screeching, but I was too preoccupied by what was happening in front of me. And it had nothing to do with the red magic pouring from her outstretched hand. With every step her appearance changed a little more. Her skin tanned. Her body slimmed. She seemed to grow taller. Her cheekbones turned sharper and higher, even her jawline sharpened. Her nose thinned. Dark eyebrows filled in thicker and sat at harsher angles. Oval, droopy eyes turned upward and into sleek almond shapes rimmed with dark eyeshadow that made pale green irises almost glow.

Melanie was gone.

In her place was the most beautiful woman I had ever seen. A woman I'd never met but *instantly* knew. I knew by the red color of her magic and the way it crippled her enemy in a split second, rendering him useless without batting an eyelash. I knew by the crown on her head. I knew by the pair of pale green eyes that were identical to Stellan's. But mostly, I knew who this was by the tears in my soulmate's eyes.

Savina Wentworth.

And she was covered in blood.

Her face had little drops of blood all over it. The entire bodice of her gown was drenched in deep scarlet blood, like Carrie at her prom. She held her chin up and something sparkled on top of her head. I looked up and my eyes widened. A crown made of teardrop-shaped rubies the size of my thumb was perched on her pretty blonde head. There had to be a dozen of them. And diamonds that glowed brighter than a full moon on a clear night wrapped around each ruby. It was gorgeous, even with the blood splattered across the stones.

Even her hair had streaks of blood in it.

Savina didn't rush or panic, she just sauntered over to him with eyes aiming lasers at his head. Ladarious shrieked and tried to push up off the ground. She lifted her other hand up and pushed more red magic out, making him flop onto his back and squirm.

His back arched as he screamed out. *"S-s-avin-n-na..."*

Her eyebrow twitched and her red-painted lips curved up into a devilish smirk. "What? Don't like my outfit, Ladarious? I've been saving it just for you."

His arms curled in unnatural angles. *"Y-y-y-ou...d-d-i-e-e-e-d-d."*

"You should have checked for a pulse," she growled. Red magic glowed brighter and thicker as she towered over him. Her green gaze was colder than ice. "Or perhaps I should tell that to your *puppet?*"

My pulse skipped beats. *Oh my God. Oh my GOD. That's Savina. She's not dead!*

Stellan sat back on his heels and swayed. His hands gripped his own chest like he thought his heart was going to fall out. *"Savina?"* His voice cracked as he shouted her name, his teary eyes latched on her face.

She didn't look at him, but I knew by the way her spine straightened that she'd heard him. Instead she held her hand out over Ladarious's face and lit him up red. I felt the pulse of electricity shock through the air. I wanted to go to Stellan, to hold him, but I couldn't get my feet to move. All I could do was watch as Savina pummeled Ladarious without break.

His screams echoed down the corridors. The muscles in his bald head twitched and his eyes rolled back. He tried to push himself up, but his limbs gave out under him. Savina flexed her long fingers and his arms and legs flopped around like a fish out of water. My jaw dropped.

Then I remembered what Melanie told me about Savina's magic – *about her own magic.* The Red Widow was a silent, perfect killer, like the most patient kind of poison slowly slithering through the victim's muscles. Like it wanted to make sure not to miss a single spot. His muscles spasmed, the knots rolled like something was crawling under his skin. Sweat pooled on every inch of his body.

Still, she didn't stop.

She was going to kill him, and I wasn't going to stop her.

Ladarious would destroy everything in sight with a smile on his face just to sit on a throne of a dying realm. He'd just been about to kill Stellan, and for that I watched carefully as she pushed more red magic into him.

He wailed and his eyes bugged out of his head. His back arched off the ground. Blood poured out of his eyes like tears. It pooled in his ears and dripped from the corners of his mouth. It gurgled in the back of his throat as he sucked in one big gulp of air and then the muscles in his body went limp and his chest fell with a single wheezing last breath.

Everything went eerily silent except for the heavy thumping of my heart.

I stared at Ladarious' body lying motionless on the dirty Penn Station floor, waiting for him to move. I'd seen too many movies. The villain was never dead the first time around. Except he wasn't moving. I stared at his chest, watching for it to rise as he breathed...but he didn't. His blue eyes stared blankly at the ceiling. He really was dead.

Savina wiggled her fingers and her red smoke flew back into her palms, vanishing like it was never there at all. Her face was a stony mask, I had no idea what she felt about what she'd just done. She just stared down at him.

My breath left me in a rush. Ladarious was dead.

Savina killed him.

Savina, not Melanie.

Because Savina is alive.

I looked to my left, to where Stellan was still kneeling on the ground. His eyes were so wide I could see the whites all the way around his pale green irises – the ones that perfectly matched his sister's. His jaw was slack and his face paler than untouched snow. He looked defeated and broken as he stared up at her in complete shock.

All this time. I shook my head. I couldn't believe it. Savina supposedly died six years ago, yet here she was. All this time she'd disguised herself as Melanie. That was how she knew so much about the other realms and the Stone Keeper. That was how she knew Araqiel and Zuriel. That was why she hung close to Maren, *her* soulmate.

Finally, Savina turned toward Stellan. Her eyes glistened as she stared across the ten feet that separated them. Her face softened and she clasped her hands in front of her bloody gown. Her lips twitched like she wanted to smile but maybe was afraid to, as Stellan was *still* just staring. She cleared her throat and took a step forward. "Hello, baby brother."

Stellan let out a strangled cry and then he was on his feet, running toward her. She met him halfway and they tackled each other. He wrapped his arms around her and lifted her off her feet. She giggled and held him tight, her eyes filled with tears. I couldn't see his face, but I saw the tension in his back muscles and the way his biceps flexed as he squeezed her tight.

I couldn't imagine what this felt like for him. The sister he adored and thought he'd lost back from the dead. I was going over every one of their interactions that I'd witnessed with new light. The kind of restraint it must have taken for her…it was unreal.

When he finally sat her back down, she smiled up at him and cupped his cheek. "I'm so proud of who you've become. You have no idea hard it's been to lie to you."

Whatever Stellan said back to her didn't reach my ears, but that was fine. This moment wasn't about me. My heart swelled for my soulmate. I knew losing her had caused him so much pain and now that could finally heal. I strolled

MIDNIGHT MAGE

over and stopped just behind him and pressed my hand to his back so he'd know I was there.

Savina chuckled and squeezed his arms. She shook her head then looked over to me. "*Ellie.*" She smiled wide and held her hand out between us. "I'm Savina Wentworth. It's nice to meet you *for real* this time."

I laughed and shook my head. "I think there's a *princess* missing there."

She opened her mouth to speak when a loud, slow clap erupted from behind us. I jumped and spun around — and gasped.

Ladarious was leaning against the wall on the other side of the corridor...*clapping.* He grinned and shook his head. "That was beautiful."

No. What? How? I glanced over my shoulder to where the body lay dead on the tile. Orange magic washed over the body and then the face changed. It wasn't Ladarious. It was one of his main henchmen. I recognized him. My pulse quickened and my stomach tightened into knots. Stellan took my hand, but Savina took a step in front of us.

"My, my. Savina Wentworth, heir to the throne herself. Guess you and I don't think that much differently, do we *Red Widow?*" Ladarious looked her up and down. Slowly. "I must say, revealing yourself to save baby brother's life? So touching. But wearing the blood-stained dress you died in? Priceless. You always did know how to make an entrance."

She took another step forward. "I know how to make an exit too. Or do you need to ask your friend here?"

"Well it's nice to finally have a worthy opponent again,

that's for sure." He chuckled and wagged his eyebrows. He pushed off the wall and rocked back on his heels. "But tell me, can you do it again?"

Savina threw a massive glowing red ball of magic the size of my head right at his chest but he blocked it with his own orange magic.

He frowned and shook his head. "Let's make this more fun…catch me if you can…"

Then he spun and sprinted down the corridor, right into the subway platforms. We cursed and leapt after him but Savina jumped out in front of us.

"*Savina—*"

"Your time has already started. Get to the other realms. Get the ingredients. You don't have any time to waste." She started running backwards, her eyes still on us. "GO. NOW!"

FORTY

ELLIE

I sucked in gasping breaths as we slid to a stop in front of the bank of mirrored elevators. Wearing this damn dress was like running through water with weights strapped around my body. The black fabric wound around my legs and I wanted nothing more than to tear at it. Stellan stood beside me and he too sucked in sharp breaths.

I looked at our reflections in the mirrored doors and shook my head. I sighed. "What the hell just happened?"

Stellan looked shell shocked. He shoved his hands in his hair and tugged at the strands. "Savina...*Savina...*" He turned and slammed his fist into the wall. It dented and fractured, tiny pieces crumbled to the ground. His brows furrowed and his face fell. All of that smooth composure I'd come to know him for was broken. His eyes were shattered. "She's alive and I left her. I shouldn't have left her."

I pressed my hand to his back and rubbed little circles, trying to comfort him. "She told us to go."

"I know, I know. But God, it wasn't enough. None of it was enough." A single tear rolled down his cheek and fell from his chin. He swiped at it and groaned. "What if something happens to her and I'm not there...*again?*"

My heart broke for him. For them. It was all so unfair. "Stellan, there was nothing you could do as a child—"

"*But I can now.*" He spun on his heels to go back toward the stairs then slid to a stop and screamed, tugging on his hair. "I-I can't go after her. She wouldn't want that, even if I want it."

I hurried over to stand in front of him and pulled his hands out of his hair. "You've watched her fight for six years *without* using her magic. You know how capable she is. And it's only Ladarious, not his army or any other army. This isn't like last time."

I didn't know the right words to comfort him, but I prayed I was helping somehow. The sister that he long thought dead was back and he had to leave her right away. I couldn't imagine how that felt. Their reunion had been short and it could've been their last, we had no way of knowing she wouldn't fall to Ladarious. *Maybe if we hurry, we can help her take him down then she can come with us?*

"No." He hung his head. "I can see it in your face, you're trying to work out how we can go back to her. But I-I know we can't. As much as I want to, we can't. Look at your wrist, time is already ticking by. Going back to her now would be the most selfish thing I could ever do."

I refused to look down at that damn timer on my wrist. We both knew there was barely any time on it, there was no need to *see it.* Not right now. Not when he was hurting like this. I reached out and took his hands in mine. We'd barely had time to take it all in before she sent us packing.

Stellan ran a shaky hand down his face. His eyes were bloodshot and teary. His cheeks splotchy and red. His hair was sticking out in every direction from how hard he'd been tugging at it. He laughed but it sounded a bit strangled. "Shit…my sister…is alive. All this time and she was right there. All these years. *Melanie.* I still can't believe it. I may never believe it."

I rested my hand on his chest, feeling the beat of his racing heart under my touch. "Do you want to go back?"

"More than you know." He shook his head. "But no, we can't. Savina – God, I can't believe I'm saying her name in a sentence in the present - she knows what's important. Bloody hell, she knows more than we do probably. She was the one who'd found the journal and it's obvious she's been in contact with Araqiel – point is, we don't have time. Especially if Ladarious is after it as well. The realm is what's most important to Savina and I'll be damned if I let her down or anyone else."

"And Savina?"

His face hardened. "You're right. She's more than capable. I've watched Melanie take down a dozen of my father's guards without breaking a sweat, and that was just with her wand. But *her* magic? Well, you saw. And that's but a glimpse. She can handle herself and him. We'll…we'll have to see her when we get back. That's all. She'll handle Ladarious."

He curled his hands into fists at his sides. The muscles in his jaw ticked and I saw the worry etched into his face. He was torn between his duty to his realm and the love he felt for his sister. He muttered under his breath, "she better be all right. Especially now that I just got her back."

"I have faith in her, Stellan, for whatever that's worth," I said softly.

"It's worth more than you know." He reached out and tucked a stray hair behind my ear. "Let's go. I have to respect her wishes, that's the least I can do. We have to do this, Ellie."

"Okay." I wanted to tell him this could wait but we both knew that wasn't true. His most beloved sister was alive, and I couldn't imagine what he was feeling. Especially now that he was parted from her all over again, and so quickly. All I could do was be here for him while we went through this together. "Okay, which one?"

He looked up at me and frowned. "Hmm?"

I motioned to the doors around us. The portal to Second Realm was glistening like it was beckoning us back home. But there were four other doors, for three other realms. Two doors on my left, two doors on my right. I had no idea which was which, or why there was a fourth. I just prayed *he* knew.

His chest heaved as he looked at all our options.

I licked my lips. "Shylock and Melanie – I mean, Savina – both thought we should go to the Vampires first since the only line from the spell we are the surest of is about them."

He nodded. "Okay. Vampires. Right. Cool. I trust all three of you. Let's do that."

Before, the other realms seemed like a distant reality. Now, standing at the threshold about to face them, my bravado wavered. *What if Shylock is right? What if I have to get bitten? What if I have to do the biting?* I didn't want anything sticking its fangs into me nor did I want to drink any blood.

Stellan glanced at me. "Are you nervous?"

"No." I lied. I ran my fingers through my hair.

"Liar." His lips pulled up into a half smile and he grabbed my hand, stopping me from pulling all my hair out. "Nerves aside, are you ready?"

"As long as I have you with me. You sure you want to do this? We can go back?" My stomach twisted in knots and my hand shook in his.

I pressed his lips into a hard line and swiped at the corner of his eye. "No, but we have to. I need to believe that I'll see her again and that she'll be safe."

"If she can hide for six years and come out like she did today I know she will be here when we get back." We were about to travel into another realm and I knew I couldn't guarantee him anything but in my gut I knew Savina would be okay. Neither of us knew what to expect but I could give him the hope he needed. I motioned to the doors around us. "Which one for the bloodsuckers?"

Stellan pointed to the first door on our right. Above it, in the place where it would've read the floor level the elevator was on, was a symbol etched in gold and chrome.

It was a square intersected by a diamond. In the center of it two vintage looking keys crossed over each other. Tiny lines that looked like rays of sunlight fanned out from the keys toward the edge of the diamond.

"Why two keys for vampires? Shouldn't it be like blood or fangs or something?"

He sighed. "I have absolutely no bloody idea."

"Well, cool. That makes two of us." I backed away. "Let's do it."

He pulled his hand out of mine and I must've made a face because he wiggled his finger with the *one ring* on it. With a cheeky smile, he pressed his hand to the middle of the mirrored elevator doors. I expected light to flash and a portal to open…instead a thick black line shot up from the ground and then the mirrors parted. Like real elevator doors.

Sure enough, on the other side was an elevator made entirely of white marble.

Stellan moved to the side and gestured for me to enter. "Here we go."

I walked inside, momentarily distracted by the click of my heeled shoes on the marble floor. I was three steps in when I heard Stellan gasp. I spun on my heels and froze. My breath caught on a scream. A dark green vine as thick as my arm was coiled tight around Stellan's throat. The sound of his strangled groan filled my ears as everything slipped into slow motion.

Stellan's eyes were wide and round as he yanked at the vine wrapped around his throat. He leaned toward me, fighting to get free, but his face turned an ugly shade of red. Thick thorns dug into his skin and blood welled as he clawed at them. I dove for him but he was yanked backwards.

And that was when I saw her.

A woman stood in front of the elevator to the right. A sharp pointed crown sat on her head. White hair hung down to her hips. Pointed ears matched the tips of her crown. Her skin was pale and silvery. Tiny icicles tipped her eye lashes and the ends of her hair. A body-hugging dress fell from her shoulders to the floor. The material was nearly translucent, with only sparking snowflakes flowing around her hips and across her chest. Blue tinged her lips as she smiled at me and reached up toward Stellan.

It was like an awful, haunting nightmare where no matter how hard you ran your feet didn't move.

She wrapped sharply tipped fingers around his throat and grinned.

"Let him go!" I screamed and took a step, but the elevator doors slammed into my arms as they started to close. "STELLAN!"

Stellan tried to scream but the fingers digging into his throat cut off the sound. He flicked his wrist and my elevator doors opened a smidge more and I flew *backward.* Like he'd thrown me.

I gasped and scrambled to my feet, screaming, "Stellan!"

She glared at me and then *threw* him. His feet lifted off the ground as he soared backward toward the open elevator directly in front of me. Thick thorn riddled vines shot out of the doors like tentacles. They wrapped around his body, pinning his arms and legs down. He crashed onto the dark hardwood floor. The loud crack of his cheek hitting the stone echoed off the walls.

I leapt headfirst toward him. "I got you—"

"NO!" He flicked bloody, cut up fingers and a wave of warm energy slammed into my face, pushing me all the way back inside the elevator. "GO!"

The doors were already closing before I managed to get to my feet again, but I charged at them anyway. My eyes were locked on Stellan. My heart caught in my throat. Those vines coiled around his body like an anaconda squeezing the life from its prey. I leapt forward as the doors slid shut in my face.

"NO!" I threw my hands between the metal then wedged half my body in the opening.

His eyes met mine and he growled. A silver wave of magic slammed into me, forcing me out from between the doors. I stumbled backward without taking my eyes off of him. I screamed his name just as the vines lifted him off the ground and sucked him into the portal elevator. The last inch of door closed in my face and I screamed. It all happened in less than a second, there was no chance of winning there. I clawed and pulled at the door, yet my fingers found no grip and tears stung the back of my eyes.

I cursed and threw my body against the closed doors, letting the screams rip up my throat. *No, no, no. This isn't happening. This isn't how this goes.* Fear, panic, and rage boiled inside me. My soulmate was gone. I didn't even know which realm he'd gone to. I rammed my shoulder into the doors and pain exploded inside my body. I smacked my palm against the cold mirror. *Oh god. He's gone.* Panic suffocated me and I collapsed on the elevator floor. "Stellan!"

WE HOPE you enjoyed entering *The Night Realm*! Don't worry, Ellie and Stellan's story isn't over yet...want to know who grabbed him? And if Ellie finds her way back to him? CLICK HERE to read Book Two in the *Magic Marked Series*, **Marvel Mage** NOW!

THE NIGHT REALM: MAGIC MARKED ❦ BOOK TWO

MARVEL MAGE

CHANDELLE LaVAUN
MEGAN MONTERO

NOW THE SPELLS ARE MINE...

. . .

I USED to say I worked better under pressure...I was wrong. This countdown clock on my arm might just break me.

STELLAN IS MISSING. Someone stole him from me. They ripped him right out of my hands and hid him somewhere I can't find. I'm desperate to save my soulmate but Second Realm is dying...without me, they have no chance but neither does Stellan. I'm being torn in two and I don't know if I can help them both.

THE ONLY CHANCE WE HAVE, is if *I* recreate the Astral Stone. But to do so, I have to brew a potion full of ingredients that are literally out of this world. The angels are sending me on a perilous journey to beg the other realms for help. And they all want a trade. Vampires want my blood, Shifters want my power, and the Fae want my life. Jumping realms was something I thought I'd only see in movies or comics, but it's real. It's dangerous. And it comes with a price. For Stellan, I'll pay anything.

BUT IF THIS clock hits zero, my time is up...and Second Realm will die.

AND IT WILL BE ALL my fault.

. . .

CLICK HERE TO read Marvel Mage!

THE NIGHT REALM has FIVE realms - Mages, Vampires, Fae, Shifters, and humans...want to know which one you belong to? CLICK HERE to join our Facebook group and take the quiz NOW!

WHILE YOU WAIT FOR BOOK TWO, HAVE YOU READ OUR OTHER BOOKS? SEE BELOW FOR LINKS TO **THE COVEN** AND **THE ROYALS**!

I THOUGHT **magic was make believe...but I was *way* wrong.**

I was nobody. No matter how hard I tried, I never fit in with anyone at my high school. Now I know why.

Turns out I'm a witch. A scary powerful one, too. Except The Coven that claimed me won't teach me how to use my magic.

Suddenly, I'm selected by the Goddess to hunt down a mythical locket needed to save the world from destruction. The only person who actually tries to help me is the alarmingly attractive Tennessee. He has immeasurable power and breathtaking mismatched eyes. I'm drawn to him on a level I can't explain...and he's forbidden from getting too close to me.

When the quest takes an unexpected dangerous turn, I

have to improvise. This supernatural world is unraveling at my fingertips and I need to master my magic fast. If I don't, I could get everyone I care about killed...

CLICK HERE TO read **The Coven: Elemental Magic** now!

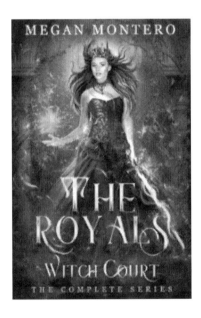

IT'S **time to claim my power...**

All my life I've lived under lock and key, always following the strict rules my mother set for me. A week before my sixteenth birthday I sneak out of my house and discover why. Turns out I am not just a normal teenager. I'm a witch blessed with a gift someone wants to steal from me.

And not just anyone...the evil King Alataris.

For a thousand years the people of Evermore have suffered under his tyranny. The Mark on my shoulder says I am the Siphon Witch, one of five Witch Queens fated to come together and finally destroy him. The only thing keeping Evermore safe is the Stone that shields the witch kingdoms from Alataris's magic...and now he's found a way to steal it. Suddenly, I'm sent on a quest to find the ancient spell to protect the Stone. My only hope for surviving is through my strikingly beautiful and immensely powerful Guardian, Tucker. The laws of Evermore state that love between us is strictly forbidden, and it appears I'm the only one willing to give in to the attraction...

When the quest turns more dangerous than expected I realize I have absolutely no idea what I'm doing. I was raised human. But I have to learn my magic fast because If King Alataris gets his hands on me he'll steal my magic and my life...but if he gets his hands on that Stone we all die.

CLICK HERE to read **The Royals: Witch Court** now!

CHANDELLE & MEGAN

Though they grew up in separate worlds Megan and Chandelle have always shared interests in the same things: art, dogs, pizza, and books. Their love of everything urban fantasy and paranormal is what brought them together in 2013. They were each hardcore introverting at their very first writing conference, in their very first workshop, on their very first day. Lucky for both of them they came together at the mention of one of their favorite authors, JR Ward. They spent the next four days talking about books, fangirling, and learning all they could about writing. Within months they were virtually inseparable and happily codependent beyond measure, despite living thousands of miles apart. After working together on their own separate projects they finally came together to bring *The Night Realm Series* to life. Strap in, it's going to be a wild ride. #YouPushedMe #YouFell

MIDNIGHT MAGE

Published by Wanderlost Publishing & Leo Press

Copyright © 2020 by Chandelle LaVaun and Megan Montero

Cover designed by **Orina Kafe**

❀ Created with Vellum